I0655042

Twelve

A novel featuring Brother XII and
his Aquarian religious commune
in western Canada in the 1930s

By

Keith Hammond

Copyright © 2012 by Keith Hammond
All rights reserved. No part of this book may be reproduced or transmitted in any form or by any means, electronic or mechanical, including photocopying, recording, or by any information storage or retrieval system without permission in writing from the author.

All characters and events in this publication, other than those clearly in the public domain, are fictitious, and any resemblance to real persons, living or dead, is purely coincidental.

Library and Archives Canada Cataloguing in Publication

Hammond, Keith, 1935-
    Twelve : a novel featuring Brother XII and his Aquarian religious commune in western Canada in the 1930s / by Keith Hammond.

ISBN 978-0-9880557-0-4

    I. Title.

PS8615.A5443T94 2012   C813'.6   C2012-905748-7

Printed by CreateSpace An Amazon.com Company
Cover watercolour of the Gulf Islands by Marjorie Thompson, Nanaimo, BC
Cover design by Turning Point Arts, Ladysmith, BC
First published 2013 by Blue Genever Publishing

Blue.Genever.Publishing@shaw.ca

To Gina:
Friend and lover,
Wife and mother.

Author's notes:

This is a story, not a history. All the characters are imaginary, all but Brother XII and Madame Zee. They were real and if the published literature and local folklore are to be believed, many of the incidents I have described actually took place. I have embroidered them from my imagination, of course, and I have moved the dates of the colony forward four years to fit in with the rest of the story. However the old Brother loved publicity and he was never too fussy about the truth, so I don't think he would have minded me taking these liberties if it allowed him to get into print.

Regarding Brother XII's appearance I could find only three photographs of poor quality, so my description has come largely from my imagination.

The existence of the jars of gold coins is well documented and some people believe they are still hidden on De Courcey Island.

I have written this story in Canadian English which differs slightly from the British version of the language. In some places this may cause confusion to British readers. In England surgeons use the title Mr not Dr, although they are of course fully qualified medical doctors. In this story everyone who is a medical doctor is titled Dr, British surgeons included.

There is a Chapter Index at the back of the book.

Principal Fictional Characters

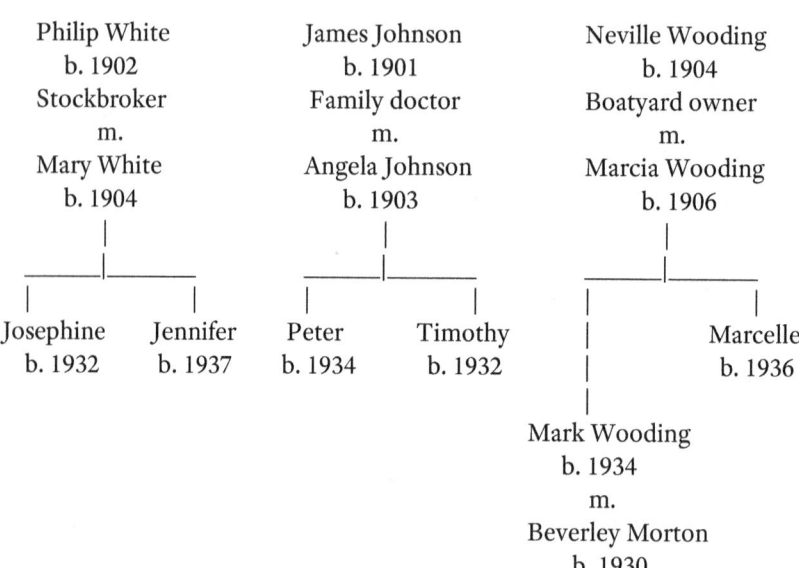

Philip White
b. 1902
Stockbroker
m.
Mary White
b. 1904

Josephine   Jennifer
b. 1932   b. 1937

James Johnson
b. 1901
Family doctor
m.
Angela Johnson
b. 1903

Peter   Timothy
b. 1934   b. 1932

Neville Wooding
b. 1904
Boatyard owner
m.
Marcia Wooding
b. 1906

                 Marcelle
                 b. 1936

Mark Wooding
b. 1934
m.
Beverley Morton
b. 1930

Chapter 1

Mary White would remember the scene for the rest of her life. It was February 1934 and she was sitting on a hard wooden chair in a simple meeting hall in southern England. A low stage ran across the front of the hall and rows of straight-backed chairs filled the floor.

She looked around furtively, trying not to attract attention. Nearly all the chairs were occupied by surprisingly prosperous-looking people. She guessed there were about three hundred altogether, and she was pleased to see several well-to-do members of the Southampton Theosophical Society. Theosophy, with its emphasis on spiritualism and reincarnation, had always appealed to her.

She turned her attention to the stage. The back was hidden by purple satin curtains which reached from the ceiling to the floor. A large golden T was embroidered in the middle of the curtains with the five-pointed Star of Egypt underneath. She recognized the symbols immediately. They came from olden times. The T was the original Greek letter Tau, and the star represented Sirius, the brightest star in the ancient Egyptian sky. In front of the curtains sat two large ebony birds, like a pair of sinister black ravens a couple of feet high. In the middle of the stage was a table draped in purple cloth like an altar, and at the front stood two big flaming torches made of brass, one on either side.

After a short while a woman stepped onto the stage and held up her hands for silence. "Brothers and sisters," she announced. "Brother XII will be with us soon. You must be quiet now."

The whispering ceased and the lights dimmed, leaving the room bathed in the eerie glow from the torches. Slowly Mary became aware of soft organ music and the smell of incense.

Mary was thirty years old, the wife of a successful London stockbroker and very well-off herself. She did not want to be noticed but there was something about her straight brown hair, her clear complexion and her delicate oval face that seemed to attract attention, particularly among men.

Just then the curtains parted and Brother XII appeared at the back of the stage in a full-length yellow robe. He had thick black hair brushed straight back, dark piercing eyes and a firm manly chin. He paused for a few moments, then he walked slowly to the front of the stage, the yellow robe flowing with his body as he moved. Mary thought he looked about forty, with the swarthy complexion of a man who'd spent years in the sun. For two long minutes he surveyed his audience in silence and she felt his charisma like a physical force.

Finally he held up his arms. "Brothers and Sisters, fellow Aquarians, welcome to this humble hall. I have returned to you to report on the great progress we have made in our colony in Canada. But first I must tell you that I have just met with the Masters of Wisdom. All our prophesies are coming true. The peace-loving Gods of ancient Egypt have risen to power once more. The age of lust and evil which has plagued mankind for two thousand years will soon be brought to a close. The Pisces Age is ending and the golden Age of Aquarius is about to begin." His voice got louder. "Brothers and sisters, first will come the fire, then a thousand years of peace . . . "

He went on to describe the wonderful new period of history which was about to unfold. Mary could picture it, a time of trust and love when the dreadful things she read about in the newspapers came to an end. She let her mind wander.

She'd read his book, *The Three Truths*, over and over again. It told how his mission to save mankind had begun with a vision several years before. He'd been lying in bed, penniless and sick, in a bare room lit only by a candle. Suddenly he'd seen a golden Tau suspended in the air near the foot of the bed. It had glowed like fire, and after a minute the Star of Egypt had appeared underneath.

When he'd seen these symbols he'd known he was about to receive a message from the Gods of ancient Egypt. After a while he'd felt knowledge flowing into his mind and he became aware of the greed and depravity which was consuming the human race. Eventually the Gods had revealed that they were about to punish mankind by bringing the present age of evil to a catastrophic end.

He'd woken deeply disturbed because they hadn't told him when the catastrophe would occur or what form it would take. For days he'd meditated in vain, and then a second trance had occurred. This time his soul had been transported to a spiritual world where he'd met a council of the eleven greatest philosophers of all time. They were called the Masters of Wisdom, and among them were Gautama Buddha, Jesus Christ, and the Prophet Mohammed. They had sat round a heavenly table and interviewed him at length. Finally they had revealed what was about to happen to the world.

The Gods of ancient Egypt were about to take command again. Eventually there would be a thousand years of peace, but first the Gods intended to purge mankind. Already they had directed the path of a meteorite called Aquarius to strike the Earth in a few years' time. Fires would spread across the globe and everyone would burn, everyone except a small group of devout people whom the Masters of Wisdom would choose. This group was to form the nucleus of a better race which would ultimately repopulate the world.

Then, to the Brother's humble surprise, they'd invited him to become the twelfth member of the council and given him the title Brother XII. As the only human member his mission was to found a colony on Earth called The City of Refuge in the one place that would be spared. There he was to assemble a group of special men and women chosen by the Masters, and after the catastrophe it was his duty to lead them forth to rebuild the human race. They would be called Aquarians, and it was they who would usher in the new age of peace on Earth, the Age of Aquarius.

Mary heard his voice begin to rise and she realized he was talking about it now. ". . . but the Gods have decreed that before the golden age begins mankind must be purged. Lust and greed must be rooted out and sinners must be burned."

His dark eyes flashed. "Even as I speak the wayward meteorite Aquarius is rushing towards us now. That great mass of rock and ice, travelling a million miles a minute, is headed directly at the Earth. The world will be engulfed in flames just as it was in ages past when the Gods demanded change . . . "

As he spoke the lights dimmed. The yellow robe and the Brother's eyes seemed to glow in the semidarkness. Above him on the curtains shimmered the golden Tau and the Egyptian star, just as he'd described them in his vision. The flames from the great brass torches flickered on either side. Mary's mind began to wander again, mesmerized by the scene.

Three years ago, she reflected, at a dramatic seance in this same hall, the Masters had revealed the sacred place where The City of Refuge must be built. How she wished she'd been there on that momentous evening, but she'd read the details many times. Brother XII's soul had departed to a higher plane leaving his body lying on the stage, and while his soul was gone another of the Masters had travelled to Earth and temporarily entered his body. Then, with the hall as silent as a tomb and everyone straining to hear, in a voice that was little more than a whisper, the Master had revealed the place that would be spared. It was a small group of sheltered islands in British Columbia on the west coast of Canada, the other side of the world.

The Brother was describing the new colony now. He was not merely talking but using his hands and his facial expression, and continually changing the tone of his voice.

". . . three years ago we purchased a green valley stretching down to the sea. It was fresh, untouched by man. There were trees, pastures, animals and birds, a little stream and a beach.

"Now we have a farm, a meeting hall, a library and a school. There are houses by the sea, and a great open-air temple where we teach the Aquarian creed. Untold millions will perish in the flames, but just as at the time of Noah, the Gods require a nucleus of good hard-working men and women to rebuild the human race."

Mary wanted to be a part of that nucleus and so did her husband, Philip. She glanced at him sitting beside her now, a slim man a couple of years older than herself. He had light brown hair and a handsome face that was slightly marred by a birthmark on his left cheek. They had learnt about the Aquarians from Theosophist friends, but they were not Aquarians themselves. Anyone could become a Theosophist, but to become an Aquarian was much more difficult. Aquarians had to be chosen. And there was another thing: it was no secret that building The City of Refuge was very expensive. Aquarians had to sell all their possessions and give the money to Brother XII.

". . . and finally I have some wonderful news," the Brother was saying. "The Masters of Wisdom have instructed me to select another small group of people for salvation. After the holocaust they will help rebuild the world. They, their children, and their children's children for a thousand years."

Mary thought of their little daughter Josephine, just learning to walk.

"The responsibility of choosing will not be left to me alone. The Masters will be watching you and they will decide, but you must look for signs within yourselves. You will know if you are worthy and if you are you should do all you can to join us now. There is nothing to lose because all worldly things will soon be burned."

Mary had spent hours brooding about the terrible state the world was in, especially since the birth of Jo. She wanted a better world for her daughter, and she couldn't bear the thought of the child being burned. She felt sure they were as worthy as any family, and life in the colony appealed to her, it sounded so simple and fresh. But Philip was a successful stockbroker and they had a big expensive house near London. How could they give away everything they owned?

And yet if Brother XII was right their home would soon be destroyed. Everything else he'd predicted had come true. The world was in a terrible state. Fascism was springing up in Europe and civil war in Spain. Hitler was persecuting the Jews, and the Japanese were slaughtering thousands in

China. No one seemed to be able to do anything about it. The traditional religions had failed just as the Brother had predicted.

He lowered his voice again and everyone strained to hear. "When I say people will be purged by fire I am talking about real fire, flames that scald the skin and roast the flesh."

As he spoke he walked over to one of the flaming torches. "It is the Gods who will send the fire," he went on, "but they have given me the power to protect you." And with that he deliberately extended his right hand into the flame.

At first Mary could not believe her eyes. The flames licked slowly between his fingers. She didn't see how it could be a trick. There was absolute silence in the hall. Then to her horror she heard a faint crackling sound and the flame changed colour as if it were burning his skin. He moved his hand back and forth. She realized the fragrance of incense had been replaced by the acrid smell of burning flesh.

She felt faint and the scene began to swim before her eyes, but just before she slipped off her chair he withdrew his hand and walked to the very front of the stage. Then he extended both hands towards the audience and flexed his fingers in and out. His right hand looked slightly charred but by some miracle it seemed otherwise alright.

"The Gods can protect you," he said. "Renounce all worldly things and trust in me."

Chapter 2

One night during that same February 1934, in the little country hospital that served the small seaport of Salcombe, Angela Johnson gave birth to her second son. Angela and her husband James had recently returned from a difficult year in the Aquarian commune in western Canada, where the baby had been conceived. James had been the colony doctor and now he looked after the Salcombe community and the nearby villages.

Angela, in her late twenties, was plump, dark-haired and attractive. She had been a nurse before she married and now she enjoyed the role of a small-town doctor's wife.

Salcombe lay on the southwest coast of England in the county of Devon, about twenty miles east of Plymouth from where the pilgrim fathers sailed. The town stood near the mouth of the Salcombe Estuary, a narrow arm of the sea that wound inland for five miles between lush green hills. For over two hundred years it had been a haven to sailors and smugglers, and lately to holidaymakers and yachtsmen.

Two babies were born that night. The other was also a boy, the son of Marcia Wooding. The Woodings were an important local family which had been prominent in Devon for generations. Angela should have welcomed the opportunity to get to know one of them better, but Marcia's assertive manner intimidated her; she would rather have had the maternity suite to herself.

The Johnsons lived in a big house called Wiscasset after a seaport of that name in America. They already had one little boy, Timothy, who was two years old, and they christened the new baby Peter. Now that there were two children at home James suggested a nanny, but Angela knew she'd be uncomfortable with the strict routine that nannies liked to impose.

She had decorated the nursery in yellow and white. Peter's crib stood in one corner and there was a spare bed that she could use if he needed attention at night. The window looked out towards the mouth of the estuary with Blackstone Rock in the middle, and the sandy beaches of Smalls Cove and Mill Bay on the far shore. There was always something to see, yachts anchoring in front of the town or fishing boats making their way out to sea. Her other child, Timmy, had previously slept in the nursery, but she'd moved him into a room of his own several weeks before so he wouldn't feel rejected.

Peter seemed to be an average baby in every way. Angela knew there was nothing very remarkable about her little son, but she loved him dearly and he seemed contented from the start.

Marcia Wooding knew it was a terrible thing but she disliked her baby boy from the moment she saw him. For one thing she wanted a girl. She had always imagined herself with a sweet little girl with blue eyes and straight blond hair. She'd even picked a name, Marcelle, and she'd pictured herself visiting friends with her little daughter in a pretty dress and ribbons in her hair.

Marcia couldn't help noticing that the other baby born that night looked much more attractive than her own even though it also was a boy. It was unusual for the hospital to have more than one delivery at a time, and she wondered if the babies could have got switched. The other belonged to Angela Johnson, the wife of the new Salcombe doctor, and she even had the crazy idea that Dr Johnson might have swapped the babies so the Johnsons would get the better one.

Her husband, Neville, didn't seem to notice the baby's ugly wrinkled skin and curly black hair. He even said he preferred to have a son, although he'd never mentioned that before. It was he who suggested the name Mark, saying it was almost the same as Marcelle. Marcia couldn't think of anything better so she called the baby Mark.

Marcia was twenty-eight. She originally came from London. She'd been a schoolteacher before she married so she was used to being in charge. She knew she wasn't pretty, but with her tall elegant figure and striking dark hair she could usually get her way with men and women alike.

The Woodings had lived in Devon for generations. They owned a lot of farmland which was rented to tenant farmers or farmed by members of the Wooding clan themselves. They had business interests too, one of which was a large boatyard in Salcombe which was run by Neville.

She and Neville lived in a fine old house called Maplehurst, overlooking the harbour. It was a big house so she employed a live-in housemaid, Ann, who she had brought from London when she'd married Neville a couple of years before.

Marcia had firm ideas about raising children and they definitely included a nanny. She'd been unable to find one locally but as her pregnancy progressed so had Ann's interest in babies. Although she was thirty, Ann had never had a serious boyfriend and it seemed unlikely she would have children of her own, so Marcia was not surprised when she asked if she could have the position of nanny.

"I love babies, ma'am," Ann had pleaded. "I've always wanted one. I may not have had much experience, but with you to teach me I'm sure I'll soon learn."

Marcia would have preferred a properly trained nanny, but with none available she hired a younger girl called Jessie as housemaid, and gave the job to Ann.

Her own mother had intended to come down from London when the baby was born, but at the last minute she had a gallbladder attack and couldn't come. Marcia was relieved because she was frightened of her mother and she thought she could manage on her own. However Mark turned out to be difficult from the start. Neville wasn't any help. He was a kind and considerate man but he didn't have much strength of will. He never disciplined the servants, and she didn't think he'd be much better with his son.

The first problem started as soon as Mark was home, when he refused to take her breast for the evening feed. No matter what she tried he wouldn't suckle. Eventually she got angry and put him down unfed, but half an hour later he was crying with hunger. She had read that success with infant feeding depended on a rigid routine, so for an hour she ignored him. He screamed and screamed, and her breasts ached with milk, but she refused to give in to her infant son.

This was just the first of many problems. Soon she realized what a mistake it had been not to hire an experienced nanny who could deal with the baby when he cried. Ann could not do much more than change his clothes.

Chapter 3

Mary and Philip returned to hear the Brother half a dozen times in two weeks. The theme of the talks was always the same but the details varied. Sometimes the flaming torches were replaced by statues of Egyptian gods. Sometimes there were ancient vases engraved with hieroglyphics, or carved animals instead of the great black birds.

After each talk a few people remained behind to tidy the room and stack the chairs, hoping to see more of Brother XII. Mary made sure that she and Philip were always among this group which grew to twenty or thirty faithful followers. Every evening after the chairs were stacked the Brother would appear dressed in an expensive suit with a crisp white shirt and a dark tie. He'd step down from the stage and go about the room talking to his flock. After the yellow robe and the dynamic sermons she found it almost an anticlimax, yet she was relieved to find he was ordinary flesh and blood. He appeared genuinely interested in the members of his congregation, their backgrounds, where they lived and what they did. She was already secretly comparing him with Jesus Christ and she worried that her affluence might put him off. It was impossible to lie when he asked about her background, but to her relief he didn't seem to mind that she was wealthy and he even seemed to seek her out.

Every evening an Aquarian couple who had accompanied him from British Columbia served refreshments. Their names were Ken and Gillian Martin and they had lived in the colony since the beginning, so she was fascinated by what they had to say.

Ken was a big friendly man, originally from Lancashire. He had an album of photos of the colony, and from him she got a picture of what life with the Aquarians would be like. There were really three separate settlements, one in a valley by the sea, and two more on small islands nearby. There were houses, roads, a farm and even a little harbour. One day, Ken assured her, they would be self-sufficient.

There were children in the colony, including a little girl the same age as Josephine, and Gillian told her they were building a school. Two of the members were teachers and they had already started classes in someone's home.

But when Mary asked about a doctor Gillian gave her a peculiar look.

"We did have one," she said. "But he left."

"Why was that?"

"Family problems. It was his wife. But we have a nurse, and there are doctors in the town of Nanaimo a few miles away."

"You don't think Brother XII could be a fraud?" Mary asked.

She and Philip were driving home from Southampton after a stunning performance by the Brother. Her father was a scientist and he had pronounced the man a common swindler, although he'd never bothered to hear him speak.

"No, he can't be," said Philip. "Three years ago, when the first group of Aquarians went to Canada, they had over half a million pounds. If he were a fraud he would have taken the money then, before they spent it building The City of Refuge."

She trusted Philip. He was a successful stockbroker and he always seemed to be right.

After a few minutes she asked, "What about the meteorite hitting the Earth and killing everyone? Do you believe that too?"

"I don't know. It's possible. Meteorites have hit the earth before."

"Well I believe it," she said. "What do you think we should do?"

"We can't do anything unless he chooses us."

They drove on in silence. The road was deserted and she watched the headlights cut through the darkness ahead.

After a while she said, "Why don't you ask him if we can be chosen?"

Philip hesitated. "I did ask him, this evening, when you were talking with Gillian and Ken."

"What did he say?"

"He said: 'It is easier for a camel to pass through the eye of a needle than for a rich man to enter the Kingdom of Heaven.'"

She felt a stab of disappointment. "Oh Philip. Does that mean he doesn't want us?"

"I'm afraid it does. And that's another reason why he can't be a fraud."

The telegram arrived the following Saturday. There was to be a special seance the very next day and it instructed them to fast after midnight in preparation. Mary was overcome with relief.

As soon as they entered the hall she could see that this was a special occasion. The stage was brightly lit, but the rest of the room was nearly dark, and there were only about thirty chairs facing the stage. There was a couch draped in purple cloth in the centre of the stage and on either side stood the familiar flaming torches. The flames had a flickering red hue which cast an eerie glow throughout the room. A hint of incense hung in the air and organ music played softly in the background.

Mary felt lightheaded from the lack of food which added to her sense of excitement. As she and Philip took their seats she noticed that only the people in whom Brother XII had shown a special interest were present. After a few minutes the music stopped, the curtains parted, and the Brother walked slowly onto the stage. This time he wore a more elaborate robe, still yellow, but trimmed with black fur. When he reached the front of the stage he stopped and stared at his audience, his eyes falling deliberately on every person, one at a time.

Finally he started to speak in a voice that was hardly more than a whisper so everyone had to strain to hear.

"Fellow believers, tonight you will know your destiny. Tonight you will know whether you are to perish in the flames or live in eternal peace. Look around you. Remember this humble hall. Tell your children, so they can tell theirs, and so on for generations to come."

He gestured towards the torches and Mary felt a twinge of fear. The flames had gotten larger, filling the room with a satanic glow.

"The fire is coming," he said. "Millions will perish, but tonight you may be given the chance to escape. The Masters of Wisdom are about to choose those who will return with me to the safety of The City of Refuge."

He went on to describe once again what would happen to those people who were not chosen. Mary could imagine it. Firestorms sweeping through the cities, people running, people screaming. Finally he paused and for two whole minutes he stood motionless, looking at his audience. Then slowly he asked, "Is there anyone here who does not believe the fire will come?"

There was silence.

His voice rose. "Is there anyone here who is not prepared to obey the Masters, whatever they command?"

Nobody stirred.

"Is there anyone who will not renounce their worldly goods? If there is, go, go now and never return."

Nobody moved. Mary sat as rigid as a post.

"It is not I who will make the choice but the Masters themselves. A meeting of the council is taking place at this very minute. Tonight my soul will make the journey into the depths of space to take its place on the council, and one of the Masters will travel to this hall. He will enter my body and speak to you directly. It is he who will reveal the names of the chosen ones."

He walked forward and took up a position directly in front of the couch. "My journey will be hard and I shall need the help of every one of you. You cannot go yourselves, but you will see the gateway to the void. Now look carefully into my eyes."

It seemed to Mary that he was staring straight at her, his dark eyes boring into her soul. Gradually she became aware of every detail of his face. His cheeks had turned pale and she noticed little beads of sweat glistening on his brow, but his eyes never seemed to waver from her face.

"Look *through* me," he purred. "There lies the road that crosses the abyss. It is an endless avenue with pillars on either side which leads on forever into eternal space. Look. Look carefully. See the avenue of pillars in your mind."

And she did see it, a road with ghostly white columns on either side, ethereal, as if it were made of mist. It stretched away to infinity, getting smaller and smaller until it disappeared into the distance. Perhaps it was her imagination, but it seemed to be really there.

"Look down the avenue of pillars," he commanded. "In the endless distance there is a light."

Yes, she could see the light, a little flicker far away. It moved a tiny fraction.

"The light is moving," he said. "The gates are opening. The cold wind from the void is blowing in."

She felt a draft on her face and the flames above the torches flickered. The lights dimmed further. Brother XII remained standing near the front of the stage.

"The Masters are calling," he whispered. "The Masters are calling me now."

Then he gave a long sigh, Ahhhhhhhh, and the breath seemed to drain from his body.

For half a minute the Brother stood like a statue, his arms stretched out in front and his face as white as chalk. Then Mary noticed a slight movement. The fingers of one hand were beginning to twitch. It was just a slight jerking motion at first, but gradually it spread into his wrist, and then his arm, and slowly his face twisted out of shape and his lips curled back in a dreadful grimace.

Then, without warning, his legs gave way and he fell backwards out of control. Fortunately he landed on the couch. Next his whole body began to convulse, writhing and shaking horribly in full view of everyone. Froth bubbled from his mouth as he panted for breath. She wanted to help him but her limbs had turned to lead.

Finally he lay still and she knew his soul had gone. All that remained was a crumpled body in a creased yellow robe lying on a couch. The avenue of pillars had disappeared and the light had vanished too. The cold draft had stopped and the torch flames rose straight up. Everyone was silent.

Just when she feared he might be dead his lips began to move. She thought she heard a whisper, but it was too feeble to make out any words. Slowly the voice became more distinct, a strange singsong voice, not Brother XII's at all.

"I am Dhyanis of the great Tutelary Deities of Egypt," it chanted. "Heed me well and then obey, or your souls will burn in hell for twenty-six thousand years, just as those of the non-chosen ones will burn.

"In every age of crisis a man has been sent who is more than a man, sent by the Gods to save mankind. Buddha, Christ and Mohammed were such men. Humble men, unrecognized by most until it was too late. Just as these, so has Brother XII been sent.

"And you, who have been found by him, are fortunate indeed. The Masters of Wisdom have examined every one of you and it is now my duty to call the names of those selected for salvation. Listen carefully for I shall call the names once only."

There was a short delay. People leaned forward expectantly. Then, with only his lips moving, Dhyanis called out the names in his peculiar singsong voice.

"Derek and Linda Watson of Christchurch. Mrs Evelyn Hiscock of Bournemouth. Arthur and Sarah Westlake . . . "

As the list went on and their names were not mentioned, Mary became alarmed, but finally she heard, "Philip and Mary White of Ashtead, Surrey."

When it was over Dhyanis continued, "Now I have some final words for the chosen ones. Since you are destined to know the joy and security of a land of sunshine, where sorrow is unknown and gain unneeded, tomorrow you will sell all your possessions and give the funds to your beloved Brother for the benefit of all. Remember that the Masters of Wisdom can see everything. Only those who unerringly obey will reach the sacred place."

With that final warning the lips stopped moving and there was silence. An age seemed to pass and then Mary heard a sigh. Eventually she saw that the body on the couch was breathing and she realized Brother XII was back.

Mary, Philip and Josephine made the long journey to British Columbia by steamship and train in the summer of 1934. It had taken longer to sell the house than she expected, and they travelled on their own, a few weeks after Brother XII and the rest of the party.

They got off the train in the city of Vancouver on the mainland and took the Canadian Pacific ferry for the thirty-mile crossing of the Strait of Georgia to Vancouver Island. Mary soon realized that Vancouver Island was almost big enough to be a country on its own. It even had a chain of mountains down the middle, and Victoria, the capital city of British Columbia, lay at its southern end.

Ken Martin met them on the dock at Nanaimo. She found it reassuring to see the big friendly man with a north-country accent. He had the Aquarian car, a large black Ford, and he drove them the last few miles south to the colony. The gravel road wound through wooded countryside for about twelve miles until they crested a hill and there was the sea, calm and blue, and dotted with little green islands.

"The Gulf Islands," Ken announced, pulling the car to the side of the road. "The Masters certainly knew what they were doing when they chose this spot for the colony."

"It's absolutely beautiful," said Mary.

"This is the most peaceful place in the world. The whole wide area is protected to the west by Vancouver Island, to the north and east by mainland Canada, and to the south by the Olympic Peninsular of the U.S.A. We sit in the middle in a huge sheltered basin."

"It's so warm," said Philip.

"Some quirk of geography draws warm air up from the south," Ken explained.

They stood by the car for a few minutes enjoying the view. The road led down a grassy slope dotted with trees, and at the bottom of the hill there was a row of neat new houses spaced along the top of a beach. Nearby was an orchard with young fruit trees growing in orderly rows, and half a mile to the south the grassland gave way to a forest of fir and cedar.

"Is that The City of Refuge?" Mary asked, pointing to the houses.

"Yes, but we usually call it Cedar-by-the-Sea," said Ken. "The colony is made up of three settlements, the one you are looking at down there, and two more on islands. Do you see that first row of islands a couple of miles away?"

She nodded. From the top of the hill she could see that many of the pretty tree-covered islets were arranged in rows.

"We own that group," Ken went on. "The settlement is on the largest one where there's a harbour. And do you see a big island beyond them?"

There was a much larger island in the distance, five or six miles away.

"That's Valdes. We bought four hundred acres at the north end. Beautiful land. We've just started a settlement there."

"How many islands are there?" asked Philip.

"Forty or fifty altogether. They stretch south for about sixty miles. The southern ones are American."

"Forty or fifty! Do many people live on them?"

"Hardly any. They're nearly all uninhabited."

They climbed back into the car.

"You'll be staying with Gillian and me for a few days, until we can fix you up with a house," he said as they drove down the hill.

The settlement looked neat and tidy. It lay at the top of a sandy bay where there was a small dock and a couple of boats. The houses near the middle faced the beach, while those towards each end stood on a low cliff. Behind them vegetable gardens and the orchard stretched up the hill. Ken stopped in front of a pretty cottage with a peaked roof and Gillian stepped out to greet them.

That evening they all attended Brother XII's sermon. There were no private cars in the colony so everybody walked. As they strolled up the road to the open-air temple the Martins introduced them to other members of the colony. They all looked happy and friendly. Ken pointed out the features of the Cedar settlement as they went along. There was a garage and workshop where they kept a truck and the big black Ford, some boathouses at the top of the beach near the dock, a store for the distribution of food, and the administration building near the top of the hill.

"That's where you pick up your mail," he said, pointing to the administration building. "And that's where *The Chalice* is printed."

"Really," said Mary. *The Chalice* was the Aquarian magazine which she looked forward to every month.

"We send out four thousand copies to places all over the world."

"That must cost a fortune," said Philip.

"On the contrary, it's a real money-maker. It costs a bit to produce but it keeps the donations pouring in."

They followed the road along the shore and then up the hill before taking a path into the forest. After a few hundred yards they came to a large grassy clearing in a hollow on the side of a hill. The ground sloped upwards on three sides, forming a natural amphitheatre which could hold two or three hundred people standing or sitting on the grass. At the focus of the amphitheatre she saw a huge old maple tree with a wooden platform at its base.

"This is our open-air temple," said Ken, "and there's the Tree of Wisdom. The Brother preaches here every evening and nearly everybody comes."

"What about the people who live on the islands?" Mary asked.

"They come by boat, and most of them get here two or three times a week. One of the reasons we all came here was to hear the Brother speak."

People were beginning to arrive. The majority were British, but some came from America and Canada. Mary was pleased to find that they were the same sort of people as herself and they were dressed in similar clothes. The men wore sports jackets or blazers and the women were in simple summer dresses.

Ken pointed to a path that led into the forest behind the Tree of Wisdom. "That's the way to the House of Mystery where the Brother lives," he explained.

Mary was curious to see the House of Mystery so she walked over to the path. The entrance was barred by a chain and the path curved through the trees so she couldn't see the house. She was peering past the chain when she heard Ken's voice.

"You can't go along there."

"Why not?"

"It's where the Brother meditates and confers with the Masters of Wisdom."

"But I want to see where he lives."

"I'm afraid you can't. It's one of his strictest rules."

"Have you seen it yourself?"

"The Earthly Council sometimes meets on the grass outside the house, but I've never been inside."

"What's the Earthly Council?"

"The committee that runs the colony."

Gillian broke in, "We should take our places now, the Brother will soon be here."

The thought of seeing the Brother again made Mary more excited than she cared to admit. She'd even bought a special yellow dress to match his robe. About two hundred people were sitting on the grass in semicircular rows up the slope of the amphitheatre. Mary took a place near the middle with Philip, Ken and Gillian.

As 8pm approached a man from the front row stood up and called for silence, and then she saw the Brother walking down the path from the House of Mystery. Her heart missed a beat. He was not wearing the saffron robe as she expected, but a simple tweed suit which looked much more appropriate in the country surroundings. Otherwise he was just as she remembered, the same swarthy good looks, the same dark eyes and black hair. Two older Aquarians moved the chain aside and escorted him across the clearing to the platform at the foot of the tree.

His talk was less formal than the ones in Southampton. There were no props, no flaming torches or big black birds. It was a practical talk about the colony and the work to be done before the meteorite struck. Mary felt his eyes on her from the beginning and at the end of the talk he publicly welcomed the Whites to the fold. It was different from Southampton, but the fire was still there. She was enormously attracted to this man, but not in a physical sense, his charisma was spiritual.

Philip wanted to see the island settlements, so the next day Ken took them for a tour in one of the motorboats.

As they waited on the dock at Cedar Philip became captivated by the beauty of the place. It was a sunny morning with no wind and a slight haze which made the distant islands look mysterious. From up the beach came the cry of gulls, and overhead a heron lazily winged its way towards some far off fishing ground.

They climbed down into the boat and Josephine sat happily on Mary's lap. Ken started the motor and they headed out towards De Courcy Island, a couple of miles away. Much of the shoreline consisted of rocks and cliffs, but Philip could see plenty of sandy beaches as well. And everywhere there were trees: fir, cedar and strange twisted arbutus trees which shed their bark as often as their leaves.

Half an hour later they were approaching a low ridge of rock between De Courcy Island and a smaller island called Link.

"This is our Panama Canal," said Ken. "These two islands used to be joined, but we dynamited a channel between them. It saves a good four miles on the trip between Cedar and the Valdes settlement."

They passed slowly through the narrow channel and then turned south along the shore of De Courcy. The fir and arbutus grew down to the water's edge, and kingfishers darted from bough to bough. Eventually they reached a fine landlocked harbour. The entrance was only fifty feet wide, but it opened out into a peaceful lagoon a quarter of a mile across. Water birds dotted the surface and herons stalked fish by the shore.

"This is Pirates Cove," said Ken. "It's the best harbour for miles."

There was a sturdy wooden dock on the far side of the harbour, with a storage barn nearby and a row of houses facing the harbour. A small tug and a barge lay at anchor and two more boats were moored to the dock.

"Who owns the tug?" Philip asked.

"Everything here belongs to us," said Ken. "We own the whole place. We need the tug and barge to transport building materials between the islands."

They tied up to the dock and Ken disappeared up the path to the houses. After a few minutes he returned with a thickset man in a check shirt. "This is John Prentice," he said. "He's the manager of the De Courcy settlement."

"Hi folks," said the manager. "Just arrived from the old country, eh? Welcome to De Courcy." They shook hands and then he went on, "Ken's going to show you around. Then we'll have lunch at the farm."

The settlement looked much like Cedar-by-the-Sea, although it was smaller. There was a row of neat wooden houses along a narrow gravel road that ran from the dock along the edge of the harbour and up to the farm. They watched a crew working on a half-finished house at the end of the row. Ken seemed to know everyone and they frequently stopped to talk as they made their way along the road. Trees seemed to thrive in the warm windless climate. In addition to the familiar fir and cedar Philip saw alder, maple, spruce and hemlock, and beneath the trees lay a carpet of salal and colourful wild flowers.

"What about animals?" he asked as they got deeper into the woods.

"There are bear and cougar in the forests of Vancouver Island," said Ken. "But they never swim out to these little islands. Deer and raccoons are the biggest critters here."

Soon they came to a small farm where a few acres had been cleared. There were cows and chickens beside a barn, and a pretty little farmhouse with a peaked roof and gables.

"This place is ideal for farming," Ken explained. "We're already producing a lot of our own food."

After a while they sat on a log to rest. To the west Philip could see across Stuart Channel to the Cedar settlement a couple of miles away. Beyond Cedar, perhaps twenty miles distant, stood the mountains of central Vancouver Island, blue and hazy in the distance. A pair of eagles soared overhead, their dark brown wings almost motionless as they floated in circles in the warm air. It was all very peaceful but the material things around them, the houses, the docks, the roads, could only have been achieved by a lot of activity.

"Who did all the work?" he asked. "Who built the houses? And the passage between the islands, who dynamited that?"

"We've done most of it ourselves. John Prentice did the blasting. He worked in the mines for years so he knows about explosives. And he was born on a farm in Saskatchewan which is where he learnt his farming."

"What about the houses?"

"Most of them were built by a contractor from Nanaimo with a lot of help from the settlers. In the end we aim to be independent. The Brother says we must use this period as a sort of apprenticeship and learn practical skills from the workmen we employ."

They had lunch at the farm with John Prentice and several others, and in the afternoon they headed out from Pirates Cove across Pylades Channel to Valdes Island.

"Do you want to see some sea life?" asked Ken. "There are usually seals basking on the rocks at the foot of the Valdes cliffs. And if we're lucky we may see sea-lions or even a pod of killer whales. They all swim through here from time to time."

They found about twenty seals lying on the smooth rounded rocks enjoying the sun, several with young pups by their sides. When Ken eased the boat in close they struggled clumsily across the rocks and plunged into the water.

After a few minutes they continued down the Valdes shore through narrow Gabriola passage until they reached a bay that was humming with activity.

"The Valdes settlement," Ken announced.

Philip saw the now familiar wooden dock with a warehouse and newly constructed houses nearby. A small bulldozer was working on a partially finished gravel road at the top of the beach.

Ken moored the boat at the dock and they got out to have a look around. "This is our most recent settlement," he said. "It's the farthest one from civilization, and we have to bring everything in by barge."

Philip was amazed. "It must be awfully expensive," he said. "Who decides what has to be done?"

"The Earthly Council makes the major decisions."

"Who's on the Council?"

"Brother XII is the chairman and there are eleven other members, people who've been here for some time. I'm one and John Prentice is another. When the Council makes a decision the Brother confers with the Masters of Wisdom. If the Masters agree we go ahead."

"What if they don't agree?"

"It's only happened once or twice, and when the Brother has explained their reasons we've realized we were wrong."

"What about financial affairs? Do you have an accountant?"

"We hardly ever discuss money. The Brother believes it has an evil influence. From a personal point of view the organization supplies everything, food, clothes, all that sort of thing, and there's never been any shortage. But one of the members is an accountant and he's on the Earthly Council."

"Where does all the money come from?"

"Donations mostly, from appeals in *The Chalice*. And a lot of the people here were very wealthy."

"You must think I'm awfully nosey."

"Not at all. You have a right to know about the colony now you live here. Is there anything else?"

Philip hesitated. "Well, yes, there is. What does the Brother do with the money? Is it properly invested in stocks and bonds? You see I'm a stockbroker. I know how to put money to work so it makes more money. Do you think he'd be interested in that?"

"Well, I'll tell you a curious thing," replied Ken slowly. "The Brother doesn't believe in stocks or bonds or anything like that. You'll never believe this, but he takes the money to the bank and changes it into gold coins. Then he puts the coins in big glass jars, seals them with wax, and packs them in special wooden boxes made by one of the carpenters. That's what he does with the money, he converts it into gold and keeps it hidden in the House of Mystery."

Chapter 4

It was not long before Marcia Wooding realized she had a problem child on her hands. She just could not ignore the temper tantrums Mark threw whenever she refused to let him have his way. She couldn't understand where he got them from. Her husband was a mild man, and her brother was so timid that he'd never even married.

In the spring of 1935 Marcia's mother, Mrs Allen, arrived in Salcombe for a visit. She was a big woman with a loud voice who was used to getting her own way. Marcia was frightened of her mother, but she was finding child care much more difficult than she'd expected and she needed help. She took care to warn her mother about Mark's behaviour in advance so she'd know what to expect.

Mrs Allen observed the scene in tight-lipped silence for a couple of days. Marcia was especially strict with her little boy so her mother wouldn't think she was weak. At lunch on the second day he dropped some food and when she scolded him he screamed. Afterwards her mother announced, "I think we should have a little talk."

"It's not my fault, Mother, I've done everything I can."

"He's a wilful little boy," said Mrs Allen. "If you don't break a little boy's will before he's one year old he'll never learn to obey you."

"But Mark's over a year old now."

"And so far you've failed. You must get the upper hand now before it's too late."

"What can I do?"

"Stop him screaming for a start."

"But how?"

"Whenever he screams give him a good hard slap; he'll soon learn not to do it. Your brother was a wilful little boy just like Mark, but I turned him into an obedient child by the time he was two."

The very next day Marcia was downstairs with her mother while Ann tucked Mark into his crib for his afternoon nap. She listened while the nanny cooed to him but he didn't go to sleep. So long as his nanny was there he was quiet, but as soon as she left he cried.

"Aren't you going to do your duty?" asked Marcia's mother after a few minutes.

"What do you mean?"

"You know very well what I mean. Your son is disturbing the entire household and you're doing nothing about it. You must make him keep quiet."

"Maybe he needs something. I'll send Ann up."

"She's just left him. Do it yourself."

They reached the nursery at the same time as the nanny, so Marcia said, "It's alright Ann, I'll deal with him myself."

Mark stopped crying when he saw her. He smiled and held out his arms. She picked him up for a cuddle, but as soon as she put him back in his crib he started crying again.

"Tell him to stop," said her mother.

She tried, but he went on crying.

"Tell him again, and if he doesn't stop give him a smack on the leg."

"Mark, stop it," said Marcia, almost shouting, but it made no difference.

"Go on," said her mother.

Marcia slapped him sharply on his naked thigh, but that made him scream louder than ever.

"Harder," said Mrs Allen. "Smack him harder. You've got to teach him a lesson."

Marcia raised her hand.

"Oh Madam," exclaimed Ann, watching in horror.

"Do it," said Mrs Allen.

Eventually they went back downstairs. Mark was screaming at the top of his voice. Ann was almost in tears as well, but Mrs Allen had forbidden her to go near him.

"I don't think that nanny helps," she said when Ann had left the room.

"What's the matter with her?" asked Marcia.

"She's not strong-willed enough to deal with a child. You should have got a proper nanny. Ann's just a housemaid."

"Mark is very fond of her."

"That's because she always gives him what he wants. The boy's been getting too much of what he wants and not enough of what he needs."

"What he needs?"

"Discipline. A good hard spanking on the bare bottom whenever he misbehaves."

Mark grew fast. He was big and strong and healthy, but the temper tantrums continued. Marcia was surprised how little they seemed to disturb Neville or Ann, but they upset her terribly. She often remembered what her mother had said about breaking a little boy's will.

Mrs Allen had long since returned to London, but Marcia told her what was happening on the phone.

"You've got to do something about it," her mother replied.

"But he's eighteen months old now. What can I do?"

"Do you remember the rhyme in *Alice in Wonderland*?"

"Which one?"

"It goes like this:
> Speak roughly to your little boy,
> And beat him when he sneezes;
> He only does it to annoy,
> Because he knows it teases."

Often it did seem as if her little boy was teasing her. When that happened she would smack him, or withhold food or love, but then he would go into a sulk which might last for days. He would sit in the nursery snivelling and asking for his mummy until Ann or Neville persuaded her to give in.

She often remembered her reaction when she first saw him as a baby. She'd never told anyone what she'd felt. She knew it was wrong but she simply did not find him a likeable child. However he seemed to love her very much indeed.

Then, towards the end of the hot summer of 1935 she realized she was expecting another baby. James Johnson looked after her during the pregnancy, and in April 1936 she gave birth to the little daughter she'd always wanted.

Marcelle was a beautiful baby with blue eyes like her father, and straight blond hair. Marcia took to her immediately. She had the nursery redecorated in pink and moved Mark into a spare bedroom at the back of the house.

Chapter 5

Mary White would never forget the day Brother XII was arrested.

It was the spring of 1936 and the Whites had been living in the colony for a year and a half. They had a nice little house on a sheltered bay at the south end of De Courcy Island, a quarter of a mile from Pirates Cove. Mary liked it because there was a sandy beach for Josephine, a good gravel path to the storehouse and the dock, and a spectacular view of the islands to the south.

The house was small but comfortable, and two other families lived nearby so she was not lonely. The pace of life was pleasant and relaxed. She drew their water from a well, fetched supplies from the storehouse at Pirates Cove, and cooked on a kerosene stove. The summer days were long and warm, and in the winter she enjoyed the cosy evenings around the wood stove with her family and friends. She found that many of the settlers had similar backgrounds to her own and they enjoyed an active social life. They played bridge every week, and there were frequent parties in people's homes or on the beach.

Brother XII's doctrine did not exclude other religions and when a group of followers humbly asked if they might hold Christian services he graciously agreed. There was no ordained minister in the colony, so the services were held by a layman in the schoolhouse, and Mary found they filled one of the last remaining voids in her life.

Philip had no skill to offer the colony except his experience with money, but the Brother handled the money himself with help from Brian Hargreaves, the trusted Aquarian accountant. So Philip worked on the farm. At first he thought the physical labour might be demeaning, but the Aquarians regarded the man who guided the plough as no less important than the one who balanced the books. Soon he found the exercise suited him and he felt healthier than ever before in his life.

One morning Mary was over at Pirates Cove chatting with friends. There were always boats coming and going so it was no surprise when a boat arrived from Cedar, however she was shocked to see the grim look on the faces of the passengers. Among them were the Martins, so she asked Gillian what was wrong.

"Brian Hargreaves has absconded with a lot of money," she said. "Ken has come to see John Prentice about it now."

"I thought the Brother kept all the money himself."

"He gave Hargreaves $5,000 to change into gold coins. But instead of going to the bank Hargreaves took the ferry to Vancouver and disappeared."

"Five thousand dollars! Surely the Masters of Wisdom won't let him get away with that."

"The Brother's consulted them already," said Gillian. "He's also called the police."

Mary took Gillian home for lunch while Ken met with John and some other members of the Council. When the meeting was over she and Philip decided to go to Cedar to see what was happening. While they were on the boat Ken explained that Hargreaves had left a note claiming the $5,000 was owed to him as wages for the work he'd done as the colony's accountant. The Brother was especially angry because no one had noticed the note for several hours so Hargreaves had plenty of time to escape.

When the boat approached Cedar, Mary was surprised to see people celebrating on the beach. Ken went ashore to find out what was happening and soon returned with a grin on his face. Apparently the police had caught Hargreaves after all.

"How did they manage that?" Mary asked.

"The ferry broke down and by the time it reached Vancouver they were waiting for him. It's strange because it's never broken down before."

Mary didn't find it strange at all, she knew the Masters would never let anyone rob the colony. As they walked up the hill to the administration building she felt a sense of jubilation. The Masters and the police had worked in harmony. The money would be returned. If only the rest of the world could run as smoothly.

The administration building was crowded and there were more people outside waiting to congratulate their leader. Everyone looked happy. She could see the Brother through a window talking on the phone, issuing orders, a smile on his face. The Aquarians had triumphed. There'd be celebrations tonight.

And then it happened.

The first thing she saw was a car edging its way through the crowd, and after a minute she realized it was a police car. Eventually it reached the administration building and three officers got out. The policemen climbed the steps and went inside. Soon she could see them through a window talking to Brother XII. At first the Brother was smiling, but gradually his expression changed and for a couple of minutes they seemed to be arguing. Then one of the policemen clipped something onto Brother XII's wrist.

At first she could hardly believe it, but then she saw the look of shock on the faces of the other people in the room. The policeman had handcuffed the Brother to himself. Next they started to lead him away. When they reached the door everyone outside could see what was happening and a hush fell over the crowd. Mary wondered if anyone would try to stop them, but they hustled him down the steps so quickly there wasn't time. She watched Ken push his way to the front, and they let him talk to the Brother briefly before they got him into the car.

Everyone was stunned. Eventually Ken returned and said, "They arrested Hargreaves alright, but he laid a counter charge, so they decided to arrest the Brother as well."

"A counter charge?" asked Philip.

"He's accused Brother XII of misusing Aquarian money when he bought the Valdes property against the wishes of the Council."

"Is that true?"

Ken looked uncomfortable. "Yes, I guess it is."

"But I thought you approved of the Valdes property," said Philip.

"I didn't at the time. We voted not to buy it, but the Masters overruled us, so the Brother bought it anyway."

"I see," said Philip thoughtfully. "Has that sort of thing happened often?"

"Sometimes. But in every case we eventually realized the Masters were right."

"What do you think will happen now?"

"I don't know. Brian Hargreaves knows a lot about the financial affairs of the colony, and maybe the Brother was technically wrong. I think I'd better go to Nanaimo and get him a lawyer."

Mary went back to De Courcy with Philip. She felt totally stunned. Brother XII in prison. It was the end of the world.

In the morning John Prentice called a meeting and announced that the Brother had been released on bail. Everybody cheered. But he would have to go to court, and the trial had been set for July. The Council was holding a rally in the open-air temple that night and they were all expected to attend.

Mary arrived at the temple with Philip just as darkness came. She had never seen the big amphitheatre so full or so elaborately prepared. On the platform beneath the Tree of Wisdom sat an altar decorated with the signs of the zodiac, and on each side stood the flaming torches and the big ebony birds. A great fire burned at the edge of the clearing casting a flickering glow over the scene. The excitement was infectious. She wanted to sit near the front but for some reason Philip insisted on going to the back.

She looked around as they waited. The firelight gleamed on people's faces and threw long shadows through the woods on either side. After a few minutes she heard a drumming sound coming from the forest. It was muffled at first but it gradually grew louder:

Bam. Bam. Bam. Bam . . .

Then, through the trees, she saw a procession of lights slowly making its way along the path from the House of Mystery towards the open-air temple. Soon she could see that the lights were flaming torches on poles, carried by a column of about forty people marching two abreast. Two of them had drums with which they beat out the rhythm. As they marched they thrust their torches up and down in time with the drums, thumping the poles on the ground.

Bam. Bam. Bam. Bam . . .

They marched slowly across the clearing to the platform at the foot of the huge old Tree of Wisdom. Some people began to stamp their feet in time with the drums while others clapped their hands. Mary felt the tension rise. Her feet were stamping out the rhythm, and sweat ran down her face.

Bam. Bam. Bam. Bam . . .

At the head of the procession marched Brother XII in his robe of black and gold, his head held high and his eyes flashing with defiance. On either side were John Prentice and Ken Martin, each carrying a flaming torch on a pole. Behind them marched the double row of men and women, their torches flashing as they thrust them up and down. Slowly they crossed the clearing and took up their positions. The Brother and his chief advisers stood on the platform. The others were spaced along the front of the crowd, still beating the drums and thumping the butts of their torches on the ground.

Bam. Bam. Bam. Bam . . .

To the left of the platform the fire threw flames high into the air casting an eerie glow on the altar and the Brother's glistening face. Gradually the tempo rose. Torches flashed, drums beat, people stamped their feet. Mary's excitement mounted and as the frenzy built she became oblivious of Philip, the crowd, everything but the lighted platform and the figure of Brother XII.

After a few minutes the Brother held up his hands and the drumming ceased. Everyone was silent. There was a long pause, then he began to speak. He started in a quiet reasonable tone that caught everyone by surprise.

"Fellow Aquarians, friends, brothers and sisters. By this time you all know what has happened in the last two days. Yesterday Brian Hargreaves stole a large sum of our money. It was only by the intervention of the Masters of Wisdom that it has been returned. The ferry does not break down every day. Hargreaves is a traitor and he must be punished. I have spoken with the Masters and they agree that he is one of you, and you must decide his fate. That is why I have called you together this evening, to decide the traitor's fate. But there is more. Hargreaves has accused me of misusing Aquarian Foundation money when we bought the land for the Valdes settlement."

His voice began to rise. "This spiteful accusation was why I was held in prison last night. When we bought the Valdes land not everyone agreed. There was honest discussion as there always should be when important decisions are to be made. But we bought the land and now it is worth twice what we paid."

He was shouting now and gesticulating with his hands. "But we are not here to make money, we are here to save mankind. The Valdes settlement is a model for all to see. It is an example of how the human race will live after the holocaust has come. Does anyone think the Valdes purchase was wrong? Stand up and have your say." He paused but no one moved. "Is there anyone here who is dissatisfied with the way the colony is run? If there is stand up. Stand up and tell me why."

Now his voice took on a cruel tone as he went on to describe Hargreaves as a filthy evil traitor. There was no compromise, no possibility of forgiveness. On and on he went, his voice gradually rising to a scream.

"And what is your verdict?" he shouted. "Do you find Hargreaves guilty? Is he a traitor and a liar and a thief?"

Someone in the front row murmured, "Guilty." Others repeated the word and soon everyone was shouting, "Guilty. Guilty. Guilty," over and over again.

Once more the Brother held up his hands for silence, and when the noise had stopped he said, "What sentence do you pass? What punishment do you want for a traitor who would destroy us all?"

For a moment everyone was quiet. Then Mary heard someone at the front say, "Death," and soon others took up the theme. "Death. Death. Death . . . "

Louder and louder came the chant, and then the drums took up the rhythm and everyone was screaming it, "Death to Brian Hargreaves. Death, Death. Death . . . "

The firelight gleamed on the sweating faces. The flaming torches flashed up and down. The chanting built to a crescendo. "Death to Brian Hargreaves. Death, death, death . . . "

Again Brother XII held up his hands for silence. He was standing on the platform by the Tree of Wisdom and for the first time Mary noticed that five small white dots had been painted on its massive trunk, making a pattern like a Christian cross.

"I can see Hargreaves now," cried the Brother. "He is in the police station cowering in the corner of a small bare cell. Now you must concentrate, everyone together, you must see him in your minds, cowering in the corner, waiting for his fate. We may not have his body but if we all work together we can certainly destroy his soul."

He paused for everyone to concentrate their minds on Brian Hargreaves. Mary could see Hargreaves easily, cowering in the corner, just as Brother XII suggested.

"Now," the Brother exclaimed, holding out his arms. "Now his soul is leaving his body like a ghost departing from the dead."

Mary could see it too, a sort of ghostly form rising from Hargreaves body. A hush fell over the crowd; they must see it too.

"Now his soul is bare," he cried. "Now is the time for us to capture Hargreaves' soul."

He paused and for two whole minutes he stood absolutely still, as rigid as a statue, his eyes fixed on some faraway point as he focused his powers. Mary imagined Hargreaves' soul struggling in vain against Brother XII's supernatural power.

Then, after the long silence the Brother cried, "I have him. I have Hargreaves soul in my power. I'm going to nail it to the tree."

Brother XII began to move his hands as if he were holding someone and nailing their hands to the white dots on the tree. It was very realistic. Mary thought she could hear the blows. The firelight flickered on the knots and whorls in the bark, and suddenly she glimpsed it, a sort of ghost of a man struggling to get free. A murmur rose from the crowd and she thought they could see it too. Finally the Brother finished his grisly task. The fire flared and she glimpsed it again, an ethereal form, the ghost of Brian Hargreaves nailed by his hands to the trunk of the tree.

"Death," Brother XII spat at the figure, raising his hand with his fingers stretched out flat like a knife. "Brian Hargreaves, I sentence you to death. I shall cut your throat so your miserable body will be severed from your evil soul."

Then he slowly drew his hand from one side to the other, exactly where Mary had seen Hargreaves' throat.

"Death."

She thought she saw the figure flinch and she was surprised there wasn't any blood.

"Now, everyone together," he commanded, holding up his hand once more as an example.

Mary's hand came up automatically.

"Death," he cried.

"Death," echoed everyone as they drew their imaginary knives across Hargreaves' throat.

Then the ghost had gone. Perhaps they'd killed it, but there had been no blood. Mary felt disappointed. Perhaps it had never been there at all.

Next an extraordinary thing happened. An animal ran out from the woods. At first she couldn't see what it was, but then she realized it was a goat from the farm. For a moment it looked confused, but then it seemed to recognize John Prentice the farmer, and it ran towards him.

"Catch that animal," ordered Brother XII.

Two men jumped forward and easily caught the goat which was quite tame. Murmurs of surprise came from the crowd and Mary wondered what was going on, but the Brother turned towards them and cried, "Here is your proof. Here is Hargreaves' soul."

Then he looked at the men who were holding the goat and told them to tie it up. One of them produced a cord, and they quickly bound the hind legs and then the fore legs and threw the animal onto its side.

"Take it to the fire," he ordered.

The two men picked up the goat, struggling with fear, and carried it over to the fire. They held it with its neck stretched out over the flames. Mary was rigid with horror.

Then Brother XII stood before his followers with his eyes blazing and sweat gleaming on his brow. With a flourish he reached inside his robe and withdrew a long steel knife. There was a look of triumph on his face, and the blade flashed in the firelight as he brandished it above his head.

"To thieves and traitors, death," he cried. "Death to Hargreaves' soul."

The men held the terrified animal facing the fire, with its head pulled back exposing its throat. Brother XII reached round its neck from behind, and with one smooth stroke of the knife he cut the animal's throat. A single piercing shriek rent the silence, and blood, real crimson blood, spurted from the severed arteries and hissed as it struck the flames.

Mary had her first serious row with Philip when they got home after the sacrifice of the goat.

"I don't know what Brother XII is up to," he said, "but I can tell you a couple of things: the world is not coming to an end, and that man is not divine. He's some sort of a madman and sacrificing animals is just the beginning. We should follow Hargreaves' example and get out of here as quickly as we can."

She could see he was upset because the birthmark on his cheek was glowing red, but she was so disturbed by what he'd said that she didn't care.

"Of course he's divine," she cried. "The outside world is getting worse every day and he's the only one who knows what to do. That animal didn't suffer and it's had an astounding effect on everyone but you. And anyway, what would we live on if we left? We've given all our money to the Aquarians."

"Well, I've never told you this, but I did keep some money in a savings account, just in case."

She was shocked. It was almost as bad as what Hargreaves had done. "How could you? We were supposed to give everything. The Masters will know. They can see everything we do, and they'll tell him. How could you be so stupid?"

"It's not me who's being stupid."

"He'll destroy our souls? He does control our souls you know."

"Nonsense. Only God controls our souls, the real God. I tell you we should leave now, before he finds out we've been discussing it. We should go straight to the church in Nanaimo and ask God for protection."

"You go if you must, but I'm staying here and so is Jo." She could hardly believe she'd said the words, and she had no idea what she'd do if he really walked out. How could she choose between the Brother and her husband? She held her breath, and when he eventually backed down she was especially nice to him in case he changed his mind.

Soon stories began to circulate that Brian Hargreaves had mysteriously disappeared. He was needed for the trial, of course, and as the date got nearer it was rumoured the police had started a nation-wide search.

Eventually the Brother called a meeting. Yes, the rumours were true, the police had even called Interpol. He had a smile on his face as he spoke, and everyone knew that Hargreaves would never be found. Mary shuddered, but he didn't seem to have discovered that Philip had been holding money back. In July the Brother called another meeting to proudly announce that with the key witness gone the charges against him had been dropped.

Mary's father had been sick with angina and she wanted to go to England to see him. She thought it might do Philip good to be away from the colony for a while too, so when Brother XII announced that he would be travelling to England, she asked if they could go along as assistants. He couldn't have heard about Philip's doubts, she guessed, because he immediately agreed.

The Brother arranged to travel by train and steamship in late July, and the Whites were to join him two weeks later. However in July Mary's father had a heart attack and the Brother asked her if she would like to travel with him instead, so she could be with her father as soon as possible. Philip and Jo would follow as originally planned.

Soon after the train left Vancouver he invited her to share his private first-class compartment so she could enjoy the view of the Rocky Mountains. At first she was nervous because she'd never been alone with him before, but his friendly conversation soon put her at ease. She sat facing him across the compartment and before long they were discussing the subject of reincarnation, something that had always fascinated her.

"Mary," he said, looking straight into her eyes. "It is not accidental that reincarnation interests you so much, nor that it came up immediately we started to talk."

"Not accidental?"

"All the major things that happen to you and me have been planned for thousands of years. We're allowed to control the little things, like what we have for lunch, but the main decisions of our lives were determined by the Gods long ago."

"You and me?" she asked. "Are we different from the rest?"

"Of course we are."

She felt a tingle of excitement. Sometimes she did feel different from other people. "I know you're different, but do you think I am too?"

He leaned towards her. She was very conscious of his dark eyes and his handsome face, and she wondered if he could sense the attraction she felt.

"Mary," he said. "Surely you believe in reincarnation?"

"Of course I do."

She often had the feeling she'd been to places before and she thought it was because she'd seen them in some previous existence. Sometimes she even thought she knew what was going to happen next.

"Do you know who you were in the past?" he asked.

That was another thing she was always wondering about. It was uncanny, he seemed to sense the very things that concerned her most.

"I almost know, but I can never quite remember. Do you know who I was?"

"Yes."

"Please tell me."

"Mary," he whispered looking into her eyes. "There's another subject that interests you, isn't there? Mythology. The Gods and Goddesses of ancient Egypt."

"How on earth did you know that?"

"The Masters told me all about you long before we met. Does the name Isis mean anything to you?"

She felt a thrill. Isis was the Egyptian Goddess of love.

"When the Masters of Wisdom revealed my mission," he went on, "they told me I would meet the reincarnation of the Goddess Isis."

Her heart missed a beat. "Do you think I might have been Isis?"

"You are Isis. Why else your interest in reincarnation and mythology? Were your parents interested in those subjects?"

"No," she replied bitterly. Her father was a scientist who thought reincarnation was nonsense.

"Isis," he whispered, taking her hand.

She had a strange sensation that all this had happened before. Isis, yes, it seemed so right. She'd always been fascinated by the Goddess Isis and now she knew the reason why.

Dusk was falling and they were deep in the mountains. Outside she could see rock and snow and ice, but in the compartment it was warm and comfortable. The cushions felt soft and the rhythmic sound of the wheels drummed in her ears. His voice was as smooth as silk and it made her want to fall asleep. Her eyes began to close.

"Look at me, Mary," he commanded gently. "Look into my eyes, my Goddess Isis. Do you not know who I am? Do you not remember when we were together in ages past?"

Yes, she thought somewhere deep in her sleepy brain, I have seen you before. Who are you? She almost knew.

He leaned closer, his eyes on hers.

"Let the mists of time be parted," he whispered. "I am Osiris."

Osiris. Of course. The great Egyptian God. He was the beloved husband of the Goddess Isis, and the father of her son.

He took her hands in his. The train thundered on through the magnificent mountains, two great Canadian Pacific steam locomotives at its head. But Mary, or Isis, they both seemed the same, was only aware of those brown eyes, those fine dark features. He looks like an Egyptian god she thought dimly. He is Osiris, there can be no doubt.

It took four days for the train to cross Canada and she spent them in a trance. She had always believed in simple reincarnation, but now he explained that not only did a person, or a soul, live many times in different bodies, but also two souls sometimes shared the same body during the same lifetime.

There had been many examples of this, he said, where the same person seemed to have two different personalities that showed at different times, like Dr Jekyll and Mr Hyde. It was quite natural for Dr Jekyll to behave differently from Mr Hyde, and there was no reason for one to feel guilty because of the actions of the other.

She was really two different people, he explained, and so was he. At present they were Isis and Osiris, and they had no reason to feel inhibited because a few days before they had been Mary White and Brother XII. Indeed, they had a sacred duty to perform in their present state. Their task was to join in holy union to produce the young God Horus, Isis' son.

This must be a spiritual and not a physical union, he assured her, but a union just the same. It was to be Horus who would eventually lead the Aquarians out of The City of Refuge, to repopulate the world with a better human race.

That very first night they started on the task, but she soon discovered there was to be no crude rough-and-tumble love making. The attendant discreetly served them a light meal with a fine white wine right in the compartment and after dinner they retired to the bedroom. With the lights turned low he very slowly, very gently undressed her, and himself too, and they lay together beneath the sheets with their bodies touching and their souls entwined.

During the next three days the whole breadth of the continent slipped by, the forests and lakes, the towns and the vast prairie grasslands, and for three days and nights the dream went on. He called her Isis all the time until the name seemed as real as her own. They talked incessantly of godly things, of Egyptian and Greek mythology, and of their central role in the great new age of Aquarius, the golden age of mankind that they would start. He was with her constantly, except for one brief period when the train stopped in Calgary and he got off to send a telegram.

Everything conspired to make her feel a different person, a godly person. Even the attendants on the train seemed to treat the two of them with special respect. They were always courteously ushered to the best table in the first-class dining compartment, the table which she herself had originally selected. Once, when they arrived late, she actually heard the head waiter telling a prosperous-looking older couple that this very table was out of service and they would have to sit somewhere else. But it was immediately available to Isis and Osiris.

From time to time vague thoughts of little Josephine and Philip and her father crept into her mind. They were ill-formed and slightly guilty thoughts, but she told herself that they were the responsibility of Mary White, not Isis, and one day Mary would come back to take care of them. Meanwhile she was Isis, and Isis had her own thoughts and responsibilities, and they were not at all unpleasant.

Although she was a goddess she became aware that she had earthly feelings and desires. One night after all fear of physical abuse had vanished, when she and Osiris were lying together naked with their souls entwined, she realized that she needed more than a purely spiritual union. She was acutely aware that in ancient Greece Osiris had been reincarnated as Adonis, the God of fertility and love, and in Roman times he had been the bull-god Apis.

As she squeezed against him she could feel the physical sign of all three, of love, fertility, and the bull, pressing firmly against her body. She wanted him physically as well as spiritually, and as they touched it was easy to tell that he felt the same desire. But Osiris insisted that earthly union, complete physical union, must wait until their souls were entirely in tune.

The train journey ended at Montreal where they were to board the *Empress of Britain* for the six day passage across the Atlantic. In the cab, on the way to the dock, Osiris told her he had telegraphed ahead from Calgary to book a first-class cabin for them both, under the name of Mr and Mrs Amiel de Valdes.

"There's nothing wrong with travelling incognito," he said with a chuckle. "One simply can't make a booking in the name of the God Osiris!"

She asked him about the different names on their passports, but he assured her it had all been taken care of, and there was absolutely no embarrassment when they boarded the ship. She enjoyed the voyage enormously. The stewards and waiters, and even the officers of the ship all seemed to treat them with the sort of regal deference she was coming to expect. The weather was calm and sunny, although quite cool, and the food was superb. Southampton appeared on the horizon all too soon.

Immediately after they had docked their steward was at the cabin door.

"Excuse me, sir," he said. "There's a telegram for Mrs de Valdes."

The name Mrs Mary White was on the envelope. It had been crossed out and Mrs Amiel de Valdes had been written above, but in that moment, even before she'd read the message, Isis vanished and Mary White returned.

The telegram was from her aunt, announcing that her father had suffered a second heart attack and died the previous night. The funeral would be in four days' time.

Mary was distraught. She had not been especially close to her father when he was alive, but now she thought of all the things she would have said if only he'd lived one more week. Even one more day and she might have seen him.

Brother XII was wonderful.

"Mary," he said gently. "Isis and Osiris have gone now. They may return, we shall have to see, but now you are Mary White and I am Amiel de Valdes, or Brother XII, they are both the same."

It was a small funeral. Mary's mother had died years before, and she had only one sister who lived in South Africa, but there were several aunts and uncles. The Brother accompanied her and he was full of compassion. She introduced him as either Amiel de Valdes or Brother XII. The other family members knew she had joined a strange religious cult overseas, so they were not surprised by the odd-sounding names; however none of them could have failed to be impressed by his smart and handsome appearance, and his obvious concern for her welfare.

When Mary met Philip and Josephine at Southampton a couple of weeks later, she knew something was wrong as soon as she saw them walking down the gangway from the ship.

Philip's first words were, "How could you?"

"How could I what?"

"You shared a cabin with that man on this very ship," he accused. "Don't deny it, I've seen the passenger list: Mr and Mrs de Valdes, first class. And all the time your father was lying on his deathbed. How could you do it?"

She nearly burst into tears, and she realized later that it would have been better if she had. It was the remark about her father that stung her most. How could she possibly have known he was going to die? And how could she tell her husband that it was not she but Isis who'd been with Brother XII, and anyway they'd never actually made love. It was impossible to explain, certainly impossible on a crowded dock with people already beginning to stare.

"I can't explain," she said lamely.

"Well you'd better try." His birthmark reddened with pent-up bitterness. "That man's a fraud. You're to come with me and never see him again."

She knew Philip was wrong. Amiel had helped her enormously during the terrible days after her father's death. She couldn't deny him now.

"He's not a fraud," she said.

"Then what is he? Your lover?" He spat out the words.

"Philip, I'm not coming with you now. Not like this. I'll phone you in a day or two, or you call me. I'll explain it then."

She turned and walked away, holding back her tears until she was out of his sight. Only then did she realize she hadn't even greeted little Jo. She had to go back, she knew that immediately, but she couldn't find them.

Then she saw Philip getting into a cab. Jo was already inside, with her little face pressed to the window and tears running down her cheeks. Mary shouted but Philip didn't hear, and the door slammed in her face. She ran after the cab but it pulled away. Desperately she hailed others, but none of them would stop, and in the end she could only stand and watch as her husband and her daughter drew slowly out of her life.

Chapter 6

Mary tried to make things up with her husband, but he refused to have anything to do with her unless she forsook the Aquarians, and there was never any question of that. She met him on several occasions and had a tearful reunion with Josephine, but they continued to live apart.

In the summer of 1936 Brother XII gave a series of talks in southwest London and she acted as his assistant. Her relationship with the Brother was now entirely proper, but as time went on she fell more and more under his spell. His talks drew a lot of attention from the press and she became terribly upset when certain newspapers suggested he was a fraud, although it didn't bother him at all.

"My dear Mary," he would say. "It makes no difference what they print; when my name is in the papers the hall is full, and when the hall is full the donations pour in."

And pour in they did. She was staggered by the amount they received. One day in August an elderly lady asked the Brother if he would accept a large sailing yacht that had belonged to her late husband. The boat was a seventy-two-foot Brixham trawler called *Lady Royal,* and the woman hoped to find a good home for her in The City of Refuge. However the boat weighed fifty tons and the Brother told Mary that the only way to get her to British Columbia would be to sail her there.

They took the train down to Chichester to have a look and Mary immediately fell in love with her. She was a big solid vessel with a shiny black hull, two masts, a long bowsprit, and a beautifully varnished mahogany cabin. Mary didn't know much about yachts but this one looked strong and comfortable.

The Brother examined every detail. He spent half a day probing the tan-coloured sails, inspecting the great wooden booms, and testing the rigging. In his early years he'd been a merchant seaman. Mary knew he could sail a boat, and as the hours slid by she realized he was planning to sail this one back to the Aquarian colony. At first she felt nervous, but he assured her that Brixham trawlers were built to handle any weather and the *Lady Royal* would make the voyage easily. His enthusiasm was infectious and before long she was looking forward to the trip.

They sailed in September. Brother XII was the captain, Mary had agreed to be the cook, and they hired three local lads from Sussex as deck hands. They ran into rough weather in the Bay of Biscay, but the *Lady*

Royal seemed perfectly safe. The Brother proved to be an excellent skipper and they arrived at their first port of call, Gibraltar, after an uneventful passage of a couple of weeks.

Mary was excited to be entering a foreign port. Gibraltar wasn't quite a foreign port because everyone spoke English, but there was a strong Spanish influence and it was sunny and hot. Palm trees dotted the waterfront, there were donkeys pulling old-fashioned carts, and the town was full of narrow streets with little Spanish shops.

During the voyage south her admiration for the Brother, or Amiel as she called him now, had grown and grown. He was a natural leader so she was not surprised by his easy command of the crew. But the skill with which he handled the ship in any weather and navigated the ocean with only the sun and the stars were talents she hadn't seen before.

They spent three weeks in Gibraltar relaxing and taking on supplies. The next leg of the voyage took them south to the West Indies on the other side of the Atlantic Ocean.

The passage was straightforward and the weather was good. On the second week they picked up the trade winds, and then the sailing was all downwind. After an ocean passage of exactly four weeks they made a perfect landfall on the tiny island of Sombrero, and within a few hours they were sailing among the palm-clad tropical islets of the British Virgin Islands. Mary found it wonderful to see land again, and that evening they anchored in the harbour at Tortola, the main island of the group.

Next day Amiel explained that he didn't want to arrive in Canada before the beginning of April because of winter storms, so they'd have to wait a month in the Virgin Islands. He gave the three lads from Sussex a month's paid leave, and for the first time in five months Mary had him to herself.

Then began one of the happiest times of her life. They were anchored in a green tropical bay with palm-clad hills on either side. At the head of the bay the quaint old settlement of Road Town nestled behind a beach of coral sand. There was a picturesque market, native houses and a store. On the hill to one side stood the old buildings of the colony, and the *Lady Royal* lay close in by the Governor's house, sheltered behind a coral reef.

She spent the afternoon shopping in the market, and in the evening she prepared a special dinner for just the two of them. She set up a table and chairs on the open afterdeck, and they sat together sipping glasses of rum and molasses and fresh squeezed limes. The tropical air was warm and she put on a pink summer dress while he wore slacks and an open-necked shirt. As dusk fell the sounds and smells of the island drifted across the water, and when the first stars appeared she began to serve the dinner.

They had been four weeks at sea and the aroma of fresh cooked food was unbelievably appealing. She brought out the courses one by one. First there was salad and newly made bread rolls, the first bread they'd tasted for a month. Next she'd cooked a dorado in a steaming casserole, with cristophenes and herbs. Finally they had a fresh fruit salad of mangos, papaya and pomegranates, with lime juice and crushed sugar cane. They ate the meal slowly, savouring every morsel, and sipped a Spanish wine shipped all the way from Gibraltar in the *Lady Royal*'s hold.

After dinner they sat drinking coffee and chatting about the voyage. There'd been no time for intimacy at sea, but now she yearned for the conversation to take a deeper vein. She sensed he had something on his mind as well.

After a while she got up to clear away the dishes. While she was below she heard him adjusting the anchor chain for the night, and feeling that the evening was over she experienced a twinge of disappointment. But when she went back up the steps she found him waiting at the top. The moon had risen over Kingstown Hill turning the water into liquid silver, and lights glimmered in the houses on the shore.

"Mary," he said, looking directly at her face.

"Yes."

"I feel something strange."

"I feel it too."

He reached down and took her hands. For half a minute her eyes were locked on his, and then he softly whispered, "Isis and Osiris have returned."

Her heart missed a beat.

For an hour they sat holding hands, kissing across the table, staring into each other's eyes. She tingled with excitement. The moon rose high above the masts and stays. A fire twinkled on the distant beach. They talked a little, but mostly they just sat and gazed at each other.

Eventually he took her hand and led her down the steps to the big aft cabin. She shivered with anticipation. Then she was in his arms, and with the moonlight streaming through the open portholes he started to undo her dress. Then, bit by bit, with care and gentleness, kissing and caressing, they slowly removed each other's clothes. Finally they lay down on the bed, half covered by a single sheet, the silvery light reflecting on the wooden beams above. All thought of Mary White and her responsibilities had gone. She was Isis, floating in a sea of pleasure, thrilled by the feel of his body, so firm and smooth and strong.

But deep inside she felt a tiny seed of doubt. Was this to be just another spiritual union? They were Isis and Osiris, but were they not also a man and a woman, a man and a woman in love? She pressed against him under the sheet, wanting him so much. She could feel he wanted her too and she pulled him towards her. And then it happened. At last they were together. For a few minutes her spirit soared, and not only her soul but also her body was satisfied.

"Isis, darling Isis," he whispered. "Forty centuries have waited for this moment."

There followed an idyllic month. Road Town was hardly a thriving metropolis but it offered a lively market in picturesque surroundings. Nearly all the islands lay within twenty miles, so they spent the month exploring them, anchoring in palm-fringed bays, lazing on beaches of the whitest coral sand, or swimming together through enchanted sunlit pools. There were almost no other yachts and apart from a few native fishermen they had the place to themselves. They ate, drank, swam and lazed in the sun, and at night they made love under the tropical moon.

One day they visited Peter Island and spent the night in Great Harbour next to Deadman Bay. Dead Chest Island was only half a mile away. The next morning they watched native fishermen make their catch with a long net pulled out from the sandy beach. As Isis bought some fish, Amiel asked the men about the names.

"Dem's Treasure Island names," said one of them with a broad West Indian accent.

Slowly Amiel extracted the story that a hundred years earlier pirate treasure really had been found in a cave on nearby Norman Island. Robert Louis Stevenson had used the location and the names in his famous novel.

"Fifteen men on a dead man's chest," chanted a young fishermen. "D'ya want a guide to see the treasure cave, Cap'n?"

His name was Emmet, and after negotiating a small fee he guided the *Lady Royal* to Norman Island. It was a hilly little island about a mile across, completely uninhabited. There were palms along the shore and groves of deciduous trees inland. They anchored in the island's natural harbour and when they had lowered the dinghy Emmet rowed them a quarter of a mile to Treasure Point.

As Isis looked back at the empty harbour she found it easy to imagine the place as a pirate haven two hundred years before. The *Lady Royal* looked something of a pirate ship herself with her black hull, her long bowsprit, and her heavy wooden spars.

Two hundred yards beyond Treasure Point they came to three caves with the sea running right inside. Emmet pointed to the southernmost entrance.

"Dat's where dey found de treasure, Cap'n," he said with a grin, his accent so pronounced that Isis could hardly understand. "D'ya want to go in?"

Although the entrance to the cave was narrow it was sheltered by Treasure Point and he was able to row the dinghy inside quite easily. Isis had brought a flashlight, but even with that it was unexpectedly dark after the bright sun. For a moment she could see nothing and suddenly she felt something brush her face. Creatures of some sort were fluttering about in the dark.

"Just bats, Miss. Dey won' hurt ya," Emmet reassured her.

After a few minutes her eyes became accustomed to the darkness. The cave was about ten feet high and fourteen wide, but it curved to the left as it went in so she couldn't see the end. Dozens of furry brown bats were hanging from the roof, moving their little heads in unison when she shone the light on them. The walls ran straight down into the water and she could see no sign of a ledge which could have held any treasure.

Emmet slowly paddled the boat in further, but after about sixty feet the cave came to an abrupt end. Isis felt disappointed. The only thing that caught her eye was some writing on the wall. At first she thought it might be a message from the pirates, but it turned out to be the names of a couple of yachts scratched into the rock.

"Where did they find the gold?" asked Amiel.

"Ah," said Emmet. "Dat's de tricky bit. Wait a minute an' I'll show you."

He slipped off his shirt and slid into the water, and after taking a few deep breaths he dove out of sight. Two minutes dragged by, then three. Isis felt a twinge of fear, no one could hold their breath that long.

"Don't worry," said Amiel. "He's up to some trick. There must be a hidden entrance. He'll be perfectly alright."

After five minutes Emmet resurfaced, not out of breath at all.

"Well, Cap'n, I thought you and the lady would be tryin' to rescue me by now," he grinned. "Truth is, there's an underwater passage to another cave just beyond this one, an' dat's where they found the treasure."

Amiel was intrigued. He asked a lot of questions and eventually decided to see for himself.

"You can swim through easily," said Emmet. "Turn off the light and look down there. Now, can you see a glimmer of light under the water? Dat's the entrance. Just feel your way through."

Amiel took off his shirt and shoes and slipped into the water. Isis thought it looked horribly dangerous. She pleaded with him to be careful but she knew he'd take no notice. Emmet dived first, disappearing immediately, then Amiel took some deep breaths and followed him.

She waited in the semidarkness. Five minutes passed but it seemed like an hour. After ten minutes she was sure something was wrong. Just when she was getting desperate there was a splash and Emmet's head appeared, gasping for breath.

"Is there a rope in the boat?" he panted.

"What's happened?"

"Cap'n got stuck."

Her head swam.

"It's alright Miss, he's in the inner cave. He's got plenty of air but he needs a rope to guide himself back."

They always carried a small anchor in the dinghy and she untied its line.

"Emmet, are you sure?"

"Yes Miss," he said. "Now shine the light down into the water to mark this end of the tunnel."

She felt frantic but there was nothing she could do. With shaking hands she tied one end of the rope to the dinghy, while Emmet swam back with the other.

This time there was almost no delay. After a couple of minutes the rope began to jerk and she guessed someone was using it to pull themselves along. A few seconds later Amiel's head broke the surface. He looked a bit shaken and there was blood on his arms where they'd scraped on the rocks, but otherwise he was alright. She helped him over the stern of the dinghy and he flopped onto the back seat.

"What happened?" she gasped.

Somehow he'd got stuck on the way through the tunnel but Emmet had come to his aid. He wouldn't tell her any more than that, but he did say he'd seen exactly where the treasure had been hidden.

"It's a perfect place," he went on. "There's an inner chamber with a small hole high in the roof that lets in light and air. The gold was on a ledge well above the water, and there's still an iron ring in the rock that they must have used to haul it through the tunnel."

Soon Emmet was back on board too. "Well Cap'n, you ain't gonna forget Treasure Island in a hurry," he said with his usual grin.

"You're right," replied Amiel seriously. "This is one of the most interesting places I've seen."

Isis was surprised. It didn't seem particularly interesting to her. But if it appealed to him so much perhaps they should leave a memento.

"Shall I write our boat's name on the wall with the other two?" she suggested.

"Alright."

"You can use my marlin spike if you like, Miss," Emmet offered, pulling a heavy clasp knife from his pocket.

He paddled the dinghy over to the wall where the other two yachts' names were written, and she carefully scratched the words, "*Lady Royal,* December 1936," into the rock.

The lads from Sussex rejoined the *Lady Royal* in the second week of December, and the following day they hoisted the sails for the voyage to Panama. The winter trade winds were blowing at full force so they made a fast passage across the Caribbean Sea, arriving at the Panama Canal just before Christmas. They anchored in the outer harbour and the official launch came alongside almost immediately. The measurer inspected the boat, issued a certificate, and gave them permission to proceed, and they finally entered the Pacific and turned the bow northwest for British Columbia.

Ever since the beginning of December Isis had suspected she was pregnant, and by January she was sure. It did not upset her physically. Even at sea she felt only the minimum of sickness and she had no difficulty carrying out her duties as cook.

Amiel was delighted. "Pleasure and duty are one," he said in his usual pedantic manner. "The Gods have willed that you shall bear a son to lead the Aquarians when I have gone."

He explained that on the passage to British Columbia a sailing ship must make a wide detour out into the Pacific to avoid the adverse winds that blew down the coast. There would be only one port of call on the long journey north, Honolulu in Hawaii.

Isis was amazed by the size of the Pacific Ocean. Day after day slipped by with never a sign of a ship, and it wasn't until their sixtieth day that they sighted Diamond Head.

They spent a week in Honolulu, resting and stocking up with supplies for the final leg to B.C. Soon after they set off the weather got cooler and for the first time in months Isis needed a sweater. On the night of April 14th they spotted the flashes of the lighthouse on Cape Flattery and she knew the voyage was almost over.

Ever since she'd become pregnant she'd been wondering how the other members of the colony would accept her as Isis, and the closer she got to British Columbia the stronger the worry became.

Isis faced her first test the evening after they arrived in B.C.

Brother XII had paid off the lads from Sussex, and the *Lady Royal* lay at anchor in Pirates Cove surrounded by familiar fir and arbutus trees. She felt comfortable hiding aboard the boat, but the Brother had called a meeting at the Tree of Wisdom and he insisted she attend.

He took her to the Cedar settlement in an open motorboat feeling conspicuous and embarrassed. Then he made her stand beside him on the platform as he reported on his fund-raising in England, the acquisition of the *Lady Royal*, and his plans to use the vessel to establish further colonies in the new Aquarian age.

Next he told his followers how the Masters of Wisdom had revealed that Mary White was Isis. He said he'd maintained for years that in a previous existence he'd been Osiris, so it shouldn't be any surprise. It was also well known, he said, that the sacred duty of Osiris and Isis was to join together in spiritual union to beget the boy-god Horus, and that was what they'd done.

"After the fire has purged the world of sinners," he cried, "you must go forth from The City of Refuge to the far corners of the earth to rebuild the human race. It is Horus who will lead you then. Horus who is both a man and a god."

Isis knew she was a different person from Mary White, but she could tell that some of her old friends could see no difference and she detected hostility from the start.

Amiel insisted she live with him in the House of Mystery. Her first impression of the enigmatic house was disappointment. She found it small, untidy and poorly furnished, quite different from her old home on De Courcy where everything had been so familiar. Furthermore she was isolated because the house was out of bounds to everyone but Amiel and herself.

She was in her sixth month of pregnancy. There was a doctor in the colony now. He came every two weeks to examine her, but she had no other visitors. She saw Ken Martin and John Prentice through the window when the Earthly Council met on the grass outside the house, but even they were not allowed inside. She called on the Martins once or twice but Gillian seemed cool. It was clear she didn't accept that Isis was any more than a Mary White who'd deserted her family for the favours of Brother XII.

And Amiel himself seemed to change. Sometimes he would be away preaching for days at a time, usually in the States. When he was home he addressed his followers nearly every evening, often on De Courcy or Valdes Islands, so he'd be away for hours while she had nothing to do.

One day Amiel told her he suspected some of the followers were showing signs of dissent, and he wanted to find out who they were. Every week his soul travelled to a higher plane to consult with the Masters of Wisdom. The process required hours of meditation, and a group of followers usually collected at the entrance to the path to the House of Mystery to give him spiritual support. He guessed that as they waited they'd be bound to talk, so he had a firm from Seattle install a secret microphone nearby for him to listen in.

Isis also wanted to hear what was being said behind her back, but Amiel would never let her eavesdrop on her own. Then one day the Brother's soul was visiting the Masters and a group of followers had gathered at the path. He lay on his couch meditating and listening to them for an hour, but eventually he got restless and went to another room. After a few minutes she picked up the headset and guiltily put it on.

Immediately the voices captured her attention.

". . . if you believe in reincarnation then it's quite possible for her to have been the Goddess Isis." It was a woman's voice she didn't recognize.

"She may have been a goddess in some previous existence," Gillian Martin's voice replied. "But she's no goddess now, she's just plain Mary White."

"She thinks she's a goddess, I'm sure of that," said the first woman.

"Yes, she really believes she's Isis." That was Ken Martin. "She's in trouble and we ought to help."

"It's Twelve who's done it," said Gillian. "And you all think he's divine."

"He's a man like the rest of us," said Ken. "A very special man, but human just the same."

"Take care," said the first woman. "He's certainly got divine connections. He knows what we're saying. Last week he repeated exactly what my husband had said, word for word."

But it was the next statement that really electrified Isis. Gillian spoke again in a voice that was little more than a sneer.

"This affair he's having with Mary is not the first one, is it Ken?"

"You mean Angela Johnson, the doctor's wife. I've told you . . . ," but Ken's voice was drowned out by static so she couldn't hear any more.

The doctor's wife, he had said. There'd been no Dr Johnson in the colony during the last couple of years but the name stuck in her mind.

Then Ken's voice was clear again, ". . . Angela Johnson. It's a good job she had to leave . . ."

But she never heard him finish. At that moment Brother XII snatched the headset from her ears. "What are you doing?" He shouted.

"Nothing," she stammered stupidly.

"Nothing. The people are rising up against you and all you can say is nothing."

She burst into tears and he softened and put his arms around her.

"I'm sorry, I really am," he said. "It will be better when our son is born. He will unite them."

As the weeks went by she got more and more depressed. One night she had a vivid dream about little Josephine far away in England. If only she could see her daughter now, what comfort that would bring.

One day in mid July her waters broke, and in the afternoon her labour began. The doctor came immediately. There was a nurse and a trained midwife in the colony too, and they took turns sitting with her. Amiel was in and out as well.

They had no special equipment other than what was in the doctor's bag, but it was her second baby and no one expected any trouble. The doctor gave her some morphine in the evening and she managed to sleep a little between the labour pains. When he examined her next morning he announced that her cervix was fully dilated, and an hour later she delivered a healthy baby.

But the baby was a girl.

Saint or sinner, true or false, Brother XII sometimes handled difficult situations superbly, and sometimes he did not. He took one long hard disbelieving look at his unwelcome baby daughter, and without a word he walked out of the room and out of the house. A group of his followers were waiting in silent vigil at the end of the path. He ignored them. He took a boat and went alone to his house on De Courcy Island to meditate and plan the rebuilding of his empire. He never set eyes on Isis or the baby girl again.

Nor did Isis have long to ponder her situation. Her first sensation was of relief that the labour was over and her baby was healthy. The first hemorrhage occurred before she realized that Amiel had gone. Her attendants thought the blood heralded the passing of the afterbirth, and the doctor held the umbilical cord waiting for it to appear. But it wouldn't come, and for ten minutes there was a steady flow of blood like water from a tap.

The attendants watched nervously, unsure what to do. The nurse suggested ergot, but the doctor didn't want to use it with the placenta still inside. Instead he gave more morphine, and made two excruciatingly painful attempts to squeeze the placenta out, but without success.

Isis groaned, and after they had failed to extract the placenta the second time she lapsed into unconsciousness.

The bleeding went on and on.

"For God's sake let it stop," the doctor prayed aloud. Then he gave the ergot anyway, with the placenta still inside.

They had no intravenous equipment to replace the blood she'd lost. Gradually her pulse got weaker as her blood pressure fell. Finally her hands and feet turned cold and white as her body made it's last futile attempt to conserve what little blood was left. There was a phone in the administration building and they called an ambulance, but by the time it arrived the doctor and nurses had given up.

Mary woke in a neat white-walled room. The smell of ether and carbolic told her she was in hospital. Her tummy was sore, and when she felt it and missed the familiar bulge the memory of her labour came rushing back. She remembered the baby had been a girl which did not fit with Brother XII's plans, and then she realized that Isis had gone forever and she was Mary White. Next she recalled thinking she was going to die, and her baby would have no one to care for it. After that everything was blank. She had just a vague recollection of an ambulance ride, blood transfusions and an operating theatre.

Gillian Martin was sitting by the bed. Mary remembered the horrible remarks she'd heard over the microphone but Gillian looked friendly now.

Mary tried to smile.

"Are you awake, dear?" asked Gillian.

"I think so."

"I'll fetch the nurse."

Mary wanted to ask about her baby but before anyone returned she dozed off.

Next she was aware of a nurse in a white uniform moving about the room, and Gillian was there again. Then she heard a man's voice and for a while she dreamed of Amiel. What a mixture of feelings his memory evoked.

And then she was awake. The man was Ken Martin and he was talking quietly to Gillian and the nurse. Slowly she remembered what she wanted, and she turned her head and whispered, "Where's my baby?"

They all peered at her and she felt a terrible sense of doom.

Eventually the nurse replied, "She's in the nursery."

"Is she alright?"

"She's fine."

Then Ken asked a curious question. "Do you know who you are?"

"Mary White," she replied without a thought.

The baby was a beautiful contented little girl whom she adored from the start. Ken and Gillian were frequent visitors and they brought her up to date with what had happened at the colony.

Brother XII had disowned Isis and declared that the whole concept had been wrong. Several people, including the Martins, had left the colony, however the majority still thought the Brother was their best path to salvation. As she talked to Ken and Gillian, Mary came to see that it had all been a terrible mistake. She didn't quite know how it had happened but she realized that Isis had only existed in her mind.

On the second day, when she was completely sure of her identity, Gillian told her that Ken had been in contact with her husband.

"If you still love him at all, dear, I think you should phone him," she said. "Ken has told him how you were totally under the influence of that dreadful man. For that matter we all were. I just can't understand how it happened."

It was still a shock to hear Amiel called dreadful, even after everything he'd done, but now she realized that she did still love Philip. She needed him more than ever, and she couldn't wait to see Josephine, so she decided to call him right away.

There was an eight hour time difference between Nanaimo and England, and it was after midnight when she got through. He answered at once and she guessed he must have been waiting by the phone. She'd never felt so grateful in her life.

It was a wonderful telephone reunion and she couldn't hold back tears. He insisted on coming to Nanaimo to fetch her and the new baby, so the three of them travelled back to England with the Martins on the now familiar train and ship.

She soon became completely reconciled with Philip so that it was hard to believe the Isis affair had ever occurred. They christened the baby Jennifer, and Philip accepted her as his own. He had already rejoined his old firm of stockbrokers, and Mary eventually settled back into Ashtead life as if she'd never been away.

Chapter 7

In the spring of 1938 the Woodings nanny, Ann, found romance. Jim Hocket had grown up in London, however he was a trained marine mechanic who worked at Woodings Boatyard. Ann met him when she took the children to see Neville one day, and before long they were dating. Jim was earning a good wage so it was no surprise to Marcia when Jim and Ann married and found a place of their own.

As soon as Ann left Mark became more difficult than ever. He wanted to be with his mother constantly, hardly letting her out of his sight. Once, when she locked him in his bedroom he scribbled all over the walls, and another time he threw all her clean underwear out of the window into the rain. Marcia could not find another nanny, so her mother, Mrs Allen, came to stay for a few weeks to help. Mark disliked his granny and she wasn't very fond of him.

One sunny day they had a picnic tea on the beach. After the meal Marcia wanted to do some shopping before she went home.

"Mummy, where are you going?" asked Mark.

"I'm going shopping. You and Marcelle can stay here with Granny. I'll see you at home soon."

"I want to come with you."

"No Mark, I'm going on my own," said Marcia.

"I'll look after you," added Mrs Allen in her usual commanding tone.

"Mummy, I want to be with you." He took a step away from his granny.

"Don't be so silly," said Mrs Allen, grabbing his wrist.

"I don't want to stay with Granny," he cried, struggling to get free. "Mummy, please let me come with you."

But his granny was strong and she wouldn't let go. "Stop making a fuss," she said. "Look, your sister's not making a fuss."

"I want my mummy," he wailed.

"Stop that at once," said Mrs Allen. She raised her free hand and slapped him hard.

Marcia looked down at her little four-year-old son. His brown eyes were wide with fear and there were tears running down his cheeks. Feeling a pang of guilt, she said, "Perhaps it would be better if I took him after all."

Mark stopped crying when he heard that, but Mrs Allen held fast to his wrist. "Certainly not," she said. "You're always giving in to the boy. That's why he's so bad. I'll hold him until you've gone."

He started struggling wildly then. Marcia knew she'd never win an argument with her mother so she turned and walked away. She could hear Mark screaming behind her and she wondered if her mother had hit him again, but she didn't dare look back.

During the next couple of weeks there were similar scenes. One day her mother said, "I warned you when he was a baby that boys were very wilful. You've always given in to him and this is the result."

"Neville thinks he's missing Ann."

"Don't be ridiculous, Ann was hardly even a nanny. What he's missing is a bit of discipline."

Marcia kept six pet budgerigars in a large walk-in birdcage in the middle of the Maplehurst grounds. A gravel path ran from the house down to the birdcage past a lawn and a shrubbery. There was something about the cage that fascinated Mark. Its strong metal frame and heavy wire netting gave him a strange feeling of power.

One afternoon, when he was five years old, he was sitting in the shrubbery near the budgerigar cage when the front door of the house opened and his mother came out. She was carrying a bag of birdseed so he guessed she was going to feed the budgerigars. He was hidden by a bush so she couldn't see him.

Her footsteps crunched on the gravel path, but he kept absolutely quiet so she wouldn't know he was there. Crunch, crunch. Her footsteps got nearer. The bush didn't hide him very well and he wondered what to say if she spotted him. He knew she'd be angry. She was always angry with him and never with Marcelle. It was so unfair. Sometimes he wondered if she loved him at all. Finally she reached the birdcage door only a few feet from where he was hiding.

He watched her take a key from her pocket and unlock the door. Then she tapped the wire netting to drive the birds to the far end of the cage. Next she opened the door and quickly slipped inside, then she closed the door behind her and took a few steps to the feeder box. She'd left the key in the lock on the outside of the door. Suddenly he had an idea. He crept out from behind the bush and tiptoed across the lawn. She might look up at any moment. He'd have to cross the path and he knew his feet would crunch on the gravel. She would be really angry if she spotted him but he was so excited he didn't care. He put his foot very carefully on the path. Crunch. She continued to pour seed into the feeder so he took another step. This time there was a louder crunch. He froze but she still didn't look up. Then he took two more steps quickly to reach the door. His mother carried on with her job. He couldn't believe his luck. He felt tremendously excited as he reached towards the lock. His hand was shaking so much he could hardly turn the key. Slowly it turned. Then he pulled it out and took a quick step back with another crunch. His mother looked up then but she was too late.

"Mark, what are you doing?" she cried. Then she saw the key in his hand. "Come here at once."

He ran to the edge of the lawn. He was frightened but he had a wonderful feeling of power. He'd locked his mother in the cage and there was nothing she could do.

"Mark, unlock the door this minute or you'll get a good spanking," she shouted.

He didn't say anything. He just stood at the edge of the lawn watching her in awe. He was completely in control and he began to experience a sensation of physical pleasure he didn't understand.

Then she stopped shouting and started to bargain. He might have given in, but at that moment Jessie, the housemaid, came out of the house. Another adult could probably force him to give up the key so he looked for a place to hide it. The gardener had rolled the lawn with a special spiked roller that left hundreds of little holes. He ran out onto the grass and pushed the key down one of the holes. Then he went to the far side of the lawn and waited to see what would happen.

Soon Jessie and the gardener were peering at their mistress locked in the cage. Mark could see she was livid with rage, but she was trying to appear dignified in front of the servants.

"I don't know what's come over the boy," she was saying. "He put the key down near the middle of the lawn. Go and find it, Jessie."

Soon both servants were crawling about the lawn on their hands and knees but they couldn't find the key. They threatened Mark with a spanking, but he knew that only his mother would spank him, and she was locked in the cage. He was safe as long as he didn't tell them where the key was hidden.

Eventually his mother promised she wouldn't spank him if he revealed the hiding place. He thought he knew exactly where it was, but he soon found that all the holes looked the same. He spent a whole hour with the servants searching the lawn while his mother sat in the cage. In the end they had to call a locksmith who freed her with a master key of his own.

That evening, when his father got home from the boatyard, he had a talk with Mark.

"Don't you like your mummy?" he asked.

"I love her," Mark replied tearfully. "I love her more than anything else in the world."

Mark often thought about the time he'd locked his mother in the birdcage and the strange sensation he'd felt. It was nearly a year before he experienced anything like it again.

The second world war began in September 1939. It didn't seem to make much difference to him until his father left to join the army. Soon the gardener joined the army too, and when Jessie left to work in a munitions factory the house seemed half empty.

One day Mother announced that Granny was coming to live with them because the Germans were going to bomb London and hundreds of people would be killed. They might even bomb Plymouth, only twenty miles away. Mark wasn't frightened of bombs but he didn't like the idea of Granny coming to stay.

Granny arrived just before Christmas and she brought presents for the children. Mark was disappointed with his present at first. It was a book of bible stories which he couldn't read, but it did have coloured pictures on some of the pages.

One afternoon the family had gathered in the kitchen to enjoy the warmth from the coal-fired Aga stove. Mark was sitting at the table looking at the pictures in his book. One of them puzzled him. There were half a dozen adults and children wearing only pieces of cloth around their waists, working by a pond with palm trees round the edge. But what really caught his attention was a woman with a long thin stick in her hand standing over a boy. She held the stick raised above her head and from the position of her body and the way the stick curved back he thought he knew what she was doing. He looked at the picture for a while. Underneath were some words but he felt too embarrassed to ask what they said.

Finally he made up his mind. "Mummy, what does it say?"

His mother looked at the book. "It says, The Children of Israel in bondage in Egypt."

"What does bondage mean?"

"It means they were slaves."

"What is that woman doing?"

"Whipping one of the slaves."

He could see exactly what the woman was doing and he began to get that strange sensation again.

"Mummy, why is she whipping that boy?"

His granny had been watching with an odd expression on her face. "That's quite enough," she said sharply. "The boy's getting a whipping and I expect he deserved it. Now turn the page and look at something else."

Chapter 8

Jennifer White silently opened her parents' bedroom door, tiptoed across the carpet, and squeezed into the big cupboard where her mother kept clean sheets and towels. She left the door open a crack so she could see out, and settled down to wait.

It was a winter afternoon in 1946, and Jenny was nine years old. Her father was at his office and her mother had gone out shopping, so she was at home with her sister Jo.

Jenny loved to play hide and seek. Jo was really too old for the game but now and then she'd agree to play. For as long as she could remember Jenny had liked to hide in this cupboard. It was warm and snug in the semidarkness, and the feel of the soft clean towels made her tingle with pleasure. She often hid there and she knew her sister would find her easily, but Jo had to wait ten minutes before she started to search, so she had ten whole minutes to enjoy the feeling. But then she heard the front door open and she realized her mother was home. Next came the sound of Mummy and Jo talking in the kitchen. The game of hide and seek was over. She was about to leave the cupboard when she heard footsteps on the stairs and her mother walked into the room.

Jenny didn't want her mother to know she'd been hiding in the cupboard so she decided to stay where she was until Mummy left. Her mother took off her coat and hung it in the wardrobe that stood in the corner, then she sat at her dressing table to tidy her hair. Next a strange thing happened. Instead of going back downstairs she opened the top drawer of the dressing table and took out a big brown envelope. For a few seconds she turned it over in her hands, and then to Jenny's surprise she quietly closed the bedroom door and locked it. She put the envelope on the bed and started to take things out, one at a time, and look at them under the light. Jenny strained to see. She thought they were old pictures, but she really couldn't tell.

Next her mother spread the pictures out on the bed. Then she knelt down and started to pray. She looked terribly sad and Jenny thought she was going to cry. Finally she put everything back in the envelope and returned it to the drawer.

When her mother had gone Jenny crawled out of the cupboard thankful she hadn't been discovered. At first she thought she'd just go downstairs as if nothing had happened, but by the time she reached the stairs she was overcome by curiosity. For a moment she stopped to think. Mummy would be busy talking to Jo, so with a thumping heart she crept back into her parents' room. She closed the door but she was so excited she forgot to lock it. Then she tiptoed across the room, opened her mother's drawer, and took out the envelope. It was bigger than she expected, so she carried it across to the bed before she looked inside.

As soon as she spread the things out on the bed she was disappointed. They were just old pictures and photos from before the war, some of them going brown around the edges. She thought they must have been taken on holiday because most of them were photos of people in some woods or on a beach. When she looked more carefully she saw that several showed a frightening looking man with straight black hair and dark staring eyes. In one of them he was beside a cute little house in a forest, and in another he was standing with Mummy by the sea.

There were also some pictures of old-fashioned statues and people wearing strange clothes. She'd seen similar pictures in a book about the pyramids, so she thought they must have come from Egypt. One of them was bigger than the rest. It showed a weird-looking woman with horns on her head and a stern expression on her face. It was scary. Two other pictures showed carvings of horrible great black birds a bit like ravens. They seemed to be glaring with disapproval as if they knew she was looking at her mother's secret pictures. She shuddered. Jo had told her of terrible things that used to happen in the olden days and she felt sure these pictures had something to do with that, especially the woman with horns.

Finally she found an old map. She didn't see it at first because it was folded up, and even when she spread it out on the bed she couldn't make much of it. A crooked red line ran all the way from the top to the bottom, but she couldn't see what it was for.

Suddenly she heard a sound at the door. She looked up and there was her mother standing in the doorway. She felt terribly guilty. Her mother's private things were lying all over the bed and there was no way she could hide them. She'd been so engrossed in the pictures she hadn't heard the door open and she had no idea how long Mummy had been there.

Her mother was furious. "Jennifer, what are you doing?" she shouted.

"Nothing."

"You're going through my personal things."

Mummy hardly ever shouted at her and she felt a stab of fear. Then her mother started across the room with her hand raised. Jenny had never seen her so angry.

"I'm sorry," she pleaded.

But her mother grabbed her and slapped her face. She'd never done that before and Jenny was terrified.

"Mummy, I'm sorry," she whimpered. "I didn't mean to do it."

"How did you know they were there?"

There was no time to make up a story so she said, "I saw you."

"You saw me?"

"I was in the cupboard when you were here."

That seemed to make things worse. "You watched me when I was in here looking at the pictures? Did you see me kneeling by the bed?"

"I didn't mean to," Jenny sobbed. "We were playing hide and seek."

"How dare you spy on me."

And with that her mother picked her up, put her across her knee, and started spanking her.

Jenny's parents almost never spanked her. She was so surprised and terrified she hardly felt the pain.

"They're wicked pictures," her mother shouted. "Don't you ever look at them again."

As soon as she could get free Jenny ran sobbing to her room and went to bed.

Nothing like that had ever happened to Jenny before. Her bottom hurt, but it was nothing to what she felt inside. She knew it had been wrong to look at her mother's things, but surely it wasn't that bad. She loved her mother and she wanted to make it up, but she'd never seen her in such a rage. Soon she felt strangely tired and drifted off to sleep.

Sometime later there was a gentle knocking on the door.

"Who's there?" she called, thinking it was Jo.

"Daddy. Can I come in."

"Yes," she said, desperately wanting attention from someone in her family. He came straight over to the bed and cuddled her, and she felt a tremendous sense of relief.

"Mummy told me what happened."

"I'm sorry," she sobbed. "I didn't mean to do anything wrong."

"Mummy's sorry too. Can she come in?"

"Oh yes."

Her mother must have been waiting outside the door because she came in immediately. They'd always been close, and now she took Jenny in her arms and whispered, "Oh, darling."

"I'm sorry, Mummy."

"I forgive you, but can you ever forgive me for spanking you like that."

"I've forgiven you already. I love you, Mummy."

"I love you too."

Mother and daughter soon made it up, but Jenny never got a satisfactory explanation of the pictures.

It was two whole weeks before she tried to look at them again. She waited until her mother was out and she had the house entirely to herself. Even then she locked the doors and drew the bedroom curtains, although there was not the slightest chance of anyone looking in.

She tiptoed across her mother's room with her heart pounding so hard she thought her chest would burst. Slowly she slid open the drawer and peered inside. It was empty. She looked in all the other drawers of course, and everywhere else she could think of, but the secret pictures had gone.

Chapter 9

Nothing in Peter Johnson's life had prepared him for the events that took place at Westgate House School in the spring and summer of 1947. Westgate was the boarding school for boys aged seven to thirteen in the country near Exeter to which Peter had followed his brother Tim.

It was January and Angela was driving Peter back to Westgate for the spring term. He was almost thirteen but his voice had not yet broken. She hoped he might become a doctor like his father, and James had already entered him for Epsom College, the senior boarding school which specialized in preparing boys for a career in medicine.

When they reached the school she parked in front of the main building among other cars discharging boys. She helped Peter unload his luggage and then she had a talk with Mr Lester-Potts, the headmaster. She was about to leave when she spotted Gordon McNair, the sports coach. He was a good-looking man in his late thirties, with black hair which he brushed straight back, and dark piercing eyes. Whenever she saw him she thought of Brother XII; the similarity was striking and he seemed to have the same effortless influence over the boys that the Brother had enjoyed over the members of his commune when she and James were there.

"Hello Gordon," she called. "You're looking very fit."

"I've just spent a couple of weeks skiing in Switzerland," he said.

"Wow. Were you on your own?"

"No, I went with an old school chum. I'd like to take a group of the boys next year if I can arrange it."

What a pity Peter would have left the school by then, she thought. Gordon McNair had a way with boys. Whether he was teaching class, coaching rugby football, or organizing expeditions, he always seemed to get the best from them.

Peter was on the rugby team which added to his stature in the school. It bothered him that he was not a star player so he was flattered when Mr McNair singled him out after rugby practice one afternoon.

"Peter," said McNair with a friendly smile. "I want to have a talk with you. Come to my room at 7:30 tonight."

"My room" meant his bed-sitting room. It was quite common for social gatherings to take place in the masters' rooms, so the request did not seem improper.

At exactly 7:30 he knocked on the door.

"Come in," called McNair.

Peter immediately sensed that something was wrong. Heavy curtains were pulled across the window and the room was in darkness apart from a single light bulb hanging from the centre of the ceiling. Two wooden chairs stood facing one another directly beneath the light. One was a straight-backed kitchen chair and the other had armrests and a padded seat.

"Sit down," said Mr McNair, pointing to the unpadded chair. He took the other one himself and sat in silence for a full minute facing Peter.

"I want to talk to you about morals," he said at last.

There was a further silence. Peter felt uncomfortable, but he'd done nothing wrong so there shouldn't be anything to fear.

"Mr Lester-Potts is concerned about immorality in the school," McNair went on.

Peter had not the slightest idea what he was talking about.

"Well? What have you got to say?"

"I don't know what you mean, sir."

"Do you know what I mean by masturbation?"

Peter had never heard the word. "No," he said, wriggling uncomfortably on the chair.

"Now, sit still and look me straight in the eye so I can see that you're telling the truth."

"I don't know what it means," Peter repeated uneasily.

"It means rubbing your penis to make it feel good."

Peter felt the blood drain from his face. How could Mr McNair know his secret? He'd discovered it by accident a year ago after a chance remark by an older boy, but he'd never told anyone, not even his best friend Mark Wooding. He tried to look steadily at Mr McNair so he wouldn't give himself away.

"Look me straight in the eye," ordered McNair. "You do it yourself, don't you?"

Peter couldn't speak.

"Answer me."

"Yes," he whispered.

"What do you do? I want to hear you say it."

"I do mas . . . " He just couldn't say the word. It sounded horrible.

"Say it," McNair demanded without sympathy. "Look me straight in the eye and say it."

Peter forced himself to look at Mr McNair's face. The mouth was set in a neutral line and the black hair was brushed straight back. He hadn't noticed the eyes before, they were very dark and they seemed to penetrate his soul. McNair had known his most private secret. Perhaps he could read people's minds.

"Say it," ordered Mr McNair. "I want to hear you say that word."

And so the interview went on. Peter longed to get off that uncomfortable chair, away from the glaring light and those terrible eyes. McNair forced him to tell the intimate details one by one, when he'd started, how he did it, even what he thought about during the act. Nothing was spared.

"Never do it again," said McNair at last. "It will weaken your body and ruin your brain. If you do it again I shall know."

Peter didn't doubt it.

After that Mr McNair took a more friendly attitude. He finished by saying, "Mr Lester-Potts has asked me to stamp immorality out of the school, but you are not to discuss this with anyone, do you understand?"

As he left the room Peter saw McNair take out a black notebook and start to make an entry.

If Peter's brother had still been at Westgate they might have discussed what had happened, but Tim had moved on to his senior school. However, the following Saturday Westgate had a rugby match against Blackwell Manor, the school that Mark attended, so he thought he might talk to his friend.

The intervening days passed uneventfully. Besides coaching the rugby and cricket teams Mr McNair taught English. Peter was in his class and McNair was his usual friendly self. On Saturday morning he briefed the rugby team for the afternoon match. No coach could have done a better job, and later he accompanied them on the school bus for the journey to Blackwell Manor. After the game they had a meal with the Blackwell team and Peter had plenty of opportunity to talk to Mark, but in the end he was too embarrassed to bring the subject up.

A week later Mr McNair again summoned Peter to his room at 7:30. He hadn't enjoyed the last meeting and he wasn't looking forward to this one, but he had not done it so he thought he'd be alright.

The room was in darkness except for the single light with the two chairs directly underneath. Once again McNair told him to sit on the hard chair while he took the padded one. Again he had to look directly into Mr McNair's eyes and after thirty seconds he felt just as intimidated as before.

"Peter," McNair began accusingly. "Do you know what sodomy is?"

Peter had heard the word Sod of course, but he didn't know what it meant.

"No."

"Don't lie to me."

"I don't know what it is," he said.

"It's the same as homosexuality," said McNair, looking straight into his eyes.

Peter knew what that was and he felt very frightened. He'd never done anything like it, but he was sure his questioner would judge him guilty just the same. It was essential to look calm but he felt faint and he wobbled on the chair.

Mr McNair's face remained expressionless. "Look me straight in the eye," he commanded. "You've done it, haven't you?"

"No sir, I haven't."

"Don't lie to me. You've done it with Blundell."

Peter was astounded. There must be some mistake. Ken Blundell was another member of the rugby team. It was totally false.

Mr McNair tapped the black notebook. "Blundell has told me all about it."

"It's not true."

McNair's eyes bored into his brain. He noticed that the muscles on either side of the man's face were moving in a strange rhythmic manner. He could hardly believe what was happening.

"No. It's you who are not telling the truth," said Mr McNair slowly. "You didn't tell me the truth about masturbation at first, did you?"

"But I didn't know what it was."

"You didn't know what sodomy was either, did you?"

"No." Peter felt utterly exhausted.

"Peter, if you didn't know it was wrong, it's not so much of a sin. But you must admit it. Ken is a good boy, he's admitted his fault. Now you must do the same."

But Peter knew he hadn't done it.

On and on it went. The hard chair, the bright light, the piercing eyes, the questions, the suggestions, on and on and on. Could he have done this awful thing and somehow forgotten it? Could he have done it in his sleep? No, it was impossible. And yet . . . ?

If only he had time to think.

After an hour of questioning he started to believe something must have happened between himself and Ken Blundell. Perhaps it had happened when he was asleep. Finally he heard himself agreeing with what McNair suggested.

But as soon as that central fact had been established Mr McNair wanted details. The dates and times and places, what they'd said to one another, exactly what they'd done. Peter knew none of that of course, but it seemed that Ken had already told him most of it. Eventually he confessed to everything McNair suggested.

At last it was over.

Mr McNair made another entry in his book. Then he said quietly, "You know, Peter, sodomy is a very serious crime. After murder it's the most serious crime there is. For your own sake you must never discuss this with anyone else, not anyone at all."

A very serious crime. Peter was terribly disturbed and he thought he'd better talk to Ken in spite of the warning he'd been given.

"Why did you tell Mr McNair that stuff about us?" he began.

"We're not allowed to discuss it."

"You know it's not true."

Ken looked frightened. "Someone will report seeing us together. I don't want to talk about it ever again."

Peter thought of going to the headmaster. But Mr McNair and Mr Lester-Potts were close friends, and anyway it was the headmaster who had ordered the investigation. And there was the black notebook. He didn't think he'd done the things written there, but he had confessed to them. If he were accused of that sort of thing he'd be expelled from the school.

He thought of telling his parents, but he wouldn't be seeing them for weeks. There was no private phone that the boys could use, and all their letters were checked by the staff, so writing wasn't any good. In the end he did nothing.

As the investigation continued the boys became suspicious of one another and personal friendships ended, but strangely they seemed to seek friendship with Mr McNair. And he remained his usual energetic self, coaching the team, teaching classes, always available.

Peter had to endure three more interrogations in the next few weeks. Two other boys had apparently confessed to doing things with him. He didn't believe these activities had really taken place but he knew the dreadful interviews would never end until he admitted whatever McNair suggested. Eventually he confessed to everything, but with a terrible feeling of unease.

After the confessions he found his relationship with Mr McNair improved. His parents thought the man was the best teacher in the school, and earlier he'd been disappointed when McNair had not shown him much attention. Now he was pleased to find he'd become one of Mr McNair's favourites.

At the end of the school term Peter sat in the train on the way home wondering how to tell his father what had been happening at school. They never discussed the sort of things Mr McNair had been investigating, and he didn't know how to begin. Even the words were embarrassing. At the beginning Mr McNair had said he was discussing morals, so he decided to use that word.

Salcombe was too small to be on the railway, so his father met him at Kingsbridge, six miles away. He was relieved to see his dad had come on his own. Talking about morals was not going to be easy.

They exchanged greetings and stowed the luggage in the car. Peter thought he'd wait until they were on the road before he brought his subject up, it would be better if his dad was occupied driving. Eventually they pulled out of the station car park and turned up the hill towards Salcombe.

"Well, we've been having good weather," said his father.

"Good."

There was a pause while Peter plucked up courage.

"Did you have a good term?" asked Father.

"Not bad."

Another silence. It was now or never.

"Mr McNair has been talking to us about morals."

"Morals, eh?"

"Yes. What do you think about that?"

Peter waited expectantly. The car reached the top of the hill and the road swung south through farmland.

"Morals," repeated his father. "That's an important subject. I'm glad they're teaching you about them."

This was going nowhere. For a wild moment Peter thought of shouting, "Masturbation," or even, "Sodomy," but of course he knew he'd never do it. Perhaps it would be easier to talk to Mark or even his brother about the subject.

"Well Dad, it's great to be home again," he said instead, putting his arm on his father's shoulder.

"And it's just great to have you back," his father replied.

The Woodings had a sailing dinghy and Peter spent most of the holidays with Mark, exploring the upper reaches of the estuary or fishing for mackerel down by the sea. He often thought of his problems at school, but he never did mention them to Mark, his brother, or anyone else.

Peter couldn't remember when he first wanted to become a doctor. The decision was certainly made before he was thirteen because by then his father had entered him for Epsom College.

One day he and Mark were playing at Wiscasset when they came across a book called *The Miracle of the Human Body*. It showed diagrams of the body, and Mark turned to a picture of the female reproductive organs. They made a few jokes about that, but soon he became absorbed in the section on anatomy.

Presently he asked, "Are you really going to be a doctor?"

"I guess I am," said Peter.

"Is that why you're going to Epsom?"

"That's right."

"I wish I could do that too."

"What, go to Epsom College with me? That would be terrific. Why don't you?"

"They've already put me down for Sherbourne. That's where the Woodings always go. But what I meant was I'd like to be a doctor." He pointed to the book. "This stuff is amazing, and your father has an awfully important job."

They discussed it for a while and Peter suggested, "Let's talk to my dad about it. He's in his study."

James Johnson listened to them carefully.

When they'd finished he said, "Well Mark, going into medicine must be your own decision, but I've found it the most worthwhile life there is."

"Would I have to go to Epsom College, sir?" asked Mark. "I've already been accepted at Sherbourne."

"You could get into medical school from Sherbourne perfectly well, but it's easier if you go to Epsom."

"They might not accept me at Epsom," queried Mark.

"They'll accept you," said James. "You've got the three qualifications that would make you acceptable at any school."

"What are they?"

"Well, first, you're school captain at Blackwell Manor. And second, you've got excellent marks."

"And the third one?"

"Ah, that's the most important of all," said James with a smile. "You've got a father who can afford to pay the fees."

Peter sat beside his mother as she drove him back to Westgate House at the beginning of the summer term.

"Do you think you'll be on the cricket team?" she asked.

The question took him by surprise because she wasn't usually interested in sports.

"I expect so."

"But will you be higher in the batting order than Mark is on the Blackwell team?"

So that was it.

"Oh Mum, you just want to brag to Mrs Wooding, don't you?"

"Of course not dear, but she often mentions Mark's achievements."

"I'll see what I can do."

But when he got back to school he found he was only in the tenth position, while Mark was sixth in the Blackwell team.

Soon after the term started one of Peter's nipples got sore and after a couple of weeks it started to swell. If he'd been at home he would have asked his father, but his father wasn't available so he ignored it. Then the same thing happened to the other nipple. He'd heard about men changing their sex, and he became terrified he was turning into a girl.

The official source of medical advice was the school nurse, but he was far too embarrassed to see her. The more usual source of advice of any kind was Mr McNair, so eventually Peter asked to see him.

"What's it about?" McNair inquired.

"It's personal, sir."

"Well, come to my room at 7:30 tonight," he said with a curious look.

Peter remembered the interviews that had taken place there last term, but this time there was nothing unusual about the room. Mr McNair's bed lay along one wall, and there was a desk for correcting school work, and a table and chairs. The curtains were pulled back to let in the evening light.

McNair was relaxed and friendly. "Sit down on the bed and tell me what's bothering you," he said, taking a chair nearby.

Peter explained what was wrong but he was too embarrassed to mention his concerns about his sex. Mr McNair told him to take off his shirt and he examined Peter thoroughly. Finally he walked over to the window and stared out silently for a couple of minutes before turning and saying, "Maybe you're changing your sex."

Peter laughed nervously, "Do you think so, sir?"

"I'm quite serious." He indicated Peter's private parts. "Is there anything wrong down there?"

"I don't think so."

"Well I don't know what it is. You're quite sure there's nothing wrong with your testicles?"

"I don't think there is, but I wish you'd take a look."

McNair hesitated, then he said, "You should go to the school nurse about this sort of thing, you know."

"Please, sir. I don't want to see the nurse."

"Well, come back here after lights-out tonight. I'll have more time then."

"Oh, thank you very much."

"Don't tell anyone you're coming. They might not understand."

"No sir." There was not the slightest risk of him telling anyone.

At 10pm he slipped out of his dormitory wearing pyjamas and a dressing gown, and crept along the corridor to Mr McNair's room. He was the prefect in charge of the dormitory, so no one questioned where he was going. McNair opened his door immediately. The curtains were closed and the room was lit by only a small lamp beside the bed. He motioned Peter towards the bed and told him to sit down.

"Now Peter, are you sure you want me to do this?"

"I don't want to go to the nurse."

"Alright then, lie on your back and pull down your pyjamas."

Peter was used to undressing in front of others so he felt only slightly embarrassed. He pulled his pyjamas down to his knees and Mr McNair sat on the edge of the bed to examine his private parts. McNair carried out a slow and thorough examination. When he had finished he said, "Well, I can't see anything wrong, but is everything working properly?"

"What do you mean?"

Mr McNair thought for a moment, then he explained, "If you want to see if a pen is working properly, you must have a look at the ink."

Peter understood exactly what he meant and the idea filled him with horror.

"But wouldn't that be wrong?"

"Not if I do it to you for a medical reason."

"I don't know what to say."

"Well, it's up to you. I can easily send you to the nurse."

"Alright," said Peter uncomfortably. "If you'll be able to find out what's wrong with me."

He was still lying on the bed with his pyjama pants pulled down. Mr McNair produced a jar of Vaseline and put some on his fingers. The procedure took a while because Peter felt so uncomfortable. When it was over McNair fetched a towel.

"I can't tell if there's anything wrong immediately," he said. "I'll have to look up some things in the library. Anyway, that's enough for now."

"When will you know?"

"Come back at the same time tomorrow evening and I'll have the answer then. And not a word to anyone, understand?"

Peter had expected to get the answer right away. He certainly didn't want to go back but he had to find out what was wrong.

Peter was deeply disturbed about what had taken place. He felt uncomfortable at the prospect of meeting Mr McNair in school next day, but McNair behaved as if nothing had happened. He taught class in his usual spirited manner and his attitude was no different than before. Not once did he mention the problem or their appointment in the evening, and Peter even began to worry he might have forgotten.

10pm finally arrived and the dormitory lights were out. He crept nervously along the corridor and up the stairs, and knocked gently. McNair opened the door at once. The room looked the same as the day before, dimly lit by the bedside lamp with the curtains pulled shut.

McNair told him to take a seat at the table, and without wasting any time he said, "Peter, I'm afraid I have bad news. Your semen is too thin, that's why your breasts are growing like a girl's. It's probably all that masturbating you used to do."

There was a long silence. Peter felt sick. Now he'd have to tell his parents. Perhaps the details in the black notebook would come out too. It was unthinkable.

"Can anything be done about it?" he asked unsteadily.

McNair waited for a while, then he said, "Yes, there is something we could do. But I'm not sure you'd like it."

"I'll do anything, sir."

"Alright then. Now look me straight in the eye."

Peter stared into those dark penetrating eyes and again he felt their power. Eventually McNair spoke. "We shall have to get all that thin semen out of your body and replace it with something that's a bit thicker."

"How can we do that?"

He could guess how they'd remove the thin stuff, but when McNair explained how he would replace it with healthy semen of his own, Peter was absolutely shocked.

"You mean like in homosexuality?" He couldn't say the word sodomy, it was all just too awful.

McNair nodded. "But you mustn't think of it like that," he said. "It's a form of medical treatment."

At that moment the first tiny doubt crept into Peter's mind. He was only thirteen and his knowledge of biology was slender, but it didn't seem likely that the treatment suggested by Mr McNair would work. Could it be he was not the fine school teacher everybody thought?

On the other hand he was a close friend of the headmaster, and his parents thought McNair was the best teacher in the school. Peter was certain of one thing, there was something terribly wrong with him; it was something too embarrassing to tell the nurse, and McNair was offering a cure.

Mr McNair looked at him across the table. "Well, Peter, what do you want?"

And so the loathsome treatments began. Peter utterly detested the procedure, but McNair assured him it was necessary and they must continue until he was cured. During the acts he thought of other things, home, sailing, anything to shut out what was going on. He became withdrawn and depressed.

One day Mr Lester-Potts called him into the headmaster's office.

"What's the matter with you?" he admonished. "This is your last term and what a disappointment you've become. I've had complaints about your work, your performance as a prefect, and even your appearance. If you carry on like this you'll never get into Epsom College. Your parents are coming for the sports day weekend. See if you can turn things around by then."

How Peter longed to tell him, tell anyone, the reason for his behaviour. But it would involve saying things that people simply didn't talk about. And the treatment was working, the swelling behind his nipples was definitely going down.

But there was worse to come. Peter was going to Mr McNair's room two or three nights a week, and one evening McNair said, "I'm getting very fond of you."

Peter felt uncomfortable with this, but he replied, "Well, I like you too, sir."

"Peter," said Mr McNair. "What I mean is that I love you."

Every fibre of Peter's body and soul was disgusted.

"Well?"

"I don't know what to say. I love my mother and father."

"Of course you do. But there are different kinds of love. It's natural for children to love their parents, but as they grow older they have to learn to love other people too. If they don't they get what's called a mother complex."

With love went full mouth-to-mouth kissing which Peter found even more disgusting than the other aspect of the relationship. But after a few weeks he began to get used to even that. Slowly he found he no longer spent all his time brooding. He started to pay more attention in class. Eventually he discovered he could exploit his relationship with McNair to his own advantage. One day he told the coach he couldn't keep his appointment that night because he needed more sleep before a cricket game next day.

"I want to get higher up the batting order," he said demurely. "My mother wants me to do better than Wooding on the Blackwell Manor team."

McNair thought for a moment. "It's funny you should mention that because I was thinking about the batting order today. You've been playing well. I was about to promote you to eighth place anyway, so you might as well come tonight after all."

After that he slowly improved his position until he was fifth.

In spite of all this he still clung to the hope that McNair was really a good teacher trying to help him get over a physical problem. The swelling was certainly getting better which helped to confirm this belief.

The dreadful school term wore on. As sports day approached he began to worry about his parents. He was sure they would guess something was wrong. Should he tell them the truth? He longed to have someone to tell.

In the end he asked the only person he could what he should do if his parents suspected what was going on.

Mr McNair sat him on the hard chair and stared into his eyes for a whole minute. The muscles on the sides of his face were contracting rhythmically in the same menacing manner as they had during the interrogations last term.

"Now you listen to me, Peter, and listen well," he said quietly. "I've been doing this for you, and it is working. You know that and I know that, but no one else would understand. They would think we were having a homosexual affair. We would both be guilty. I would go to prison and you would be sent to a dreadful reform school."

"But what if my parents can tell?"

"You must insist they are wrong."

"Well, I'll try, but I don't know what I can do if they guess."

McNair walked over to a cupboard and took out a black cane about three feet long and three quarters of an inch thick.

"Do you know what this is?" he asked.

Peter had seen it before. It was a Mafia sword-stick which Mr McNair had obtained in Sicily during the war. The top six inches formed the handle of the sword, and the rest was a sheath that concealed a long thin three-sided blade with a wicked point. There were stains on the blade, and he'd told the boys he'd used it to kill an Italian spy.

"Peter," he said slowly. "If you tell anyone what we have done, for any reason, I shall kill you with this sword-stick."

Peter had no doubt at all that he would do it.

To Peter's immense relief his parents did not come to the sports day weekend after all, and he never had the embarrassment of seeing them in company with Mr McNair. The ghastly summer term finally came to an end. He passed his exams in spite of everything and he was accepted into Epsom College. Even by the end of the term he was not sure whether Mr McNair was a pervert or a saint. His medical problem had gone away completely, so he tended to believe the latter.

A few days after the holidays had started his mother said, "Peter, I met Mrs Wooding in the town this morning, and we talked about the cricket teams. You were fifth in the batting order, weren't you?"

"That's right."

"Mark never got higher than sixth. I felt so proud of you."

Peter said nothing. Mr McNair was fifty miles away but he still didn't like to think about what had happened.

One sunny morning he was on the quay with Mark, watching the boats prepare for the summer regatta.

Mark turned to him and said, "I saw your father yesterday."

"Really, so did I."

"No, dumb bum, I mean professionally. Didn't he tell you?"

"We only talk about important things."

"OK, big shot. Then I won't tell you about my disease."

Peter's curiosity got the better of him and he said, "You might as well tell me, 'cause my dad'll tell me anyway." Although he knew it wasn't true.

"Well, I've got adolescent mastitis."

"What the hell's that?"

"Sore tits. God, you're ignorant. A doctor's son too."

Peter was really interested now.

"Are they swollen?"

"Yea. So you do know about it. Well it's quite common according to your dad."

"Did he examine your balls?" said Peter with a smirk.

"Yep. Said they were the biggest he'd ever seen."

"How come you didn't mention this before?"

"Well, I wasn't sure what it was before. I thought it might be something serious."

Peter didn't quite know how to approach the next question. "Did he say why your tits were swollen?"

"Hey. Why are you so interested? Have you got the same thing?"

"Of course not. I'm just interested in medical subjects, that's all. I'm going to be a doctor."

"Well, he said it's due to hormones. Something to do with my age."

"What about treatment?"

"No need for treatment, it'll get better on its own."

About a year later Peter got another shock. The Johnsons were at breakfast and Angela was opening her mail. A friend who lived in Exeter had sent her a copy of the Western Morning News. She read it carefully.

"Look at this," she said eventually. "Gordon McNair has been convicted of homosexual assault at Westgate School. There's a whole section about the trial. It mentions the cricket team and the rugby team, but it doesn't give the names of the boys. Did you know anything about it, Peter?"

Once again Peter felt the blood drain from his face. But it didn't give the names of the boys.

"No, I didn't know anything about it," he spluttered.

"Look at this," Angela went on. "He's been sent to Dartmoor Prison for fifteen years hard labour. Apparently it was not his first offence."

Chapter 10

It was a cold windy day in September 1947. Mark's father had just driven him the two hundred miles to Epsom College for the start of his first term. They had an appointment to meet Mr Prescott, his new housemaster, but they arrived early to have a look around. Mark put on an air of confidence but he was secretly apprehensive.

The school grounds covered several acres. The major buildings stood in a group at the top of a slope. Several had high peaked roofs that reminded Mark of a medieval town, an impression strengthened by their arrangement around a large asphalt quadrangle. As they looked around they passed groups of older boys, and Mark imagined hostile stares.

There were five hundred boys at the school ranging in age from thirteen to eighteen, and for accommodation they were divided into houses with about fifty boys in each. Mark had been assigned to Holman House, and he was grateful that Peter had been placed in the same one. At least he'd have one friend. Eventually they found Holman and an older boy showed them to Mr Prescott's study. They knocked and were asked to enter. The study looked old-fashioned with wood panelling on the walls, an oak desk and some leather-covered chairs. Mark looked around uncomfortably aware that this was one of the places where corporal punishment was administered.

Mr Prescott was a large man in his fifties with greying hair. "Ah, yes, Mr Wooding," he said as he shook Neville's hand.

"This is my son, Mark."

Mark held out his own hand showing no sign of the nervousness he felt. "How do you do, sir," he said firmly.

He was determined to make a good impression at Epsom College and he intended to start right there.

Peter Johnson's first impression of the school was quite different. Where Mark had imagined a medieval fortress, Peter saw a collection of classrooms and laboratories, a swimming pool and a gym. Where Mark had seen hostile stares, Peter saw potential friends. He was a little nervous when he met his new housemaster, he didn't want another Gordon McNair, but Mr Prescott looked reassuringly ordinary.

There were ten other new boys in Holman House that year. The prefect in charge of their dormitory explained the rules and traditions of the school. The system of bells and roll calls that controlled nearly every detail of their lives was familiar from their junior schools. The rigid system worked because the invariable result of missing a roll call or the summons of a bell was five strokes with a cane after lights-out that night.

All this was no more than the boys expected. They might not have liked it but they believed that British boarding schools provided the best education in the world. Indeed, the classrooms, the laboratories, and the quality of the staff were all first class, and the complete control over body and mind that the system provided made it hard not to get educated. The school specialized in the sciences, and there was good reason for the medical schools of Britain to favour students from Epsom College.

Mark was obsessed with trying to impress his mother. She often bragged about her own school achievements so he threw himself into every school activity with a dedication that certainly impressed the staff even though his mother hardly seemed to notice.

Rugby football was the major sport in the autumn term. By playing hard and drawing attention to himself, Mark managed to get onto the Junior Colts team for fourteen-year-olds although he was only thirteen. Thus he ensured he'd be captain of the Junior Colts the following year, and set his course towards the eventual captaincy of the school First XV.

He pursued his academic studies with no less energy. Boys were streamed according to their performance in the entrance exams. Mark was placed in the highest class accessible to thirteen-year-olds. He was average at languages but gifted at the sciences where he usually came top.

Peter Johnson did not have the same drive to succeed as his friend. He tried reasonably hard at sports, but rarely made the team. In classes he started in form Upper Four B where he remained comfortably in the middle. His parents had been concerned he'd be overshadowed by Mark, but in spite of his average performance Peter's personality made him very popular in Holman House. People respected Mark's achievements and they learned not to get in his way, but it was Peter who made the most friends.

In the summer of 1951 Mark and Peter were seventeen years old and nearing the end of their time at Epsom College. They both hoped to go on to Guy's Hospital Medical School in the fall. Their marks were good and they'd already been accepted, provided they passed an interview.

The evening before Mark's interview at Guy's Hospital, Pissy Prescott, as the housemaster was affectionately called, gave him some advice.

"You've passed the exams and you shouldn't have any trouble," he said. "But you never know how interviews will go. Dress neatly in a school suit or a blazer, and sit squarely on the chair. At Guy's they often have a human bone on the table. It's not an exam, the bone is just a talking point, but it wouldn't do any harm to check your anatomy."

Next day Mark caught the train to Waterloo and took the underground to London Bridge. The wrought-iron gates of Guy's Hospital reminded him of his first sight of Epsom College and he remembered how frightened he had been. He was nervous now, but this time he was eager to cast off the bonds of boarding school and get on with his life.

The front courtyard of the hospital was enclosed by impressive old buildings of stone and weathered brick. In the centre stood a statue of the founder, Thomas Guy, and around the periphery Rolls-Royces, Bentleys and Jaguars were neatly parked. Ahead a broad flight of steps led up to the triple arch which formed the main entrance to the hospital. Mark climbed the steps and found himself in a great covered colonnade, twenty feet wide and twelve feet high, supported by stone pillars along each side. Near the entrance was an office with an inquiries wicket.

"Which way is the medical school, please?" Mark asked a middle-aged porter in a blue uniform.

"On through the colonnade," he said. "It's the big building in the far corner of the park."

"Is that where medical students go for interviews?"

The porter smiled. "Go to the medical school office and ask for Mr Jimmy Barnett."

Mark thanked him. At the far end of the colonnade he came to a small park surrounded on all sides by hospital buildings. The park was a green oasis of grass and trees, isolated from the noisy city outside but buzzing with activity of its own. There were nurses in uniform, medical students wearing sports jackets, white-coated doctors, porters and others hurrying about their business or sitting on benches and chatting. But what caught Mark's eye most, after years in a boys only boarding school, was the number of young women on the hospital staff.

He found the medical school easily, a four-storey building with ivy covering the lower half. Mr Barnett was kind and helpful. After some preliminary paperwork he said, "This interview is an important part of the admission process, so take it seriously. I'm afraid you've got old Dr Potts as the chief inquisitor today. He can be very difficult."

There were two other lads sitting nervously in the cold oak-panelled waiting area. The interviews were running late, and it was forty minutes before the second one came out of the room. His face was pale and he shook his head ominously as he left.

Eventually a secretary called Mark forward and solemnly ushered him into a large room where two elderly men sat behind a mahogany table. There was more oak panelling and portraits on the walls. Lying on the table he saw a human femur. Good old Pissy. He'd looked up the anatomy just last night.

The elder of the two doctors motioned Mark to sit down. He had thin white hair and a grim-looking face. He didn't smile or utter a word as he picked up a folder and started to read. Two or three minutes passed in silence while the second man looked at his watch. Eventually the elderly doctor passed the folder to his companion, still in silence, and then he looked up.

"Good afternoon, Wooding," he said. "I'm Dr Potts, and this is Dr Wotherspoon."

"Good afternoon, sir." Mark sat squarely on the chair going over the details of the femur in his mind.

"Wooding," said Dr Potts, indicating the folder. "You have a very impressive school record: captain of rugby, house captain, the school prize for physics, and you've got excellent marks in biology and chemistry as well."

"Thank you, sir."

"But why do you want to be a doctor? Are you interested in people or test tubes?"

The question took Mark completely by surprise. Why didn't you ask about the femur, he thought. Why indeed do I want to become a doctor? I'm really not very interested in people. I like science, but that's not the real reason. I really want to impress my mother. And I'd like to be a great surgeon, so everyone will think how important I am.

Epsom College gave its students a fine education in the sciences; but it must have done something more, because with no delay that the interviewers could discern Mark replied, "People, sir," thereby uttering the two words that Dr Potts wanted to hear.

Chapter 11

Mark's formula for success was simple: get good marks and make sure you're noticed by anyone of importance higher up. But getting noticed in a big place like Guy's Hospital was not as easy as it had been at boarding school.

For the first two years he and Peter were preclinical students who spent their time in laboratories and lecture rooms. They did not go on the wards of the hospital. Mark found he had no contact with the senior doctors he was keen to impress, so in the long summer vacation of 1953 he took a job as an orderly on Astley Cooper ward. He did not enjoy the work. The junior orderly got the jobs that no one else would do, but it allowed him to make contacts, and there was an unexpected bonus, Helen Metcalf.

Helen was a pretty student nurse. She had short brown hair, bright sparkling eyes, and a quick smile, and she gave him encouraging looks as soon as he started on the ward. He took her out a few times, usually to the movies or for a drink at a local pub, but every evening she had to be back at the nurses' home before the doors were locked at 11pm.

Mark shared a flat in West Kensington with Peter and another student named Roy Whitfield. They had the lower two floors of a Victorian row house on Comeragh Road. It wasn't luxurious, but they each had their own bedroom and there was a large living room with a balcony that overlooked the Queen's Club tennis courts, providing a view of grass and trees.

One morning in July Mark woke early. It was his day off, and Helen had a couple of days off too, so he was taking her for a picnic in the country. Roy had told him of a secluded spot on the Thames a few miles west of London where they could picnic on their own. She'd arranged to spend the night with a cousin in Chelsea so she wouldn't have to be in by 11pm.

Mark had an old red MG sports car and at 9:30 he parked it in the Guy's courtyard. Helen was waiting at the entrance to the colonnade wearing a blue and white summer dress, and as she ran down the steps to meet him he thought how lovely she looked.

"What a wonderful day," she cried. "Where shall we go?"

"There's a place on the Thames beyond Henley."

She shot him a smile. "I hope we can swim. It's going to be hot."

They drove west, through St. James's Park, past Buckingham Palace, and out of London along the great west road. They bought food for their picnic in Henley and stopped for coffee at a picturesque old pub on a tributary of the Thames. Willows lined the banks and there were reeds growing in the shallows. The river meandered past a couple of islands and under an old red-brick bridge. A rowing skiff idled by and a group of swans begged for food.

After coffee they crossed the old bridge and turned right along a lane which followed the river. Mark soon found the track Roy had described. It was narrow and overgrown so that branches brushed both sides of the car, but eventually they came to a clearing by a peaceful backwater. Willows and aspen provided shade, and a grassy bank ran down to the water which looked wonderfully cool.

"I can't imagine a more perfect spot," said Helen.

They unpacked the car and Mark spread a blanket on the grass. There was no one in sight and they settled down side by side.

"I love being out here in the country with you," said Helen after a few minutes. "You are lucky to have a car. It's like a magic carpet that you can climb onto and go anywhere you want."

"And you can climb on it with me whenever you want."

He leaned over and kissed her.

"I do want," she said.

He slipped his arm around her waist.

"I definitely do want," she whispered as she pulled him down towards her. The warm air smelled of flowers and in the background came the chirp of crickets.

"How about a swim?" Mark suggested about half an hour later.

They changed by the car. Helen wore a pale blue one-piece swimsuit that clung closely to her body. Mark couldn't keep his eyes off her. They played about in the water for a quarter of an hour, then climbed out to warm up in the sun. In a few minutes they were kissing and cuddling again and Mark was in heaven. He'd never been like this with a woman before. Presently he said, "Helen, sweetheart, I want to make love to you."

"Alright," she replied, giving him a kiss.

He hadn't expected it to be so easy and a shadow of doubt crossed his mind. He was still a virgin, although he didn't care to admit it, and he'd always imagined making love for the first time in the privacy of a bed.

She ran her fingers down his back.

"We can't do it here," he said.

"Why not?"

"Someone might come along."

"Don't be silly. No one's going to come along."

She was right of course, but he felt awkward out in the open and he feared he might fail. What could he say if that happened? It would be better back at the flat.

"Let's wait till we get home."

She looked at him and said, "You're a funny boy."

After they'd eaten their picnic, had another swim and spent a little more time on the blanket, they headed back to London.

"What would you like to do this evening?" he asked on the way home.

"What do you suggest?"

"How about a movie? *The Glen Miller Story* is on in Hammersmith, and you've got to take your things round to your cousin's place."

"I don't really have to do that, Mark," she said with a wicked little smile. "I could stay at the flat with you."

Again he felt that little doubt, but he said, "That would be wonderful."

The Glen Miller Story was full of the music of the great band leader of the thirties. They held hands in the theatre, but now they were on their way home and that little doubt persisted. He wished he'd done it before so he knew what to expect. He wished they could just kiss and cuddle without the expectation of actually making love.

Mark parked the MG outside the flat and they went in. Peter was away but Roy was sitting in the living room in semidarkness sipping scotch and listening to Eartha Kitt on the record player. The double doors to the balcony were open to let in the cool night air.

Roy had met Helen before, and now he looked at her admiringly in her pretty summer dress.

"Hi Helen, you look absolutely gorgeous," he said. "But aren't you going to miss the curfew at the nurses' home and turn into a pumpkin or something?"

"I'm on days off and I'm staying here," she replied. "Didn't Mark tell you?"

The three of them sat around chatting and sipping coffee for half an hour. Eventually Helen went to take a shower.

Roy knew Mark hadn't gone the whole way before, and when she'd disappeared he said, "So you're going to dip your wick at last, you lucky old bastard."

This was it; there could be no going back and his doubts were as strong as ever.

After Mark had showered he found Helen waiting for him on the balcony. It was a warm night and she wore only a loose chiffon nightie. He put his hand on her waist and she slipped into his arms.

"Mark, you've given me a wonderful day," she said. "Now I want to do something for you."

He led her to his room and they lay down on the bed to cuddle. After a few minutes he turned out the light and started to remove her nightie and his own pyjamas. Presently he realized she could feel he was ready.

"It's perfectly safe," she whispered. "It's the safe time of the month."

She rolled onto her back and he awkwardly climbed on top. He felt clumsy in the dark and it was much more difficult than he expected. He didn't want to hurt her but he didn't want to fail, and that's just what seemed to be happening. The harder he tried the softer it became. For a few minutes he lay beside her in silent embarrassment, searching for an excuse.

"I think I'm too hot," he stammered.

"Yes, you are rather hot," she replied awkwardly.

He threw off the sheets and after a few minutes he started again, but he feared that when the time came he would fail once more and that's just what happened.

For a while they lay in silence, then Helen asked, "Is it me?"

"No, it's me," he said, feeling utterly inadequate.

"Don't worry about it. Let's just go to sleep."

In a few minutes she was sound asleep, but sleep did not come easily to Mark. If only they hadn't talked about doing it out in the open. That was when he'd first thought of failure, and once the idea was implanted in his mind it wouldn't go away. If only it had all happened differently. And yet the conditions could hardly have been better: a lovely girl who cared for him, a beautiful day together, a quiet room and a comfy bed. If it didn't work then, would it ever work at all?

In the morning he felt wretched. Apart from the effect of his failure on his relationship with Helen, there was the problem of what to tell Roy. He was bound to ask what had happened, and Mark couldn't tell a direct lie. A poor performance by a beginner was one thing, they could laugh about that, but impotence was quite another matter.

He decided to make one more attempt. Helen was cautious, which was hardly a surprise, but they touched and kissed and soon he became aroused. He was more experienced now and when she turned onto her back he knew what to do. He supported himself on his knees and elbows as he gently got into position.

And then the same dreadful thing happened all over again, just as it had before.

Chapter 12

It was a warm sunny day in the summer of 1954 and Salcombe harbour was sparkling in the sun. Peter Johnson opened the gate to the waterfront garden of the Ferry Inn. The place was full of people enjoying a lunchtime drink and he spotted his friend, Jack Ross, with a couple of girls. One of them was Jack's girlfriend Jo White, but it was the other who caught Peter's eye. She had smooth shiny brown hair which swung in a wave when she turned her head.

The Rosses lived in the village of Portlemouth, across the estuary from Salcombe. Jack was pursuing a career in the army having recently graduated from Sandhurst.

"Hello Peter," said Jack as he introduced the girls. "You already know Jo and this is her little sister Jenny. They're on holiday with their parents."

Jenny shot him a smile.

They chatted for a while and then Peter went over to the bar to buy a round of drinks.

Salcombe had become a popular yachting resort and the little town was bustling with people. There were holidaymakers looking for boats to hire, yachtsmen ashore to visit the pubs, and fishermen hurrying to catch the tide.

Peter was twenty years old now, a medical student at Guy's. His fair hair and blue eyes were unchanged but his face had matured. He was dressed for boating in blue jeans and a white T-shirt, and he'd spent the morning working on the family's sailboat, a twenty-foot sloop moored in the harbour.

As he waited for the drinks he looked back at Jack and the girls. Jenny was very young, no more than seventeen he guessed, but she looked stunning in blue gingham shorts and a white Aertex shirt. She had a pretty oval face with dark eyes and smooth clear skin, and her shoulder length hair was cut with a slight inward curl that perfectly framed her face. He walked over to the phone and dialled his parents number. His mother answered.

"Hello Mum, it's Peter. Is anyone using the boat this afternoon?"

"I don't think so."

"I'd like to take Jack Ross and a couple of girls out sailing."

"A couple of girls?" He could almost hear her chuckle.

"They're friends of Jack's. No one special."

"Of course you can, dear."

He wished she wouldn't call him dear.

Peter and Jack drank beer and the girls had Babychams. In the sunshine, on empty stomachs, the alcohol soon went to their heads and the conversation flowed easily. Peter didn't want to make a fool of himself, so he tried to conceal his interest in Jenny, but the more they talked the stronger the attraction became. When lunch time approached he mentioned his plan to go sailing.

"We haven't done any sailing," said Jo.

"That doesn't matter."

"Well, I certainly want to go," said Jenny.

"That's settled then," said Jack. "And Peter, we're having a party on the beach tonight."

"A beach party?"

"On Fisherman's Cove."

"What about the girls?"

"Jo's going, but Jennifer wanted to take a look at you before she decided." He turned towards her. "I guess now you've seen him you'll want to stay home."

"I'll put up with anything for a party," she laughed.

They arranged to meet on the quay after lunch and Peter walked home with a spring in his step.

The afternoon was ideal for sailing, sunny and hot but with just enough wind. Peter and Jack showed the girls what to do and soon they had the sails set.

First Peter took them inland towards Kingsbridge, five miles away. The estuary wound between the lush green hills of Devon, past woods and farms. On the way back he kept close in along the sandy beaches of Portlemouth dodging swimmers. As they got nearer the open sea the wind freshened, but the girls were used to sailing now and they sat on the windward deck as the boat heeled to the breeze.

Peter was enjoying himself immensely. During the afternoon he learned that Jenny wanted to become a ballerina. In the fall she was going to the London School of Dance and Drama in Holland Park, not far from his flat on Comeragh Road. He wondered how she'd fit in with his friends. She was very young but she was pretty and she had self-confidence so they probably wouldn't notice her age.

Eventually he took them into Starehole Bay where they anchored for a swim. An old four-masted sailing ship had been wrecked in the bay and they could see the remains of her hull through the water. Peter was a good swimmer so he dived down to get a souvenir but nothing would come loose. After a few minutes they all climbed back on board to warm up in the sun.

"Now tell me about this beach party," asked Peter.

"It's a funeral party," laughed Jo.

"What?"

"You know that leaky old green dinghy of ours?" said Jack.

Peter nodded.

"The poor old thing's come to the end of its life, so we're going to have a bonfire on the beach to launch it into the next world."

While they were swimming they'd noticed some people in a rented motorboat fishing for mackerel, and now the boat headed into the bay. There were half a dozen people on board curious to see what was going on.

"What's down there?" one of them called.

"The wreck of an old four-masted barque," said Jack.

"An old windjammer? Do you mind if we take a look?"

They anchored nearby and Jack pointed out the remains of the ship twenty feet below. There were two little girls on the boat, aged about five and three. Peter watched them climb onto the foredeck with their mother to get a better view. Suddenly the younger one fell feet first into the water. She went in with hardly a splash and disappeared at once.

The mother screamed, but the other adults were listening to Jack and they hadn't see what happened. Peter dived off the foredeck and swam straight down. He had no face mask and everything looked blurred, but just as his breath was running out he spotted the child lying between the sand and the side of the ship. Her eyes were open and her hair was drifting eerily in front of her face. He grabbed her and with bursting lungs he headed up. As soon as his head broke the surface people reached down to take her, but her limbs were limp and her face was blue. As they lifted her into the boat her eyes lolled open and vomit trickled from her mouth.

Peter took a breath and called, "Hold her by the feet. Keep her upside down."

Hands helped him into the boat. The mother was holding the child but no one seemed to know what to do. Out of the corner of his eye he saw Jenny climb aboard.

"Quick," he called. "Get a floor board."

Jenny pulled up one of the loose boards that covered the bilge of the motorboat. Peter placed it with one end on a seat and the other on the floor to make a firm sloping platform. Then he picked up the little girl and laid her on the board with her head down the slope. Without a word Jenny held the child's legs to prevent her sliding down, while he opened her mouth and scooped away some vomit with his fingers. He grasped her head with one hand beneath the chin, placed his mouth over hers, and exhaled. Nothing happened. No air would go into her lungs.

He heard Jack explain that Peter was a medical student with training in resuscitation, but he couldn't get it right. For half a minute he adjusted the way he held the child's head but nothing happened. No air would go into the lungs. He felt everyone's eyes upon him. Desperately he pulled the chin up to straighten out the child's larynx and suddenly it worked. The little chest rose as he exhaled and when he took his mouth away the air came rushing out. He went on with this for several minutes and gradually the girl began to breath on her own.

"I can feel the pulse now," said Jenny. "It's getting stronger all the time."

Gradually the child's colour changed from blotchy blue to pink, and she started vomiting water mixed with food. Peter turned her on her side with her head down the slope so she wouldn't inhale the vomit. Finally she opened her eyes and whimpered, "Mummy."

Her mother knelt over her with tears streaming down her face. "Oh, my little Susie," she sobbed. "You saved her life."

The child was shivering wildly and Peter realized they were all waiting for him to take the lead.

"I'm just a medical student," he said. "My father's a doctor in Salcombe and I think we'd better get her there as quickly as we can. Jack, will you and Jo take the sailboat home. Jenny and I will go in this boat to keep an eye on Susie. I'm worried about hypothermia."

Jenny found some blankets in a locker and she helped Susie's mother strip off the girl's wet clothes and wrap her up. She still felt cold so the mother cuddled her while Jenny covered them both with a piece of canvas to keep out the wind.

It took forty-five minutes to get back to the quay and another half hour to find Peter's father. It looked as if Susie was going to make a complete recovery but James Johnson put her in the hospital for the night to make sure.

By this time Jack and Jo were home and they were watching when Susie's father turned to Peter and Jenny and said, "Thank God you were here. You two make a wonderful team."

Fisherman's Cove was a small sandy bay directly opposite Salcombe. In the evening Peter rowed Jack and the girls across the estuary in the Johnsons' dinghy. They arrived early to help collect driftwood for the fire and soon they had a big pile stacked on the sand. Jack's brother, Barry, trimmed the old green dinghy with red bunting and set it on the beach nearby.

As dusk came the breeze died and the estuary grew totally calm. Guests arrived in boats and eventually there were twenty or thirty people on the beach.

When the first stars appeared Barry put a match to the pyre and everyone gathered round to watch the flames grow. People fetched bottles of beer and wine from their boats, and someone produced a guitar. Then they sat on the sand talking and singing as darkness fell.

The story of the little girl's rescue spread and Jack had to re-tell it several times as different groups arrived. Peter sat close to Jenny. He slipped his arm around her waist and she squeezed up close.

Eventually Barry stood up, a little drunk, and called for silence. Then with mock solemnity he announced, "Ladies and Gentlemen. We are gathered here to send this boat, which has been a member of the Ross family for fifty years, on her last voyage to that great harbour in . . . "

"Get on with it, Barry," someone called. "You're making me cry."

"Insensitive landlubbers," he retorted. "Alright, send her on her way."

They scrambled up and carried the heavy old boat to the fire. Then, as the guitarist attempted the funeral march, they launched her into the flames. Her bottom planks were steeped in tar, and soon the flames rose around her in a column that lit up the beach for a hundred yards.

Peter found it strangely moving to see the old boat gradually disappear. For a while everyone stood in silence watching the fire. He glanced at Jenny. The firelight was glinting on her hair and she looked more appealing than ever.

"Let's go for a walk down the beach," he suggested, and when she nodded he felt a thrill.

He led her down to the water's edge and they strolled along the beach until their path was blocked by the ferry pier. There they paused to look at the lights of the harbour. Then she was in his arms. Her body felt light and firm, and she had a lovely childlike scent. Her face turned up and they kissed for the first time.

"Don't talk," she whispered. "I want to remember this moment."

He put his hands around her waist and pulled her gently against him. Then he felt her fingers behind his neck as she drew his head down to her face.

The firelight flickered along the beach. To the left the great headland at the mouth of the estuary stood out against the starlit sky, and in front the lights of the harbour shimmered on the water.

They went on for an hour, kissing, caressing, sometimes gently, sometimes passionately, standing back and holding hands while he looked into her face.

Chapter 13

Mark Wooding felt uneasy as he climbed the steps at the entrance to Guy's Hospital and made his way to the notice board in the colonnade.

It was 1954 and the students had begun their apprenticeship on the wards. At this stage the Guy's students were joined by another group who'd done their preclinical training at Cambridge University. There was usually no rivalry between the two groups, but among those who came from Cambridge this year was an ambitious young man called Paul Ellison. He was intelligent, fast and opinionated, and he was determined to be recognized as the leading student of the year, an unofficial position hitherto held by Mark.

On the notice board Mark found a message from Paul, a simple list of three patients' names with their wards and admission diagnoses. He turned the paper over but there were no details. His firm made their weekly ward round that morning, and now he had three new patients to examine before 10am. Ellison must be up to one of his tricks.

The medical staff were organized into firms, each one like a pyramid, with a senior doctor at the top and layers of juniors below. Beneath the chief of the firm came the registrars, trainee specialists who might one day have firms of their own. Below them came the housemen, young doctors who'd just finished their exams. The students, about a dozen to each firm, were at the bottom of the pile. The most junior students were called ward clerks, and Mark, Peter and Paul Ellison fell into that category.

Mark hurried along the colonnade and across the park to the medical school. He loved the Guy's Hospital park in summertime; it was peaceful and green, with lawns, trees and flowers. Usually he would find friends sitting on the benches chatting to student nurses, but today he didn't stop.

Each ward clerk was allotted half a dozen patients, and it was his duty to examine them and write up their notes. Once a week the whole firm went round the wards with their chief. They would stop at each bed in turn, and it was the student's job to describe the details of that patient's illness to the rest of the firm. A student's prestige depended on how well he gave these presentations. The chief of Mark's firm was Dr Cudmore, a senior consultant surgeon whose weekly ward round was an important event. All the doctors on the firm attended and most of the nurses too.

Mark climbed the steps to the medical school and made his way to the library. There he found a copy of Bailey and Love's *Practice of Surgery* and he took a seat at one of the tables. Before he opened the book he reread Paul Ellison's note: "Waites, Astley Cooper Ward, goiter. Webber, Astley Cooper Ward, varicose veins. McIntosh, Queen Ward, cholelithiasis." So he had to read about goiter, varicose veins, and gallstones, and write up the medical histories of three patients, all before 10am.

Patients varied enormously. They could be pleasant and cooperative or miserable and mean. Some had interesting diseases which would generate a lot of discussion and give a student a chance to shine. Others had routine conditions that would hardly raise any comment from the chief.

A student's reputation could depend upon the patients he was given, and a senior student was usually designated as controller to distribute the patients fairly. However, at the beginning of this term none of the senior students had wanted the chore. Paul Ellison had volunteered and he never failed to use the position to his own advantage.

Mark opened the textbook. He'd studied goiter a couple of weeks before, and varicose veins were so common that Cudmore probably wouldn't discuss them at all, so he turned to the chapter on gallstones and started reading that.

At 9:15 he made his way to Astley Cooper. The ward reminded him of Helen Metcalf. She'd been transferred long ago, but he still hadn't overcome his failure as a lover. There were nineteen beds on the ward, but it was big and airy with tall windows that let in plenty of light. The sister in charge ran it in the old Victorian style, so everything was neat and clean.

He said good morning to a blue belt, a third year student nurse, and explained why he hadn't seen the patients before. She was a friend of Helen's and he wondered if she knew his secret.

"Mr Waites is in bed eleven," she said, "and Webber's in fifteen. You'd better see Waites first, he's getting snarly."

Mr Waites was a thin nervous man with wide staring eyes and a swelling on the front of his neck.

"Good morning," said Mark. "I'm Mr Wooding, your medical student. It's my job to take your medical history and examine you before Dr Cudmore's ward round."

"About time too," Waites retorted. "I been 'ere since yesterday, and the only doctor I've seen was a young 'un for ten minutes last night."

It's not my fault, thought Mark. He looked in the patient's chart for a letter from the referring doctor giving the details of his condition, but there was nothing there. He'd have to do the best he could without it in the ten minutes that were left. He tried to take a medical history and carry out a proper examination, but Waites was uncooperative, and eventually he moved on to bed fifteen to see Webber.

The stripping of varicose veins was a straightforward operation usually done by a registrar, so he explained to Mr Webber that they probably wouldn't stop to see him that morning. He promised to come back in the afternoon to examine him then.

That left twenty minutes for Mrs McIntosh, the patient with gallstones. He walked across to Queen, the women's ward, and apologized to a staff nurse for coming so late.

"There's a referral letter about Mrs McIntosh," said the nurse. "And some X-rays from another hospital."

A bit of luck at last. He read the letter carefully and learned another lucky fact, the patient had been in Guy's Hospital before, so she'd know what to expect. He walked over to her bed and introduced himself.

She smiled at him cheerfully. "Good morning, laddie," she said with a Scottish accent. "So you're me ward clerk. Just in time for rounds, eh? Better late than never, that's what I always say."

Mark could tell she was going to be cooperative. He quickly went through her medical history, confirming the details outlined in the letter. Then he drew the curtains round the bed and discreetly carried out a physical examination.

When he'd finished he said, "Mrs McIntosh, you're here to have your gallbladder removed. It will probably be a straightforward operation, but if you have any problems I'll do my best to help."

"Thank you," she said. "I appreciate that."

"In a few minutes Dr Cudmore will be coming round," Mark continued. "It's my job to present your medical history to all the doctors, and I may need a little help myself."

She smiled broadly. "I'm used to ward rounds, laddie. You can depend on me."

He drew back the curtains, and he was about to leave when she stopped him.

"There's one more thing you ought to know. Me little sister died of Weil's disease when she was a girl. The doctors are always interested in that."

"What's Weil's Disease?" he asked.

"You'll have to look that up, won't you, laddie?" she grinned. "But she went yellow, just like I do when I have gallbladder attacks."

"Thank you Mrs McIntosh, that may be very helpful."

He put the referral letter in the patient's chart. Weil's disease, what on earth was that? The girl had become jaundiced, so it was likely something to do with the liver, and if she'd died it must be serious. He didn't have time to go back to the library, but he had a copy of Davidson's *Textbook of Medicine* in his briefcase so he went to look at that.

Mark waited with a dozen other students and junior doctors for their chief to arrive. Dr Cudmore was a big man of about fifty-five with curly reddish hair and a beard. The group hushed when he appeared. He had a brief talk with the sister before leading them briskly down the ward to the first patient.

The round served a double purpose. It kept the chief informed about his patients, and it acted as a forum for teaching the students and younger doctors. Many of the patients were recovering uneventfully from operations carried out by Cudmore and the registrars, and these got little more than a passing nod. New patients and those with complications took longer, but most of the two-hour round would be spent on bedside discussions of the four or five patients who had the best teaching potential.

The first patient was Mr Waites, and soon the group was standing round his bed. Mark usually welcomed the opportunity to show off his knowledge, but today he was unprepared. However Waites' case history was still fresh in his mind, and he thought he did a good job of reciting it and describing what he'd found when he'd examined the man.

"So what's your diagnosis?" asked Dr Cudmore.

"Nodular goiter, sir."

"And what treatment would you recommend?"

Mark had not had time to get all the information he required, but patients were admitted to a surgical ward for one thing only.

"Surgery, sir. Partial thyroidectomy."

"Wooding," said Dr Cudmore. "Did you notice anything unusual about this patient's face?"

Waites had been so bad tempered that Mark had hardly looked at his face, but now that the patient was staring at the group of doctors no one could miss the unusual bulging of his eyes.

"Well, I . . . "

"Exophthalmos," Paul Ellison butted in. Paul was a big good-looking lad, slightly taller than Mark, with straight dark hair and a handsome face. He always wore expensive suits which was unusual for a student.

"Well done, Ellison," said Dr Cudmore. "And what does that mean?"

"Thyrotoxicosis, sir," replied Ellison at once.

"Wooding," said Cudmore. "Do you know what thyrotoxicosis is?"

Of course I do, thought Mark miserably. "It means that Mr Waites' goiter has started to produce too much thyroid hormone."

"And what might happen if we rush into surgery?"

"He might go into heart failure," said Mark.

"That's right. Exophthalmos is an important sign, and if you'd examined him properly you'd have found other clues. Mr Waites, hold out your hands," he ordered.

The hands trembled perceptibly.

"There, he has a tremor. These are important observations, Wooding. I'm surprised you missed them." He looked at the patient, "Don't worry, we'll give you a course of medical treatment before the surgery. I won't operate until I'm sure everything's alright."

Then he turned back to Mark, "What's his sleeping pulse rate?"

"We'll be doing that tonight, sir."

The patient's nurse looked at the sister, who nodded, giving her permission to speak.

"Actually we kept a sleeping pulse chart last night, sir," she said.

"That was very efficient of you," said Dr Cudmore approvingly.

"Mr Ellison asked us to do it."

Cudmore raised his eyebrows.

"As controller of the firm I like to check all the patients when they come in," said Paul casually. "I couldn't help noticing that Mr Waites was thyrotoxic, so I ordered a sleeping pulse and a BMR as well."

Mark was really embarrassed now. He guessed why there'd been no referral letter in the patient's chart, Ellison must have removed it because it warned of thyrotoxicosis.

They moved on to the next patient. Paul Ellison recited the history and the details of his examination in a very professional manner. He'd obviously taken a lot of trouble and at the end Dr Cudmore congratulated him on his presentation.

Then they went on down the ward, and to Mark's dismay, when they got to Webber's bed Cudmore smiled and said, "Good morning, John." It was unusual for a consultant to have personal friends on a public ward.

"Which student is looking after Mr Webber?" he asked.

"I am, sir," said Mark uncomfortably. "But I haven't had time to do his history and examination yet."

Dr Cudmore looked annoyed. "Why not?"

"Because I wasn't told about him until an hour ago," he blurted. "And I had two other patients who seemed more important."

"Every patient is important," said Cudmore sharply. "If you ever want to be a doctor, Wooding, you'd better remember that."

A look of satisfaction crossed Paul Ellison's face, and he gave a little cough.

"What is it Ellison?" asked Cudmore.

"Well sir, I don't wish to embarrass Wooding, but as controller of this firm I don't want you to think I allot patients only an hour before rounds."

Cudmore looked at Mark.

"I didn't get a note until this morning," he stammered.

"Really?" said Ellison. "I put the notes on the board yesterday, but I have no control over what time people go home in the afternoon."

"Wooding," said Mr Cudmore angrily, "get your act together. These patients come in early so we can make sure they don't have thyrotoxicosis or some other complication."

He looked at his senior registrar. "Brooks, you're responsible for the students. Don't let this happen again. Is that perfectly clear?"

The registrars were trainee surgeons, overworked and underpaid. Alan Brooks had put in years under consultants like Dr Cudmore, waiting for a consultant's post himself. The last thing he wanted was to displease an important surgeon who could ruin his career.

They finished on Astley Cooper and walked over to Queen Ward, and eventually they arrived at Mrs McIntosh's bed. They made an impressive group, Cudmore with his reddish hair and beard, very much in charge, the doctors and students, the sister in her plain blue uniform and the nurses dressed in white.

"Good morning, Mrs McIntosh," said Dr Cudmore.

"Good morning, sir," she replied in her Scottish accent, obviously enjoying the attention.

"Which student is looking after this patient?"

"It's Dr Wooding," answered Mrs McIntosh.

Cudmore liked patients who took part in the proceedings to some extent, it added to the show-business atmosphere of the round.

"Well Wooding, let's have Mrs McIntosh's history," he said.

Mark related the details of her illness with no hesitation. She'd been getting attacks of pain in the right upper abdomen, and sometimes there was jaundice. He described her previous history too, including two pregnancies during which she'd been anemic. He even mentioned her little sister, and how she'd died of Weil's disease.

"Did you find anything abnormal when you examined her?" asked Cudmore.

"Well, the gallbladder wasn't enlarged, but I did think I could feel her spleen."

"Her spleen? I couldn't feel it when I saw her in the outpatient clinic three weeks ago. Brooks, have you examined this patient yet?"

"Yes, I saw her last night."

"Was her spleen enlarged?"

"I didn't notice it," said Dr Brooks.

Mark saw a smirk on Ellison's face.

"Alright," said Cudmore. "Let's assume the spleen is normal for the time being. What's your diagnosis, Wooding?"

"Gallstones, sir."

"Very good. Now give me five common characteristics of patients who have gallstones," asked Dr Cudmore. "They all begin with F."

Mark knew that one. "Fair, Female, Fertile, Forty and, well, the last F doesn't apply to this patient, sir." He looked at Mrs McIntosh sitting up in bed, good-natured and plump. "The last F stands for Fat."

"Very good, laddie," she beamed.

Dr Cudmore looked at her and smiled too. "Now Wooding, how would you confirm the diagnosis of gallstones?"

"With X-rays, sir. I'd do a cholecystogram."

He remembered the X-rays the nurse had mentioned, but he hadn't had time to look at them. They might not be films of the gallbladder at all.

"Well, do we have this patient's gallbladder films?"

It was the student's duty to make sure that X-rays were ready for rounds, and Mark wondered if Ellison had tampered with them as well. But they were all looking at him now. He'd have to take a chance.

"They're in an envelope with the patient's chart," he said.

"Well, let's have a look at them," ordered Cudmore impatiently.

Mark saw Paul watching him. He felt sure it was a trap, but there was nothing he could do. He picked up the big envelope marked X-RAYS, and reluctantly reached inside.

"Hold them up to the light, man, so we can all see them," said Cudmore.

He took the top film and shakily held it up. To his amazement it was a picture of a gallbladder, and inside were three large stones. The other members of the firm peered at it with satisfaction.

When they'd finished looking, Dr Cudmore asked, "What treatment would you recommend?"

"Cholecystectomy, sir. Removal of the gallbladder."

"Very good. Well, I assume the routine blood tests are being done, and she's on my operating list for Friday?" said Cudmore as he prepared to move on to the next patient.

Mark could see Paul fidgeting. He was obviously aware that no tests had been ordered yet, and he seemed to be wondering how to let everyone know.

Mark said quickly, "The history of Weil's disease in the family is interesting."

"Possibly," said Cudmore. "Does anyone else have an opinion?"

"I think it's irrelevant," said Paul. "I'd like to know what blood tests Wooding has ordered."

"You have to be careful before you dismiss anything as irrelevant," replied Cudmore. "What do you know about Weil's disease?"

"Well, not a great deal, sir," said Paul vaguely.

"Come on, Ellison. Tell us what you do know."

He looked uncomfortable. "Well, I don't actually know anything about it."

"Then how can you dismiss it as irrelevant?"

Paul stared at his feet.

"Does anyone know about Weil's disease?"

"I know a little about it," volunteered Mark, who'd just looked it up. "It's a rare infection that's carried by rats and is sometimes transferred to humans. It's almost unheard of nowadays, but it used to occur among fish workers in Glasgow."

The patient looked at him with admiration. "We used to live in Glasgow, and my father worked in the fish market. He often caught jaundice, and sometimes he passed it on to my sister."

This sort of diversion was just what Cudmore liked on a teaching round, it made medicine interesting.

"That's very impressive, Wooding," he said.

Ellison gave a cough. Mark felt sure it was about the blood tests. He had to divert their attention so he said, "What about the spleen?"

Paul looked at him with contempt. "The spleen's perfectly normal. You heard Dr Brooks say so."

Cudmore appreciated a little controversy, it stimulated discussion and helped the students learn. "Draw the curtains round the bed," he ordered. "Mrs McIntosh, there seems to be a difference of opinion about your spleen. Do you mind if some of us examine it? Three will be enough. Ellison, Dr Brooks, and myself."

Paul leant over the patient and placed one hand on the front of her abdomen, high up on the left side, and the other behind her back. He squeezed the upper abdomen between them, probing under her ribs with his fingers.

"Take some deep breaths," he said. "Let your muscles relax." For a few moments he looked doubtful.

"Well, what do you feel?" asked Cudmore.

He hesitated. "Nothing sir. I don't think the spleen's enlarged."

He was followed by Brooks and Cudmore. The rest of the firm crowded inside the curtains looking on.

"Well, what do you think, Allen?" asked Cudmore finally. For the first time he seemed to be asking a question to which he didn't already know the answer.

"I think the lad's right, sir," said Dr Brooks. "I don't know why I missed it, but I think the spleen is definitely enlarged."

"So do I." There was a pause. "Well, what do you make of that?"

"I don't know. She could have portal hypertension, but there are no other signs. I'll look into it this afternoon," said Brooks.

"Mrs McIntosh," said Dr Cudmore. "Mr Wooding has discovered that your spleen's enlarged. It may not be important, but we'll have to check into it before I operate."

He started to move on to the next patient.

"Excuse me, sir," said Mark. "May I make a suggestion?"

"Certainly."

"Perhaps she has congenital spherocytosis."

"Go on."

"It's an illness that runs in families, and it causes repeated attacks of mild jaundice often with abdominal pain, just like this patient has. Also it makes the spleen enlarge, and it often leads to gallstones."

"Quite right," said Dr Cudmore.

"There's another thing. Perhaps her father and sister didn't have Weil's disease at all. Maybe their jaundice was due to spherocytosis."

"Very good, Wooding. I think that's a very good suggestion."

He turned to the houseman. "Routine blood tests won't be of much help in this case," he said. "Talk to the people in hematology and have the appropriate tests done for spherocytosis. And cancel the surgery for Friday."

Then he looked at the students. "Well done, Wooding. A few minutes ago I thought you were losing your grip. I'm pleased to see I was wrong."

Chapter 14

For a moment Jennifer White couldn't remember why she felt so happy. Then, as she lay in bed in the hotel room she shared with her sister, the details of the evening on Fisherman's Cove came rushing back. She thought about the day ahead. She was going to walk round the cliffs to Gara Sands with her parents and Jo. She'd much rather spend the time with Peter, but he was taking her to the Kingsbridge fair in the evening.

She got out of bed and made her way to the bathroom. She took off her pyjamas to shower and looked at herself in the mirror. She wondered if Peter would like the way she looked. She was only seventeen and he was a sophisticated twenty on his way to becoming a doctor. After showering she slipped on a pink flowered dress and combed out her hair. Jo was still pretending to sleep, so she gave her a shake and went down to breakfast.

They crossed the estuary on the ferry and followed the narrow cliff-top path to Gara Sands. It wound back and forth round headlands and bays, sometimes dropping to sea level and sometimes climbing a few hundred feet. On the right the cliff dropped away to the sea where gulls swooped and soared on the wind. To the left the ground rose in a steep bank covered with gorse and heather, alive with small birds flitting from bush to bush.

But Jenny was aware of none of these things. All she saw was Peter's wonderful face, his fair hair, his blue eyes and his firm manly chin. She pictured the details of his body and his smooth suntanned skin.

Eventually they came to the beach where they spent the day exploring the rocks and swimming in the sea. Jo and her parents talked, read and lay in the sun, but Jenny just sat and stared out to sea.

Eventually her mother asked, "You're very quiet, Jennifer. Is anything the matter?"

"She's in love," Jo laughed, but Jenny hardly heard.

Mary White was worried. She liked Peter and at first she was pleased that Jennifer had found such a suitable boyfriend. But as the weeks went by she noticed a certain dreamy happiness which made her wonder if her daughter really had fallen in love. Jennifer was too young for a love affair, and she didn't want to lose her little girl.

Whenever she saw Jenny and Peter together Mary felt a twinge of jealousy. Her mind would flash back to that idyllic time in 1936 with dear darling Amiel. Once more she'd see his handsome face, his dark compelling eyes. She'd picture Road Town harbour and the old *Lady Royal*. Again she'd feel the warm tropical air and see the islands and the beaches. Oh, what emotion it awakened in her mind. For a few weeks she'd glimpsed paradise, and she'd give the earth to live those weeks again. She could not discuss these thoughts with Philip, of course, and Jenny must never know.

There was another thing that bothered her, something much easier to discuss. Richard Gordon's best-selling novel *Doctor in the House* had just been published. It was based on his experiences as a medical student, and although the book was hilariously funny she believed a lot of it was true. It made medical students look an immoral group, and she was concerned her daughter might get hurt.

They argued about it.

"Why can't I go to Peter's flat? There'll be other people there."

"There'll only be other medical students."

"Well, they're people aren't they? And anyway what does it matter if there are other people?"

"Something might happen to you."

"Do you mean I might get raped or something?"

"You've read that dreadful book."

"You enjoyed the book," Jenny protested. "You kept reading bits out to make us laugh."

"It was funny in a way, but those sort of things actually do go on."

"Oh Mum, don't be so old-fashioned."

When Jenny saw the flat on Comeragh Road she realized it was very similar to the one described in Richard Gordon's book and shown in the subsequent movie. Medical books, microscopes, human bones, and even an outdated bottle of blood lay around. The walls were decorated with signs borrowed from the streets of London, and there was a record player and even a bar. None of the students' parents had ever seen the flat, and Jenny immediately decided that hers would be no exception. She liked it though, and the connection with Gordon's notorious book gave it a certain romance.

The flat encouraged an active social life, and hardly an evening went by without something happening. Groups of students and nurses would drop in for a drink, and impromptu parties were common. These generated invitations to other parties, so there was always something to do. Jenny slipped into the scene very easily, delighted with the opportunity to make friends in London where she'd just started at the School of Dance and Drama.

One evening in September she and Peter were at the flat with Mark and Roy Whitfield. By this time Roy had a steady girlfriend, a Guy's nurse called Christine, and she was there as well. Jenny had to catch the 11pm train home to Ashtead, and Peter drove her to the station in Mark's car. They arrived early, so they went for a coffee in a little restaurant nearby. Christine's relationship with Roy had been bothering her and eventually she asked, "Christine has three days off from the hospital?"

"That's right. She's been on night duty and now she's got time off."

Jenny hesitated. "I noticed she had a bag with her."

"Well?"

"Is she staying at the flat?"

"Yes," he replied.

"You mean with Roy?"

"Yes."

There was a pause. Then she asked, "She's sleeping in his room? In bed with him all night?"

Peter wanted to be honest but not too blunt.

"Well," he said. "She's his girlfriend, and he's her boyfriend. And it's not as if they just met."

"Are they engaged?"

"No."

"I don't think I approve of that," she said finally.

He looked out of the window. It was dark and the lights of London were flashing their many-coloured messages.

"I don't think they need your approval," he replied slowly. "Mine neither."

"But isn't it wrong?"

"I know our parents would think so, but how can something be wrong if it doesn't do any harm?"

"Suppose she has a baby?"

"They'll use a contraceptive. They've done it lots of times before."

"Peter," she said. "I hope you don't want me to . . . , well, you know, go the whole way. I've always thought it should be saved for marriage."

He reached across the table, put his hand on hers, and looked into her face. Her hair was smooth and glossy, with that slight inward curl beneath her chin. Her dark eyes looked serious. She was very young and very beautiful.

"Jenny," he said. "I love you, and I'd adore to make love to you, but I would never make you do anything you didn't want. Maybe one day we will be married, but until then it's up to you. However, I can't control what my friends do, that's got to be left to them."

They made love for the first time three weeks later in Peter's bedroom at Comeragh Road. It happened almost by accident after a strange evening, and it was not very satisfactory on that first occasion.

When Jenny looked at Peter and his friends she saw young people living on their own, away from the influence of the previous generation. They had a lifestyle that would never have been approved of at home, but no awful fate seemed to overtake them. And when she started at the London School of Dance and Drama she found the students there valued virginity no more than those at Guy's.

There were other things that influenced her too. One evening she brought a couple of her fellow drama students over to the flat for a drink, and when she showed them around they were impressed.

"Your boyfriend lives here?" said one. "Wow, maybe you should move in."

She could hardly ask her mother for advice, but there was an older girl called Jessica Clark at the drama school whom Jenny liked. She was a vivacious black-haired woman of twenty-one, experienced in worldly matters, so Jenny sought her opinion.

"What would you do?" she asked.

"You've got to make up your mind if you really like this guy," Jessica replied.

"I really do."

"Well," she said. "It'll be love him or lose him I expect."

At last Peter had a car of his own. After negotiations with his father he'd bought an old 3 litre sports Bentley with a dark green body and wire spoked wheels. It was a car that attracted attention wherever it was parked.

Every year the drama school held a reception and dance, and Peter thought it would be a good opportunity to show off his car. Jenny was still living at home in Ashtead, so he picked her up at Waterloo Station and drove her to the flat on Comeragh Road to change her clothes. She looked perfect in a simple cocktail dress of cream taffeta, with a silver belt and shoes.

The school was in an impressive Edwardian building made of marble faced with brightly coloured tiles of blue and green and grey. It looked more like an exotic palace than a college.

The Board of Directors were using the reception for publicity so there was a photographer outside to snap the guests as they arrived. The dark green Bentley and the cream colour of Jennifer's dress went perfectly with the marble and the tiles. He was about to snap Jenny beside the car when a Rolls-Royce drew up with Mr Baltzan, the grey-haired Chairman of the Board, and his wife. The photographer was delighted to have a Rolls and a Bentley in front of the school and soon he was clicking away with Jenny and the Baltzans in the picture. After a few minutes Baltzan said something to Jenny, and she walked over to Peter.

"Mr Baltzan wants me to go in with him and his wife," she announced.

"Wait while I park the car, and I'll come with you."

"But they're going in now."

Baltzan glanced at Jenny.

"I can't miss an opportunity like this," she said, and she trotted off to the chairman's side.

Peter parked the Bentley and followed a group of students into the building. He found himself in the most striking room he'd ever seen. It was a great round hall three storeys high, built of marble inlaid with coloured tiles, brilliant blues and golds and greens. The tiles formed pictures of exotic birds and flowers, strange symbols from olden times, and elaborate mythological scenes. The roof was a marble dome which curved up to a stained-glass skylight at the peak. A gallery ran round the hall one floor up, and arches of blue-grey marble reached to the ceiling. Running round the dome was a circle of unfamiliar letters, a long quotation in ancient Greek.

A band was playing at the far side of the hall, but there was no sign of Jennifer. Soon he became aware of a woman in a slinky black dress by his side.

"You look lonely," she said, giving him a smile.

"I think I've been deserted."

"So have I. Would you like to dance?"

She was taller than Jenny, with long black hair, dark eyes and a pale creamy complexion. She danced beautifully with movements as smooth as a cat's.

"My name's Jessica," she said after a minute. Her voice had a mysterious tone.

"I'm Peter."

After fifteen minutes the music stopped and they were left standing under the marble dome.

"Well, Peter, what do you think of our pagan temple?" she asked.

That's right, he thought, it is like a pagan temple, and you're the high priestess.

"What does it all mean?"

"Most of the murals are scenes from Greek mythology." She pointed to them one by one. "That's Orpheus. And there's Jason with the Argonauts, and the monster Scylla. And over there are the Sirens, . . . "

As she went on they became the centre of a group of curious spectators.

"Can you read Greek?" he asked.

She nodded.

He pointed to the lettering above the gallery. "What does that say?"

She took his hand. "It's from the Odyssey and it says: For sailors who bring their ships to this place there is no chance of escape whatever."

She squeezed his hand mysteriously as if she were giving him a message, and then she asked, "Do you know the signs of the zodiac?"

"I've heard of them."

"Let me see what I can tell about you."

She drew his hand up in front of her and slowly opened his palm. They were the centre of attention now and everyone was silent. Then she drew her fingertips gently back and forth across his palm sending shivers down his spine. He spotted Jenny in the crowd. She had a strange look on her face.

"Peter," asked Jessica, regaining his attention. "When were you born?"

"Nineteen thirty-four."

"The day?"

"February the fifteenth."

She looked up at the dome. The signs of the zodiac were depicted in coloured tiles and she pointed to one of them.

"There's your sign, Peter," she said. "It's Aquarius."

Jenny's face looked pale.

"Do you want me to tell your future, Peter?"

She stroked his palm again and he felt another shiver.

"I can tell your future," she repeated softly. "You and I are very close, because I'm an Aquarian too."

Suddenly Jenny stepped forward and snatched his hand away.

"Leave him alone."

"Take it easy, Jenny," said one of her friends. "It's just a bit of fun."

Peter felt embarrassed. "This is Jessica," he said. "She's telling me about the school."

"I can see exactly what she's doing, and you're just making it worse." And with that she ran out of the room.

He followed her across the hall and into the library. She sat down at a table in the corner. He sat beside her and put his arm round her shoulder.

"What's the matter?"

"It's Jessica," she sobbed. "And you. I saw the way you were dancing with her, and the way she stroked your hand. Why doesn't she get a man of her own?"

He slowly made it up. They danced, and later there was a buffet supper which they ate in the library with some of her friends. Soon everyone seemed to have forgotten the incident, everyone but Jenny. She remained pensive for the rest of the evening.

When Jenny went to get her coat she found Jessica waiting.

"I'm so sorry," Jessica began.

"It's alright."

"I wasn't trying to steal your boyfriend. That would be impossible anyway."

"What do you mean?"

"He's in love with you. It's obvious."

"How can you tell?"

"The way he looks at you all the time, and at no one else."

That made her feel better.

"Is he the one?" asked Jessica. "The one you were telling me about."

"Yes."

"I think he's gorgeous."

"I noticed."

"Oh, Jenny," she said. "Give me a break. You should remember what I told you a couple of weeks ago."

Peter could hardly get a word out of Jenny as they drove back to Comeragh Road. Roy was in the living room listening to the record player as usual, but she walked straight through to Peter's bedroom to change.

Peter followed, and when he'd closed the door she gave a little smile and said, "I'm sorry. I guess I got jealous."

He kissed her. "You don't have to be jealous of anyone."

"Don't I? Do you really mean that? I need to be reassured."

He sat on the bed and pulled her gently down after him. "Then I'll reassure you."

The lights were low and he lay on the bed facing her. The sound of Ella Fitzgerald singing *Just One of Those Things* drifted through from the living room next door. He ran his fingers over her back, and then slowly up her thigh, inside her dress.

"I'll take it off," she said. "I've got to change anyway."

Bit by bit they both undressed and eventually she was wearing only her bra and tight bikini panties. He looked at her in the dim light, so young and pretty.

She shivered. "I don't feel reassured yet. Let's get into bed."

He slipped off his shirt and trousers and soon they were cuddling in the warm soft bed. For a few minutes he caressed her and she murmured, "Oh, I love you so."

They'd gone this far before, but now he said, "Let's take off all our clothes so we can get closer."

Without a word she undid her bra and slipped off her panties, and he discarded his own underwear.

"How could you ever think I'd be interested in anyone else," he whispered.

"That's what I want to hear," she said as she snuggled up against him.

They were very close now. At first he pretended it wasn't happening. He could tell she felt nothing but pleasure as their hips moved back and forth, and gradually he realized her virginity had gone.

Suddenly he knew what was going to happen.

"Oh, God," he said, straining to hold back, but it was all over in a minute. Then he lay limp and useless in her disappointed arms.

Ella Fitzgerald's voice drifted through the wall, *"It's the wrong time, and the wrong place, though your face is charming . . . "*

"I'm sorry," he said. "It'll be better the second time."

"There won't be a second time," she replied icily. "They'll kill me if I miss that train."

Again she was silent as they drove across London to the railway station. He parked the car and bought her ticket to Ashtead. She took a seat by an open window. He waited on the platform to be with her until the train pulled out, but he couldn't think of anything to say. A porter walked down the platform slamming the doors ready for the train to leave.

"Jenny," he began uncertainly.

The engineer blew his whistle.

"Yes."

"That was the wrong time and the wrong place. We can't leave it like that."

There was a clanking as the engine took up the slack between the coaches, and then the train began to move.

"Yes," she said again. He was walking down the platform now, keeping level with her as the train gathered speed.

"I wish we could go away together," he said. "Even if it were just for a weekend. Then we wouldn't have to worry about stupid trains and things like that."

He started to run to keep up with her. The other passengers began to stare.

Without any hesitation she called out, "The weekend after next I'm supposed to be going away with the school. I'll tell them I can't come, and we'll go somewhere together. Mummy and Daddy will never find out."

People were grinning. There was no privacy.

"You're sure?"

"Of course I'm sure," she shouted to him as he ran. "It's the most important thing in my life."

"Where shall we go?"

"Anywhere. You fix it."

He was running fast now, losing ground.

"I love you, Jenny."

"I love you too," she yelled.

But he didn't hear. He'd run into a trolley full of mail bags, and a cheer rang out from the other passengers as he floundered on the top.

Chapter 15

Mark Wooding could never discuss his problem with his friends. His sexual orientation was entirely normal, but since his failure with Helen Metcalf he had avoided intimacy because he feared it would happen again. His friends never seemed to have any doubt about their ability to have sex at any time. Confidence was the secret of their success just as fear was the cause of his failure. For as long as he could remember he'd been frightened of failure, a fear that was somehow connected with his mother.

In the autumn a curious little incident occurred which only made things worse.

Late one Friday afternoon Mark staggered down the steps of the Guy's Hospital Dental School, the side of his face numb from local anesthetic. Medical students got free dental care provided the work was done by dental students or housemen. Lydia Kennedy was only a junior houseman but she'd just filled a cavity in one of his molars.

He walked across the park to the students' cafeteria called the Lower Spit, and there he found Peter, Roy, and some friends drinking coffee.

"Where've you been?" asked Peter.

"Getting a tooth filled. And now I feel exhausted."

"Did Lydia do it?" Peter smirked.

He nodded.

"Lydia's got the biggest tits and the shortest arms in the dental business. I expect you enjoyed it, you old pervert."

They all laughed.

We're going for a beer," said Roy. "I'm meeting Christine and a friend at six o'clock."

"Who's the friend?"

"A girl called Ann Henderson from Samaritan Ward.

I've heard she's hot stuff," said Bill Weaver, another student in the group. "But I thought she had something going with one of the housemen."

"Christine says that's finished."

"Really?" Bill grinned. "Maybe I'll come too."

"We're going to the Admiral Cod. Then we can have spaghetti at the coffee shop on Kensington Road afterwards."

The fifth student called Andy Polanski decided to go as well, and they arranged to meet at the pub at 6:30.

The Admiral Codrington was a small pub favoured by the students because the publican didn't stick to the official closing time. Mark found the others already at the bar, so he joined them and ordered a pint of bitter.

"I'd like you to meet my friend Ann," said Christine, as he waited for his drink.

Ann Henderson was a pretty girl with short blonde hair. She smiled at Mark and asked, "Are you the Mark Wooding on Dr Cudmore's firm?"

"That's right."

"I've heard all about you. Aren't you friends with Paul Ellison?"

Everybody laughed.

"They're mortal enemies," said Roy.

"Really?"

"They both want to be top dog."

The conversation continued mostly about the hospital; the prospects for the rugby team, the proposed new Guy's tower, gossip about students and nurses. Bill Weaver placed himself next to Ann, but she was obviously more interested in Mark. One round of drinks followed another. As the evening progressed the prospect of a spaghetti dinner seemed to recede.

By 8:30 they'd decided to give up on the spaghetti and return to the flat to eat whatever was there. Bill seemed to finally realize that Ann was unimpressed, and he and Andy chose to go their own way. But before they left the pub Mark went to the washroom. There were three open urinals in a row along a tiled wall, and he stood in front of the middle one and began to unzip his trousers. Before he had time to get started Bill and Andy came in, and of course they took the two remaining places. Mark was not particularly shy, but he sometimes found it difficult to pee if people were watching. Bill was standing on his left, and he started without the slightest delay. Andy was on the other side and he had no difficulty either.

"My," said Bill. "What a relief."

Andy glanced at Mark. "Hey, you don't seem to have much of a stream," he laughed. "Having trouble with your prostate?"

Bill was already zipping up his fly. Mark stood between them in embarrassment, with no sign of anything happening at all.

"Well," said Bill cheerfully. "If it don't work for peeing, it won't work for screwing. That's what Prof Howard says. Poor Ann Henderson, but you can't win 'em all."

And with that remark Bill and Andy left. When they'd gone Mark had no difficulty whatever, but Bill's comment upset him deeply. Professor Howard was a psychologist. Had he really said that? It could be true.

They walked over to the cars to drive back to Comeragh Road. Roy and Christine went with Peter in the Bentley, and Ann went with Mark in his MG. It felt good to have a girl by his side in the car.

When they reached the flat Peter had a sandwich and went to bed. The others ate their sandwiches with coffee in the living room, and listened to the record player with the lights turned low. Ann sat close to Mark on the couch. Soon he put his arm around her back, and when she rested her head on his shoulder he felt happier than he had for months. After a while he went out to the kitchen to make more coffee.

"Ann," said Christine, while Mark was out of the room. "If we're going back to the nurses' home tonight we ought to leave soon."

Ann was curled up comfortably on the sofa. "It's so nice here I don't want to move," she replied. "But I guess you're right, we've got to beat that curfew."

"Well actually we don't have to beat the curfew at all," said Christine. "That's why I'm saying this while Mark's outside."

"What do you mean?"

"We could spend the night here, and go back to Guy's early in the morning."

There was a silence. Eventually Christine added, "What do you think?"

"Well, I haven't been asked," said Ann.

"Oh, for Christ's sake, I'll ask you," said Roy. "I'm officially asking you on behalf of my friend. Look, Christine and I are comfy here. We don't want to go back until the morning."

"I only met Mark today," said Ann. "I think he's great, but I'm not sure I'm ready to spend the night with him."

"Just keep your knickers on if you don't want to do anything," said Roy. "He won't rape you."

"Roy's quite right," said Christine. "You won't have to do anything you don't want to."

"Well," she replied. "Let's wait and see what Mark thinks about it."

But as soon as Mark heard the plan he felt a wave of panic. The incident at the pub was fresh in his mind and he couldn't bear another failure.

"Well," he stammered, searching for an excuse. "I've got a lot of studying to do, and I really don't want to get tired. I'll run you both back in the car right now if you like."

They were all taken aback.

"You don't have any studying to do," said Roy with disbelief. "And tomorrow's going to be an easy day."

Mark started to mumble something else but Ann interrupted. "I really think I should get back," she said in embarrassment, and Christine reluctantly agreed.

He drove them silently over to Guy's, and when he got back he found Roy angrily waiting.

"What did you do that for?" he exclaimed. "Too tired! I've never heard such bullshit. What the hell's the matter with you?"

"I don't know," replied Mark miserably. But he knew very well.

Chapter 16

Peter heard about The Mermaid from Christine who had stayed there with her parents.

"It's a quaint little inn in the old medieval port of Rye," she told him. "There are crooked stairways and lovely old rooms with oak beams in the ceiling. It used to be a smugglers' haunt in the olden days and there's even a secret passage to the harbour."

He was nervous when he phoned to make the reservation.

"Your name, sir?"

"Er, Johnson."

"Mr and Mrs Johnson?" came the voice on the phone.

Could they tell he was lying?

"Yes, of course. Do you have a room with a four-poster bed?"

"That would be the Elizabethan Chamber, sir."

"I think we'll take that one."

The weather was fine, so they folded down the Bentley's top for the seventy-mile drive through the countryside of Kent. They must make a good-looking couple, he thought, as they thundered along, Jenny with a red Paisley scarf covering her hair, and he with his blue and gold scarf flying in the wind.

They spotted the ancient town of Rye from miles away. It was built on a hill that rose abruptly from the surrounding flat farmland. At the top of the hill stood an ancient church tower, and around the base were the remains of the massive wall that had once protected the town from the French. Inside were cobbled streets and gabled buildings from Elizabethan times, and at the end of the High Street they came to the quay where fishing boats were moored in the river. When they saw Mermaid Street they knew they'd arrived.

"Let's not go in yet," said Jenny. "I want some time to think."

"Are you having second thoughts?"

"No, but I'm nervous."

He took her hand. "I'm a bit nervous too."

Three hundred years ago Rye had been an important seaport, but the sea had receded and now the quay faced only a river. Peter parked nearby and they sat in silence looking at the boats.

Eventually she said, "I hate deceiving my parents. They've always been so good to me."

"Jenny, if you don't want to go through with this I'll understand."

"But I do want us to be proper lovers."

There was a pause. Then he said, "I've got a present for you."

He produced a little box and inside was a gold plated ring. "We can't book in without a wedding ring."

He slipped it on her finger and it fitted perfectly.

"One day I'll put a proper ring on your finger. That's what I really want."

"Oh, that's what I want too."

Mermaid Street was a narrow cobbled hill with cottages along the sides. The inn was a black and white Tudor building with a red tiled roof. He pulled up outside and they went in to register. Peter still thought they might be exposed, but the receptionist smiled pleasantly and the porter seemed more interested in the Bentley than the youthful appearance of Mrs Johnson.

"What a lovely old machine, ma'am," he said to Jennifer as he collected their bags. "I expect your husband will want to park it himself."

Peter parked in the courtyard and the porter showed them to their room. The inn was every bit as romantic as Christine had described. Their room was quaint and cosy, with a pretty latticed window and a big four-poster bed. As soon as the porter had gone Jenny jumped onto the bed and started bouncing up and down.

"We've got this beautiful room all to ourselves for two whole days," she cried, and soon they were both on the old four-poster, romping like a couple of kids.

Presently she lay back and sighed, in a pensive mood again. "You do love me, don't you?"

"Of course I do. How many times have I got to tell you?"

"Lots of times. Being here with you is only alright if you love me."

He leant over and kissed her, and soon they were in each others arms. Slowly her skirt crept up and she started to unbutton his shirt.

"Jenny," he gasped. "We've got all night."

"This is just an appetizer," she giggled. "It's a taste of what's coming later on."

But after ten minutes she panted, "We must stop now. My whole body's tingling as it is."

They showered separately and dressed for dinner. He wore a sports jacket with grey flannel trousers, and she a light grey skirt and a pink lambs' wool twin set, with lipstick and earrings to match. Peter thought the pink suited her perfectly.

"I'm so proud of you," he said. And when they walked into the bar for a drink before dinner everyone glanced in her direction.

The bar had a huge open fireplace which looked very old and as Peter ordered the drinks he asked the barman about it.

"Fourteenth century," the man replied. "When they rebuilt the inn after the French raided Rye."

"The French?" queried Peter.

"They burned the town and stole the church bells."

They finished their drinks and walked through to the dining room. It was lit entirely by candles and the light from two fireplaces, each with a small log fire. The head waiter looked approvingly at Jenny and showed them to a nicely decorated table.

They had a delicious dinner of lobster bisque, followed by fillet of sole caught that morning, and a rack of local lamb which was as tender as butter. Between the courses they sipped glasses of Riesling, and talked a little, but mostly they just gazed at each other in the candlelight. After dinner there was coffee in the lounge. Jenny asked the waiter about the coat of arms above the fireplace.

"That's to commemorate Queen Elizabeth's visit," he replied.

"The Queen stayed here?" asked Peter in surprise.

"No, that was the first Queen Elizabeth," replied the waiter.

"Elizabeth I, the virgin Queen," whispered Jenny when he'd gone. "What a lot she missed. Let's not take too long over coffee, I want to go upstairs."

"So do I."

But when they finally reached their room Peter sensed a certain shyness and he went into the bathroom first so she could undress on her own. When he got back he found her already in bed, her clothes neatly folded on a chair. He climbed in beside her and turned out the light. With the sudden darkness came a sense of anticlimax, but it lasted only a minute. Soon her nightie and his pyjamas were discarded, and for the first time they were naked together in a big double bed.

"Not too quickly," she said, and he knew she was thinking of the last time, but now he knew what to expect. When it was over she said, "Oh, I love you so much. That was the most wonderful feeling I've ever had."

"Do you want to do it again?" he joked.

"I couldn't possibly do it again tonight."

But in the middle of the night he felt her shaking him. The bedside light was on.

"Jenny, what on earth's the matter?"

"Oh Peter," she said. "I had a dreadful dream. We could never get married. There was always something to hold us apart. And now I've woken you for nothing."

She was sitting up in bed, still naked, her breasts young and firm, her tummy smooth and flat. The shyness had finally gone.

"You will marry me?" she asked.

"We can get married tomorrow if we can find someone to do it."

"Don't be silly, I'm under age," she said unreasonably.

He put his arm around her and she pressed herself against him.

"Do you feel like making love again?" he asked.

"Yes, I do."

"I thought you couldn't possibly do it again tonight."

"Tonight's full of surprises," she said, light-hearted again. "It's the most surprise-filled night of my life."

He pulled her towards him until the full length of their naked bodies touched.

"Now, darling," she whispered. "Do it now."

The next time he woke it was morning and light was streaming through the small leaded panes of the window.

Jenny couldn't understand why Peter was trying to steer her towards one end of the High Street. Finally he stopped outside a jeweller's shop.

"I want to buy you a ring," he said.

"We can't get an engagement ring. We're not engaged. And I'd want more time to choose it."

"Well, I want to get you some sort of ring, so whenever you look at it you'll remember this weekend."

In the very first tray she saw a little silver eternity ring. It had translucent blue enamel inlaid around the outside, and she knew immediately it was the one she wanted. She watched Peter pay for it, but she was disappointed when he put it in his pocket. She wanted to wear it out of the shop.

"You can't," he said.

"Why not?"

"You'll see."

He led the way up Lion Street to the church. They went inside and she was awed by the quiet dignity of the ancient building. She still wasn't sure what he was up to, but he took a pew near the front.

Finally he said, "Last night you had that silly dream about us never being able to get married. Well, one day we'll be married properly. But I'm going to give you this ring, and if you accept it, then in our own way we'll be married now."

Her eyes felt moist. "Oh, sweetheart," she stammered.

"Do you accept it?"

"Of course I do."

She held out her hand and he slipped the ring onto her finger. She felt a profound significance and a tear ran down her cheek.

"Let's say a prayer," she whispered. " Somehow I know there are hard times ahead."

They were walking round the old church looking at the stained-glass windows when Peter saw a man with a white clergyman's collar approach.

"Good morning," said the man pleasantly. "I'm the vicar of St. Mary the Virgin. Can I be of assistance?"

Jenny's eyes still looked a little moist and Peter wondered if he'd seen them kneeling near the altar. He had a sudden urge to ask the vicar to marry them, but of course it would be impossible.

"We were admiring that stained glass window," he said instead.

"That window," replied the vicar. "It illustrates the Benedicte. It was given as a memorial for Mr A.C.Benson. He lived in Rye, you know."

"Really?" said Peter, with no idea who A.C.Benson was.

"Very stirring words, don't you think."

"Yes, I do agree," said Peter.

"Do you sing the hymn often in your church?"

"The hymn?" asked Peter stupidly.

"Yes. The hymn written by Mr Benson." The vicar stared at him as if he were an idiot. "*Land of Hope and Glory*, of course."

Jenny squeezed his hand and he glanced down at her. All sign of tears had gone and she was trying to suppress a giggle.

The vicar ignored Peter's stupidity and showed them several other features of the church, including the donation box. After Peter had contributed five shillings he took them up the church tower.

The view was magnificent. For the first time Peter realized what the old seaport of Rye must have been like before the sea receded. Now there was nothing but flat green farmland to the east and west. Only to the south could they see the shore, three miles away. Rivers ran along the sides of the town and combined to form the broad estuary that was Rye's only remaining connection with the sea.

"Imagine all that grassland replaced by tossing waves," said the vicar. "Little Rye standing on its hill jutting out into the ocean. This church was here then. People stood on this very spot to watch for foreign ships."

"What's that fort down there?" Peter asked, pointing to a massive stone tower at the southeast corner of the town.

The vicar looked at him with surprise.

"You have heard of the Cinque Ports, I suppose?" he said. "The five seaports which were fortified in medieval times to guard against the Vikings." He'd accepted the five shillings readily enough but he obviously didn't think much of Peter's intelligence.

"Yes, of course I have."

"Well, Rye is one of them. It was fortified back in the eleventh century, and that's the Ypres Tower."

When they left the church Jenny grinned. "You have heard of the Cinque Ports, I suppose!" she mimicked, and burst out laughing.

"He treated me like the village idiot," Peter retorted. "And to think, I almost asked him to marry us."

"Did you really?"

"Yes, really. When he first spoke to us and asked if he could be of assistance."

"Oh darling," she said, fingering the ring. "But we are married now."

Chapter 17

Mark hurried across the park and ran up the stairs to the maternity ward. If he was going to be late for a birth he didn't want it to be this one.

Every three months the students changed firms so they'd get experience in all the departments of the hospital. Mark, Peter, Roy and Paul Ellison were among a group of students recently assigned to obstetrics where they were on Victoria ward. There was a suite of labour and delivery rooms which opened onto a central lobby where doctors, students and midwives gathered to discuss their patients.

Mark's firm was looking after a patient called Mrs Driver whose baby was presenting as a breech. The largest part of a baby was its head and most babies were born head first. If the buttocks came first the head sometimes got stuck, then it took a lot of skill to deliver the baby before it died.

Mark glanced around the lobby. There were bookshelves along one wall and a table and chairs in the middle. Peter was sitting at the table reading. He looked up and said, "Mrs Driver's cervix is fully dilated."

A cry came from Mrs Driver's room and Mark guessed she'd begun to feel the urge to push the baby out. Nurse Morton put her head out of the labour room door to call for assistance. Beverley Morton was the youngest of the staff midwives. Her position in the hospital hierarchy was much higher than Mark's so he didn't expect her to know his name, but he was well aware of hers. She was an attractive woman with a lovely figure, three or four years older than himself. What always caught his eye was her thick ash-blonde hair which she wore in a ponytail high on the back of her head.

"You students," she called. "Get a stretcher and help us move this patient into the delivery room."

She'd done her training at the Middlesex Hospital and only recently come to Guy's. Dr Weeks, the obstetrical registrar, had been trying to attract her attention, but to the amusement of the students she ignored him.

By the time they'd collected a stretcher the patient's contraction had subsided so they had no difficulty moving her to the delivery room with its special obstetrical bed.

Just then Dr Weeks arrived. He knew Mrs Driver from the prenatal clinic so he had a brief talk with her and told her what to expect.

He turned to Nurse Morton. "Beverley, give her the trilene inhaler during her pains. I'm going outside to talk to the students."

They sat at the table in the lobby while he described the twists and turns a breech baby had to make as it passed through its mother's pelvis.

"Now that the cervix is fully dilated the baby will start to come down," he explained. "Soon you'll see its buttocks and then its legs. You may be tempted to pull the baby out by its legs, but if you do that the arms may drag behind and get stuck above the head. The head and arms together are too wide to pass through a woman's pelvis, so they may get stuck. It's best to let the mother push the baby out on her own, then the arms are pushed down with everything else."

Back in the delivery room the patient was resting between contractions. Beverley was attending to her, and a student nurse held a cold cloth to her forehead.

"Mrs Driver," said Weeks. "I'm going to examine you internally now to see how the baby's coming."

He pulled on sterile rubber gloves and carefully inserted the first two fingers of his right hand into the vagina. He described what he could feel to the students as he went along so they would know just how the baby was lying.

Soon Mrs Driver began to pant as another contraction began. She drew up her knees and gripped the handles at the sides of the bed while the nurse held the trilene inhaler to her face. Beverley Morton encouraged her to push, but the contraction subsided before they could see the baby. This went on for an hour, a series of weak contractions with long intervals in between. Eventually they could see the baby's buttocks when the patient strained but they disappeared back inside between the contractions. Weeks began to look worried.

"This is just what I wanted to avoid," he told the students outside the room. "The baby's half way through the pelvis and the mother's getting exhausted."

During the next thirty minutes the baby hardly moved at all. Nobody spoke. Mark could feel the tension build. Presently Weeks called them outside again, and this time he included Beverley Morton in the discussion. He seemed to be seriously weighing his options rather than teaching the students.

"As a baby gets weaker, its heart rate slows," he said. "If the fetal heart drops below a hundred we'll have to intervene."

"A Caesarean section?" Paul suggested.

"It's too late for a Caesarean, we'd have to do a breech extraction. That means pulling the baby down by its legs which is what we try to avoid. Let's hope she can push it down a bit further before fetal distress sets in."

"Do you want me to call an anesthetist?" asked Beverley.

Her face was covered by a surgical mask but Mark couldn't help looking at her eyes. They were warm and grey, with lashes a little darker than her hair. He was sure she must have noticed because she looked straight back at him.

"No," said Weeks. "I'll use local anesthetic, but not too soon in case it stops her pushing."

They went back into the room just as another contraction began. This time the buttocks remained in view after the labour pain stopped and a feeling of relief ran through the room. But there were no more contractions for ten minutes and when the fetal heart rate dropped to ninety-two Mark realized the baby was in danger.

Weeks turned to Nurse Morton. "Beverley, I think we'd better get this baby out before it's too late. I'm going to do a breech extraction. I'll need a full delivery set with local anesthetic, episiotomy scissors and obstetrical forceps."

"Yes, sir," she replied.

Mark glanced up. He was sure Weeks would have preferred her to say, "Yes Dennis," but she always treated him professionally. Most of the nurses would have snapped him up, but it seemed she didn't want to get close.

He fantasized about being out with her himself, driving through the countryside in his MG, or arriving at a hotel like the one Peter had stayed at in Rye. But she was so far above him in the hospital hierarchy that she didn't even know his name. Perhaps that was why he could imagine himself with her. It could never really happen so there was no risk of things going wrong.

Mrs Driver was groggy but still conscious so Weeks explained what they had to do. When he'd finished he turned to the students.

"Johnson, get your hands scrubbed and put on a sterile gown and gloves. Ellison, look after the trilene inhaler. And Wooding, check the fetal heart every couple of minutes."

The nurses put the patient's feet up in stirrups and folded down the lower part of the delivery bed.

"Xylocaine," called Weeks, as he picked up a syringe from the instrument tray, and Nurse Morton held out a bottle for him to draw up the local anesthetic.

"Mrs Driver, I'm going to put the anesthetic in now," he said. "Take some breaths of trilene so you don't feel the needle."

He waited for a few minutes for the xylocaine to work, then he said, "Johnson, episiotomy scissors," and Peter put the big scissors into the palm of his hand.

When Mark listened to the patient's abdomen again he got a shock. The baby's heart was so faint he could hardly hear it and the rate had dropped to eighty-four.

"The fetal heart rate is eighty-four," he called.

Weeks made a two-inch incision in the back of the vagina where the skin was stretched over the baby's buttock. The tissues sprang apart and immediately there was less pressure on the baby and more room for him to work.

"The first thing is to bring down the legs," said Weeks, with one hand in the vagina and the other on the outside of the patient's abdomen. "Johnson, keep some downward pressure on the uterus. I don't want to push the baby back inside."

After a minute he said, "I've got my fingers behind one of the knees and I'm bending the leg so I can bring it down."

It looked traumatic, but Mrs Driver was breathing deeply from the trilene inhaler and she didn't seem to feel any pain.

"Here is the foot," said Weeks as a tiny foot appeared. "Now for the other one."

Soon he had both legs outside the mother, and Beverley gave him a warm towel to wrap them in. The baby came down further then and everyone relaxed as he prepared for the next stage.

"The fetal heart has dropped to eighty," said Mark. The baby was short of oxygen, but he expected it would soon be breathing on its own.

Weeks pulled gently on the infant's thighs, angling it backwards and forwards as he eased it out, trying not to let the arms get above the head. Presently Mark could see the place where the umbilical cord was attached, and he watched Weeks pull down a loop of slack cord so it wouldn't draw tight as the baby descended.

"Now that the umbilicus is outside, the cord will get compressed," said Weeks. "The baby will get no more oxygen until it breathes. That gives us about five minutes, so Wooding, call out the time every minute."

The baby was lying on its side within its mother, with one hip towards the front and one at the back. Its arms, shoulders and head were still inside, and it seemed as if the shoulders were preventing it from coming out any further.

"We've got to deliver the shoulders next," said Weeks as he angled the body forward, trying to lever the rear shoulder out from the back of the vagina, but it wouldn't come.

"One minute has gone," said Mark quietly.

Next, Weeks angled the baby towards its mother's back in an attempt to get the front shoulder out, but that didn't work either.

"Two minutes," called Mark.

Weeks glanced anxiously at the clock. "Something's stuck," he said. "Johnson, hold the fetal trunk while I find out what it is."

Peter supported the baby's body parallel to the floor, while Weeks felt inside.

Eventually he said, "Both arms are up above the head, that's why the shoulders won't come out."

Mrs Driver groaned, shifting her buttocks on the bed. Weeks told Ellison to give her more trilene. "And Beverley, call the anesthetist," he added with an edge to his voice. "You'd better get someone from pediatrics too."

"Three minutes," said Mark.

"Are you sure?"

"Yes."

"Well, call out every thirty seconds. I'm going to try rotation and we're running out of time."

He removed his hand from the vagina and it was followed by a gush of blood. Then, using both hands, he grasped the infant by the thighs and firmly turned it until it faced its mother's back. Finally Weeks slipped his hand back inside.

"Three and a half minutes," said Mark.

"Good," Weeks announced. "Rotating the baby has moved one arm in front of the face. Now I think I can get it down."

But delivering the arm took longer than expected, and by the time it was outside four minutes had passed.

"Now for the other arm," he said, turning the baby back the other way.

There was more bleeding and time was getting short. "Four and a half minutes," Mark called.

Mrs Driver groaned.

"More trilene," called Weeks. Then he pushed his fingers back inside to bring down the remaining arm.

"Five minutes are up, sir," said Mark, but Weeks was still struggling with the baby's arm.

"Do you want forceps to deliver the head?" asked Beverley, anticipating the next move.

"Yes."

He finally got the second arm and both shoulders delivered. The baby came out further then, but its head was still trapped inside so it couldn't breathe. He grasped its body, turned it until it faced its mother's back, and told Peter to hold it while he applied the obstetrical forceps. It didn't move.

"The left blade," said Beverley, handing him one half of the forceps.

He slipped the broad nine-inch blade into the vagina until its curve fitted snugly around the side of the baby's head. Then he applied the right blade and latched the two together so they gripped the head, with the handles protruding below the baby's body.

"Alright Johnson, I've got the baby now," he said as he grasped the body and the forceps together and began to ease the head out of the vagina.

He moved the forceps up and down as he pulled, and soon the infant's mouth and nose appeared, although most of its head was still inside.

"Wooding," he called. "Clear the mucous from the infant's mouth. Don't wait for the head to come right out."

Mark quickly cleared the mouth and nostrils using a small suction tube, but the baby didn't breathe. Weeks soon had it completely delivered, but still it didn't take a breath. He clamped and cut the umbilical cord and handed the baby to Beverley. She wrapped it in a warm towel, then she too suctioned its mouth and nose.

Nobody spoke. Mark had seen newborn babies that were slow to breathe, but usually the stimulus of the suction got them started. He'd never seen one that didn't breathe in the end. He looked at Mrs Driver. She was fast asleep.

"Johnson, you look after the mother," said Weeks.

He quickly rinsed the blood from his gloved hands, then he listened to the baby's chest.

"I'll need an infant laryngoscope and endotracheal tubes," he said.

Mark had not seen a tube passed through a newborn baby's larynx and down into its lungs before. He expected it would be difficult, but Weeks carried out the procedure smoothly, using a small rubber tube which fitted snugly into the trachea. He put his lips to the end of the tube and gently inflated the tiny chest. The baby's ribs rose and fell as he forced air into the lungs, but it still didn't breathe on its own.

Just then the anesthetic registrar arrived, still dressed in surgical greens. Resuscitation was a part of his specialty so he took charge. Instead of his own lips he used a small rubber bag and oxygen to inflate the lungs, and he injected drugs into the stump of the umbilical cord. It looked more professional than the obstetrician's technique and Mark expected the infant to breath at any moment.

Five minutes passed, and then ten. Mrs Driver remained asleep, oblivious to the struggle, while Weeks and Peter Johnson delivered the placenta and sutured the episiotomy.

Next a registrar from pediatrics appeared, accompanied by his houseman and a student. He wore a long white coat and had a serious look on his face. He listened carefully to the infant's chest. Then he shone a light into its eyes to observe how the pupils would react. Next he raised the limbs and let them fall to see how limp they were. Finally he scratched the soles of the little feet to test the reflex curling of the toes. After all that he shook his head, and it was only then that Mark realized they had lost Mrs Driver's baby son.

Chapter 18

It was a fine night with a full moon in November 1954. Peter and Jenny were driving down to Salcombe. A few miles beyond Basingstoke the road divided so he asked Jenny which way she would like to go.

"Does it matter?"

"Well, the A303 goes past Stonehenge and I've always wanted to see what it looks like by moonlight."

"That place gives me the creeps by daylight," she said. "Did they really sacrifice people on the altar stone?"

"Absolutely. Whenever the moon was full the druid priests would sacrifice a virgin."

"A virgin, eh? Well, I should be quite safe." But she added, "I'll look at it from the road but I'm not going inside."

Peter took the north fork which passed through the market towns of Andover and Amesbury. The streets were dark as midnight approached, with hardly a light in any of the windows. A couple of miles beyond Amesbury they reached the open grassland of Salisbury plain and in the distance the ancient ruin of Stonehenge shimmered in the moonlight. A few hundred yards before the main road reached the monument he turned off to the right and parked close to a fifteen-foot rock beside the road. The main body of Stonehenge was only a hundred yards away.

"Here we are," he said, opening the door.

"You're not getting out?"

"Why not?"

"Oh Peter, horrible things have happened here."

"We'll just look from the road."

The full moon was high in the sky and the ring of thirty huge stones glimmered in its ghostly light. They looked enormous, twenty feet high and four feet wide, some with stone lintels across their tops. A few had fallen during the past three thousand years, but most of them were intact.

"That's called the heel stone," he said, pointing to the big rock close to where they'd parked. "If you stand in the middle of the circle on midsummer morning the sun rises directly above it."

After a couple of minutes Jenny said, "My sister says that if you run round Stonehenge at midnight you'll be married in the eyes of the Gods."

Peter glanced at his watch. "Well, it's five to twelve, so let's get married in the eyes of the Gods."

He could see she wished she'd kept her mouth shut but eventually she said, "Well, I'll walk round the outside if you like, but I'm not going inside the circle."

The grass was short so it was easy to walk and soon they came to another enormous rock.

"What's this one?" asked Jenny.

"It's called the slaughter stone," he replied, as casually as he could.

"Oh my God, is that where they made the sacrifices?"

"No, that was the altar stone."

"Where's that?"

"Inside the circle."

She shuddered. "Well, I'm not going in there to look."

Peter felt a bit uneasy himself as they left the car behind. The moon was very bright so he could see for miles. The undulating grassland stretched into the distance with an occasional clump of trees but there were no lights or other signs of civilization. The great circle of stones cast black shadows and it was easy to imagine the ghosts of priests and their murdered victims lurking in the dark.

A few smaller rocks and some grass-covered mounds stood outside the main circle, and outside these a low bank ran round the site. It took a quarter of an hour to walk right round and by that time Jenny's confidence had returned.

He bent and kissed her. "How does it feel to be married in the eyes of the Gods?"

"Well, I can see why Christian marriages are more popular."

"How about having a look inside?"

To his surprise she agreed, and they walked over to the great stone circle. Most of the uprights were still standing, and nine of them were still connected by lintels. They paused in the dark gap between two of the uprights. The grassy area inside the circle was about fifty yards across. It was brightly lit by moonlight and it contained a jumbled ring of smaller stones about six feet high, and five colossal arches, three of them intact.

"What are the smaller stones?" asked Jenny. "They look different from the others."

"Bluestones. The ancient Britons brought them all the way from Wales."

Then Peter thought he saw a movement. He paused but it didn't happen again and he decided his eyes were playing tricks.

"What's the matter?" asked Jenny.

"I thought I saw something move," he whispered.

"Oh come on, no jokes."

They went inside and soon they came to the famous altar stone. She looked at it in awe.

"Do you think people were really murdered here?"

"I'm sure they were," he said seriously. "Stonehenge was an active pagan temple for over five hundred years."

"Doesn't it scare you?" she asked.

"Not really."

"Well, I dare you to lie on the altar stone and count to a hundred with your eyes closed."

He climbed onto the cold hard altar wondering if he really had seen something move.

"No jokes," he said.

"Just shut your eyes and count to a hundred."

He did shut his eyes, but he expected she would play some trick so he opened them a fraction.

"You're cheating," she cried at once. "What a chicken. Now you'll have to let me blindfold you."

He reluctantly let her tie his thick scarf round his head. Now he could see nothing at all and he couldn't hear much either.

"Count to a hundred slowly," she said. "If you take less than two minutes you're a chicken."

He counted very slowly and it seemed to take an age. Finally he sat up and pulled the scarf off his head.

It was almost dark. A cloud had covered the moon and he could see only a few feet.

"Jenny," he said.

There was no reply.

"Jenny, where are you?"

He waited in the semidarkness, but there was no sign of her.

At first he thought she was playing a trick to pay him back for pretending he'd seen something move.

"Come on Jenny," he said. "I know you're there." But he had a horrible feeling she wasn't there at all.

"Jennifer," he called. "Please answer me."

There was a slight scuffling noise. He strained his ears but now his heart was pounding so hard he could hardly hear a thing. He tried to shout her name but his voice dried up in his throat. He began to climb off the altar stone, but he slipped in the dark and fell into a gully between the rocks. Suddenly he was too frightened to move. He could see nothing and hear nothing but the thumping of his heart.

It was ten minutes before the clouds thinned and the moonlight returned. Gradually his panic receded. But there was still no sign of Jenny. He crept over to a nearby arch, trying to keep in the shadows. There was nothing there. Then he tiptoed to the next arch and peered behind that. Slowly he walked from rock to rock calling her name. There was nothing, not a piece of clothing, a shoe, not anything to show she'd ever been there.

Perhaps she was outside. He ran to the edge of the ruin and looked out across Salisbury plain. The moon shone on a scene of perfect tranquillity. There was not a person in sight. He felt sick with fear but he could only see in one direction, so he started round the outside of the ruin. When he had gone half way round he spotted something strange. A horse was standing on the grass, tethered to a rock by its reins. It had not been there when he'd walked round with Jenny twenty minutes earlier.

Then he remembered the movement he'd seen and the scuffling he'd heard, and he was gripped by fear. So they had not been alone in the ruin after all. But the horse was still there, so whoever owned it must still be there as well.

Then, without warning, a strong pair of hands gripped him from behind.

Jenny was annoyed with Peter when he pretended he saw something move. Well, two could play that game, so when he laid down on the altar stone she crept off to hide, and when clouds covered the moon it took her completely by surprise.

Next she heard footsteps and her heart began to pound. It couldn't be Peter, he was still lying on the altar stone. She kept perfectly still hoping that whatever it was would pass her in the dark. Then there was a footstep right behind her and a hand clamped hard across her mouth. A powerful arm wrapped around her body and someone kicked away her feet.

"Any noise and you're dead," came the coarse whisper of a man. Then she was dragged across the grass and pushed behind a rock.

Next she felt a knife against her neck, and the man said, "One sound and I'll cut your throat."

He rubbed himself against her and she knew what he wanted. He kept the knife at her throat with one hand, and with the other he felt up her skirt.

"Keep quiet and I won't hurt you," he said.

Now he had his hand inside her pants. He was getting more excited every minute as he explored her with his fingers. Gradually it got lighter as the clouds shifted. She knew that Peter would come looking for her, but they were hidden between the rocks. Eventually she heard Peter's voice.

"Jennifer," he called. "Jennifer, where are you?"

The man froze. Then he pressed the blade to her neck. "If you make a sound I'll cut your throat," he repeated.

But Peter's voice gradually got fainter. Then she heard him outside the ruin, running in the wrong direction, still calling her name. Finally there was silence.

The man waited a long time before moving. Eventually he told her to turn around and for the first time she could see his face. He was a big man, about thirty, with lank greasy hair.

"Alright Jennifer, look at this."

He picked up a piece of wood and sliced it with his knife. It was as sharp as any razor.

"If you're a good girl and do what I say, you won't get hurt. Do you understand?"

"Yes," she whispered meekly.

"Now, Jennifer, take off your coat."

She hesitated.

He stepped forward and slapped her face hard.

"Do what I say, Jennifer, or you'll get some more of that."

"Please don't hurt me," she whimpered. "I'll do anything, but please don't hurt me."

He held up his hand and slapped her again. "Take off your coat and spread it on the grass."

She obediently took off the coat and laid it down. Underneath she was wearing a woollen dress.

"Alright bitch, pull up your dress," he ordered.

She pulled it up until the hem was above her knees.

He hit her a third time. "Higher. Pull it right up."

This time she did as she was told revealing her brief bikini panties.

"Take off your pants," he said. She was shivering with fear but she took them off.

He reached down to feel her with his fingers and soon he was panting with excitement.

"Lie down on your coat."

He put the knife down and started to unzip his pants. For a moment he turned away and Jenny saw her opportunity. She was shaking with fear, but she grabbed the knife and threw it as hard as she could. Then she watched in dismay as it hit one of the stone lintels and bounced back onto the grass only thirty feet away.

"You'll be sorry you did that, you little bitch," he said. "Now I shall have to punish you."

He walked over to the knife, but as soon as he bent to pick it up she ran, and as she ran she screamed. At first she thought she might get away but he was faster and eventually she fell. He was on her in a flash, crushing her against the ground. She was still screaming as he turned her roughly onto her back. The knife was in his hand. He held it to her throat and snarled, "Shut up."

When Peter felt someone grip him from behind he thought it must be the owner of the horse, but then he heard a voice that could only belong to a policeman.

"We want to ask you some questions, sir."

There were two policemen in uniform. They must have parked their car in the road and approached silently across the grass.

"Officer," he began. "Thank God you're here. My girlfriend has disappeared."

"Really," said the older policeman. "And just where are you going on that horse?"

"It's not my horse. I think it belongs to whoever's got my girlfriend."

"Then why were you getting on it?"

"I wasn't."

The older policeman turned to his companion. "Hold him tight, Fred."

"Yes, Sarge."

A sergeant on a night patrol, thought Peter. Something must be wrong.

The sergeant walked over to the horse. Attached to the saddle was a leather bag, and when he felt inside he pulled out a pair of handcuffs and a coil of rope. He held them up for Peter to see.

"Are these what you were looking for?"

"For God's sake officer, those things must belong to the person who's got my girlfriend. We've got to find her quickly."

"If this isn't your horse, then how did you get here?"

"By car. It's parked over there." Peter pointed to the road by the heel stone, but the car was hidden by the rock. He could see the police car further up the road. They must have come from the opposite direction.

"I don't see a car," said the sergeant.

"It's behind that rock. But what about my girlfriend. He may be raping her right now."

"Listen," said the sergeant, holding up his hand. "Keep quiet for a moment."

Peter was bursting with frustration but he stood still. The only sound was the wind in the grass.

"I don't hear anyone being raped," said the sergeant at last. "We're going to take you over to the car for questioning."

"Why? What have I done?"

"Suspicious loitering. We've had complaints."

He thought of trying to bolt. If he ran towards the circle of rocks they'd be bound to follow, but the younger policeman was a big man. Soon he found himself being marched off to the police car. When they were half way there he realized that now he could see the Bentley.

"That's my car over there," he said.

The sergeant looked doubtful. "What's the licence number?"

"AH 2693. It's a Bentley."

"A Bentley eh?" repeated the sergeant disbelievingly. He turned to his constable. "Fred, run over and check the licence plate of that car. Be quick now."

The constable walked off, leaving Peter with the sergeant. Peter was beside himself. Handcuffs and a length of rope. Jenny was in mortal danger. And why were the police snooping around Stonehenge at midnight anyway? They must have suspected something too.

Suddenly there was a loud scream.

At that moment the constable reappeared, running hard, and for the first time the sergeant looked disturbed.

"What was that licence number?"

"AH 2693," the constable panted. "And it is a Bentley, an old one."

The screaming went on and on. It came from the middle of Stonehenge.

"Come on," shouted the sergeant, but Peter was already running towards the circle of rocks.

Jenny thought she was going to die. The man had taken away her shoes so she could never outrun him even if she managed to escape. Now he twisted her arm up behind her back and started to march her back towards the place where her coat lay on the ground. Punish her, he had said. And what else was he going to do? With every step she felt more terrified. But then he paused and looked over his shoulder. He seemed to be listening to something. Then she heard it too, the sound of feet thudding on grass. Next she heard Peter shout her name. Then her assailant let go of her arm and dashed off so quickly she could hardly believe she was free. Next she saw Peter running towards her with two policemen close behind. She called and in a moment she was in his arms.

"Oh thank God you've come," she sobbed.

"Thank God you're alive. Are you alright?"

"Yes. No. I don't know."

She told them she hadn't been physically injured, but she couldn't stop sobbing.

The policemen chased the man, but he reached his horse ahead of them and cantered off across the grass. They had no way of following him, but Jenny didn't care. She insisted she wasn't injured and refused to go to a hospital. Her only desire was to be left alone with Peter.

The sergeant explained they'd had complaints about someone prowling around Stonehenge, and they took her to the station in Amesbury to make a statement. She told them most of what had happened, but some of it was just too horrible to describe.

Peter phoned his parents to warn them what had happened. He wanted to phone hers too, but she wouldn't let him. Her mother would panic and she couldn't face a confrontation.

When they arrived in Salcombe Peter's parents were waiting up. Jenny was still in a state of shock and Dr Johnson gave her a sedative. She slept until mid morning and when she came down for coffee with Peter and his mother she was quiet and withdrawn; the sparkle had gone from her eyes and she'd hardly combed her hair.

After lunch they all went for a drive across Dartmoor in the Johnsons' Humber. They took the main road to Buckfastleigh and branched off across the open moor. There were miles of rolling grass and heather, with rocky crags at the tops of the hills and little streams in the valleys. Peter sat in the back with Jenny. He did his best to draw her out but nothing seemed to work.

The road passed through Princetown with its grim nineteenth century prison. This part of the moor had more fog and rain than anywhere else in England, which was probably why the magistrates had chosen it for the prison. He shuddered when he saw the buildings, square dreary structures built of granite, with small barred windows in ugly rows. It was a fortress of a prison that offered no hope of escape.

Then Peter remembered that Gordon McNair was there. He'd been sentenced to fifteen years hard labour so he was bound to be in there still. He imagined McNair dressed in prison clothes, toiling alongside thugs and thieves, with heartless guards to drive him on for year after endless year. Child molesters were hated by the other inmates so he probably had no friends.

By this time Peter knew that McNair was a pervert who'd been satisfying his own desires. The experience had been devastating at the time but he had no desire for revenge. He was more ashamed of his own gullibility than angry with McNair. It had made no difference to him in the end, although he was still too embarrassed to tell anyone the story.

He would like to meet Gordon McNair again. He was curious to find out more about the man. What could drive a man to take such risks when he was bound to get caught in the end? What could possibly be worth fifteen years in jail?

McNair had talked of love. Just the thought of it was revolting. But he loved Jenny, there was not the slightest doubt about that. He longed to see her, hear her, touch her. He would take any risk to be with her. Was it so very different? Perhaps that was what McNair had felt.

He wondered if he himself was any better. What would Jenny's parents think if they knew what he did with their daughter. She was barely seventeen. Perhaps they'd think he was just as much a criminal as Gordon McNair.

He shuddered.

"What's the matter?" asked Jenny.

"It's a secret."

"You mustn't have secrets from me."

For the first time he'd caught her interest.

"Something happened to me a bit like what happened to you last night."

"Like what happened to me?"

"Well, not as bad."

"What's it got to do with Dartmoor prison?" she asked.

"I'm sorry, I just can't say."

They drove on in silence.

Jenny was depressed. It was not a fear of being attacked, because she felt perfectly safe. She hadn't actually been hurt at all, so there was no excuse for feeling that way.

In the evening the Johnsons went to a bridge party. Jenny wanted a quiet evening with Peter, so they went for a meal at The Captain's Table, a trendy little restaurant in Fore Street. As they drove down the hill from Wiscasset she felt a change of mood. She looked forward to having a drink, and she was curious about the experience that Peter had alluded to in the car.

The Captain's Table was a small place run by an ex Royal Navy quartermaster and his wife. It was expensive but good, with neat discreetly lit tables and a bar at the back. Some of the other diners greeted them as they entered, but she insisted on a table in a corner where they'd be on their own.

They ordered a simple meal of lobster thermidor and a French white wine. Jenny waited until she could feel the effect of the wine before she put her question. The lights were low and there was music in the background.

"Peter," she said at last. "What did you mean this afternoon when you said you'd had an experience like mine?"

At first he seemed reluctant to talk, but she persisted, and eventually he made a joke about how other boys got seduced by older women, but it was just his luck to be fancied by a man.

After that she thought she knew what was coming. But then he described the long interrogations in Mr McNair's bedroom under the single light. How he'd been forced to stare into the man's eyes and answer questions for hours on end. How he'd confessed to masturbating, which was true, and how that had led to other confessions which were not. He described the false confessions McNair had extracted from other boys, confessions of disgusting things they said they'd done with him. He told her how confused and frightened he'd become, and how McNair had threatened to expose what he was supposed to have done. He described the black notebook, and the order not to talk to anyone else. And he finished by assuring her that she was the first person he'd ever told.

She was amazed. It was not what she'd expected at all, and she felt truly touched that he'd confided in her. But it was Dartmoor prison that had reminded him of it, and she sensed there must be more. They ordered another bottle of wine, and as they sipped it she asked him gently, "But why did you think of this when we passed the prison? Why did that remind you of it?"

He looked at her warily. "Because Gordon McNair is in there now."

"In Dartmoor? Because he extracted false statements from schoolboys?" It didn't make sense. "He must have done something else."

There was a pause. Peter seemed to be weighing something in his mind.

"Jenny," he asked. "Do you find this disgusting? Does it make you despise me?"

"No. I'm surprised you didn't tell anyone at the time, but it doesn't make me love you any less. More perhaps, because you've shared a secret."

There was another silence. But now she was really curious and eventually she asked, "There's more, isn't there?"

"Yes," he said, and slowly he told her the sordid details of his forced homosexual affair with Gordon McNair.

When he'd finished he said, "Jenny, I've told you my closest secret. Now I want you to talk about what happened to you last night."

The wine was having its effect and it didn't seem so terrible anymore.

"It's nothing compared to what you've just told me," she said.

"Well, tell me anyway. Everything that happened. I do want to know."

She started slowly because she couldn't think of the right words, but soon all the details came pouring out. She'd given the police only an outline of what the man had done. She'd said nothing about what he'd done with his hand inside her pants. Peter asked why she hadn't told them.

"I don't know," she replied. "I intended to, but when it got to that part I just couldn't. I was humiliated and embarrassed, but it was more than that. It was a private thing and I couldn't tell anyone else."

"But you didn't mind telling me?"

"That was because you told me about what happened to you."

She leant forward and kissed him gently on the lips. It was the first proper kiss she'd given him since the Stonehenge incident.

Finally they finished the wine and the waitress brought their coffee. Louise, the owner's wife, had known Peter for years, and she came over and sat with them. They talked for a few minutes, and then she looked at them thoughtfully and asked, "When are you two going to get married?"

"We're already married in our own way," Jenny replied, holding up her hand with the blue and silver ring.

"Yes, that's easy to see," said Louise. "But I meant in the proper way. If you don't get married in the proper way things can go awfully wrong."

Chapter 19

Mark heard Paul Ellison shouting as soon as he entered the college. The Guy's college was where the housemen lived and it also housed some of the students' facilities.

"It's my turn. Give me the bag," Paul's voice came from the students' common room.

"No way," came Roy Whitfield's reply.

Mark turned into the common room. It was a large room with low tables and padded couches where students could relax. Paul and Roy were standing near the door and Roy held a black leather obstetrical bag in his hand.

"What's going on?" asked Mark. "You'll have everyone in the college here in a minute."

"We've been called to a home delivery," said Roy. "It's my turn, but Paul wants to go instead."

Paul glared. "Keep out of it, Wooding."

"He missed his last case," said Roy. "So now he wants to take mine."

"You know the rules, Paul," said Mark. "The case counts as yours whether you get there or not."

"Give me the bag," Ellison demanded .

"Go to hell," said Roy, gripping the bag more tightly than ever.

Ellison glared, then he stomped out of the room.

"Whew," said Mark. "Where's this delivery?"

"Wilcott Road, about a mile from here."

He looked out of the window. Dusk was falling and it was pouring with rain. "You should have let him take the case after all."

Maternity patients attended the prenatal clinic at the hospital, but if the pregnancy was straightforward many of them preferred to have their babies at home. Each home delivery was carried out by a staff midwife with a medical student to help. Groups of students lived in the college for a week at a time so they could take the deliveries in turn. The hospital supplied a medical bag with rubber gloves, an apron, and a few other things, and there was a rusty old bicycle on which they were expected to find their way to the patient's home.

"Well," said Roy. "Rain or shine, I'll have to go now."

"Come on, I'll take you in the car," said Mark.

Five minutes later they were making their way through the rain down St. Thomas' Street in the red MG. Mark had an A-to-Z street atlas of London and he found Wilcott Street quite easily, but he couldn't see the midwife's car.

"Oh my God," said Roy. "I can't go in there on my own, will you come in too?"

"There's only supposed to be one student for each case," said Mark. "You can wait here in the car until the midwife arrives if you like."

But almost immediately the door burst open and a man ran out. "Are you the doctors?" he called. "She's about to 'ave the baby."

"Is the midwife here?" asked Roy.

"No one's here except me and her mum."

"You're Mr Brooker?"

"That's right. Please hurry."

"Come on, Roy," said Mark. "I'll come with you after all."

Mr Brooker led the way up a narrow flight of stairs to the bedroom. In the middle was a double bed with a woman lying on her back covered by a sheet. The bulge of her abdomen was obvious and she grunted as they came in. A table with a basin stood along one wall and there were some plain wooden chairs. Sitting by the patient's head was an older woman with a plump good-natured face, who Mark guessed was Mrs Brooker's mother.

"Oh, Doctor, I'm so glad you're here," she said. "I'm Mrs Gerrard. Me daughter's waters broke a couple of hours back and she's getting strong contractions. This is 'er fourth baby and they usually come pretty quick."

"Have you called the midwife?"

"Bert called her an hour ago. I thought you must 'ave come instead."

A look of panic crossed Roy's face. "We're just medical students. We'll have to wait till the midwife arrives."

At that moment the patient started to breathe heavily and her face twisted with pain. She bent her knees, placed her hands behind her thighs, and started to push in a manner which told Mark the baby would soon be born.

He looked at Roy. "I've done more deliveries than you. Perhaps I should take over?"

"I wish you would."

He felt excited. They could handle a normal delivery on their own, and it would certainly put Ellison's nose out of joint. When the contraction was over he told Mrs Brooker what he was going to do. "I've delivered babies before," he finished up. "And I'm sure we'll manage perfectly well even if the midwife doesn't arrive in time."

"All me daughters have easy labours," said Mrs Gerrard cheerfully.

"I'll need some clean towels and a basin of hot water," Mark replied as he put on the apron from the students' bag.

Mrs Gerrard turned to her son-in-law. "Well Bert, you heard what the doctor said."

The baby came quickly, a healthy girl that started to cry at once. Mark handed it to Roy to clean up while he waited for the placenta. Ten minutes passed and then some bleeding started. At first it was just a trickle and Mark thought it was the placenta separating from the uterus. He gently pulled on the umbilical cord to help it come out, but it seemed to be stuck. Another fifteen minutes passed and the bleeding gradually got worse. He tried massaging the uterus through the abdominal wall to make it contract but that didn't make any difference. The patient's pulse was rising and her blood pressure was beginning to fall. It was not an emergency yet but it could easily become one. There were no drugs in the students bag so he couldn't use ergometrine, and there was no intravenous equipment either.

Bert Brooker was standing by the door awkwardly looking on. Mark asked him if they had a phone.

"There's a phone box at the end of the street," he said.

"Roy," said Mark. "I think we'd better call Weeks. Get him on the emergency line and tell him we have a postpartum hemorrhage at 58 Wilcott Street. The midwife's not here and we have no drugs or transfusion equipment."

Roy nodded and hurried out of the room.

"Is she going to be alright, doctor?" asked Mrs Gerrard when she heard Mark's message.

"I'm just taking precautions," said Mark, but he wasn't at all sure.

"It took an age to get hold of Weeks," said Roy when he returned. "He's just finishing a Caesarean section and he'll be here in a few minutes. He's sending an ambulance with some O-Negative blood."

The bleeding went on and on. Mark was sure it would not stop until the placenta came out. He considered doing a manual extraction. That meant putting his hand up into the uterus and using his fingers to strip the placenta off the uterine wall. It was a painful procedure, and it could send the patient into shock. It was a last resort, but he doubted if she could survive much more loss of blood.

"The systolic blood pressure is only 90," said Roy. "I can't get the diastolic at all."

Mark made a decision. "I'm going to do a manual extraction."

"What do you want me to do?" asked Roy.

"Put the patient on her back with a cushion under her buttocks and her knees drawn up. I'll need a clean bowl of water and a fresh pair of surgical gloves. And Mrs Gerrard, you'll have to look after your daughter. She's quite drowsy from loss of blood, but this will be painful and she'll need your support."

"Of course. Do everything you can, doctor."

Mark used the umbilical cord to guide his right hand up into the uterus. He could feel the body of the placenta but it was hard to discern the edges. For a couple of minutes he palpated it in silence. In the distance he thought he heard a bell.

Next he began to prise up the edge of the placenta with his fingers. It was difficult at first, the uterine wall was soft and he was frightened he might tear it. The main body of the placenta came away more easily, but as he proceeded the bleeding seemed to get worse. He had almost finished when he heard footsteps on the stairs. The door opened and Paul Ellison burst in. Then he heard that bell again and he realized it was the ambulance.

"What are you doing?" demanded Ellison.

"Mark's doing a manual extraction of the placenta," said Roy.

"You can't do that here. It's got to be done in hospital. You'll kill the patient like that. You should never have gone to this delivery."

Mark's heart was racing and his hands shook.

"There's O-Negative blood in the ambulance," he said. "Go and fetch it."

"You've gone too far this time, Wooding," said Ellison.

There were more footsteps and Mark heard other people come in. He glanced up and saw Weeks, with Beverley Morton close behind.

"What's going on here?" asked Weeks as they crowded into the room.

"Wooding's trying to do a placental extraction," said Paul Ellison loudly. "Wooding, you'd better stop that immediately. Dr Weeks is here now."

Mark looked at the patient, gradually bleeding to death. There was no time to lose and in another few seconds he'd have the placenta out.

Ellison carried a large obstetrical bag from the ambulance. "I said stop that, Wooding," he demanded. "Wait until I unpack the instruments, then Dr Weeks can take over."

There was a silence as Weeks took in the scene. Finally he said, "Be quiet Ellison. Get me the ergometrine from the obstetrical bag and then fetch the blood from the ambulance."

Next he turned to Mark. "Gently now. Gently pry the placenta off the uterine wall. Try to get it out in one piece. I don't know where you learned this, but you seem to be doing it right."

Then to Paul he said, "Come on Ellison, let's have that egrometrine. Then fetch the blood."

Finally Mark got the placenta free. He gently drew it down the vagina and lifted it into a kidney dish from the instrument bag.

"What are you going to do next?" Weeks asked.

"Inject ergometrine, take blood for cross-matching, set up a rapid transfusion of O-Negative blood, and examine the placenta to see if it's complete. If any of it is missing we'll have to examine her under anesthetic in the hospital."

They didn't have to wait long. With the placenta out, and the ergometrine making the uterus contract, the bleeding soon stopped.

Weeks wanted to know everything and Mark gave him a detailed account of what he'd done. As he talked Mark realized that Beverley Morton was watching him, but he was too concerned about what Weeks would say to pay much attention.

When he had finished Weeks said, "Well, Wooding, I must congratulate you. You've done a great job."

Then he turned to Mrs Gerrard who was holding her little granddaughter wrapped in a blanket.

"I'm sorry the midwife let you down. I'll look into that as soon as I get back to the hospital, but you were lucky this young lad was around. I don't think any of the others would have saved your daughter."

His words gave Mark a boost, particularly with Paul listening. But there was a patronizing tone to his voice, and he didn't like the way Weeks had referred to him as a "young lad," it was as if he were talking about a schoolboy.

Then Weeks looked at Beverley and said, "Well Bev, if we leave the boys to clean up the mess we'll be able to make that dinner party after all."

For the first time Mark noticed that underneath their surgical greens they were dressed for going out. Weeks was wearing an expensive suit and Beverley looked great in a black velvet cocktail dress.

To his surprise she replied, "I don't think we're quite finished with this patient yet. You go to the party, Dennis. I'll stay here and help the boys, as you call them."

"But you won't be able to get back to the hospital."

She looked at Mark and smiled. "I expect the boys will give me a ride in their car."

"But it's only a two-seater."

Mark was surprised he knew what sort of car it was. They must have seen it in the road outside.

"Well, I'll just have to sit on one of their laps," she said with a chuckle. "I wasn't really invited to the party anyway. It's much better if I don't go, particularly now this has come up."

"Suit yourself," said Weeks curtly.

Beverley sent Bert Brooker off to get fresh hot water. Then she bathed the baby while Mark and Roy prepared the patient for the ambulance ride to Guy's. Mrs Gerrard helped them with their various tasks and attended to the baby.

They all worked together smoothly. Beverley was in charge, of course, but she wasn't the least bit bossy. Mark had hardly seen her out of uniform before and he couldn't help staring at her whenever he thought she wouldn't notice. She looked superb in the black dress with her blond ponytail. An hour passed before everything was done. Finally they were ready to go.

It was crowded in the MG on the way back to the hospital. There was no back seat so all three of them squeezed into the front. It was still pouring with rain.

"Why was Paul Ellison so upset?" asked Beverley.

"He arrived too late for his last case, so he wanted to take mine," replied Roy. "He was just being his usual unreasonable self."

"Is he always like that? He has a good reputation as a student."

"He's a good-looking fellow who thinks he's better than everyone else."

"I don't think he's good-looking at all," said Beverley.

"You don't like that straight black hair and that big firm chin? He looks just like Dennis Weeks," Roy teased.

"So?"

"So who do you think is good-looking, then?"

She laughed and said casually, "I like men with curly hair like Mark."

Mark could hardly believe his ears. He thought she'd been looking at him in a funny sort of way. Usually he avoided women who showed an interest in him, in case they expected him to ask them out and perhaps to bed. That was what was always on his mind. He couldn't stand another failure. But Beverley couldn't possibly expect him to ask her out. He was much too junior for that, so he felt quite safe. It was nice to think about it, though.

Roy was sleeping in the college while he was on obstetrical call so he got out there. Beverley lived in a flat near the Elephant and Castle which was a ten minute drive.

When they were alone in the car Beverley said, "Dennis Weeks was right Mark, you saved that patient's life. None of the others could have done it. What branch of medicine are you going into?"

"Surgery," he answered. "I want to be a surgeon."

She was silent for a while.

Then he asked, "Do you live on your own in the flat?"

"I share it with a staff nurse called Pamela Goslin." She hesitated. "But she's away tonight."

He had a sudden intuition she was going to ask him in. He was surprised that he felt none of his usual nervousness, but if it were she who asked him, then there was no obligation for him to do anything. With Helen Metcalf he'd spent all day preparing her for seduction, so when he couldn't do it he could hardly pretend he didn't want to.

They were driving south on Borough High Street. "Take the next turning on the left," she said. "It's on the right-hand side."

He pulled the car up to the curb and looked across at her. She was peering into her handbag looking for her keys. He could see her face in profile and he wanted to kiss her, but she would have to make the first move. She seemed to take a long time to find the keys and he guessed she was trying to make up her mind. Finally she had them in her hand.

"Mark," she said, and then she paused.

"Yes."

"Would you like to . . . ?" She tailed off and turned her face towards him.

Perhaps he should kiss her. He hesitated, unsure what to do. The rain beat on the outside of the car.

"Would I like to what?" asked Mark.

"Oh, nothing. Thank you for the ride."

Chapter 20

The story of how Mark had successfully treated a postpartum hemorrhage in a patient's home got passed around. Dr Gilbert, the Chief of Obstetrics, congratulated him in front of all the staff. Paul Ellison's face looked like thunder, and Mark saw Roy give him a dig in the ribs to make sure he understood.

Mark also noticed that Beverley was watching him with a curious smile, and during the next few weeks he caught her doing it several more times. The others noticed it too. "She can't have such good taste as everyone thinks," Roy joked.

But Peter took a more serious line.

"Just be careful," he cautioned. "Weeks is dating her, and he's got a lot of influence with Dr Gilbert. If you want a good report at the end of this rotation you'd better not step on Weeks' toes. Ellison will spill the beans if you get up to anything. He's pissed off with you for stealing the limelight."

However Mark had no intention of doing anything. The most desirable woman on the ward was paying him attention, and all his friends could see. If Beverley Morton had been a student nurse they would have expected him to take her to bed, but she was a staff midwife being dated by a senior registrar, so they didn't expect a thing. He could enjoy the prestige of her attention without the slightest risk. And it was more than the prestige he enjoyed. Beverley was a very attractive woman. He spent hours dreaming about her, the way her ponytail swung when she turned her head, her alluring voice and her soft grey eyes.

When the students changed firms in the middle of January he missed her terribly. Mark, Peter and Roy were transferred to the children's ward, and for a whole month he didn't see her at all. Then, one evening, he met her in a pub.

On Friday nights students and nurses gathered in The Miller, directly across the road from Guy's. One evening in February 1955 Mark and Roy squeezed their way into the crowded bar, ordered beer, and joined a group of friends. For an hour they drank and chatted until the crowd began to thin.

"Look," said Roy, "Your girlfriend's over there."

And there was Beverley Morton with a party of doctors and nurses. She was wearing a dress of royal-blue needlecord which went beautifully with her ash blond hair. He thought she looked absolutely lovely. She was with some senior housemen and a couple of registrars, but Dennis Weeks was not among them.

He watched her for a few moments and she looked up and smiled.

"She really likes you," said Roy. "It's a pity she's out of reach."

Beverley's group were leaving and as they passed she stopped and said, "Mark and Roy, how nice to see you. We've missed you on Victoria ward. The students we've got now aren't nearly as much fun."

She didn't seem to be with anyone in particular and her friends went on without her.

"Would you like a drink?" Mark asked, too shy to use her name.

"Let me get them," she said.

Mark and Roy each had a beer and Beverley a gin and tonic. They chatted for another half hour, and when it was time to go she asked, "Mark, do you remember once you gave me a ride home to the Elephant and Castle?"

"Yes."

"Would you do it again tonight? Dennis Weeks was supposed to meet me but he got called away. I don't want to go home on the bus."

"Of course."

He remembered the last time he'd taken her home, when she'd spent an age looking for her key. He wondered what would happen this time, but she had it in her hand before he stopped the car.

"Would you like to come up for a coffee?" she asked casually. "Pamela's away and I'm on my own."

It was an old four-storey row house that had long ago been converted into flats. She lived on the top floor and he followed her up three flights of dingy stairs, his attention focused on her legs as she climbed ahead of him. He didn't know what would happen when they reached the top, but it would depend on her. He wouldn't start anything himself.

She unlocked the door and they went inside. They were in a large bed-sitting room, but before he had time to look around she turned towards him with her face tilted up and a slight smile on her lips. Her shoulders were back and she clasped her hands behind her so there was not the slightest doubt what she wanted. To his own amazement he bent his head and kissed her, and she kissed him back. He felt the most wonderful thrill. She went on for half a minute, pressing herself against him. His body began to respond and he drew away in embarrassment, but she put her hands behind his back and pulled him gently forward.

Presently she let go.

"Sit down while I make some coffee," she said, as if nothing had happened. "Do you take milk and sugar?"

She slipped off her coat and hung it on a hook by the door. There was a gas fire in the wall opposite and she walked over and lit it before disappearing into a tiny kitchen.

Mark looked around the room. There was a bed which doubled as a couch along one wall, a couple of easy chairs in front of the fire, a coffee table with some magazines, and a bookcase with books and ornaments on the shelves. It was not unlike the flat on Comeragh Road, but smaller and neater and without the student things.

He took off his own coat and hung it beside hers, and after a few minutes she returned with a mug of coffee in each hand.

"Good, it's getting warm in here at last," she said. "Do you like Benny Goodman?" And without waiting for a reply she put a record on.

He sat in one of the easy chairs and she sat on the bed. They sipped their coffee and talked. Mark realized they were talking mostly about himself and his ambition to become a surgeon at one of the big London hospitals. He longed to kiss her again but he wasn't sure how to begin. After the beer he needed to go to the bathroom and when he got back she had turned out the lights and the room was lit by only the flickering glow from the fire. She was sitting on the bed.

"Come and sit over here," she said, patting the bed with her hand.

He sat down and kissed her, and soon they were lying in each others arms. He hadn't dared to be like this with a woman since Helen Metcalf eighteen months ago, but this time he could back off without embarrassment if he had to. He tingled with pleasure as her body pressed against his. After a few minutes she started to unbutton his shirt and then she said, "Mark, will you undo my dress. There's a hook and a zipper at the back of my neck." She climbed off the bed and stood facing him with her arms above her head.

He sat on the edge of the bed and reached round behind her with one arm on each side of her chest. As he fumbled with the hook his face brushed against her breasts. Finally the dress slipped to the floor.

"Now my bra."

Soon she was standing before him dressed in nothing but panties and nylon stockings. Her nipples were level with his face.

"Kiss me," she whispered. "Kiss me there."

His heart was pounding. He was sitting on the edge of the bed in just his underwear while she stood facing him almost naked.

"Now my panties."

He slipped them slowly down her legs.

"Stockings."

Mark had never felt anything like this before. He slipped off his remaining clothes as she climbed onto the bed, then she began to run her fingers all over his body. Finally she rolled onto her back. So this was the time. He slid gently on top.

How ridiculous his fears of impotence seemed now. What a sheer impossibility. But there was another fear at the back of his mind. There was no legal way of getting an abortion, and the private clinics which did the operation illegally were unbelievably expensive. He carried a condom in his wallet for just such a situation as this.

"Wait a minute while I get a condom."

"Don't bother," she panted. "I've just finished my period. It's perfectly safe."

"Better to be sure," he said as he climbed out of bed.

He sat on the edge of the bed to put on the condom, but as the tight rubber rolled over the sensitive skin he suddenly realized what was going to happen. He did his utmost to stop it, but it wasn't any good. When it was over he sat there in silence wondering what to say.

"What's the matter?" said Beverley. "Do hurry up."

"I'm awfully sorry," he stammered. "It's the condom. Putting it on made me . . ."

He got up and walked miserably to the bathroom. What was he supposed to do now? Should he put on his clothes and leave?

When he returned Beverley said, "You'd better not go home now. You can sleep here if you like."

She got out of bed and put on a nightie, and they washed, made more coffee, and drank it by the fire. Eventually they got back into bed, and pretty soon they were cuddling again.

This time Mark did lose his virginity and even this second time it was over too soon.

Mark didn't understand the meaning of his encounter with Beverley at all. Their meeting had been accidental, but she'd made love with him, and now he could think of nothing else. He left a message in her mail slot in the colonnade, and every day he waited for a reply. Her name was not in the phone directory, and the sister in charge of Victoria would not allow personal calls at work. He crept up to the ward to find her but nobody seemed to know where she was. He could hardly believe it had meant nothing to her, but as the days slipped by his hopes began to fade.

For a year and a half he'd feared he was impotent. It was an enormous relief to have conquered that problem, although even now slight doubts remained. He had not been a very good lover. Perhaps that was why she was ignoring him now. As the week progressed he became desperate, but when he got home on Friday he found a letter.

"Dear Mark," she'd written. "Something happened and I had to go away. I enjoyed the evening and I hope you did too. I've got tickets for *Salad Days* at the Aldwych Theatre on Friday next week. If you'd like to come phone me at the flat, HOP 8217. Don't try to see me on the ward. Love, Beverley."

Chapter 21

James Johnson was not happy. It had been a long drive from Salcombe and darkness was falling. He was not looking forward to their annual shopping trip to London this spring; these days they could buy almost anything they wanted in Plymouth. But what was really upsetting him was that Angela had arranged for them to stop in Ashtead for dinner with Peter's girlfriend's parents. Jennifer was a lovely girl, but Peter was much too young to get married, so he didn't see the need to meet her parents.

There was another thing. The girl's father was a successful London stockbroker with a big expensive house. James wasn't very fond of stockbrokers, they seemed to make a lot of money without doing much work. And he was suspicious of Londoners too.

They passed Guildford and took the side road to Ashtead where they found the Whites' house, Strathbrook, with no difficulty. Peter's old green Bentley was already parked in the driveway. As they walked over to the front porch he noticed how nice the house looked, but it was no bigger than Wiscasset so perhaps the Whites wouldn't be too bad after all.

Jennifer opened the door with Peter by her side.

"Please come in," she said. "My parents are just coming."

They walked into the hall as the Whites appeared. Jenny's father smiled immediately and held out his hand.

"I'm Philip White," he said. "Welcome to Ashtead."

He was a slim man of about fifty with greying hair, casually dressed in a tweed sports jacket. He certainly didn't look like a slick London businessman, James thought. Jenny's mother seemed alright too, she had her daughter's good looks and the same friendly smile.

Perhaps they were going to have a pleasant evening after all.

Mary White was delighted that Peter and his parents were coming to dinner, but she sensed that Philip was not very enthusiastic. She knew he thought doctors were pompous and overpaid; they often made stupid investment decisions and he doubted if they were as intelligent as people supposed. However when the Johnsons arrived James did not seem to be at all pompous, and Mary was relieved that Philip showed no sign of his prejudice against the medical profession. In fact she sensed the men took an immediate liking to one another. But when she heard that Mrs Johnson's first name was Angela she got a shock.

Angela Johnson.

She'd often thought about that name over the years, especially during the last few months when she'd seen her daughter in love. Jennifer radiated happiness, and that evoked powerful memories of the intoxication she'd felt with Amiel all those years ago. But they were bittersweet memories tinged with jealousy. She recalled the House of Mystery and the secret microphone.

She remembered Gillian Martin's voice, cruel and unexpected: *This affair with Isis is not the first one, is it Ken?*

And she remembered Ken's reply: *You mean Angela Johnson, the doctor's wife.*

She would never forget that name.

That was the day her love had begun to fade. She had tried to find out more, but the older Aquarians were evasive, and there'd been no Dr Johnson in the colony while she was there. Could this be the woman? She was about the right age, and a doctor's wife too, but Angela and Johnson were common names.

Jenny showed them into the living room where Mary seated them in front of the fire. Philip poured drinks and soon the conversation flowed.

"Angela, have you always lived in Devon?" Mary asked.

"We moved there towards the end of 1933."

"Where were you before that?"

Angela hesitated before replying, "We spent a year in Canada."

"In British Columbia?"

"How on earth did you know that?"

"Just something I heard," said Mary.

It sounded suspicious, but Angela was looking uncomfortable so Mary decided to back off; she'd ask more questions later. The men began to discuss their wartime experiences and soon everyone relaxed. Presently Mary announced that dinner was ready and Philip led them through to the dining room. It was a large room with an oak table attractively set with crystal and Georgian silver. When they were seated Jenny brought in a dish of smoked salmon while Philip poured the wine.

The first part of the meal went smoothly. Jenny described her dancing classes and the magnificent building that housed the school, and Peter entertained them with stories of his life at Guy's. After a few minutes Mary came in carrying the main course of the dinner. She held the dish up proudly for everyone to see, a sizzling roast leg of lamb. Then she placed it on the buffet for Philip to carve. Jenny followed with a bowl of roast potatoes and another of fresh green peas.

"Roast lamb," said Angela. "Wonderful. And fresh green peas. Where did you find those at this time of year?"

"They're frozen," said Mary. "We can get them in Epsom now."

Philip carved the lamb and Jenny carried the dishes of vegetables round. There was a lull in the conversation as James helped himself to mint sauce and Angela spooned peas onto her plate.

Mary saw her opportunity. "Angela, were you an Aquarian?" she asked.

Angela looked up in surprise and spilt her peas all over the table.

"Do you mean, was I born under the sign of Aquarius?" she stammered.

"No, I mean a true Aquarian, a follower of Brother XII."

"Well, yes, James and I were Aquarians. How did you know?"

"We were Aquarians too and I remember someone mentioning your name. I didn't realize it was you until just now."

Angela blushed. "I hope you didn't hear anything too bad about me," she said. "There was a lot of malicious gossip in the commune when we were there."

"Were you very close to Brother XII?"

Angela hesitated before replying: "I worked closely with him on a project to start a nursing facility in the commune. Some of the other women didn't like it and in the end we had to leave."

"When was that?"

"Towards the end of 1933."

Mary looked at Angela with hostility. So this was the woman Gillian Martin had been talking about. She'd had an affair with Amiel. It made her feel sick.

"So you were Aquarians too," said James. "What an extraordinary coincidence. When were you there?"

"We joined the commune in 1934," said Philip. "And we left about three years later."

Peter looked puzzled and there was an expression of horror on Jennifer's face.

Then Jenny spluttered, "Peter's an Aquarian."

"Peter?" Mary queried. "An Aquarian? When were you born?"

"The fifteenth of February," he replied.

"But which year?"

"Nineteen thirty-four."

If the Johnsons had moved to Devon at the end of 1933, and Peter was born in February 1934, he must have been conceived in the colony. Suddenly she realised that if Angela had been intimate with the Brother then Peter was probably Brother XII's son. That would mean he and Jenny were half brother and sister.

She must know, tonight, before whatever was between them went any further. But how could she ask without revealing her own involvement with Amiel? Jenny had been brought up to believe that Philip was her father. It would be unthinkable to risk disillusioning her now, at a dinner party, in front of strangers.

When the main course was finished she got up to take out the dishes and bring in the dessert. Jenny followed her into the kitchen. As soon as they were alone she demanded, "Mum, what is the matter with you? Why did you have to ask Mrs Johnson all those questions?"

"I just want to find out as much as possible about Peter's parents, that's all."

"It sounds as if you just want to make them hate us."

"What I want is to make sure Peter is right for you."

Jenny was on the point of tears.

"Peter is right for me. I love him, don't you understand? And I don't want you to mess it up."

"You may think you love him," said Mary calmly. "But you're much too young to know what love really means. There may be reasons why Peter is unsuitable for you. It's something we'll have to discuss."

Jennifer stared at her in disbelief.

"You don't want me to love him, do you?" she said at last. "You want to drive him away. That's why you're being deliberately rude to the Johnsons."

"I wasn't rude to anyone," said Mary. "But I certainly don't want you to fall in love with someone who's unsuitable."

"What could possibly be unsuitable about Peter?"

For a moment Mary considered telling her daughter everything, including her fear that she and Peter were brother and sister. Then the girl would be able to see what she was trying to do. But it was all too complicated, and she couldn't reveal that Philip was not Jenny's true father without discussing it with him.

"Come on," she said. "I'll carry the dessert. You take in the plates."

Back in the dining room Angela was outlining her belief that the climate of South Devon had changed.

"Before the war," she was saying, "fuchsias grew wild with no special attention and there were palm trees in Sharpitor Gardens."

"There's been a change in the sea life too," said James. "We used to get porpoises in the estuary every summer, but never any more. They say the Gulf Stream has moved offshore and that's what's made it cooler."

The conversation ran on and Mary served the chocolate mousse she'd prepared for dessert. Finally there was a pause.

"Angela," she asked, "I wish you'd tell us more about your life with the Aquarians."

"Well, I'm a nurse and I worked closely with Brother XII when we were setting up the nursing facility in the commune."

She still wasn't quite certain what Angela's role had been, so she asked, "Did you have a very close relationship with the Brother?"

Angela's face reddened and she seemed unable to reply, however James came to her rescue.

"The Brother had a lot of influence over both of us," he said. "But when Angela became pregnant I persuaded her it had gone far enough and we left the commune soon after that."

Mary felt a chill in the pit of her stomach. "I see," she said. She wanted to throw up, but she forced herself to put a spoonful of mousse in her mouth and they all continued to eat.

"Who on earth was Brother XII?" asked Peter after a few minutes.

"He was a religious leader," said James. "Your mother and I lived in a sort of religious commune in Canada for a while before the war. I was their doctor."

"A religious commune?" Peter looked surprised. "I didn't think you believed in God."

"I used to, more than I do now. But it wasn't an ordinary church thing. More of an experimental colony really."

"An experimental colony?"

"A different kind of community where everyone was equal, and we shared the material things of life."

"Who was Brother XII?"

"He was our leader. He started it all."

"Well, I had no idea," said Peter. "How come you've never mentioned this before?"

"I don't know. I don't like to talk about it, I guess. We started off with such good intentions. We donated a lot of money, everything we had, and in the end we lost it all. I was very stupid and now I feel rather ashamed of the whole affair."

"Was Brother XII a religious nut?"

"It's not as simple as that. He was a bit of a nut, and a bit of a con man too, but at the same time I'm sure he was sincere. He thought the world was going to end sometime in the nineteen-thirties, and his colony was the one place that would be spared."

Peter looked at his father with amazement. "You fell for that? I can hardly believe it."

"You never met Brother XII. The man had an incredible personality. He had dark piercing eyes that seemed to bore into your soul. Believe me, he could convince anyone of anything."

"Were you there too, Mum?" asked Jennifer.

"Yes."

"With Dad?"

Mary felt uncomfortable, "Yes, of course."

"Did you meet the Johnsons there?"

"No. We must have been there after they left."

"When were you there?" asked Jenny.

"Before you were born," she said. It was almost true.

"I wish you'd tell us more about it."

"There's nothing more to tell," said Mary with finality. "The Johnsons and ourselves were members of the same commune a long time ago. Dr Johnson said he doesn't want to talk about it and nor do I. Now, finish your dessert, and then go and put the coffee on. I think we should talk about something else."

All four parents seemed relieved to get away from the subject of Brother XII but no one could concentrate on anything else. The rest of the meal dragged by with a series of awkward silences. They had coffee and liqueurs in the living room, and soon after that Angela made the excuse that they were tired after the long drive from Salcombe, and the Johnsons took their leave.

Angela had booked a suite at the Hotel Russell in Russell Square, where they always stayed when they went to London. As soon as they'd got on the road she began to think about the extraordinary evening they'd had. She and James were on their own because Peter had to drive the Bentley back to London.

"What did you make of them?" she asked as they turned onto the London road.

"I liked him," said James. "But I wasn't so fond of her. In fact I thought she was rather rude."

"I thought so too."

"Fancy them being Aquarians."

"I wonder how they knew about us?"

"Perhaps they heard about us from one of my patients."

They drove on in silence. It had started to rain and Angela stared through the windshield at the dark road ahead, still puzzling over Mary White.

"James," she said at last. "What did she mean when she asked if I'd had a very close relationship with Brother XII? It almost sounded as if she thought I'd had an affair with him."

"Oh, I don't think she meant that."

"He did have an affair with one of the women, you know," she said.

"Of course I know, I was her doctor." He was silent for a minute, and then he asked, "There never was anything between you and the Brother, was there?"

Angela stared through the window. There wasn't much traffic and they had already reached the Kingston Bypass in spite of the rain. She'd worked closely with the Brother on several projects when he'd needed her expertise as a nurse. At first he'd given her hints, little signs that he would welcome a more intimate relationship. He was a very attractive man and she'd been flattered and shocked both at the same time. However she'd never taken up his propositions.

She put her hand on James' knee. "Of course not, dear," she said. "I've never been unfaithful to you."

Jenny was crying as she said goodbye to Peter. They were standing in the driveway by his car.

"What an awful evening," she sobbed. "I just don't understand what happened."

"I think our fathers liked each other," said Peter optimistically.

"I'm afraid my mother was very rude. And what was all that stuff about Aquarians and Brother XII? Did you ever hear that before?"

"No."

"I'm sure that's got something to do with it," she said.

"But it happened ages ago before we were born."

"Will you ask your parents about it?"

"Of course I will, and you must do the same."

She put her arms around him for reassurance.

"We mustn't let this make any difference to us," she said.

"Of course it won't."

She buried her face in his shoulder. "Peter, I'm frightened they'll try to separate us."

"Look sweetheart," he said, kissing the top of her head. "There's been some silly little misunderstanding, that's all. It's not going to make any difference to us."

"You promise?"

"I love you and there's nothing anyone can do to stop us seeing each other."

But then she had another thought. Next weekend Jo would be home, and they had planned that Peter and Jack Ross would spend the weekend at Strathbrook. They were all going to a dance on Saturday night.

"You'll still come next weekend, won't you?" she asked.

"Do you think I ought to?"

"You must come. We've got to carry on as if nothing has happened."

"Then I'll come."

She put her arms around him and gave him a long hug which made her feel better. He was right, it was probably just a little misunderstanding which would soon be forgotten.

As he got into the car it began to rain, and by the time she'd watched the tail-lights disappear down the road her face was soaking wet. Well, she thought, at least they won't be able to see she'd been crying.

Mary White was in the kitchen with Philip, clearing up. She did not feel very comfortable about the way the evening had turned out. Eventually she'd got the information she needed, but she wondered if she'd been too clumsy.

She filled the sink with hot soapy water and put in a pile of dishes. "Well, what did you think of them?" she asked guardedly.

"I liked them. And imagine them being taken in by that charlatan and living in the Aquarian colony. It makes them rather like us," Philip replied with a smile. "How on earth did you guess?"

"Something I learned about a woman called Angela Johnson while I was there. That's why I had to find out if she was the same Angela Johnson. Did I sound rude?"

"Well, she obviously didn't want to talk about it, and you almost asked her if she'd been intimate with Brother XII. I hope Jenny didn't understand."

"Where is Jennifer?" she asked. "She should be in here helping with the dishes."

"She's outside seeing Peter off."

Even thinking about her daughter with Peter made Mary feel uncomfortable, but it was a good thing to have her out of the way while she talked with her husband.

"When did Angela say they were there?" Philip asked.

"Nineteen thirty-three. And Peter was born early in 1934, so she must have got pregnant while they were there."

"Well, I don't suppose all this will make much difference to Jenny and Peter."

Mary took her hands out of the sink and looked at him in surprise. "Of course it will."

"What do you mean?"

"They can't possibly continue their relationship now."

"Why not?"

She was surprised he didn't understand. "Because they're brother and sister. Half-brother and half-sister, anyway."

He stared at her. "You mean . . . "

"Yes. When I was . . . , when I was mixed up with Brother XII, I discovered there had been another woman before me who thought she was Isis, and her name was Angela Johnson."

She broke down and put her arms round him, her hands still dripping with water from the sink.

"Oh Philip," she sobbed. "It was so awful, and I was so stupid. I can hardly bear to think about what happened. If you hadn't saved me I would surely have died. And now little Jenny seems to be falling in love with her own brother, and it's all my fault."

Philip tried to calm her. "Perhaps you're wrong about Peter. He doesn't look like Jenny."

"They've got different mothers. Jo and Jenny don't look alike either, do they?"

"No, I suppose they don't," he admitted.

"There's no doubt about what I heard when I was in the colony, and look at the way Angela behaved this evening. She's the same woman alright. Peter has to be Brother XII's son. Oh, Philip, what are we going to do?"

"I think you're just going to have to sit down with your daughter and tell her the truth."

She looked at him in horror. "You mean tell her that you're not her real father. Tell her that in the middle of a happy marriage I started to believe I was a goddess and went off with a religious maniac who convinced me he was the reincarnation of an Egyptian god?"

"Well, you'd better just tell her a little bit at a time!"

"Philip, I'm her mother. She's seventeen years old, and she needs me to steer her through the most difficult period of her life. If I tell her all that she'll have no confidence in me whatever. It's out of the question. Somehow I must put an end to her relationship with Peter Johnson, but I can't simply tell her the truth."

"You've got to be gentle. It's going to take some time to end a relationship like that."

"Maybe," said Mary. "But in the meantime I must watch them like a hawk to make sure they don't go too far."

Just then she heard the front door open and she knew Jenny was back.

"Jenny will be in here in a minute," she said. "Leave this to me. I'll deal with it in my own way."

Chapter 22

Mark was sitting in the library trying to concentrate on the *British Medical Journal*. Outside there were leaf buds on the trees and sparrows were chasing each other as if spring had arrived. They were thinking about mating, he realized, and he was thinking about it too.

A week had passed since he'd received Beverley's note. She'd sounded reserved when he'd phoned, but she did have tickets for *Salad Days* that evening, and he was picking her up early so they would have time for dinner.

He couldn't concentrate on the *BMJ* so he decided to go for a coffee. He put the magazine back on the rack and made his way across the park to the Spit.

For two weeks he'd thought of nothing but Beverley, but now he was apprehensive. She could have any man in the hospital and he couldn't understand why she was interested in him. Peter and Roy were mystified too.

He reached her flat sharp at 6pm. She looked gorgeous in a pale blue dress. Blue seemed to suit her, he thought, as she climbed into the MG. She'd bought the theatre tickets so the meal was his responsibility. He couldn't afford an expensive restaurant so he thought they'd eat at a pub. He suggested the old George Inn because it had character and it was near the hospital.

She hesitated. "Let's go further away," she said. "I've had a row with Dennis Weeks and I don't want to meet any of the registrars."

They settled on The Prospect of Whitby, an old pub overlooking the Thames a mile east of Tower Bridge. There were only a handful of customers and the barman entertained them with stories of the river.

"That's Execution Dock," he said, pointing to a wharf a couple of hundred yards along the bank. "They'd chain pirates there at low tide, so when the water came up they'd slowly drown."

Mark made sure they reached the theatre in plenty of time. Their seats were near the front of the dress circle and as they made their way down the aisle people turned their heads.

Salad Days was a light-hearted musical. He didn't think much of the story but the music was catchy. She held his hand as they went to the bar in the interlude, and he wished his friends were there to see.

She talked about all kinds of things, but one thing she did not mention was what had happened between them a couple of weeks before. After the show he asked if she would like to go somewhere for a nightcap, but she wanted to go straight home. The Aldwych Theatre was near the Strand, and it took only a quarter of an hour to drive across Waterloo Bridge to the Elephant and Castle. He parked outside the door wondering what would happen next.

She leant across and kissed him. For a moment he thought that would be all, but then she asked, "Do you want to come in?"

"What about Pamela?"

"She's away," she said, and he felt a shiver of excitement.

They climbed the stairs and she unlocked the door, took off her coat and flopped into one of the easy chairs.

"Well, that was a lovely evening," she said. "But now I feel grubby and tired."

He felt a twinge of disappointment as he took off his coat and hung it on the hook.

"Shall I light the fire?" he asked.

"Please do. Then I think we should both take a bath."

She stood up and stretched. The blue dress showed her figure beautifully. He wanted to undress her as he had before, but she disappeared into the bathroom and soon he heard the water running. She returned wearing a pink dressing gown with nothing underneath. He yearned to kiss her but she seemed to be avoiding him.

"I'll get into the bathtub first," she said. "You can get undressed here in front of the fire."

He watched her go into the bathroom and close the door, then he slowly took off his clothes, folded them, and put them on a chair. He felt too self-conscious to go completely naked, so he kept his underpants on. After a while she called and he gingerly opened the bathroom door. It was warm and steamy inside. She was lying on her back in the bathtub with her hair tied up in a knot to keep it dry. She sat up when he came in and her breasts glistened with soapy water. She didn't seem at all embarrassed.

"Would you wash my back," she said. "I can't reach the bit in the middle."

She handed him a bar of soap and he knelt on the floor outside the tub and started to wash her. The feel of his fingers sliding over her slippery wet skin was very exciting.

Then she said, "Now wash under my arms."

He slid his hands into her armpits from behind and moved them backwards and forwards, but he couldn't help touching the sides of her breasts.

"That was nice, Mark," she said. "Now I want you to wash the rest of me."

She stood facing him with her legs slightly apart and her hands clasped behind her back. Her beautiful body looked firm and smooth.

Then she said a peculiar thing: "This isn't supposed to be sexy. I think you'd better take your pants off so I can see you don't get too excited."

He obediently removed his underpants but the sign of his excitement was already obvious for her to see.

"I'm serious," she said with just a hint of a smile. "Now start washing my tummy."

He didn't know if she was teasing but he was already tremendously excited as he knelt in front of her, stark naked, sliding his hands over her slippery body.

"A bit more soap," she ordered. "Go a little higher. More to the left. Now to the right. Now you can do my breasts."

He slid his hands up and down over her nipples and she shivered with pleasure.

"I thought I told you not to get excited," she said, panting with excitement herself. "Now wash my legs."

She was still standing in the tub with her legs apart, while he knelt on the floor before her. He put more soap on his hands and then with shaky fingers he began to wash her ankles.

"Go a bit higher."

He moved his fingers up to her calves and then her knees, desperately trying to keep control.

"Higher," she ordered. "Go higher."

He felt her muscles tighten as he slid his hands up her thighs, and she was gasping when his fingers reached the top.

"Now my bottom," she breathed.

He slipped a soapy hand between her buttocks and slid it back and forth. She hadn't even touched him but he was so excited that it hurt.

Suddenly she said, "That's enough," and she lay down to rinse herself off. Then she looked at him as if nothing had happened and said, "That was a lovely wash, Mark. Now I'm going to wash you."

She got out of the bath and dried herself while he ran more hot water and then climbed in. She looked at him for a few moments, then she said, "Dip your head under the water, I'm going to start by shampooing your hair."

When his head was thoroughly wet she told him to sit up and poured on some shampoo.

"Keep your eyes closed," she said. "If the soap gets in them it will sting. And don't get excited, you're just having a bath."

He felt her rub her fingers through his hair as she lathered his whole head and most of his face as well.

"Now stand up and keep your hands behind your back," she said. "And don't open your eyes, they're covered with soap."

It was a strange sensation, standing in front of her, naked, with his eyes tightly closed and his hands behind his back. He felt her soapy fingers explore his body and he imagined her studying him in the bright bathroom light.

Soon her hands began to move lower, creeping down his tummy, slowly, bit by bit. She had told him not to get excited but that was quite impossible.

He heard her dip her hands in the water and pick up the bar of soap. He imagined her sliding it between her fingers, and he guessed what she was going to do next.

"Mark, I told you not to get excited," she said.

Then he felt her fingers moving just a little at a time. More, he thought, move them more.

Keep your hands behind your back, she'd said; keep your eyes shut; don't move; don't get excited. For two whole minutes he tried, but in the end it was impossible to obey.

"I'm sorry," he said when it was over and he'd washed the shampoo off his face.

"You don't have to be sorry," she replied. "It was wonderful."

"I tried not to come."

"But I wanted you to."

"Then why did you keep telling me not to get excited?"

"I wanted to see what would happen. Anyway, that made it better in the end."

In a way it had.

"But why did you do it?" he asked.

"Because, darling, I want us to make love properly later tonight. And I want to come this time, so I thought I'd do something to slow you down."

"Slow me down? I'm completely exhausted. I shan't be able to make love again tonight."

"Yes you will," she said. "I'll make coffee, and we'll sit in front of the fire and have a drink. And when we're ready we'll get into bed and everything will be alright. I love you."

Beverley could feel the effect of the alcohol. She was sitting on a cushion by the fire with a glass of Drambuie in her hand. Mark sat in the easy chair nearby and they were both sipping their second glass of the sweet liqueur. He had put his shirt and pants back on, but she was wearing just her dressing gown. Mugs of coffee sat on the table, and Mantovani's Orchestra played quietly in the background on the record player.

"Why did you have a row with Dennis Weeks?" asked Mark.

"It was about you."

"About me?"

"He discovered I spent the night with you," she said.

"How on earth did he do that?"

"I was with his friends the night we met in the Miller and they told him I stayed behind with you. Later in the evening he drove round here and saw your car outside."

"Are you having an affair with him?"

"No," she said, but it wasn't the whole truth.

Six months ago, when she'd left the Middlesex Hospital, she'd been heartbroken over the end of her engagement to Jeremy Blakelock, and as soon as she'd arrived at Guy's, Dennis had shown an interest. He was a good-looking man in a classical sort of way, an important doctor who should have made an ideal replacement. But there'd never been any spark in their relationship. He didn't turn her on.

"If you're not having an affair with him, then what business is it of his if my car was outside your flat?" asked Mark.

"That's just why we had a row. It's none of his business at all."

But she knew that wasn't quite true either. Her friends had worked on her. Pamela in particular had kept telling her what a splendid catch Dennis Weeks would be. Beverley could hear her now: "You're nearly twenty-six years old and he's good solid husband material."

Dennis had kept asking her out, and in the end she'd gone. At first it was alright, although rather dull. He was attentive and considerate, and he didn't interfere much with the rest of her life. He was not a patch on Jeremy, but she got quite fond of him just the same and eventually she let him sleep with her. But as soon as that happened his behaviour changed. Now he seemed to think he owned her. He would get upset if she so much as went to the pub without him. Well, he didn't own her, and now he never would.

Mark was quiet for a while. Mantovani's rendering of *Beautiful Dreamer* drifted lazily around the room. She sipped her coffee. He finished his Drambuie and she got up to refill his glass. She moved her cushion nearer to the chair and when she sat down again she laid her head on his lap.

"Have you had many affairs?" he asked.

She was glad he'd asked. She didn't like secrets and she wanted him to know. "I used to be engaged," she said.

"Can you tell me about it?"

It took her a few moments to decide how much to tell. The music had stopped and just the gentle hiss from the gas fire filled the room. Eventually she said, "He was a doctor at the Middlesex Hospital. A surgical registrar."

"You're not still engaged to him?"

"Of course not. Would I be here with you if I were engaged to someone else?" But she felt a stab of guilt because it wasn't that simple.

"What happened?"

"He fell out of love with me. He went off with someone else. That was why I left the Middlesex."

She felt his hand touch her cheek.

"Do you still love him?"

"I don't know," she said. "For a while I did. But now I've met you I feel better."

Her eyes filled with tears. She felt one spill down her cheek and she wondered if he could see it. He leant forward and kissed her, and then he climbed off the chair and knelt facing her in front of the fire. They touched softly, and she felt a combination of tenderness, love and desire that had eluded her for half a year. Jeremy had left a terrible hole in her life, and now Mark had come along. He even looked like Jeremy. She'd hardly been able to keep her eyes off him when he'd started on Victoria ward in October. He was going to be a surgeon too. It was uncanny.

But Mark was nearly ten years younger than Jeremy, and four years younger than herself. Pamela had told her she was baby snatching. But what was four years really. It would seem like nothing when they were twenty-eight and thirty-two.

"Hold me tight," she whispered, and she tucked her face into his shoulder so he wouldn't see her tears. They were tears of happiness, but he might not understand. Earlier she had said, "I love you." She hadn't meant to say it, the words had just slipped out. But was it true?

What she'd done when they were in the tub was kinky. She'd never done anything like that before. Well, not quite like that. She and Jeremy had done some pretty way-out things. But Mark had enjoyed it. And now perhaps she loved him, and perhaps he was falling for her as well.

But then she felt that stab of guilt again, because on the very day that Mark had phoned she'd received a card from Jeremy. He was in Switzerland skiing. "I'll call you when I get back," he'd written. He'd done that before and never called, but it had given her heart a wrench.

Her tears had gone. Mark was still kneeling in front of the fire, and she leant forward and kissed him. He slipped his hand inside her dressing gown and she felt a thrill. "Let's get into bed," she said.

Chapter 23

Peter Johnson felt nervous as he parked his car at Strathbrook. He was relieved to see that Jack Ross's car, an old two-seater Morgan, was already there. It was a cold afternoon in the spring of 1955, a week after the Whites' dinner party.

He was still intrigued by the Aquarian affair but his parents knew no more than they had already told, and Jenny said hers refused to talk about it at all. He wondered if they had something to hide but he had no idea what it could be.

Jenny ran out to meet him and he bent to give her a kiss.

"Better wait till we're inside," she said. "My mother's watching from the window. She wants us to see less of each other."

"Why?"

"I don't know. She didn't want us to go to the dance tonight, but Jo and Jack are going so I insisted."

The annual Young Conservatives Ball was held at the Drift Bridge Hotel near Epsom. The next day was Sunday, so there could be no dancing after midnight. The band played the last waltz at 11:50 to leave time for *God Save the Queen.*

On the way home Peter chose the route across Epsom Downs and he pulled the car to the side of the road under some trees.

"Why are you stopping here?" asked Jenny.

"Because you were the most beautiful girl at the dance, and I don't think I should come to your room tonight."

"Of course you must come."

"But what about your mother?"

"She's not going to be watching us in the middle of the night. You must come. I want you."

When they reached Strathbrook the light was still on in her parents' bedroom.

"Wait for ten minutes after they turn out their light," she said. "They never take long to go to sleep."

He walked down the corridor to the spare bedroom he was sharing with Jack and began to undress. Jack got in a quarter of an hour later and when he heard the plan he laughed.

"You're going to get caught," he said.

"Well, what would you do?" asked Peter.

"Do? I already did, old boy, on the way home." He patted his chest with pride.

"What, in the Morgan? With Josephine?"

"Of course it was with Josephine. I didn't pick up a whore."

"But in a two-seater car?"

"We Rosses are pretty athletic," he said immodestly. "But now I need some sleep."

Soon after that Peter saw the light in the main bedroom go out and he crept along the corridor to Jenny's room. The glow of her pink night-light glimmered under her door.

"Sweetheart," she whispered as he came in.

She was lying on her back, naked, with her arms above her head, her young body glowing in the dim pink light. He let his pyjamas fall to the floor and climbed onto the bed. They came together immediately. He was a long way down the path to bliss when he became aware of a light in the passage outside. Jenny must have seen it too, because he felt her stiffen. Then he heard someone go into the bathroom next door.

"Keep still," she whispered. "It's my mother."

He thought Mrs White was unlikely to come in, but he daren't move. It was a strange sensation lying there naked, fully aroused but forbidden to move, and he hardly heard Mrs White leave the bathroom.

Then there was a knock on the door. They were still locked together on top of the bed. He started to disengage while Jenny frantically tried to pull up the sheet, but before they were even half covered the door opened. Bright light from the corridor streamed into the room as Mrs White peered in.

"Are you alright, dear?"

"Yes," Jenny answered shakily. "What's the matter?"

Peter lay rigid. But gradually he realized Mrs White's eyes had been blinded by the bright light outside. She could see nothing in the dim glimmer that filled the room. He held his breath.

"I saw a pink glow under your door. I thought there might be a fire."

"It's just my night-light."

"That's a relief. Well, goodnight dear."

She started to close the door, but when it was almost shut she seemed to have another thought and she opened it again. Once more the light from the passage streamed into the room. Luckily it didn't fall directly on the bed.

"What does a great big girl like you need a night-light for?"

"I like to use it sometimes. It reminds me of when I was little," said Jenny.

"Oh, that's nice." Mrs White lingered in the doorway, peering into the room as if she couldn't quite decide what to do. Peter's heart was pounding.

"You were a lovely child, you know. I often think about those times."

Jenny didn't seem to know how to answer that. Eventually she said, "And you were a wonderful mummy."

Peter thought she said it with a finality that would end the conversation, but instead Mrs White took a step into the room.

"I'm so glad I've got you for a daughter," she persisted. "Let me give you a goodnight kiss, just like when you were a little girl."

"Don't be silly, Mum. I'm not a little girl anymore, and I want to go to sleep."

But then her mother stumbled on Peter's pyjamas. "Well, you still leave your clothes all over the floor like a little girl. I'll pick them up for you."

"Don't bother," said Jenny. "I'll pick them up in the morning."

"Better do it now. They'll be all creased up by the morning." She bent down.

"Leave them where they are," said Jenny, with an edge to her voice.

"It'll only take a minute." Her mother picked up the pyjamas and Peter watched her turn them over, wondering what they were.

"I'll have to switch on the light," she said at last.

All this time Peter had not moved. He was lying on the bed, half on top of Jenny. Both of them were naked apart from the sheet, which barely reached to the level of their hips.

Suddenly harsh cold light flooded the room. There was a moment's silence while Mrs White stared at them with wide-eyed horror. Then she screamed. She let out a single long shriek, slammed the door, and ran back along the passage to the main bedroom. Her scream was so loud that Peter knew it must have wakened everyone in the house.

Jenny sat stunned, her mouth half open, her face as white as a sheet.

"Come on," he said. "Get your nightie on. Everyone will be in here in a minute."

He started to pull on his pyjamas.

Slowly she came to her senses. "Oh my God. Poor Mummy. What am I going to do?"

"Get your nightie on and get into bed so everything looks normal. Now, do you want me to stay with you, because I will if you like?"

"No, you go to your room."

As he moved towards the door she asked, "Peter, will you marry me?"

"Of course I will."

He reached the room he shared with Jack before anyone else appeared, and when he'd closed the door he felt a tremendous sense of relief.

"What the hell's going on?" demanded Jack.

He explained what had happened and Jack began to grin.

"Why can't you do it in the car like everybody else?" he asked, and they both started to snicker. Then there was a loud knock on the door and Philip White stormed in.

He stared at Peter with fury. "Put your clothes on and get out of my house," he shouted. "You accept my hospitality and then violate my daughter right under my nose. My wife's so upset she can hardly speak. The girl's almost a juvenile. I've a good mind to call the police."

Peter was taken aback. He'd expected to be bawled out but not like this. "Can I say something?" he asked meekly.

"No you cannot. Just put your clothes on and leave." And without waiting for a reply he marched out of the room.

Peter started to dress, but after a few minutes there was another knock, more gentle this time, and Josephine came in. She looked very serious.

"You've really done it this time," she said. "Everyone's in a terrible state. Mother is hysterical and Jenny is in shock. She says the two of you want to get married. Is that right?"

"Yes it is."

"Why didn't you tell Daddy that?"

"He didn't give me a chance."

"Well, perhaps I can give you a chance. Wait here. I'll try to get Mum and Dad together so you can explain."

She left the room, and ten minutes later she returned and escorted Peter downstairs to the living room. Mr and Mrs White were standing in their dressing gowns. Jenny was nowhere to be seen.

"Well?" asked Mr White.

"I'm awfully sorry," Peter began.

"You're sorry. I suppose you think that makes everything alright."

Peter was exasperated himself. "No, I don't," he said. And then he blurted, "I want to marry her."

"Marry?" Mary White almost shrieked. "You two can't possibly get married."

Peter was astonished. "Why not?"

"Because . . . ," she hesitated. "Because you're a Catholic. That's one reason."

"I could change."

"You can't change your religion on a whim."

"It's not a whim. We love each other and we want to get married."

Mrs White looked shocked. It seemed that talk of love and marriage made things worse.

"Jenny is much too young to know about love," she said.

"I wish you'd bring her down here and ask her," said Peter.

"No. You're not to see her. You've influenced her far too much already. She's only seventeen and she's much too young to marry. She couldn't marry without my permission, and I'd never agree to it. Never."

"But I just want to see her for a minute," Peter pleaded.

"No. You are never to see her again."

Josephine was standing by the door. She looked just as surprised as he felt.

"Come on Peter," she said softly. "You'd better go now."

As she escorted him across the hall, she added, "Jenny's upstairs. Of course you'll see her again, but I don't think you'd better try tonight. Go home now and I'll tell her to call you tomorrow. You'd better not phone here."

Peter spent all Sunday waiting for Jenny's call. He considered ringing her, but her mother was sure to answer. Why had her mother been so shocked at the suggestion of marriage? She'd said she'd never give consent. Never. It just didn't make sense.

The phone rang and he snatched it up, but it was Josephine.

"You sound disappointed."

"Well, I thought Jenny was going to call."

"She can't. They won't let her near the phone and she can't leave the house. But she'll call you tomorrow evening. And Peter, she really loves you. I hope you deserve it."

"I love her too."

Mark and Roy arrived back at the flat soon after she'd rung off. They hadn't eaten, so Mark went out to get some fish and chips and a jug of beer, and soon they were all having a meal.

Peter told them what had happened, but they didn't take it very seriously. Roy's affair with Christine was fairly superficial, and now that

Mark was sleeping with Beverley Morton he'd developed a more flippant attitude too. When Peter got to the part where Jenny's mother saw them naked they burst out laughing, and Peter chuckled a bit himself.

The next morning he considered going to the dancing school, but one of his patients was having a gastrectomy. It was a big operation and medical students were expected to assist. Afterwards he sat in the library staring through the window, seeing nothing but Jenny's face.

In the evening he decided to risk a call to Strathbrook in spite of Josephine's warning. He prayed that Jenny would answer the phone, but it was Mrs White's voice he heard.

"Ashtead 2915."

He said nothing.

"This is Ashtead 2915. Peter, is that you?"

He took a chance. "Yes, Mrs White, it is. Please may I speak to Jennifer?"

There was a pause. Perhaps it was going to be alright.

"No, I'm afraid you can't," she said.

"Mrs White," he pleaded. "I'm very sorry about what happened. I'm not asking to see her. I just want to talk to her. Just a few words. I miss her so much."

"That's just the problem. Talking to her will only make it worse for both of you. I think it's much better if you don't."

He wanted to tell her to go to hell.

"Is she alright?" he asked politely.

"Yes. But I don't want you disturbing her. Please don't phone again." And before he could tell her what he really thought she rang off.

He had to go to the hospital in the morning, but after lunch he drove over to the dancing school. He parked outside and walked up the brightly coloured corridor to the students' entrance. There was no official reception desk, but he saw several people and one of them went to find her.

Peter waited in the great domed hall. The marble walls threw back echoes and eventually he heard someone hurrying down a corridor towards him. His heart beat faster, but when the footsteps got near he recognized Jessica Clark's thick black hair.

She smiled warmly. "You're looking for Jenny?"

"Yes," he said, disappointed again.

"Well, she's not here. Apparently her mother called on Monday to say she was sick and she hasn't been here since."

Peter was shocked. Her mother was always one step ahead.

Jessica looked at him curiously. "Is everything alright between you two?"

He got the feeling she hoped everything was not alright. She took his phone number and promised to call if she heard anything.

"Maybe I'll call you in a few days anyway," she suggested with a smile.

As he walked back to the car he decided to drive down to Ashtead. He didn't have any plan, but he was angry with himself for letting Mary White outsmart him.

It took an hour to reach Ashtead. He parked the Bentley up the hill from Strathbrook where it was unlikely to be seen. He watched the front of the house for ten minutes but there was no sign of life. Then he went round the back and still there was nothing.

A balcony ran along the back of the house one floor up with a door and a window opening onto it. The window belonged to the bathroom and it was always left slightly open. Mr White kept a ladder beside the garage so Peter used that to reach the balcony. He crept over to the window and slipped his fingers inside to undo the latch.

The window was small, hardly big enough to squeeze through. He took off his coat but even then it was tight. He eased himself through carefully making as little noise as possible. Then he gently opened the door and stole into the familiar passage that ran between the bedrooms. Jenny's door was closed and he stood outside for a minute recalling the love they'd shared within.

Finally he opened the door and gasped with surprise.

Philip White looked at his watch. It was only 4:15 so he decided to take the long route home across Epsom Downs. He thought the drive across the open countryside would help him think. It was an extraordinary coincidence that Jennifer should fall for someone who was apparently Brother XII's son. He didn't think Mary was handling it in the right way at all. He'd told her she should have a frank talk with Angela Johnson and explain the truth about her daughter. He was sure Angela would understand and be frank in return, and then the two of them could come up with a plan to separate Peter and Jenny. They might even decide to tell their children the truth.

Philip believed the truth had a way of overcoming problems. He'd even offered to act as an intermediary and tell Angela himself, but Mary had refused. She had not merely refused, she'd gone almost apoplectic at the very idea. They must never tell anyone what she had done, and if

Angela had done the same thing she would never admit it either, so there was no point in asking her.

As Philip threaded his way down the hill to Strathbrook he was surprised to see Peter Johnson's old sports Bentley parked a little way up from the house. He entered his driveway and put his car in the garage. He was still thinking about the Bentley, but there was no sign of anyone at the front of the house. He tried the front door and found it locked as he expected, but instead of using his key he decided to have a look around the back.

He walked round to the back of the house and immediately spotted the ladder up against the balcony. The bathroom window was open too. He stood and thought for a minute. It had to be Peter and he was already inside. Then he made his way carefully back to the front door and let himself in.

When Peter opened the door to Jenny's room he was astounded to find it almost bare. It was not just empty; nearly everything had gone. The furniture was all that was left to show that she had ever lived there. It was a child's furniture really, but it reminded him of her.

The top of her dressing table was clear. It had always been cluttered with tiny bottles of makeup, trinkets, photos and all the little things of her life. To see it empty shocked him beyond words. Her bed had been stripped. Even her sheets were gone, those soft cotton sheets between which they'd made such perfect love. All that remained were the blankets folded neatly on the end of the bed.

The cupboard door hung open and her clothes had been taken too. He pictured her wearing them: the Aertex shirt she wore when they first met in the garden of the Ferry Inn; the pink flowered dress she'd worn to the Kingsbridge fair; the little taffeta cocktail dress he liked so much. They were a part of her, and now they were gone.

He walked over to the chest of drawers and pulled them open one by one. They were empty too. It was as if she'd never lived there. His heart sank. He loved her so much and now there was nothing. For the first time he thought he might never see her again.

But what could have happened? Perhaps there was a note for him somewhere. He searched the room for a clue, but all he could find was a crumpled white blouse on the floor by the bed.

He put it to his face. It smelled of her, a wonderful scent of everything he longed for. Then he sat down on the bed, buried his face in the blouse, and wept.

Peter was not sure how long he'd been in the room when he heard footsteps on the stairs. His first impulse was to hide in the cupboard, but then he couldn't see the point. What more did he have to lose? They could call the police, he supposed, but he hadn't stolen anything so what did it matter? Also, he had to know what had happened to Jenny. Perhaps a showdown would be the best way to find out.

The footsteps came straight along the corridor to the bedroom, as if whoever it was already knew he was there. It sounded like a man so he wasn't surprised when Philip White opened the door. Mr White didn't look surprised either.

"Hello Peter," he said gently. "What are you doing here?"

"Looking for Jenny."

"How long have you been here?" He didn't sound angry.

"I don't know. Maybe half an hour."

"Well, you just missed her. I took them to Epsom Station about an hour ago."

"Where has she gone?"

"She's taking a holiday with her mother."

Peter was amazed. "A holiday?"

"Just a few weeks."

"But, where?"

"I'm afraid I can't tell you that," he said. "I know you're upset, and Jennifer is too, so her mother has taken her away for a while to help her get over it."

"But why? I accept that what we did was wrong, but why have you sent her away?"

Philip White walked slowly over to the bed, sat down, and put his hand on Peter's shoulder. It was quite different from the last time they'd met.

"There's something you don't know," he said. "And I can't tell you what it is. Wait till she comes back. It'll only be a few weeks."

"How many weeks?"

"I don't know exactly." He paused for a minute, then he said, "You'll have to go now, Peter. You shouldn't be here at all, you know."

Peter remembered that he'd broken in. Mr White had been very understanding. They went downstairs, but before Peter left he made one more attempt to find out where Jenny was.

"I wish you would just tell me where she is."

"They'll be spending the night on the south coast. I can't say more than that."

The next evening was the first that Peter did not spend by the phone. He'd given up expecting Jenny to call, and Mark persuaded him to go to the pub to cheer himself up. Roy had some studying to do, so he stayed behind, and when they got home at 10:30 he looked excited.

"Your girlfriend called twice," he said. "She sounded pretty upset you weren't in."

Peter jumped for joy. "Jennifer? Where is she?"

"In Southampton, on the *Pretoria Castle*."

"The *Pretoria Castle*? What on earth's that?"

"A steamship, dummy."

"A ship? What's she doing on a ship?"

"Going to South Africa. She sails at midnight."

They were in the living room of the flat. Roy's medical books littered the table. Peter slumped onto the couch.

"South Africa?" he repeated. "Tonight? Can I call her?"

"Apparently not. There's a phone on the ship, but it's for outgoing calls only and it'll be disconnected before they sail. She was a bit upset when I told her you were at the pub having a good time."

"How can I contact her?" asked Peter desperately.

"You can write to her on the ship. It calls at Las Palmas and Cape Town. I've got the address."

"I'll try to phone the ship."

"She said don't do that because you'll tie up the line. She's going to call again if she can."

By 11:30 he'd almost given up when the phone rang. His hand shook as he put it to his ear.

"Hello," he said.

"Hello." The voice was indistinct, but it was her at last.

"Jenny!"

"Is that you, Peter? I've only got a minute."

The line was awful, he could hardly hear.

"Can you speak a bit louder? I can't hear you properly," he said.

"I'm shouting already, and there are other people listening. I'm going to South Africa with Mummy."

He was talking to her at last but he couldn't think what to say.

"Yes, Roy told me," he shouted. "Why are you going so far away?"

"Mum wants me to. We're going to stay with her sister in a place called Kokstad in Cape Province. Have you got a piece of paper? I'll give you the address."

He wrote down the address in South Africa and checked the ship's address as well. He wanted to tell her that he loved her and how much he missed her, but he was embarrassed shouting at the top of his voice with Mark and Roy listening through the wall.

"I do wish you weren't going away," was all he managed to say.

"Well, I wish I wasn't going too."

"Couldn't you have run away?"

"No. It would have hurt Mum too much. She's upset enough as it is."

"What about us? Do you think I'm not upset?"

"Are you? It didn't stop you spending the evening in the pub."

There was a crackling noise on the line, and he heard Jenny arguing with someone. Then her voice came through again quite clearly, "They're going to disconnect the phone," she said hurriedly. "Promise me you'll write."

"Of course I'll write, but I just want . . . "

"I'll always love you," she interrupted.

He started to say, "I love you too," but the words were lost.

Peter wrote his first letter immediately, before he went to bed. In it he put down all the feelings of love, hurt and loneliness he'd failed to express on the phone. He read the letter through. If only he'd said those things on the phone.

The *Pretoria Castle* took only four days to reach Las Palmas in the Canary Islands; he worried that his letter might not arrive in time, so he sent another to Cape Town, and to be sure he mailed a third to Durban, the final port.

It was exactly a week before her first letter arrived. He took it downstairs to open in the privacy of his room, and he held it to his face hoping there'd be a trace of her own sweet smell.

The first part was dated the day the ship had sailed.

Darling Peter,

What an awful phone call. I'm so sorry darling, I've left you with all the wrong words and thoughts.

What I meant to say was that I've thought of you every minute since we were parted. I don't want to go to Africa, except with you. I should have run away, but I've failed you even in that. How can I ever make it up? I love you with all my heart.

There's a steamship schedule here. It takes three weeks to get to Durban, and three more to get back. If we stay with Auntie for a month we'll be home in just ten weeks. That's seventy days. I've marked them in my diary so I can cross them off one by one.

After that I will have done my penance, and if my mother still tries to stop me seeing you I shall definitely leave home.

With all my love,

Jenny.

But she'd added more each day, and gradually her style had changed. It remained just as affectionate, but as the days progressed she began to describe the ship and the other passengers. And on the fourth day, after they'd docked at Las Palmas, she could not conceal her disappointment when she found there was no letter from him. She'd received one from her sister but the steward said mail to the Canary Isles was unreliable. Peter was devastated to think she hadn't heard from him. If only he'd sent two letters. He immediately wrote again to both Cape Town and Durban.

A few days later Peter heard from Jessica Clark. She phoned to say she'd received a card from Jennifer.

"Would you like to see it?" she asked.

"Yes," he said.

"Well, I was going dancing tonight with friends, but my boyfriend has let me down, so if you come as my partner I'll show you the card."

It wasn't quite what he wanted but he agreed.

"We're going to the Blue Angel, the nightclub in the West End. Will you pick me up in that gorgeous Bentley?"

Jessica's friends turned out to be fun. They went to a pub first and they didn't arrive at the Blue Angel till 11pm. The card was just an excuse to get him to take her dancing; Jenny hadn't even mentioned his name.

When they eventually reached the nightclub the hostess showed them to a table close to the small dance floor. The lights were low and the drinks were expensive, but they'd already had several before they arrived.

Jessica was wearing the same slinky black dress he'd seen at the dancing school reception. The music was soft and they did little more than sway back and forth, her face nestled against his shoulder and her body touching his.

When they sat down Peter spotted Josephine watching from another table.

Peter sensed that something was wrong as soon as he opened Jenny's second letter. The envelope was postmarked Cape Town and it contained two separate letters, one much longer than the other. He saw that the long one was unfinished and he read that first.

She'd written it in the form of a diary, adding more each day. The *Pretoria Castle* was a big passenger liner carrying travellers from England to South Africa. Most of them were under thirty, and she had become friendly with two girls, Ann and Virginia, who were returning home to South Africa from a finishing school in Switzerland.

Not a very appropriate name, she'd written when describing Virginia. Ann was being chaperoned by an older brother, and there were plenty of other young men to escort them to the Captain's cocktail party, the fancy-dress ball and the other activities on the ship. Peter could imagine the scene, but it didn't make him jealous because the letter was full of her love for him.

When they reached the tropics the crew had rigged a canvas swimming pool on deck, and when the ship crossed the equator there'd been an elaborate ceremony. If only you were here, she'd written, what fun we would be having.

South of the equator it had got steadily cooler, and after the ship crossed the Tropic of Capricorn they could no longer sunbathe on deck. As they approached the southern tip of Africa great swells called cape rollers had swept in from the Southern Ocean. She described how the ship's huge bow buried itself in the oncoming swells and threw sheets of spray back as far as the bridge. The crew had to drain the swimming pool, and for a day and a half she'd been sick.

On the fourteenth morning after they'd left England she'd got up at dawn to catch her first sight of Africa.

As we entered Table Bay, she'd written, the sea became calm, and now the ship is steady. I am writing this as we wait for the tugs to take us into the dock. The city of Cape Town lies ahead, shining in the early morning sun. Behind the city stands flat-topped Table Mountain, covered by a white cloud like a tablecloth. Here the sun rises in the north making the mountain and its cloud glow like gold.

Darling, I ought to be having a wonderful time but it's all wasted because I can't share it with you. I love you and I can't wait to hear from you.

The letter was unfinished. It looked as if she'd intended to write more after the ship had docked, but she'd changed her mind.

The shorter letter was lying on the bed beside him, so he picked it up.

Dearest Peter,

Now we are in Cape Town and still there is no letter from you. I can't believe you wouldn't write to me, but all the other passengers have got mail.

Darling, I'm frantic with worry that you're angry with me for going to Africa. I had no choice, although I would certainly have run away if I'd known this would happen.

And that phone call from Southampton. Perhaps you thought I rang off because I was annoyed you went to the pub. I was disappointed when I couldn't get you on the phone, but that was all. And I didn't ring off, they disconnected the line while I was trying to explain. That dreadful call was the last contact I've had with you. How I wish I'd never got through. If only I could see you for just one minute, I know I could make you understand. Now the ship is in port everyone is happy, but I've never felt so miserable in my life. This afternoon Ann and Virginia are going to show me around Cape Town, but I just want to be on my own.

My mother says men fall in and out of love with hardly a thought, and that I'd best forget you. But Peter, I still love you and I can't believe you've just stopped loving me. But even if you have, please write. Please don't leave me like this.

I wrote this letter separately because Mum wants me to throw the other one away. But when I wrote the first one, day by day, I thought we were lovers, and I can't bear to tear it up.

I love you still,
Jenny.

Peter was horrified. He knew he must contact her straight away. By now the ship should have docked in Durban, so he called the Union Castle passenger office and asked how he could contact a passenger there.

"Durban, sir? You can place a call direct to our ships in Durban but it must be arranged in advance."

Peter leaped for joy.

"How do I do that?"

"We'll make the arrangements, sir. There'll be a charge of course."

"I'd like to place a call as soon as possible."

"The passenger's name, please?"

"Miss Jennifer White. She's in tourist class, cabin T 36."

"Very good, sir. I'll call you back when she's on the line."

Peter was elated. If only he'd done this when the ship was docked at Cape Town. How delighted she would have been if he had called her then.

The phone rang only ten minutes later.

"Is that Mr Peter Johnson?" The voice sounded distant.

"Yes, it is."

"Did you want to speak to Miss Jennifer White on the *Pretoria Castle*?"

"Yes, that's right." His excitement mounted.

"The *Pretoria Castle* docked this morning, on schedule. Durban is the final port of destination and Miss White has already disembarked," the voice said. "There's a two-hour time difference between Durban and London, you know."

"Oh. I didn't know."

"We had to contact the ship so there will be a charge of five pounds," said the voice. "Would you like us to put it on your telephone bill?"

Five pounds, thought Peter miserably, a fortune, and for nothing.

"Alright."

"Very good, sir." The phone went dead.

Ten days passed and no more letters came. Peter knew that if she'd received either of the letters he'd sent to Durban he would have heard by now. Five consecutive letters could not have gone astray so they must have been intercepted.

Jenny's mother had taken her to Africa to break up their relationship, but he never dreamed she'd go so far as this. He had written to the address in Kokstad a week ago, but if Mary White could intercept letters to the ship, she could certainly do it in a private house owned by her sister. And she could probably stop them going the other way too.

He heard nothing for a month, then a letter arrived from Mary White:

Dear Peter,

Jennifer is young and easily influenced. You persuaded her to do things which should be reserved for marriage because they have such a profound effect upon a girl. For months I watched her fall under your spell, and now I understand why.

I hope that now she is away from you she will take a less emotional interest in a number of young men, as is normal for girls of her age. It was hard for her at first, but there are several suitable men here and I'm pleased to say it is already beginning to happen.

I'm writing to ask you to stop trying to communicate with her. We are living with my sister and she understands the situation. Censorship is common in this country so I have no difficulty keeping track of Jennifer's mail. However, for your own good it would be better if you stopped thinking about my daughter and found yourself somebody else. Perhaps you already have. Josephine told me she saw you at a nightclub with Jessica Clark, Jennifer's friend from the dancing school. I have told Jennifer this to help her understand that your relationship has truly come to an end.

What you did to her was inexcusable, and now I'm asking you to leave her alone so she can get over it. I have no intention of allowing her to return to England while you are still showing an interest in her.

Yours sincerely, Mary White.

By the time Peter had finished the letter he felt physically sick. He'd never placed a phone call to another continent before, but that was what he decided to do. He called the operator and half an hour later the phone was ringing in Kokstad, South Africa.

A man answered, and for a moment Peter thought he was speaking in a foreign language, his accent was so strange.

"I want to speak to Jennifer White, please," he asked as clearly as he could.

Next a woman came on the line. His heart fell. It was Mary White, and he knew he had failed again. He hung up without speaking, another five pounds wasted.

The last straw came a month later. A tiny parcel arrived from South Africa. He did not recognize the writing on the label but he opened it with trembling fingers, hoping for a message from Jenny. Inside there was no message, only a small cardboard box. He lifted the lid, and there lay the blue and silver ring he'd given her in the church at Rye.

Chapter 24

When Paul Ellison slyly announced he'd seen Beverley Morton at the Middlesex Hospital the previous evening, Mark guessed the remarks were aimed at him. He was with half a dozen other students sitting round a table in the Spit drinking coffee. They all knew about his affair with Beverley.

"I was visiting a friend who's doing research on cystic fibrosis," said Paul. He always made it sound as if he had important friends. "A white Jaguar pulled up, and who do you think got out?"

Everyone looked at him expectantly.

"Our Miss Morton, dressed to kill. I must admit she's a good-looking woman. I'm not surprised she has several irons in the fire."

Mark felt his face redden.

"Was she by herself?" someone asked.

"Of course not. Midwives don't drive Jaguars. She was with a doctor. He looked a bit like young Mark here, except he was older, better dressed, and a lot better looking."

He paused for them to laugh.

"I don't know who he is, but he must be important because the porter treated him with great respect. Yes, Dr Blakelock. No, Dr Blakelock. That sort of thing. Our porters don't treat Weeks like that."

Well, Mark knew who Jeremy Blakelock was, and it upset him to hear that Beverley was still seeing him. She continued to go out with Weeks sometimes too, although she swore it was only for social reasons, whatever that might mean.

He got up in disgust and went out to the park. He loved the Guy's park in summertime. The trees and lawns were beautifully green and the flowerbeds a mass of colour. It was a warm sunny afternoon and he sat down on a bench and let his thoughts wander.

His relationship with Beverley had been going on for nearly five months. He recalled the first few weeks with nostalgia. They'd slept together at her flat whenever Pamela was away. He'd been unable to study or do anything but think of her. He laughed about it now, but it had been wonderful at the time. He'd thought the feeling would go on forever and he'd been disappointed when it began to fade. But his feelings had only partly cooled. He still felt jealous when she went out with someone else.

Well, to hell with Jeremy Blakelock, he thought. And to hell with Beverley Morton too. He'd watched Peter moping about after Jenny went away and he wasn't going to fall into that trap. Beverley had given him back his confidence and she would always have a place in his heart, but he was no longer her slave.

"And who's looking after this patient?" asked Dr Wood.

" I am, sir," said Mark. "This is Mr Wiggins. He's a fifty-five-year-old machinist who developed a productive cough with fever two weeks ago."

Mark went on to describe a typical case of pneumonia which was a bit slow to recover.

The students were attached to a medical ward called Addison now, under the direction of Dr William Wood, a respected internist. Wood was a tall serious man of sixty, with straight iron-grey hair and glasses which he often wore on the end of his nose. He had none of the flamboyance of a surgeon like Cudmore, but he'd got a solid reputation for accurate diagnosis and good judgement. In fact it was well known that he despised surgeons, thinking they were too quick to cut and too keen to show off.

They discussed Mr Wiggins case and looked at his X-rays, then Dr Wood had several of the students listen to the patient's chest.

When they had finished he asked, "Well Wooding, what do you think?"

"It looks like a straightforward case of pneumonia that's a little slow to respond to treatment," said Mark.

"There's nothing in the history or examination that might concern you?"

"Nothing I could find."

Paul Ellison had been unusually quiet but now they were about to move on to the next patient he suddenly spoke up.

"May I say something, sir?"

"Of course."

"I think we should consider a diagnosis of psittacosis."

"Psittacosis is a rare disease, what makes you think of that."

"Well sir, his lack of response to penicillin, the low white blood count, and the patchy appearance of the pneumonia on the X-ray are typical of psittacosis. Don't you agree, Wooding?"

Mark could hardly agree since he'd finished his presentation with no mention of psittacosis. He felt his face redden.

"Psittacosis only occurs in people who've been in contact with infected birds, usually parrots." said Dr Wood. "Wooding, does the patient have any birds?"

"No," replied Mark. "He told me he has no pets at all."

Paul looked at the floor. He seemed to have been put in his place, but the patient was bursting to say something.

"What is it, Mr Wiggins?" asked Wood.

"I have no pets myself but my sister has a parrot. She was visiting yesterday and she told me it died last week."

Now Mark's face was really red.

"Why didn't you tell us before?" asked Dr Wood.

"I did. I told that doctor there." He nodded at Paul.

"Well Ellison, you didn't tell us you already knew the patient had been in contact with a sick bird," said Wood with a smile. "And it seems you forgot to mention it to Wooding as well."

"I didn't want to embarrass Wooding," said Paul. "But psittacosis is a serious disease so I thought I'd better ask a few questions myself." He glanced smugly round the group, obviously delighted by what he'd done.

"What have you got to say about that, Wooding?" asked Dr Wood, still smiling.

Wood turned to his houseman. "Run the appropriate tests," he said. "Psittacosis responds to tetracycline, but don't use it unless the diagnosis is confirmed."

Then he looked at the patient, "Mr Wiggins, you've probably just got ordinary pneumonia that's a bit slow to respond, but if you do have this disease which people catch from parrots we'll soon find out."

Mark liked Dr Wood in spite of his prejudice against surgeons. His ward rounds did not have the show business atmosphere that Dr Cudmore enjoyed, but they were an excellent learning experience. However, today's round seemed to drag on and on. It was a good thing Helen Metcalf had recently been transferred to the ward; exchanging glances with her was all that kept him awake. How pretty she looked, he thought, with her dark brown hair and dusky eyes. Judging by the looks she gave him she was keen to renew their friendship, and with his new-found confidence Mark was keen to renew it too.

It had been over two years since the picnic they'd had by the river. That was the first time he'd been unable to make love. Well, he no longer had that problem, and as the ward round wore on he found himself thinking about Helen more and more. Perhaps he would ask her out, and perhaps they would have an affair. What a wonderful thing was self-confidence, but buried in his mind there was still a small seed of doubt.

Chapter 25

"Knife," ordered Cudmore, and the scrub nurse placed a scalpel in his hand.

Peter looked around the operating theatre. In the centre stood the table with the patient covered by green drapes. The patient's head was exposed, attached to the anesthetic machine by a black rubber hose, and there was a strip of exposed skin down the middle of the abdomen. Three men and a woman leaned over him, all wearing caps, masks and green surgical gowns.

The room smelled of ether, and the anesthetist sat by the patient's head with a grim look on his face. Peter watched him check the blood pressure for the third time in five minutes.

The leader of the team was Dr Cudmore, his reddish hair and beard nearly covered by his mask and cap. Next to him stood his scrub nurse, whose job was to keep the instruments ready for use. Across the table were Alan Brooks the registrar, and Mark Wooding the second assistant. Behind them two more nurses and an orderly waited to fetch equipment and run errands. To one side stood the theatre sister, there to oversee her nurses. Round the edges of the room hovered the students. Everyone was dressed in green and they all wore masks and caps.

"I shall make a right paramedian incision," announced Cudmore as he drew the scalpel's razor-sharp blade down the middle of the abdomen. The skin and flesh sprang back leaving a clean-cut furrow from the ribs to the navel. Blood spurted from a dozen small vessels and Brooks hurried to clamp them with artery forceps.

"Diathermy," ordered Cudmore.

"Not yet," protested Dr Mondale, the anesthetist.

"Why not?"

"Too much ether," said Mondale. "You might start an explosion."

"Look, this man has a bleeding ulcer. If I don't stop the bleeding immediately he'll probably die." Then he added with a mixture of humour and contempt: "Those idiots on the medical ward have been trying to cure him with pills."

"I'm sorry," said Mondale.

"I told you I needed the diathermy, so why use so much ether?"

Both Cudmore and Mondale were full members of the consultant staff. Theoretically they were equals, but anyone could see who carried the most weight.

"You know I have to use more at the beginning," pleaded Mondale. "I'll reduce it as soon as I can."

"Well, I'll give you five minutes to get it down to a safe level."

Peter felt sorry for Dr Mondale. Technically he had the right to forbid the electric diathermy if he thought the sparks might cause an explosion, but few anesthetists could stand up to a surgeon like Cudmore. He was a big man with a loud voice, but he showed great skill as he used scalpel, forceps and fingers to separate the layers of the abdominal wall.

This part of the operation was routine and Peter's thoughts drifted. It was the summer of 1957 and the students would soon be taking their final exams. After that they would become housemen. His thoughts turned to Mark. His friend wanted to be a surgeon and a major stepping stone would be an appointment as Dr Cudmore's house surgeon. He needed to impress the chief, but so far on this rotation his performance had not been good. Something was wrong. There wasn't a woman involved and his on-again off-again affair with Beverley Morton didn't seem to be the problem. Peter glanced at him now. He was bending over the operating table holding a retractor. Most of his face was covered, but there was sweat on his forehead and his eyes looked hollow and dull.

"Now for the moment of truth," announced Dr Cudmore. "I'm about to open the peritoneum. Is it a bleeding ulcer, or have we made a mistake?"

Everyone strained forward. At the bottom of the wound lay the peritoneum, the translucent membrane that stretched tightly across the patient's bowels. Peter watched him use a pair of forceps to pull up a fold.

"Knife."

He made a small incision with the scalpel and there was a sucking sound as air was drawn into the abdominal cavity. Next he enlarged the hole and soon he had his hand inside, examining the organs one by one. He announced his findings as he went along in a voice loud enough for all to hear. Everyone else was silent.

Finally he came to the stomach. For a while he palpated it in silence. "The X-rays show an ulcer near the gastric outlet," he said at last. "I can't feel the ulcer, but I think the stomach's full of blood."

He enlarged the opening in the peritoneum until Peter could see a glistening pinkish-white bag about the size of a grapefruit, with its surface streaked with blood.

"What do you think of that, Wooding?" he asked.

Mark hesitated. Peter looked at him in surprise. He was holding a retractor to separate the edges of the wound but he didn't seem to be paying attention at all.

"What was that, sir?"

"I asked you what you thought of the patient's stomach. What's the matter with you, Wooding?"

But before Mark could reply Dr Mondale broke in. "The blood pressure's falling. You'd better get the bleeding stopped as quickly as you can." He adjusted the blood transfusion to make it run faster.

Ignoring Mondale, Cudmore said, "The ulcer is in the posterior wall of the stomach. First I'll stop the bleeding. Then I'll do a partial gastrectomy. That will remove the ulcer and also the part of the stomach that secretes most of the acid, so another ulcer won't develop."

He turned to Brooks. "Come on, Alan. Let's get on with it."

He cut through the front of the stomach and inside it was full of clotted blood. Brooks scooped out the solid clots with his fingers while Mark used the suction tube to remove the liquid. Soon the ulcer came into view, a circular white crater half an inch across with a small bleeding artery near the middle.

"Suction," called Cudmore. "Wooding, keep the stomach clear while I catch that bleeder."

He deftly clamped the end of the spurting vessel with a pair of artery forceps.

"Diathermy," he ordered, with no reference to the anesthetist.

Peter could smell ether and he wondered what would happen when the diathermy sparked. Dr Mondale looked worried too.

"Burn," called Cudmore.

Brooks touched the diathermy to the metal artery forceps and pressed the pedal on the floor. There was a crackle of electricity and a puff of smoke rose from the ulcer.

"Alright," said Cudmore. "That's stopped the bleeding. Now let's finish the job."

He and Brooks began the task of freeing the stomach from its attachments, while Mark assisted by securing the blood vessels they cut. It was slow meticulous work, dangerous to hurry. After a while they divided the duodenum, and then Cudmore began the delicate task of separating the body of the stomach from the pancreas.

A nurse came in with two bottles of blood. "That's all there is left," she announced.

Mondale looked shocked. "There are supposed to be another four units?"

"Apparently they used them on the medical ward before the patient was transferred to surgery."

"What's the matter?" Even Cudmore sounded anxious.

"The blood pressure's dropping and we're short of blood. Are you sure you've got the bleeding stopped?"

"Of course I am."

Dr Mondale looked at the nurse. "Tell the blood bank we need four more units. They can send O-Negative if they like, but we can't wait for a full cross-match."

Mondale must be really worried, thought Peter. Even O-Negative blood was risky if it wasn't fully cross-matched. He glanced at Mark and got a shock. The little of his face that was visible looked white and there was sweat all over his forehead. He even seemed unsteady on his feet. No one else had noticed, they were all concentrating on the operation.

Cudmore was still trying to dissect the back of the stomach off the pancreas but it was firmly stuck. "The ulcer has penetrated through the gastric wall into the pancreas and stuck the two together," he explained.

Suddenly the stomach came away from the pancreas and blood spouted up like a fountain. It flooded the operation site so fast that no one could see where it came from.

"Pack," called Cudmore.

Brooks held up the stomach while Cudmore pushed a gauze pack into the hole and pressed it down with his fingers to control the hemorrhage.

"I think we've torn the gastro-duodenal artery," he announced.

The hemorrhage was temporarily controlled by the gauze pack, but they would have to tie off the bleeding artery.

He turned to his assistants: "Wooding, use your retractor to hold the stomach out of the way. And Brooks, when I remove the pack, quickly clamp the bleeding artery before the wound fills with blood.

The scrub nurse handed Brooks a pair of artery forceps.

"Are you ready?"

"Yes," said Brooks, but Mark was silent.

"Wooding?"

Mark seemed to be staring into space.

"Wooding, what's the matter with you. Use your retractor to hold the stomach out of the way."

But slowly Mark's legs buckled and he slithered down the side of the table. He was still holding the retractor which pulled the gauze pack out of the wound. Blood squirted from the torn artery. Cudmore was as quick as a flash. He removed Mark's useless retractor and pushed the pack back into place before anybody moved. Then he looked down at Mark lying on the floor.

"Johnson, Whitfield," he called. "Put Wooding on a stretcher and get one of the housemen to see what's wrong."

"He's fainted, sir," said Ellison before the others could respond. "Would you like me to take his place?"

"Well, he picked a bad time to faint. Yes, Ellison, get scrubbed as quickly as you can."

By the time Peter and Roy had got Mark onto a stretcher he was conscious again, and Paul was gowned and gloved ready to take his place.

As they wheeled Mark out of the room they heard Cudmore say, "You're not going to faint on me, are you Ellison?"

"Of course not sir, you can rely on me."

"I tell you I'm perfectly alright," Mark protested.

"Well, Cudmore told us to get the houseman to check you over," said Peter.

"Look man, you've caused enough trouble already," added Roy. "Just stay where you are. We want to go back to the theatre to see what's happening."

They disappeared leaving him on a stretcher in the corridor. He felt miserable. There was something wrong and he knew what it was.

He had started to feel ill six weeks ago and at first he thought it was flu. The lymph nodes in his neck enlarged and his throat became sore. Then four days ago he discovered enlarged lymph nodes in his groin. He laid on his bed to feel his spleen and it was enlarged too. That was when he'd thought of leukemia.

He spent a sleepless night and in the morning he'd gone to the students' hematology lab on the top floor of Hunt's house. There he placed half a dozen glass slides on the workbench, pricked his finger, and smeared a thin film of blood on each. Then he stained the slides and as he waited for them to dry he wondered what to do. Acute leukemia meant certain death, nobody ever survived.

When the slides were ready he put the first one on the microscope and adjusted the focus. The red cells looked normal, but between them were dozens of abnormal white cells. Some of them were grossly enlarged with big distorted nuclei. There wasn't any doubt, he had acute lymphatic leukemia.

He'd gathered up the slides and walked across the park looking for a quiet spot to think. Perhaps he should consult a doctor, but there was no effective treatment so he couldn't see the point; the last thing he wanted was more medical investigations and tests. The final exams started in a couple of weeks, but they didn't matter anymore, and impressing Cudmore didn't matter either. His only desire was curl up and go to sleep.

He was about to get off the stretcher when he heard the houseman coming down the corridor. He wore a short white coat with a stethoscope draped round his neck and he looked very young.

"Hello, Mark. I got a message you'd had an accident or something."

"I fainted, that's all. I'm perfectly alright now."

"Are you sure?"

"Quite sure. I think I've had a touch of flu."

He looked doubtful. "I'd better listen to your chest."

"Go ahead." Mark was relieved, there was nothing wrong with his chest.

"It sounds alright," he announced after a minute. "Well, if you're feeling better now I guess you can go."

Mark swung his legs over the side of the stretcher trying to look as healthy as he could.

Just then Roy came out of the theatre to see how he was getting on.

"Are you OK now?"

"I'm fine."

"He just fainted, that's all," said the houseman. "He's had a touch of flu." And he hurried off down the corridor.

"Thank goodness for that," said Roy. "I thought you looked quite ill."

The last thing he remembered was blood spurting from the patient's abdomen. "What happened when I fainted?"

Roy explained exactly what had happened.

"Oh, my God. How's the patient now?"

"Much better. They've stopped the bleeding. Mondale's got transfusions running into both arms and the blood pressure's finally coming up. Cudmore's still working on the gastrectomy, but I'm sure the patient will survive."

By the summer of 1957 the students had finished their training and they were preparing to take the final exams. Students from all over London assembled for the written papers at the examination hall in Kensington, a huge place filled with rows of school desks and hard wooden chairs.

The oral exams were more of a game. The students went in groups to different hospitals to examine patients and answer questions on what they thought was wrong. These were not ordinary patients; they'd been selected because of the strange diseases they had, and many of them were regulars who'd learned to act their part. Often they exaggerated their symptoms or dropped hints about what was supposed to be wrong.

For the last exam, surgery, Peter had to go to St. Mary's Hospital in Paddington in a group that included Paul Ellison, and he took them in his car. He thought he was dressed neatly enough in a tweed sports jacket and grey flannel trousers, but Paul wore a new suit from Savile Row and his Cambridge college tie.

They parked the Bentley at St. Mary's and followed the signs to the examination hall, a big room that had once been a hospital ward. There were about twenty patients on beds separated by screens. At the far end of the room three pairs of examiners sat at tables strewn with human bones, surgical instruments and specimens in jars.

An official explained what they had to do, allotting each student three patients to examine. "You'll get fifteen minutes with each one," he said. "You won't see the examiners till you've finished all three."

Peter's first two patients were straightforward. One had gallstones and the other was waiting to have a hernia repaired. His third patient was a man of fifty called Baxter, whose abdomen was crisscrossed by operation scars. It seemed he'd had surgery on almost every organ. Now he had pain deep in the middle of the abdomen just above the navel.

"It's my pancreas," he confided. "I've got a pancreatic cyst. At least, that's what the doctors say. They're going to take it out, but I wasn't supposed to tell you that."

When Peter examined his abdomen Mr Baxter winced with pain. Peter thought he could feel a lump above the umbilicus where the pancreas lay, but with all those operation scars it was difficult to be sure. He jotted down some notes and then the bell rang indicating that he had to move on to the examiners.

He found himself sitting nervously in front of a pair of poker-faced men with greying hair. At first they questioned him about the specimens on the table, and he thought he did quite well. Then they dealt with the patients Peter had examined. The first two were easy and he had no difficulty making a diagnosis and suggesting treatment. Finally they came to Mr Baxter. First Peter listed the man's many illnesses and the operations he'd undergone. Then he described the present complaint of abdominal pain, and the examination finding of a lump in the pancreas.

"Could you feel the lump yourself?" asked one of the examiners.

Peter hadn't been quite sure, but Baxter had told him it was there so he thought he'd better say yes.

"So what's your diagnosis?"

"A pancreatic cyst."

"And what would you do about it?"

"Well, I think he needs another operation."

Both examiners stared at him. "Johnson, have you ever heard of Munchausen's Syndrome?" one of them asked.

"Munchausen's Syndrome. No, I can't say I have."

He was about to ask them what it was when the bell rang, signalling that his time was up. The rules were strict, no talking after the bell.

"Thank you, Johnson," said the chief examiner without a smile. "The results will be posted the day after tomorrow."

On the way home in the car the students discussed their cases.

"What's Munchausen's Syndrome," asked Peter as casually as he could.

"Did you get the Munchausen case?" asked Paul.

He nodded.

"So did I. All those operation scars on his abdomen! And he told me he needed yet another operation for a pancreatic cyst. Can you imagine anyone believing that?"

Peter's heart fell. But he wanted to know the answer, so he thought he'd try another approach.

"But who was Munchausen?"

"Baron Karl von Munchausen, the German storyteller," said Paul confidently. Then he looked directly at Peter with a sly smile on his face. "Hey, Johnson, you got it wrong, didn't you? You missed the Munchausen's. What did you give for a diagnosis?"

They were driving east on Oxford Street. Peter shifted the heavy gear lever of the Bentley as they went round Oxford Circus.

"A pancreatic cyst," he replied miserably.

"No."

"He told me his doctors had found a cyst and he needed an operation."

"They'll say anything to get into hospital."

"But why? Why do they want to be in hospital?"

"Nobody knows. They just want to be patients. Maybe they like the attention."

He couldn't help being impressed. "Where did you learn all this? It's not in Bailey and Love's textbook of surgery."

"Cambridge, of course," Paul replied. "Did you know Cudmore's daughter is at Cambridge? She's coming to Guy's next year."

"Cudmore has a daughter who's coming to Guy's as a medical student?"

"Her name's Pat. Pretty girl. A redhead like her father. I aim to be Cudmore's house surgeon in July. It can't do any harm to date the boss' daughter, can it?" Paul chuckled.

"You old rat," exclaimed one of his friends. "You'd do anything to get ahead."

"Yes, I guess I would."

That evening Peter told Mark what Ellison had said. All these years his friend's single ambition had been to get to the top in surgery, and he needed the Cudmore job. Three months ago he would have got it, but now it was slipping away. Perhaps this would shake him into action.

Mark stared silently out of the window for a long time. It was dusk and the last of the tennis players at Queen's Club were finishing their games. Finally he said, "It doesn't matter anymore."

"Why not?"

"Because I'm not interested in surgery any longer."

"What do you mean?"

There was a long silence, then finally Mark said, "I'm ill."

"You're depressed, that's what it is. You need a psychiatrist."

"No, Peter, I don't need a psychiatrist. I've got leukemia."

"Leukemia?" Peter felt a chill. "What makes you think that?"

Mark told him about the lymph nodes in his neck and groin, the enlarged spleen and the blood slides he'd prepared. As the story unfolded Peter felt ill himself, but when he heard his friend had consulted no one else, he wouldn't accept the diagnosis.

"But what else could it be?"

"I don't know. But I do know that doctors always make mistakes when they treat themselves. You've got to see someone else. What about Willy Wood? He's the best there is."

Mark phoned Willy Wood's secretary next morning. She told him there was a long waiting list, but in five minutes she called back to say Dr Wood insisted on an appointment that same afternoon.

Wood did not seem to be in any hurry. He sat with his glasses halfway down his nose listening carefully to the story, and then asked some questions of his own. Next he carried out an examination, not just of the lymph nodes and the spleen, but a thorough scrutiny of the entire body. All the while Mark searched for clues as to what he thought, but like a good poker player he gave nothing away. Finally he got out his microscope and looked at the blood slides.

Mark sat in silence, waiting for the verdict.

"Wooding," he said at last. "I assume that from all of this you've come to a diagnosis of acute lymphatic leukemia?"

Mark's heart fell. "Yes."

"I can see why. Raised lymph nodes, enlarged spleen, abnormal lymphocytosis in the peripheral blood. It doesn't look very good, does it?"

"No."

Dr Wood sat for a minute studying him over the top of his glasses. He seemed to be wondering what to say.

"Wooding," he went on. "What I ought to do is publish your case in the Guy's Hospital Gazette, because it's a perfect example of how not to behave."

Mark could hardly believe his ears, he'd expected a little sympathy at least.

"You have been one of the best students we've had at Guy's but even you have fallen into the old trap of trying to diagnose yourself. You don't have leukemia at all. What you've got is a bad case of mononucleosis."

Mononucleosis? Glandular fever? He'd been much too ill for that.

"But what about the blood smears?"

"Tricky, I agree, but the abnormalities in the lymphocytes are not those of leukemia and I've sometimes seen them in severe mononucleosis."

"Are you sure?"

"We'll confirm it with a Paul Bunnell test and a bone marrow puncture, but I'm quite sure."

Mark felt a surge of relief. He was amazed how quickly he adjusted to this development, already he was interested in surgery again.

Willy Wood seemed to read his mind.

"Mark," he said, using his first name for the first time. "I know you've set your heart on becoming a surgeon, and so has Ellison, and you both want Dr Cudmore's house job. Well, I'm going to tell you something in confidence. I'm afraid Ellison is going to get it."

Mark caught his breath. Wood was bound to be right. At this time of year the consultant staff spent a lot of time discussing the students and picking the ones they wanted for housemen.

"A lot of people have been surprised by your poor performance lately. I know the reason now, but Dr Cudmore has made up his mind. However I thought you were a much better student than Ellison and I'd like to have you work for me. Who knows, you might decide to become a consultant physician instead. Anyway the jobs change again in six months, and if you were my house physician I could probably arrange for you to get the Cudmore job next January."

Another surge of relief.

"That's if you pass the exams, of course. You don't imagine you failed any of them?"

He wasn't sure. For a moment he wondered if Wood already knew, but that would be impossible.

"No, I don't think I failed, but I wasn't feeling well. I may not have got high marks."

"That doesn't matter. I know your work and I know you've been ill."

Mark was waiting by the notice board in the medical school hall with Peter and fifty other students. It was a solemn occasion, the culmination of five and a half years work. They stood in groups, some talking quietly, others fooling around and making nervous jokes. Paul Ellison stayed to one side with his friends, quietly aloof.

Dr Wood had told Mark to rest in bed for a couple of weeks, but he was already feeling better and the exam results were so important that he couldn't keep away. He'd told Peter about Willy Wood's offer and they were discussing it now.

"I'd really rather have the Cudmore job," said Mark.

"But Wood's houseman is just as important as Cudmore's," said Peter.

"But Ellison will seem to have won."

"Nonsense. You'll be Cudmore's houseman in six months time when the jobs change over. Willy Wood doesn't like Ellison, so he'll have to take a less important position. You're the one who'll come out on top."

"That's why I'm so excited," said Mark. "Have you decided what you're going to do yourself?"

"Well, I think I failed the surgery exam, so I'll probably have to remain a student for another six months and take it again in November. After that

I'll get a house job in a provincial hospital where there's less work and more play."

There was a hush as Mr Barnett, the medical school secretary, appeared at the end of the hall. He held some papers in his hand and everyone stood aside to let him reach the notice board.

"I've got the results of the medicine, surgery and obstetrics exams," he announced as he pinned the papers on the board. "The pathology results will be here in a few minutes."

Everyone surged forward, but he held up his hand for silence. "Remember, only students who have passed all four subjects can become housemen."

Mark felt a twinge of fear. There was such a crush of people that he found it difficult to see, but the surgery results were pinned higher than the others. The names were typed in two columns under the headings Passed and Failed. Towards the top of the Passed column he saw Ellison's name and further down was R. Whitfield, so Roy had passed as well. His heart beat faster, but finally he spotted his own name near the bottom. They were not in any particular order, so there was nothing wrong with that. Peter's name was in the Failed column which was a disappointment, but no more than he expected.

All about him people were either cheering or groaning. He craned his neck to read the medicine results, and again both he and Ellison had passed. He didn't expect Ellison to fail anything although he hoped he might. Peter had passed medicine, but Roy had not, so both his friends would have to continue as students for a while.

Eventually he reached the obstetrics list. That was the subject which worried him most because he'd been feeling particularly grim that day. He was getting quicker at finding the names by now, and in the Passed column he saw Ellison, Johnson, Whitfield and finally his own name. All that remained was pathology.

He heard Paul's voice behind him. "Well Wooding, three all and one to go. But we won't know who's the real winner until we see who gets the most important house job."

He had a patronizing smile on his face and Mark wondered if he already knew he was going to be Cudmore's houseman."

They probably all knew, thought Mark, but they couldn't know what Willy Wood had offered him. He was going to be the real winner as everyone would eventually see.

He smiled back. "You're right, we'll have to wait until the house jobs are announced. I guess a combination of Dr Wood's job and Dr Cudmore's, one after the other, would be the biggest prize of all."

Mr Barnett had gone back to his office, but now he returned with the fourth list. "Here are the results of the pathology section of the exam," he announced from the doorway.

This was the final hurdle. Everyone crowded towards him.

"Come on lads, let me through. No one's going to see the list until it's posted on the board. You've nearly all passed anyway."

He squeezed his way to the front and pinned up the paper. Mark heard a hiss as people drew their breath in surprise, but he was thinking of his arrangement with Willy Wood and he didn't look immediately. When he finally glanced up he saw that there were only five names under the heading Failed, so they all stood out conspicuously. A dreadful feeling gripped his stomach. One of them was M. Wooding.

"Well," grinned one of Ellison's friends. "We shan't have to wait till the house jobs are announced after all."

Mark saw Dr Wood professionally one week later. Physically he was feeling better. His swollen lymph nodes were going down, and the lab tests had confirmed the diagnosis of mononucleosis. He was depressed about the exam results, of course, but he still hoped Wood might come up with an alternative plan.

Dr Wood finished his examination and said, "Well, from a medical point of view you're doing fine, but what about your career?"

"I'm sorry, sir. I just don't know how it happened. I was feeling especially ill the day we wrote the pathology exam."

"I'm sorry too, but the fact is you failed and our arrangement cannot stand."

There was a pause. Mark hoped he might offer a job in six months time, after the repeat exam, but Wood went on, "I can't promise you anything in January either. Any number of promising young doctors may come along by then, and I'm afraid you've spoilt your record."

"I don't feel it was entirely my fault, sir."

"Getting sick wasn't your fault, but deciding to treat yourself certainly was. If you'd come to me earlier I might have got you better in time for the exams. At the very least I could have stopped you making a fool of yourself on Dr Cudmore's firm."

"What can I do now?"

Willy Wood finally gave a friendly smile. "It's a setback, but it's not the end of the world. If you really want to be a surgeon you'll get there in the end. Use your six extra months as a student to polish up your weak points, and I expect I'll be able to find you some sort of job at Guy's in January."

Chapter 26

Peter Johnson had never felt more nervous than when he started his first job. From the moment he stepped inside his new hospital he felt that everyone's eyes were on him.

He'd passed the exams in November with Mark and Roy. Mark had secured a house job at Guy's. It was not a very important job, but enough to keep his foot in the door.

Peter didn't want to become a specialist and nor did Roy, so they'd taken jobs at the Royal Sussex County Hospital in Brighton, where they thought they'd have a better time. Peter was house surgeon to Dr Radcliff, the chief of surgery, while Roy became house physician to a consultant named Dr Crawford.

They drove down to Brighton on the day before they were due to begin. The hospital stood on the side of a hill, about a mile from the middle of the town and a quarter of a mile from the sea. There was a big central building of grey stone which must have been impressive when it was new. Over the years the hospital had expanded and an assortment of buildings of various styles stretched along the road and up the hill. Peter parked the Bentley outside the Casualty Department, and they made their way past a row of ambulances to the administration office. After they'd filled out the forms to become members of the hospital staff, the administrator arranged for Dr Radcliff's departing houseman to show Peter around, while one of the house physicians did the same for Roy.

The departing houseman's name was Daphne Westlake and she had a superior air. "Your first job?" she asked Peter without a smile. "I hope you're a fast learner. I'm leaving tomorrow sharp at noon."

She decided to show him their living quarters first and they plunged into a maze of corridors behind the main block. It reminded Peter of a rabbit warren and he wondered how he'd ever learn his way around. Soon they emerged into a lane at the back, and a little higher up the hill he saw a large red-brick building.

"That's the nurses' home," Daphne announced.

"It's very big."

"The hospital is a nurses' training school so there are a lot of student nurses. And that's where the house staff live as well."

"The housemen live in the nurses' home?" He asked with a grin.

She looked at him icily. "We have the west wing. The doors between the two sections are locked, of course."

"Oh, of course."

She led him up an enclosed walkway to show him the doctors' accommodation. The rooms were bright and modern, and at one end there was a big lounge with a view of the sea. During the tour they met a few of the people he'd be working with and eventually they went to the doctors' lounge for coffee.

"How many doctors are on the house staff?" he asked.

"Well there are fifteen living here," she said. "And two or three married ones who live outside."

After a few minutes a thickset man in his early thirties came in.

"Good," she said. "Here's Gordon Bishop. He's the surgical registrar."

Bishop had curly brown hair and a ruddy complexion, as if he'd spent a lot of time in the sun.

Peter stood up. "Good afternoon, sir."

"No need to call me sir," he said with a smile. "Just plain Gordon will do. This isn't one of your big London teaching hospitals." Peter noticed a distinctive accent, South African perhaps.

"So you're taking over Vallance and Jowers?" Bishop went on as they shook hands.

"Vallance and Jowers?"

"Those are Dr Radcliff's wards," explained Daphne.

"You haven't shown him the wards yet? Let me have a coffee, then we'll all go down together."

Bishop helped himself to coffee and then asked Peter if it was his first job.

"Yes, it is."

"Nervous?"

"A bit. And I haven't even started yet."

"I remember my first job. It was in Bulawayo."

"Where's that?"

"Africa," he drawled. "You limeys would call it the bush."

They talked about the hospital for a few minutes and Peter took an immediate liking to his new registrar. When Bishop had finished his coffee he said, "Come on, Daph, let's get down to the wards and show this lad around."

Vallance and Jowers were male and female surgical wards next to each other in the west wing of the Main Block. Vallance had twenty-four beds and Jowers a few less. They were similar to the wards at Guy's except the ceilings weren't as high.

"You're responsible for the admission and discharge of the patients, and all their medical treatment," Daphne explained. "But the ward sisters run the wards, so there may be a bit of conflict."

"What are the sisters like?" he asked.

"Sister Yelland's in charge of Vallance. She's in her fifties and she's been doing the job for years. She'll probably try to mother you."

Peter felt intimidated by the prospect of pitting his untried knowledge against a fifty-year-old woman's lifetime experience. He was quite prepared to put up with a bit of mothering if it led to harmony.

"What about the sister who runs Jowers Ward?"

"Pat Hooper. She's younger, about thirty. She can be difficult too."

"Don't let Daphne scare you," Gordon put in. "Those sisters aren't nearly as bad as she thinks. They can actually be quite helpful."

Just then the hospital loudspeaker paged Dr Westlake, and Daphne took the phone. It was the houseman in the Casualty Department calling to say he had a girl with possible appendicitis who might need to be admitted.

"I'll come and take a look," said Daphne.

"We'll all go," said Bishop. "Peter, take a white coat from the office."

They made their way down the main staircase to the entrance hall and turned into Casualty. It was crowded with people. There were patients sitting on chairs, nurses, orderlies, and other patients on stretchers with worried relatives looking on. A couple of black-belted staff nurses were directing the activity and a sister in a blue uniform sat at a table writing notes.

Bishop led the way to a cubicle where a man lay on a stretcher, his lacerated arm stretched out on a stand. A houseman wearing a surgical mask and gloves was about to stitch it up.

"Hello, Gordon," he said. "The appendix is in bed twelve but I can't come with you just now."

"What's the story?"

"She's had abdominal pain for a few days and her family doctor thinks it's appendicitis."

"Her name?" asked Bishop.

"Julia Sparks. Sister's got the details."

They walked over to the desk where the sister handed Bishop the patient's notes. She called a junior nurse to accompany them to bed twelve.

"We've got only one empty bed on Jowers," said Daphne as they walked across the room. "This had better be a genuine emergency. Do you want to examine her, Gordon? Then you can decide if she really needs to be admitted."

"No, you do it. It's an opportunity for our new houseman to see you in action. After all, he'll have to do this himself tomorrow."

They made their way towards a row of cubicles closed off by curtains. There were patients everywhere.

"I don't suppose you've seen a place like this before," said Daphne with an air of superiority.

Casualty at Guy's was often just as chaotic, but Peter replied politely, "Well, it is pretty busy."

"And I don't suppose you've had to make decisions like this, either."

He was getting fed up with her condescending attitude so he said, "I expect I'll manage perfectly well."

She glared at him and Bishop smiled, but at that moment the overhead speaker announced a call for Dr Westlake.

"Well, in that case," she replied curtly, "perhaps you'd like to examine this patient while I answer the phone."

Peter laughed. "No, I don't think so. I don't officially start until tomorrow."

"That doesn't matter. I'm sure Gordon will supervise."

He felt a twinge of fear. He wanted to see his first patient on his own, with plenty of time to prepare.

"No, really. I think it would be much better if Dr Bishop did it."

But to his horror he heard Gordon say, "You've got to take the plunge sometime, Peter. Let's see what you can do."

The nurse was already pulling back the curtain, and inside the cubicle he glimpsed a girl of sixteen or seventeen on a stretcher with her mother sitting by her side. They both looked hostile.

"I'm really not quite ready to deal with a patient yet," he said to Gordon.

"Why not?" demanded the mother. "We've already waited an hour. All you have to do is admit my daughter to hospital."

Bishop cleared his throat. "I'm sorry we've kept you waiting, Mrs Sparks. Dr Johnson has to ask your daughter a few questions and examine her. We must be sure she really needs to be admitted."

"Of course she needs to be admitted, she has appendicitis. I don't see why this young man has to see her at all."

"It's hospital regulations," said Bishop reasonably. "Dr Johnson is the houseman."

"Well, please hurry up. I don't want to wait another hour just because Dr Johnson is not quite ready."

Peter was taken completely by surprise and his mind went blank. Everyone was staring at him but he couldn't think what to say.

"I'm Dr Johnson," he mumbled stupidly, trying to collect his thoughts.

"The pain . . . " he began, but the words dried up.

"The pain?" the girl repeated.

"Er . . . Where . . . ?"

"It's in my back."

There was a pause while he tried to pull himself together. Appendicitis didn't usually cause back pain. The curtains parted and Daphne returned from her phone call.

"When?"

"About a week ago."

He waited for her to continue but there was another long delay. He just couldn't think what to say. Sweat was running down his face. They must all be able to see it. Daphne was staring at him in amazement. She seemed about to intervene, but Bishop held up his hand.

"What about your periods?" Peter stammered.

"My periods?"

"Yes, you know, your monthly periods?"

"They're alright, I think."

"You're not pregnant?"

"Of course she's not pregnant," exploded Mrs Sparks. He could see she thought he was an idiot, and the girl gave him a peculiar look as well.

"I think my periods are alright," she said uncertainly. "It's just that. . . "

"Her periods have got nothing to do with it," Mrs Sparks interrupted. "Dr Block's already diagnosed appendicitis and he didn't have to ask a lot of personal questions. Just admit her to the hospital so a proper doctor can see her."

Peter thought he'd have to admit her anyway, but the regulations demanded an examination first.

"I'm sorry, Mrs Sparks," he said. "But I'll have to look at your daughter before I can admit her."

"Look at her?"

"You know, examine her. Feel her tummy and that sort of thing."

The girl started to blush. "You don't mean . . . ?"

He guessed what she was thinking. He was embarrassed too, but it was part of a proper examination.

"An internal," he stammered. "Yes, I'll have to do that."

He moved closer to the bed and started to pull down the sheet, but she grabbed it with both hands. "Not here. Not with everybody watching."

His face went red. "I'm just going to examine you on the outside first," he said.

Mrs Sparks looked desperately at Gordon and Daphne, and out of the corner of his eye Peter saw Bishop take a step forward. The game was up. He'd never be able to work here now.

But in the back of his mind he did know what to do. He simply had to go through the medical history in the systematic manner he'd been taught. Finally he remembered how to begin, but at that moment Gordon Bishop held up his hand to intervene.

Just then the curtains parted and a nurse came in.

"Mrs Sparks," she said. "Would you please come over to Sister's desk, she wants to ask you some questions."

"Just a moment, Nurse," said Bishop. "I have something to say to Mrs Sparks myself."

It was now or never.

"Julia," Peter interrupted. "Would you like to tell me in your own words just how your illness began?"

Bishop looked at him in surprise.

"When did you first feel unwell?" His confidence was beginning to return.

Bishop turned to Mrs Sparks, "Perhaps you'd better see the sister after all. I'll have a word with you later."

"I was alright until two weeks ago," said the girl. She paused while her mother left the cubicle.

"What happened then?" Peter prompted.

"Well, it started with a burning sensation when I went to pee."

"Have you ever had that before?"

"Sometimes. But it always got better on its own."

"And this time?"

"It did get a little better, but then the pain started in my back."

"Did you tell Dr Block?"

"I told him about the backache."

"What about the other?"

She looked embarrassed. "No."

Peter knew he was on to something. "Why not?"

She looked round to make sure her mother really had gone. "Because it usually happens after I've been with my boyfriend. I can't tell the doctor that, he might tell Mummy."

"I see."

"Doctor," she went on anxiously. "Do you really think I'm pregnant?"

"I don't know yet." He felt better now. "You'll have to tell me more about it."

She told him the rest of her story and then he examined her abdomen and back. Finally he said, "Julia, one of us will have to examine you internally, you know. Are you prepared for that?"

She nodded solemnly. There was no blushing this time.

He turned to Bishop, "Do you want to do it?"

"No, you go ahead."

When he'd finished and washed his hands, the girl asked, "Doctor, am I going to have a baby?"

"No, Julia, you're not."

"Oh, thank God for that. Do you know what's wrong with me?"

"I think so. But I want to talk with Dr Bishop and Dr Westlake, and we may have to do some tests."

"You won't tell Mum. I mean about my boyfriend."

"No, we won't tell her."

Bishop led the way to a small consulting room. "Well?" he asked, when he'd closed the door.

"I don't think it's appendicitis at all," said Peter. "I think she's got pyelitis. She obviously gets cystitis after intercourse, which is common enough, but it's never been treated and now it's spread to her kidneys."

"How would you confirm that diagnosis?"

"A urine test."

"And if that's positive, would you admit her to hospital?"

"Not onto a surgical ward. You could put her on one of the medical wards, but I expect she could be treated at home."

At last Gordon Bishop smiled. "Welcome aboard."

It was 6pm when Peter met Roy down by the Bentley. He had toured the hospital, visited the operating theatres, been introduced to the doctors, met the nurses and seen all the patients who'd be his tomorrow.

His friend looked worried.

"What's bothering you?"

"I screwed up a bit, that's all," said Roy.

"Screwed up a bit?"

"I had to go on a ward round with several doctors, the ward sister and a bunch of nurses."

Peter could imagine it. He thought of his own experience in Casualty. "Did they make you examine any patients?"

"No, but they kept asking what drugs I would use."

"Well?"

"Have you ever heard of Aludrops?"

"You mean Aludrox, dummy. It's a liquid antacid. You give it by mouth for treating stomach ulcers."

"Oh my God," said Roy. "I thought it was eye drops. No wonder they all laughed."

Peter laughed himself. He felt much better.

"Did they ask you about the dose?"

"I said you put two drops in each eye four times a day."

"What? To treat stomach ulcers?" Peter tried to keep a straight face. "Now I see what's bothering you."

"Even the student nurses were laughing. I'll bet it's all over the hospital by now. Let's go for a drink."

"Where shall we go?"

"The registrar told me they usually drink at the Bristol," said Roy. "It's just down the hill from the main entrance."

"He told you where to go drinking? You couldn't have been that bad."

"He probably thought it's all I'm fit for."

They walked the short distance down to the Bristol Bar. Peter ordered a couple of pints of Worthington, and they sat at a table near the window overlooking the sea.

After a while Roy grinned sheepishly. "I expect they're used to new housemen making fools of themselves."

"Well, they didn't throw us out, did they?"

Then he went on, "You know, this place is a training school for young nurses, it's near the beach, there's a pub just down the road, and the housemen live in the nurses' home."

"And we're stuck here for a whole damn year," added Peter.

They both began to laugh.

One evening in May an incident occurred that changed Peter's life. It started with a call to Casualty to see a woman with abdominal pain. As he walked down the stairs he recalled his first day at the hospital and the girl he'd seen then. Things were different now. After five months as a house surgeon he knew exactly what to do. He'd even learned to carry out straightforward operations, although usually he had Gordon Bishop to assist.

The sister smiled when he walked into the Casualty Department. Everyone was friendly now; he'd become a part of the team. "Your patient is in bed four," she said. "Her name is Violet Smith."

He found Mrs Smith with her husband and two small children. The husband looked worried and the children clung to their mother's side. He was used to situations like this and he did his best to put them at ease. First he listened to Mrs Smith's story, then he examined her abdomen.

"It's your appendix," he said at last. "I'm afraid you need an operation."

"Will she be alright, Doctor?" asked the husband. "We couldn't bear to lose her."

"Stop worrying," said his wife. "Now come here and I'll tell you all what to do while I'm away." And as Peter left he saw them huddle together while she gave her instructions.

But when he looked for a surgeon Peter found that Bishop was off duty and Dr Haley, the registrar at Brighton General Hospital, was tied up with emergencies all evening. In the end he phoned Dr Radcliff.

"I've got an appendix here, sir. Bishop's off duty and Haley's busy at the General."

"I'm afraid I'm busy too. Can you handle it on your own? You've done several appendices with Bishop helping."

Peter felt a surge of excitement. He'd have the whole operating theatre at his command.

"Don't worry, sir. I can do it," he replied.

"Call me if you have any problems."

Next he called the theatre sister to set up for the operation. Sister Spalding had worked in hospitals for many years and she did not approve of housemen doing surgery. Her tone was cold.

"Are you sure Dr Radcliff gave permission?"

"He actually asked me to do it."

"Very well."

But when he tried to arrange for an anesthetist he found the registrar was away and a trainee anesthetic houseman named Steve Hendricks was on call. He didn't have much confidence in Hendricks but there wasn't any choice.

An hour later he entered the operating suite. There was a wide central corridor with theatres on the left and changing rooms on the right.

Hendricks was already there, dressed in green overalls, preparing the anesthetic machine.

Peter went into the changing room and when he emerged the porters had arrived with Mrs Smith. He walked over to reassure her before Hendricks injected pentothal into her i.v. tube to send her to sleep. Then he watched anxiously as Hendricks tried to slide a curved rubber endotracheal tube through her mouth and larynx to carry the anesthetic gas and oxygen to her lungs.

Peter had a staff nurse and a student as surgical assistants. When they were gowned and gloved they swabbed the patient's abdomen with antiseptic and covered it with drapes. He chose a spot low down on the right side, stretched the skin between his fingers, and made his incision. That was when he got his first surprise, the blood looked unusually dark.

"Steve, are you sure she's getting enough oxygen?" he asked.

"Forty percent," said Hendricks. "That should be plenty."

It was not too late to stop. He could put the operation on hold and call Dr Radcliff.

"You're sure she's alright?"

"Relax," said Hendricks. "Everything is fine. Just get on with the surgery."

He divided the tissues of the abdominal wall, but then he encountered another problem: the abdominal muscles were so tight he couldn't get his fingers inside to find the appendix.

"Steve," he said eventually. "You'll have to get her more relaxed."

"Can't you make a bigger incision?"

"It's not the incision. Her muscles are too tight. "Why don't you try some curare?"

"I don't want to use muscle relaxants. It's safer if the patient breaths on her own."

Peter enlarged the incision but it made no difference, the abdominal muscles were too tight. Curare would relax them but it would also stop the patient breathing. Hendricks would have to pump the gas into the patient's lungs by squeezing the anesthetic bag which was a more complicated procedure.

After five frustrating minutes Peter felt sure there was something wrong with the anesthetic. "Perhaps you should call Dr Grant," he said.

Hendricks made some adjustments to the anesthetic machine. Then he said, "I don't think I'll call Dr Grant just yet. I'll do what you say and try some curare."

"Are you sure you should?"

"You suggested it yourself," he said, breaking the top off a small glass vial and sucking the liquid into a syringe. "I wish you'd make up your mind."

"Well, why don't you start with half a dose," said Peter. "That couldn't do much harm."

"If that's what you want."

He injected the curare into the i.v. tube. Nothing happened for a couple of minutes, then to Peter's relief the abdominal muscles relaxed and he was able to find the appendix. For a few minutes he concentrated on what he was doing, but then the staff nurse whispered, "Peter, the patient's awfully dark."

Peter looked up and got a shock; her face and lips had turned purple. She must be critically short of oxygen. Monitoring the patient's condition was the anesthetist's job.

"Steve, what the hell's going on," he said.

Sweat was running down Hendricks' face. He was pumping the anesthetic bag as hard as he could but the oxygen wasn't going into the patient's lungs.

"It's that half dose of curare. It stopped her breathing, but it didn't relax her lungs enough for me to pump the gas. Giving half a dose was a silly idea, I'd better give the other half."

He drew the rest of the curare into the syringe, injected it rapidly into the i.v. tube, and then he went back to pumping.

"Why don't you finish the operation?" he said.

But now there was another problem. The patient was relaxed enough, but her bowels began to bulge out of the incision as if they were being pushed from inside. Peter had never seen anything like it. Suddenly he was gripped with fear.

"Steve, there is something wrong."

He turned towards Hendricks and got another shock. Mrs Smith's body was covered by drapes, but her head was exposed and now her lips were almost black. His pulse raced.

"My God. Turn up the oxygen."

"I'm already using 100 percent."

Hendricks was squeezing the bag desperately now, trying to force oxygen into the patient's lungs, but it wasn't doing any good. Peter felt sure she was going to die. He had no idea what was wrong but every second she looked worse. It was too late to call Grant. His heart was pounding so hard he could hardly think.

"Nurse, cover the wound with a drape," he said. "Then get Sister Spalding in here. I'm stopping the operation."

He pulled off his gloves and ran round to the head of the table. The first thing he checked was the oxygen but it was turned fully on.

He looked at Steve. "Maybe it's this anesthetic machine."

"No," said Sister Spalding, who'd just come into the room. "They've been using that machine all day. It's perfectly alright."

Hendricks pulled down his mask. His face was white. He was still pumping the useless anesthetic bag but the patient was dying and he seemed to have no idea what to do.

Peter did have an idea in the back of his mind, but if it failed he'd be held responsible for the death.

"How about disconnecting the machine altogether?" he suggested.

"Don't be silly," said Hendricks. "If we take away the oxygen she'll die for sure."

"And there's nothing wrong with the machine," repeated the sister.

"Look," said Peter, "I don't know what's wrong, but she's surrounded by fresh air and if we can just get it into her lungs she should be alright. Unplug the machine."

Hendricks glared at him. "You heard what Sister said, there's nothing wrong with it. Unplugging the machine would be like murder. I won't do it."

An image of the little family flashed through Peter's mind. "Then I'll do it," he said. "I'll take full responsibility."

He heard Sister Spalding draw her breath and the nurses stared at him in surprise. He had no authority over the anesthetist in something like this and for a moment he thought they were going to stop him.

Then Hendricks said, "Alright, do what you want. But it'll be your fault if she dies."

With shaking hands he disconnected the machine. Now the patient lay motionless on her back with the endotracheal tube sticking out of her mouth. Instinctively he felt her pulse. It was still just there, but if she didn't breathe soon she'd be dead.

He remembered the little girl on the boat whose life he'd saved by forcing his own breath into her lungs, and now he confidently put his lips to the tube. But this time it didn't work. Hardly any air would go in. He couldn't believe it. He removed his mouth, took another breath and tried again, but it was just the same. When he'd done this to the little girl her lungs had inflated easily.

He was beaten. She was going to die and they'd all blame him. Already they were staring at him accusingly.

"The pulse has almost gone," said the staff nurse.

Desperately he tried again but still it didn't work. The girl's lungs had taken much more air than this. But there'd been no tube in her throat.

He straightened up and started to take out the endotracheal tube.

"What are you doing now?" demanded Hendricks.

He didn't answer. When he'd removed the tube the patient lay completely motionless as if she were dead. He felt a wave of despair.

"Airway," he called.

The staff nurse put one in his hand and he slipped the short rubber airway into the patient's mouth. Still there was no movement. He drew a breath and placed his lips on hers. The smell of ether was nauseating. He pinched her nose with one hand and used the other to hold up her chin. For a moment he hesitated; if this didn't work there'd be no second chance.

Then he exhaled and immediately he knew he'd got it right. The air went in easily. He removed his lips and it whistled out again, pungent with ether. Again and again he forced air into her lungs. Her chest rose and fell but there was still no sign of life. No one said a word. Perhaps he was working on a corpse.

Then he heard the door burst open and Gordon Bishop's voice talking rapidly to Sister Spalding. He tried to hear what they were saying but he was dizzy from the ether and he could only catch an occasional word: incompetent, negligent, death. He couldn't see much as he bent over the patient and at that point he almost gave up.

But a few moments later the staff nurse said, "I think I can feel the pulse."

"Well, that's something," said Bishop, taking charge. "Peter, keep that going for another minute while I get organized." Then, politely but firmly, "Sister, we'll have a different anesthetic machine no matter what you say." And then, "Steve, get me the laryngoscope and another endotracheal tube."

Bishop inspired confidence. Soon Mrs Smith was connected to another anesthetic machine with oxygen flowing into her lungs. Peter was surprised how quickly she returned to normal and he felt an enormous sense of relief.

"Well lads," Bishop said to Peter and Steve. "Let's get that appendix out before the bosses arrive."

"The bosses?"

"Dr Grant and Dr Radcliff are on their way. Sister Spalding's put the fear of God into them. You've had a very close call. Sister thinks you shouldn't have been operating on your own, and she's perfectly right."

"Dr Grant told me to go ahead," said Steve defensively.

"Yes, I know Radcliff and Grant gave you the nod, and we'll talk about that later. But you're supposed to be responsible doctors. If you're asked to do something that's beyond your ability, it's up to you to say no."

He re-intubated the patient himself. Then he handed the anesthetic over to Steve and helped Peter remove the appendix. The operation went smoothly and at the end Violet Smith seemed none the worse for what had happened.

When they'd finished he told Peter to meet him at the Bristol Bar in half an hour.

Peter expected a ticking off, although the pub didn't seem an appropriate place for that. When he arrived Gordon Bishop was already sipping a pint of beer.

"I'll just have a half," he said. "I'm still on call."

Bishop paid for the drinks and said, "Now, start at the beginning and tell me exactly what happened."

Peter described everything that had taken place. When he finished, Bishop asked, "Do you know what was wrong?"

"Well I didn't know at the time, but now I wonder if the endotracheal tube was in the wrong place. Perhaps Steve accidentally put it into the esophagus instead of the trachea. Then the oxygen would have gone into the patient's stomach instead of her lungs."

"I hoped you'd figure it out. That's exactly what was wrong."

"How can you be so sure?"

"Because I've seen it happen before, in a hospital in Africa. The anesthetic Steve was giving was going into the patient's stomach. When the stomach was full it came back into her mouth, and from there she breathed it in. That's what kept her alive at first, but when he injected the curare it stopped her breathing. Then everything went wrong."

"It's a good job you arrived," said Peter.

"Not at all. You saved her life, not me. That's what I want to talk to you about. But if you hadn't guessed the tube was in the wrong place, what made you take it out?"

"There was nothing to lose. She was dying anyway. And I thought, she's dying from lack of oxygen but we're surrounded by air. All we had to do was get the air into her lungs."

"That's what I like about you, Peter, you're full of common sense. That's why I've decided to talk to you now."

He was silent for a minute, then he asked, "Have you thought about what you're going to do when you finish your year as a houseman?"

Peter wondered what was coming. "I haven't done my national military service yet," he said. "I'll have to go into the army."

"That'll mean a couple of years working in a military VD clinic, or examining new recruits. It would be a terrible waste of someone like you."

"I don't have any choice."

"Yes you do. We need doctors like you in Africa. I've been watching you, Peter. You don't spend much time reading books, but you're practical and you're good with your hands. There was nothing wrong with what you were doing tonight. It was the anesthetic that was wrong, and when the chips were down you even dealt with that. You're just what we want."

Peter felt flattered and the thought of working in an exotic place appealed, but he was supposed to go in the army.

"What about my national service?"

"Oh, to hell with that, there are plenty of ways to get around it."

They each had another beer, and then they talked about Africa until the bar closed and they had to leave.

Gordon Bishop was a good talker and he painted an exciting picture. For years he'd worked as a government medical officer in Rhodesia and Nyasaland, and he'd travelled all over South, Central and East Africa. He talked of dark forests, snow-capped mountains and plains teeming with animals. He described the health service, the small rural hospitals and the tremendous challenge that medicine in Africa provided. Every day seemed to bring an opportunity to save lives and treat disease on a scale which couldn't be imagined in England.

"I'm not suggesting you go there for the rest of your life," he said. "But I can't describe the satisfaction that two or three years would bring to someone like you."

They left the Bristol and walked back up the hill. Peter went to Jowers Ward to see that Violet Smith was alright, and then he made his way up to the residents' quarters. There were people in the lounge and he heard the clink of glasses. For a moment he considered joining them, but he had a lot on his mind so he ran himself a bath instead. He liked to spend time in the bathtub thinking, and he lay there for three quarters of an hour, topping up the hot water from time to time.

He hadn't given much consideration to what would happen at the end of the year. All his life the major decisions had been made for him. This was the first time he'd had a real choice. He could stay in England and join the army, or go to Africa, or anywhere else in the world. For the first time he was free.

Jenny White had gone to Africa. But she was in South Africa, a civilized country so far as he knew. The places Gordon had described were wild, untamed, full of challenge and excitement. That was what he wanted to see.

He thought about Jenny for a while. He didn't love her anymore, but he didn't love anyone else and he wondered if he ever would. That was another thing about Africa, he might bump into Jenny. The chances were remote of course, and it really didn't matter after all these years, but it was curiously appealing just the same.

By the time the bathtub had gone cold for the third time he'd made up his mind.

Chapter 27

It was the summer of 1959 and Mark Wooding was at the Royal Sussex County Hospital where he was starting his first appointment as a surgical registrar. He'd been lucky to get a registrar's job so soon. Fortunately Dr Wood had given him a good reference from Guy's, and Peter and Roy had been popular at the Royal Sussex County, so when Gordon Bishop returned to Africa he'd been given the position.

"Sister Spalding, this is Dr Wooding, our new surgical registrar," said Dr Radcliff as he introduced Mark to the surgical staff.

The sister looked about forty, Mark thought, with a stern face and an air of authority. "How do you do, Doctor," she said rather formally.

He looked her firmly in the eye as he shook her hand. "Mark Wooding," he replied with just a hint of a smile. He hoped his serious expression would establish his position, and he used his first name to show he wasn't too aloof. The relationship between the surgical registrar and the senior theatre sister could be a struggle for power.

Sister Spalding introduced her nurses as they walked round the theatre suite. He felt self-conscious as they looked him up and down. Oddly, the attention he felt most came from the most junior person there, a young student nurse whom the sister hadn't bothered to introduce. She had dark hair and dusky eyes which reminded him of Helen Metcalf.

It was the same when Radcliff took him round the wards. Everywhere he sensed the scrutiny of the staff nurses and sisters and their desire to establish their positions. He felt something else as well. He was an unmarried surgical registrar and he could tell that some of them were eyeing him in quite a different way.

Each day he did ward rounds with the sisters and housemen until he knew every detail of the patients and the staff. He assisted the senior surgeons with the complicated operations and did most of the easier ones himself. Another part of his job was supervising the housemen. He had to know their strengths and weaknesses, so he tried to do some surgery with each one of them in turn.

One of the people who seemed to pay him special attention was Pat Hooper, the sister on Jowers Ward. She was an attractive woman and in a way she reminded him of Beverley. But the person who really caught his eye was the student nurse he'd seen that first day in the operating theatre. She had an innocent childlike face with an upturned nose, and she looked at him in a way that seemed to offer an invitation. Her name was Shirley Fuller but she was too junior for him to ask her out.

Roy had left the hospital the previous fall when his year as a houseman was up, but Peter was still there, working in Casualty to gain experience before he went to Africa. After a year and a half he knew just about everyone in the hospital, so Mark found him an enormous help.

One evening they walked down to the Bristol Bar for a drink. There were several other doctors and nurses there, and among them Mark spotted Shirley Fuller. Before long she came up to him to chat and by the time the pub closed he wondered if she was as innocent as she looked.

"Do you think she's too young?" he asked Peter when they were on their own.

"Well, Sister Spalding might object if you have an affair with one of her student nurses. Pat Hooper would be disappointed too."

"I think she's stunning."

"Me too," said Peter. "The consultants call her Midnight."

"Why do they do that?"

"Black underwear. She wears little black panties and a bra. Sometimes you can see them through her theatre clothes."

Mark's first problem with Shirley came a couple of weeks later.

It was a warm evening and Peter suggested a drive in the country and dinner at a pub. "There's a nurse in Casualty I'd like to take out," he said. "Why don't you ask Shirley?"

"I thought you said it would upset Sister Spalding."

"Just don't start a scandal, that's all. We can all go in my Bentley, it's a perfect evening for an open car."

They drove out to the Plough Inn in the quaint little village of Rottingdean, a few miles along the coast. There were old-fashioned cottages, a thirteenth-century church, and a pretty village green. They had a nice dinner and the more they had to drink the more fascinated Mark became with Shirley. She looked as innocent as a little girl, but her personality was more complex. One minute she'd be soft and submissive like Helen, and the next she'd want to take charge.

It was hot in the pub and he suggested a stroll. They walked hand in hand across the village green in the moonlight, and when they reached the duck pond they stood silently in the shadow of a tree. She wasn't very tall and when they kissed she had to stand on her toes.

Holding her felt wonderful. During the eighteen months he'd been on the house staff at Guy's he'd been with no one but Beverley, and since his arrival in Brighton there had been no time for anyone at all.

It was almost closing time when they returned to the bar and the others were ready to leave. They climbed into the car and she snuggled up to him during the drive. They got back at 11:15, a quarter of an hour before the nurses' home door would be locked.

"How about having the girls up to the lounge for a nightcap?" Peter suggested.

"I'm afraid there isn't time," he said. "The nurses' home will be locked in fifteen minutes."

"Nonsense," said Peter with a laugh. "They lock the main door, but I've got a key to the side door from the doctors' wing."

Shirley looked at him expectantly but he felt a twinge of fear. He couldn't risk a failure, it might be whispered all over the hospital in no time at all.

"No," he said, as casually as he could. "I've got a hard day tomorrow and I want to get some sleep."

He accompanied her up the passage to the nurses' home and kissed her outside the door.

"You're a funny man," she said before she went in.

He knew she meant peculiar, and she was perfectly right.

Mark spent part of every day in the operating theatres. Every day he saw Shirley at one time or another and word spread that a romance was brewing between the registrar and the pretty young nurse the consultants called Midnight. Being in the hospital limelight didn't help him overcome his problem and he avoided taking her to his room.

Peter was due to leave the hospital at the end of the summer and the house staff planned a party to send him off. The lounge in the doctors' wing of the nurses' home made an ideal location. They didn't plan anything formal, but they invited the more important senior doctors and some of the nurses as well.

Mark did not like the idea at all. He'd have to ask Shirley, but he didn't want Dr Radcliff to see his registrar with a first year student nurse from the operating theatre. He tried to dissuade her from coming. "Hospital parties are a bore," he said. "I've got to be there to talk to Dr Radcliff, but you don't have to come."

"You don't want me."

"Look, some of the senior surgeons will be there and I'll have to talk to them. Perhaps I can do it better on my own."

"Are you ashamed of me?"

He was trying to think of a better excuse when her temper flared.

"Well, it's Peter's party and he's invited me, so I'll be there whether you like it or not."

She arrived looking lovely in an emerald green blouse and a full black skirt, and she was soon the centre of attention of a small group of admirers. Mark was talking with the senior doctors, but when he glanced in her direction he noticed that one of her admirers was a junior houseman who'd arrived only the previous week.

The senior staff slipped away a few at a time. After an hour someone turned down the lights and people began to dance. Eventually Mark looked around for Shirley, but she was flirting with the new houseman. He tried to attract her attention but she ignored him. He was left standing awkwardly by the bar watching her, feeling embarrassed and out of place.

Peter came up to him and said, "You'd better do something."

"What do you mean?"

"Dance with her, you idiot. You're a registrar now. You can't afford to let a junior houseman make a fool of you with everyone watching."

But she seemed determined to make a fool of him. She'd dance with him for a while, but just when everything seemed alright she'd go back to the junior houseman, and Mark would be left on his own.

When he tried to speak to her about it she replied, "Nonsense. I can dance with whom I please."

Finally he managed to corner her. He asked her to come to his room to talk and to his surprise she agreed. As they walked in silence down the corridor he wondered how to begin. They went into his room and he closed the door.

"I'm sorry, Mark," she said before he could open his mouth. "I've behaved very badly."

He felt a surge of relief. They were going to make it up.

"Well, I didn't behave very well either," he said. "But if I'm going to make a career as a surgeon I do have to talk to the consultant staff."

He sat down on the edge of the bed expecting her to sit down too, but she remained standing, facing him, with her hands clasped demurely in front. She looked like a naughty schoolgirl waiting for a scolding.

She smiled very slightly and said, "I know that."

He thought she was going to say more, so he waited.

"I . . . , I deserve a good spanking," she went on.

He was so relieved they were joking about what had happened that he laughed and said, "Well, just a small spanking perhaps."

She gave a little smile and pulled up her skirt. Then she climbed onto the bed, and before he could do anything she was lying face down across his lap.

"Give me six of the best," she whispered. "That's what I need."

Her skirt was up around her waist. She wore no stockings and her bottom was bare apart from black lace panties which were tight and very brief. Mark wasn't sure what to do so he gave her a gentle smack with his open hand.

She giggled and said, "You'll have to do it harder than that if you want to make me behave."

He smacked her again, quite hard this time, and she wriggled about on his lap.

He waited.

"Go on," she whispered.

He slapped her again.

Of course he knew what was happening. He could hardly believe it, but he knew what it was. She was breathing faster now, panting with excitement. She squirmed about like a worm and he started to feel excited himself. He felt guilty but he didn't want to stop. She had a slim waist, but her buttocks were full and firm, and her panties covered only a narrow strip down the middle. He noticed the cheeks were pink where the three smacks had landed.

"You ought to make me take my pants off," she said, climbing off his lap.

"Perhaps I'll remove mine too," he suggested shakily.

"If you wish."

She got up and slowly pulled down her panties. Her buttocks were pink. He knew it was wrong but he was much too excited to care. He slipped off his trousers and underwear and sat on the edge of the bed, aware that the sign of his own feelings was easy to see. She looked at it but said nothing. Then she climbed across his lap with her skirt pulled up and he felt her naked skin against his own as she squirmed about.

"Now," she said. "Give me six hard spanks on the bare bottom and I'll never be bad again."

He hesitated.

"Go on," she panted.

He gave her bottom a single smack with his open hand. She gasped and her muscles tightened. He was throbbing with excitement, but he thought he might have hurt her so he waited to see what she'd do.

"Go on," she said again. "Go on, you mustn't stop."

So he spanked her bottom hard five more times, with a pause between each stroke. She twisted and squirmed and let out little gasps, but she didn't tell him to stop.

When he'd finished she lay panting for a minute, and then she whispered, "You can have me now."

She climbed off his lap and laid on her back with her skirt pulled above her waist. He was on her in a flash. The speed and intensity of her passion surprised him. Beverley had always been rather slow, but Shirley was quite the reverse.

Mark's relationship with Shirley progressed normally. During the next few weeks she became a frequent passenger in the red MG as they explored the Sussex countryside.

For six weeks he never mentioned what had happened on the night of the party. Then one evening they went to his room after drinking at the Bristol. She seemed strangely quiet, lost in a world of her own. He expected they'd soon be making love, but suddenly she demanded, "Spank me. Spank me until I cry."

He hesitated but she insisted, "Spank me. Now. Don't stop until I cry."

So he sat on the edge of the bed and put her across his knees, and afterwards she gave herself to him with the utmost passion.

Later he lay awake wondering what private fantasy had engulfed her and what his role had been. He felt puzzled and guilty at his own reaction, because he'd enjoyed it too. He remembered the bible picture when he was a child, and he could see the Egyptian woman with her arm above her head. The very next day he had the afternoon off and he took Shirley for a drive. They were sitting on the beach at Burling Gap throwing pebbles into the sea when he brought the subject up. It had happened twice and embarrassing or not he was curious to hear what she had to say.

Her explanation was simple and she didn't seem ashamed. "Yes, sometimes I do find it sexy," she said. "My father used to spank me when I was a girl. I loved my dad and I liked it when he spanked me. Sometimes I was naughty on purpose just to make him do it."

Was it really as simple as that? The power of fathers over daughters and mothers over sons?

Chapter 28

Peter Johnson sailed for Africa in the fall of 1959 on the *Pretoria Castle*. He had taken a job as a government medical officer in Rhodesia. For the first ten days it was warm and calm and he enjoyed making new friends, but as they travelled south the weather got cooler and his mood began to change.

Late one evening he stood alone on the passenger deck staring out across the sea. The ship was ploughing into big swells that rolled in from the Southern Ocean. The voyage was coming to an end and soon the new friends he'd made on board would be gone. He was feeling lonely and his thoughts drifted to Jennifer White.

She'd described these same long swells sweeping up from the south. He recalled her letters so clearly he could remember the actual words. Perhaps she'd stood at this very spot, thinking of him. Did she ever think of him now? He'd had no contact with the Whites for years, but now he wished he'd called Jo to find out where Jennifer was. He still had the little blue and silver ring in a box where he kept odds and ends.

Her cabin number was T 36. He'd sent so many letters he'd never forget that number. As he walked back along the deck he thought he'd like to see the place where she'd lived and slept, and perhaps dreamed about him. There was a diagram of the cabin layout in the tourist class lobby and he found T 36 easily enough. The mahogany door was closed of course, but he waited outside picturing her in his mind. Perhaps there was still something of hers inside, hidden in the back of a drawer. Perhaps the cabin was empty and he could lie on the bed where she'd slept. He put his hand on the doorknob and waited, imagining he could feel her touch. Eventually he plucked up enough courage to turn the knob, but the door was solidly locked.

The first thing that struck Peter about Cape Town was the natural beauty of the place. Jenny had described the fair city at the foot of Table Mountain, but she hadn't mentioned the colours. The flat-topped mountain was a mixture of greens and browns and subtle greys, with white clouds across its crown and white buildings at its foot. The sea and sky were azure blue, and everywhere there were flowers.

The next thing that struck him was the number of Africans. He hadn't thought about it before, but now he realized there had been none on the ship. The waiters and porters and cleaners had all been white, and so had all the passengers. This was South African policy, but it came as a bit of a shock.

An official from the Rhodesian Ministry of Health met him on the dock with his railway ticket and instructions for the journey into the interior.

"You're being sent up north," he said. "There's a malaria epidemic and you're to go straight to a place called Ndola."

"How far is that?"

The man smiled. "Four days on the train."

For the first day the train ran through pretty countryside, with hills and even some low mountains. It looked quite like England, or France perhaps, with farms, vineyards and woods. Everything was pleasantly green. But then they climbed to the central plateau of Africa where the track ran across hundreds of miles of veld. For two days he saw nothing but dry undulating grassland and small stunted trees. The heat and dust were terrible. The only things to break the monotony were a couple of rivers with lush green banks, and a few small dusty towns.

After Mafeking the train left South Africa and ran on north through the vast waterless plains of Botswana. Peter began to wonder what he'd let himself in for, but when they reached Southern Rhodesia the country became greener and more attractive. The rainy season was early that year, and soon after they'd passed the Victoria Falls they ran through their first tropical rainstorm.

He got off the train at Ndola in Northern Rhodesia and looked up and down the platform. He had travelled a quarter of the way up Africa and by this time he was used to the assortment of people who met the train. There were Africans of all types, from ragged barefoot boys to women in colourful robes. There was a wide variety of white people too: farmers with wide-brimmed hats, army officers in uniform, and government officials in white shorts which reached down to their knees. On the Ndola station he saw an Englishman. Peter recognized him immediately by his neatly cut sports jacket and grey flannel trousers. The recognition seemed to be mutual because he came forward with his hand outstretched.

"Peter Johnson?" he asked. "I'm Jim Dawson. Glad you're here."

Dr Dawson was head of the Ndola Hospital. He looked about thirty-five, short, with dark wavy hair and a serious expression on his face. After a brief inquiry about the journey and an invitation to dinner that evening, he got straight down to business.

"I'm very pleased to see you. We're in the middle of a malaria epidemic."

"I don't know how much use I'll be," said Peter. "I've never actually seen a case."

"Don't worry, you'll soon learn."

"I didn't know malaria came in epidemics. I thought it was endemic, always around."

"It is a bit unusual, but that's what it seems to be. Now, let me drive you to where you're staying. I'll show you the town on the way."

Ndola had a white population of only ten thousand so Peter was surprised to see wide paved streets with big modern buildings and well stocked stores. The residential areas were attractive too. There were neat new bungalows surrounded by lawns and flowering shrubs. It looked much more prosperous than the small South African towns he'd seen from the railway.

"This part of Africa is called the Copperbelt," explained Dawson. "Rhodesia is the world's second largest copper producer, and it all comes from here."

"There don't seem to be many Africans."

"There are sixty thousand of them actually, but they live in a separate township outside the city."

They pulled up in front of a modern two-storey building.

"Londonderry House," said Dawson. "It's a hostel for government employees. I've booked you in here until you can find a place of your own."

A native houseboy took Peter's bags and showed him to a large airy bed-sitting room with a veranda along the back. Soon he was relaxing in the shower, his first for nearly a week. Then he unpacked, slipped on an open-necked shirt and a pair of slacks, and waited for Dawson to pick him up at 6:30.

There was another couple at dinner, Alan and Susan Melfort, Rhodesians not much older than himself. Their clipped accents reminded him of Gordon Bishop. Alan was a government doctor. He'd been in Ndola for three years and Jim Dawson had been there six, so they spent most of the evening discussing the health service and the job Peter was about to begin.

"How can the three of us look after sixty thousand Africans?" he asked when the houseboy had cleared away the dishes.

"We can't," said Jim. "Not in the way you'd treat patients in England. Our main job is to supervise an army of semi-trained native medical assistants. They do most of the actual work and refer the more complicated cases to us."

"What about the ten thousand whites."

"We just look after the government employees, the police and the civil servants. Most of the whites go to private doctors. There are several in town."

He poured them all a brandy while the houseboy brought in coffee.

"Just a small one for me," said Peter. "I want to be fit for work tomorrow."

"Good. With an epidemic like this you're going to be in the thick of it from the start."

"You know, Jim," said Alan. "I'm still not convinced it's malaria at all."

"Of course it's malaria. I've been in Africa for nearly six years and I know malaria when I see it."

"But what about the negative blood smears?"

"Oh, there are always some negative blood tests, you just have to ignore them." He turned to Peter. "In Africa, if a patient has a headache and a fever you'd better regard it as malaria unless you can prove it's something else."

"But Jim," Alan protested. "The white patients have been taking prophylactics."

"They say they take them, but half the time they forget."

"What do you think is the cause of the epidemic?" asked Peter.

"The rains came early this year. The Public Works Department is supposed to carry out a spraying program, but this year they weren't ready. I've never seen so many mosquitoes."

Alan was conspicuously silent and eventually the subject changed to cars. Peter knew he'd need transport and Jim promised him a hospital Land Rover for a few days, until he had time to buy something of his own.

At the end of the evening the Melforts drove him back to Londonderry House. As soon as they were in the car Alan said, "Sometimes I could wring Jim Dawson's neck."

Susan laughed, then she mimicked Dawson's British accent. "I've been in Africa for six years and I know malaria when I see it!"

"Bloody limey," Alan exploded. "Sorry Peter, no offence, but I've lived here all my life and it doesn't look like simple malaria to me."

"Well, what do you think is the explanation?"

"I don't know. A lot of things can give you aches and pains and fever. Perhaps it's some kind of flu. I just wonder . . . " He stopped.

"What do you wonder?"

"Well, it sounds a bit far-fetched, but strange things happen in Africa. Perhaps we've got some new disease, some sort of mutation on our hands."

Next morning Peter was ready at 8am for Alan Melfort to take him to the African Hospital. It stood at the edge of the town, a collection of long white single storey stucco buildings with corrugated iron roofs, surrounding a square central compound. Peter was surprised to find that the sides of the buildings which faced in towards the compound were open. The beds were protected by the roof, but there was no wall.

"A lot of old colonial hospitals were built like that," Alan told him. "It gives plenty of fresh air and the weather is always warm."

The wards were full. The patients lay or sat on old-fashioned iron beds covered with dark grey blankets. Several of them had visitors even at this time in the morning, but it was quiet and reasonably clean. Alan and Peter went round accompanied by an African medical assistant, neatly dressed in khaki shorts and shirt. Hardly any of the patients spoke English and the assistant acted as an interpreter.

"There are half a dozen different native languages in this area alone," Alan explained. "Not many of us know more than one, so we rely on local interpreters."

They went up to a bed occupied by a middle-aged man with a heavily bandaged leg suspended by ropes and pulleys. He grinned as they approached and said something Peter couldn't understand. The medical assistant laughed. Alan grinned too and turned towards the assistant.

"Well Amos, what did he say?"

Amos hesitated, "Something like: Another young Englishman come out to see the colonies."

They all laughed then. Peter realized he'd never know what these people were really saying about him, but they seemed to be friendly.

"He was bitten by a crocodile," said Alan. "He's lucky to be alive. Crocs don't usually let go."

He turned to Amos. "Tell him: Any more cheek from him we'll throw him back in the river."

Amos said something and they both laughed again.

"The language isn't as much of a problem as you might expect," Alan said as they moved on. "With most patients it's obvious what's wrong."

Looking round the wards Peter couldn't see much sign of an epidemic. "Where are all the cases of malaria?" he asked.

"Well that's another strange thing. Most of them have been among the whites and better educated blacks, like Amos here. Malaria is endemic among the poorer blacks, and that hasn't changed."

"I thought poor people usually came off worst in epidemics?"

"They usually do, but not in this one."

They finished their ward round and went to the outpatient clinic at one corner of the compound. Like the wards, it had a roof and three walls but was open at the front. Peter was surprised to see a line up of thirty or forty natives waiting for attention. At the head of the line a medical assistant dressed in khaki was seeing the patients with the help of a couple of African nurses.

"Most of them have minor things," Alan explained. "The medical assistants deal with them. If there's anything serious they're told to wait for one of us."

The assistant stood up when they approached. Alan introduced him and then they moved deeper into the clinic where Peter saw half a dozen sick-looking Africans sitting on a bench. Alan dealt with them quite quickly, arranging for most of them to be admitted to the hospital. Then he escorted Peter over to the European Hospital to meet Jim Dawson.

The hospital for whites stood next to the native one, and the two were connected by a covered walkway. They found Jim in the doctors' lounge.

"Help yourself to coffee," he said to Peter. "Then I'll show you around. I'm going to put you on the European side for the first few weeks. It'll give you a chance to settle in."

Peter took a chair and Dawson began to explain in more detail what his duties would be, but there was a knock at the door and a nurse burst in.

"Sullivan's collapsed," she said to Jim. "You must come at once."

"Collapsed?"

"We found him unconscious a few minutes ago."

"Alright." Dawson looked upset. "Peter, you'd better come too."

"Who's Sullivan?" he asked, as they hurried down the corridor.

"One of our malaria cases. An important one. He's a Police Inspector."

They reached the end of the corridor and turned into the medical ward. The European hospital looked newer than the African one. There were walls on all sides of the building and Peter thought the wards looked much the same as hospital wards in England. He could see no sign of African medical assistants and all the nurses were white.

They hurried through the ward to a small private room with just one bed. The patient was lying on his back unconscious with his eyes sunken like a corpse. His skin had a yellowish tinge and his face was covered with sweat. A nurse with a stethoscope was trying to take his blood pressure.

"The systolic is only eighty and I can't get the diastolic pressure at all," she said. "The pulse is a hundred and forty."

"What about the temperature?"

"A hundred and three."

"I'll need the i.v. trolley with saline, plasma and intravenous chloroquine. And get the oxygen as well. We don't have a minute to spare."

Next he looked at Peter. "We've got to get the blood pressure up. Crank up the foot of the bed."

As Peter turned the handle to raise the patient's feet he watched Dawson carry out his examination: eyes, mouth, ears, heart, lungs, abdomen, reflexes, and finally the neck to see if it was stiff. Everywhere he seemed to draw a blank.

"The systolic has dropped to seventy-five," said the nurse.

Now Dawson examined the abdomen more thoroughly, pushing his hand up under the ribs. "The spleen is enlarged," he said. "But the abdomen's still quite soft so I don't think it's ruptured."

The nurse was taking the blood pressure again. "It's still falling," she announced. "Do you want me to call the relatives?"

He nodded. "In a minute. Right now I need you here."

Just then the door banged open as an orderly pushed in a trolley with bottles of intravenous fluid. "The oxygen's on it's way," he said.

"Peter," said Jim. "Start an i.v"

He wrapped the rubber tourniquet around the patient's arm, and while he waited for the veins to distend he asked Dawson about the blood smears.

"Negative," came the reply.

"Well, what do you think is wrong?"

"Malaria, of course. We're in the middle of an epidemic. What else could it be?"

"Perhaps it's meningitis. What about a spinal tap?"

"Of course it's not meningitis, the neck's not stiff."

"But have you done a spinal tap?"

"No I haven't, and there's no time now. The patient's in shock so hurry up with that i.v. Put up a unit of saline and run it as fast as you can. Now, let's have some chloroquine and hydrocortisone."

The porter arrived with the oxygen tank and Peter soon had oxygen running into a mask on the patient's face.

Dawson injected the chloroquine and hydrocortisone into the i.v. and after the saline he ran in two units of plasma. With the fluids, drugs and oxygen, the blood pressure finally started to rise and within an hour it was normal. During the afternoon the patient regained consciousness and they all breathed sighs of relief.

But the blood smears remained negative for malaria.

"How do you account for that?" Peter asked Dawson.

"The chloroquine we were giving him before suppressed the malaria parasites in his blood."

"Then why didn't it cure his malaria?"

"I don't know. Maybe he didn't get enough. Anyway it worked when we gave it intravenously. After all he's better, and he hasn't had anything else."

"He's had hydrocortisone, oxygen and intravenous fluids."

"Well, I'm sure it's malaria. I'm not going to do a spinal tap, if that's what you want. Not now he's getting better."

Peter spent the afternoon with Dawson preparing for the job he was about to begin. By the evening he was exhausted so he had dinner at the hostel and relaxed on his veranda, listening to the sounds of the African night. Steps led down to a wide lawn dotted with palms and flowering shrubs shimmering in the moonlight. Beyond the lawn there was a hedge, and beyond that the untamed bush stretched away for hundreds of miles. The air was warm and still, and fragrant with the scent of flowers.

He took the steps down to the lawn. The moon was bright and the trees cast black shadows on the grass. There was not a movement anywhere, but in the background came the rustle of a thousand insects and the faint croaking of frogs. After a while he walked across the lawn and hid, deep in thought, in the shadow of a tree. It was very beautiful and he was filled with a bittersweet emotion. He'd hardly thought of Jennifer for years, but now he was in Africa he could think of nothing else.

When he arrived at the hospital in the morning he found an older man in police uniform deep in conversation with Alan and a haggard looking Dawson.

"... and you do plan to do an autopsy?" the policeman was asking.

"Yes, of course," said Dawson.

"If you do it yourself, make sure one of your colleagues is present."

"Surely you don't think . . . ?"

"Not me, the family. They think you should have transferred him to Lusaka."

"It was just a simple case of malaria."

"He's dead, you know. He's the first police officer we've lost to malaria in three years. You're quite sure it wasn't something else?"

"Of course I'm sure."

"Well, I hope you're right. I'll have to order an inquiry if you're not. I won't have any choice."

When the police chief left, Dawson explained that Sullivan had died during the night. His blood pressure had fallen again and by the time Jim reached the hospital he was dead. They arranged to do the autopsy that afternoon.

"Have you done autopsies before?" Alan asked Peter as they walked over to the morgue.

"I've watched them but I've never actually done one."

"Well, you're going to have to do them here."

When Peter had watched autopsies in England the body had been prepared in advance by the mortuary attendants. The clothes had been taken off, the chest and abdomen opened, and the top of the skull removed for the pathologist to inspect the internal organs. The body had looked more like an anatomical specimen than a person.

Here it was different. When they entered the morgue he immediately smelled the odour of the dead, a cloying mixture of human tissue, fat and feces that could not be hidden by any amount of antiseptic. His stomach turned. Then he got another shock, the body had not been prepared in any way. Sullivan lay on his back on the stained wooden mortuary table wearing his pyjamas, just as if he were still alive.

"Rule number one," said Alan. "Do everything yourself. Most of the autopsies are requested by the police to see if there's been foul play. Often your best clues will be on the outside: blood on the clothes, cuts, bruises, broken bones and that sort of thing. Look at the outside first."

They donned thick butchers' aprons and rubber gloves. After they had removed the pyjamas Dawson took a large knife and with a single steady stroke he slit the abdominal wall down the middle, from the chest to the pelvis. Peter shuddered. Loops of bowel distended with gas bulged through the incision. It was entirely different from surgery, the body naked and the tissues lifeless and cold. There was very little blood but a horrible stench of death.

Dawson examined the abdominal organs one by one. The diagnosis of malaria would be made by sending samples of the liver and spleen to the pathologist in Lusaka, two hundred miles to the south, so he removed the appropriate samples and dropped them into a jar of formalin.

Next he took a pair of metal shears and crunched through the ribs on each side of the chest, one by one. When the last rib had been severed he divided the remaining tissues with the knife and removed the entire front of the chest as a single piece. Next he severed the tissues behind the heart and removed the heart and lungs. He cut the lungs into slices, and opened the heart so they could look at the valves.

When he'd finished he breathed a sigh of relief.

"Well that proves it. I always thought it was malaria and there's no sign of anything else."

The autopsies Peter had seen before had been done by professional pathologists, and they had always looked at the brain. Perhaps it was meningitis. Dawson's autopsy would not have detected that. Maybe they all had meningitis, some new mutant form of the disease. Perhaps he, Peter Johnson, would be the first to recognize it. They'd call it Johnson's Disease. He'd be famous.

"Don't you think we ought to examine the brain?" he suggested.

Dawson looked annoyed. "Why?"

"It might be meningitis."

"You're not going on about that again."

"It's just that at the autopsies I watched in England they always looked at the brain."

"Well, this is Africa and we don't open the head unless there's a good reason. It's messy and unproductive."

He replaced the heart and lungs and laid the section of chest wall back on top. The mortuary attendant would stitch it roughly into place before the funeral.

"What do you think, Alan?" he asked Melfort.

"This case could cause a lot of trouble. The family are dissatisfied and the police chief's involved. Perhaps it would be a good idea."

He grunted.

Peter had never seen the top of the skull removed before and he soon discovered why they didn't want to do it now. Dawson made a long incision across the top of the head from one ear to the other. The knife made a grating noise as it scraped the surface of the skull. Then, with fingers and knife, he stripped the scalp off the skull in two flaps, as if he were skinning an animal. The front flap he dragged forward until it lay inside out over the face, and the back one he pulled down behind the neck. The whole top of the skull was exposed, a dome of bare white bone streaked with blood. Next he marked out a circle round the skull just above the ears. Then Peter and Alan had to grip the head as he sawed through the bone with a 14 inch carpenter's hand saw. Ground up bone and fat kept clogging the saw's teeth and it took twenty minutes to cut right round the head. When he had finished the top of the skull was loose. Peter felt excited. Soon they would know the truth.

Next Dawson inserted a chisel into the groove and levered up the bone. There was a tearing sound as a few remaining tissues gave way, and then the top of the skull lifted off like a tight round cap. Underneath lay the brain, shiny and white.

They all peered at it for a minute. The surface was clean and Peter could see no sign of pus. In a way he was disappointed.

"It doesn't look like meningitis to me," said Dawson at last.

He separated the convolutions with his fingers to examine the spaces between. "Perfectly normal," he added triumphantly. "But we'll pickle the brain in formalin and send it to Lusaka. They can have the final word."

The final word came a few days later in the form of a written report from the pathologist. He had examined the tissues under the microscope and found the patient was heavily infected with Plasmodium falciparum, malignant tertian malaria. There was no evidence of meningitis or anything else.

"Why didn't he respond to treatment?" asked Alan when the three of them discussed it.

"Does Plasmodium falciparum ever become resistant to chloroquine, like staphylococci get resistant to penicillin?" asked Peter.

"It's never been reported," said Dawson. "Chloroquine's a wonderful drug, safe and effective."

"Then why didn't it work on Sullivan?"

"We were giving it by mouth. Maybe his stomach didn't absorb it."

"He was getting it intravenously towards the end, straight into his blood."

Jim Dawson had no answer to that. But the epidemic seemed to be abating, probably because the Public Works Department had starting spraying at last.

During the next few months Peter learned more about practical medicine and surgery than ever before in his life. He was amazed by the variety of diseases among the Africans. They suffered from all the illnesses he was used to and all the tropical diseases as well. Sometimes he had to visit native villages and then he needed four wheel drive. At first he used the hospital Land Rover, and he liked it so much that he bought one of his own. The country he explored was flat and lightly wooded, and dotted with twelve-foot anthills left by a race of giant ants now long extinct. Streams with lush green banks meandered through the bush towards the Kafue River a few miles to the west, and along their sides he found African villages of round thatched huts unchanged since the time of the missionaries.

In the spring of 1960 Jim Dawson went on leave. Peter had learned a lot from Dawson but he was happy to have a change. The next head of Ndola Hospital was an older man with a softer personality. His name was Gerry Rossiter and he'd been in Africa for many years. Peter loved to go round the wards with him, or sit on the veranda drinking beer and listening to his adventures.

One morning early in 1961 Gerry called Peter into his office.

"How would you like to go to Nyasaland for a month? I've just had a call from the Ministry. They need someone temporarily while one of their regular doctors goes on leave."

"Nyasaland?"

"A place called Zomba. It's a small town on the side of a mountain. There are three doctors. One looks after the whites and the other two run the African hospital."

"What would I be doing?"

"The African hospital. Surgery and obstetrics."

"Do you think I could handle it, Gerry?"

"You're the perfect man for the job. There's a fully trained surgeon in Blantyre, forty miles to the south. He comes to Zomba once a week for the difficult cases, so you'd only have to do the straightforward stuff."

"I'm not sure."

"Well, you'd better be sure because I've already told them you'll be arriving the week after next." He smiled and before Peter could object he went on, "And I've just had a call from Gordon Bishop. He's living in Salisbury now."

"You've been talking to Gordon?"

"Yes. You could drive to Nyasaland via Salisbury and stay with the Bishops for a few days. Gordon wants to show you the fleshpots of Southern Rhodesia."

"Alright," he said. "I'll go."

"Good. Nyasaland is the most beautiful place in Africa. It's all mountains, forests and streams. Lake Nyasa is like an inland sea. I wish I could go myself."

Peter found it a hot dusty 500-mile drive to Salisbury down the main north-south road of Africa. He spent a night in Lusaka, stopped for a swim in a lake outside Karoi, and reached Salisbury just after dark on the second day. It was the first big city he'd seen for over a year and he was impressed by the rows of attractive houses on lighted streets. Gordon and his wife Norma gave him a warm welcome.

"I expect you're tired tonight," said Gordon. "Tomorrow I'll show you round Harare Hospital, and in the evening you've got a date."

"A date?"

"We're going out to dinner and then on to the Zimbabwe Club. It's the latest Salisbury nightclub, so you'll need someone to dance with."

"Who's the date?"

"A friend of Norma's. Her name is Melanie, but I call her Melons for obvious reasons."

"Don't you dare," said Norma.

Melanie was pleasant enough, and they had a nice dinner at the Jameson Hotel in the centre of Salisbury. After dinner Gordon led the way down some steps between two modern buildings, and at the bottom Peter was surprised to find a nightclub in the traditional style. The lights were dim, an African band played soft romantic music, and people crowded together on a small dance floor or sat at tables attended by waitresses with very short skirts.

The club was decorated to resemble the inside of a ruined temple, with stone walls, little alcoves, and dark mysterious passages. There were exotic African carvings of animals and birds on display, and strange clay pots from ancient Egypt with geometric designs in black, red and gold. Standing in an alcove was an old wooden altar with sinister stains down the front and a large black bird on either side.

Gordon led them to a table, and a waitress brought them drinks. Norma explained that the club had been decorated to resemble a ruined temple which had been discovered in the bush two hundred miles to the south.

"The temple is just a part of a whole ruined city called Zimbabwe," she said. "It's one of the great mysteries of Africa, a thousand years old and no one knows who built it. The things in here are copies of real ones that were actually found at the site."

Peter had always been fascinated by ancient ruins. "Perhaps I'll drive down there and see it," he said. "I've got a few days."

Norma suggested that Melanie might like to go with him, but to his relief she declined. He'd rather be on his own. Presently they danced. He held her close and they talked of this and that, but he had the feeling she was merely there to keep him company, conscripted by her friends.

And then it happened.

Their table was at the far side of the club from the entrance. Peter was sitting with his back to the wall, idly watching as a group of people came in through the door. There were three men and three women. The doorman took their coats, and one of the men, older than the others, handed him some money. The lights were dim, but across the room something caught Peter's eye. Perhaps it was the way one of the women walked. Perhaps it was her smile, or the way her hair swung smoothly in a wave when she turned her head. It was straight shiny hair with a hint of an inward curl. Her face was a perfect oval. His heart missed a beat.

She looked straight at him. He could see her eyes, dark and serious, and her mouth without a hint of a smile. She was staring directly at him and his pulse began to race. He held her gaze and on her face he saw a look of shock.

Without a word he stood up and began to walk towards her, squeezing past tables and chairs, his eyes never leaving her face.

She stood completely still, her eyes on his, her face a blank. Out of the corner of his eye he saw her companions follow the waiter to their table. One of them went back to fetch her, a young man in a suit. He touched her arm but she ignored him.

She wore a simple blue cocktail dress with a thin gold belt. Simple clothes had always suited her because she'd been so pretty. Now she looked more beautiful than ever.

Then he was in front of her, looking into her face. She stared back as if she were looking at a ghost.

"Jenny."

"Peter."

He reached down and brushed her hand, and she moved her fingers in return. Moisture filled his eyes.

"Do you feel it too?"

"Yes," she whispered.

For two minutes they stood motionless as he gazed at her face. People began to stare. The man who'd come back to fetch her was shifting his feet in embarrassment. Gradually Peter realized he needed to hold her in his arms.

"Would you like to dance?"

"Alright."

He took her hand and led her towards the floor.

"I'll join you in a minute, Archie," she murmured to the young man in the suit.

The band was playing a selection from *My Fair Lady*. The music was soft and slow, and immediately she nestled close. They swayed slowly back and forth as the vocalist crooned, *"People stop and stare, they don't bother me . . . ,"* but he was unaware of anything but her. He danced with her like that in silence for some time, but gradually his senses began to return.

"I love you," he murmured.

"I love you too. The instant I saw you it started all over again."

"I must see you on your own," he said.

"But where?"

"There's a little hidden alcove at the back."

He took her hand and led her across the floor. The alcove was designed for privacy and as soon as they were alone she fell into his arms.

"You too," she murmured as she pressed against him. "I wanted you the moment we touched."

They sat in silence for five minutes, holding hands and looking at each other. Eventually she put her hand up and touched his face. "I can't believe this is happening. We only met ten minutes ago. What are we going to do?"

"Will you marry me?" he asked.

"Of course I will."

"Well then, that's what we'll do."

"But I can't marry you immediately, you dope," she chuckled. "There are things we must see to first. My job for example. And my mother will probably want to give us a big wedding back in England."

He thought her mother had done enough harm already. He could plainly remember her saying she would never agree to them marrying. Never. He still had no idea why. But he didn't want to argue at the moment, so he said, "Well, let's announce our engagement anyway. We can buy a ring tomorrow."

"Oh yes, darling, yes." She gave him a kiss.

"You know, it's an extraordinary thing," she went on. "I feel I already know you just as well as I did before. It's as if we've hardly been apart."

"But we have been apart, and we've got a lot of catching up to do." He paused. "Who's Archie?"

She laughed. "Archie Clayton-Jones, my boss' son. You're jealous. I love you."

"Is he . . . ?"

"My boyfriend? No. Although Mr Clayton-Jones would like that. And so would Archie, I think."

A serious look crossed her face. "What about you?"

"There's no one. Only you."

"Has there been anyone?"

"Nothing serious."

"Oh Peter, I'm so glad. I don't want to share you with anyone."

She turned her face up and kissed him.

"What are you doing here?" he asked.

"I'm Mr Clayton-Jones' private secretary. He owns a mining company in Johannesburg and we want to expand into Rhodesia. And you, Peter, what on earth are you doing here?"

"I'm a doctor."

"I know. My sister told me."

"Your sister tells you what I'm doing?"

"Usually. But she didn't tell me you were in Africa."

"Why didn't you write?"

She looked terribly sad. "At first, when I heard nothing from you, everyone said you'd deserted me and gone off with Jessica Clark. By the time I guessed what had really happened I thought it was too late."

"I never deserted you. I wrote and phoned and telegraphed. But let's not talk about that now."

But the sadness lingered in her face. "Peter, I've always carried a flame for you, ever since we kissed on the beach at Salcombe when I was only seventeen."

"We've got so much to talk about, let's spend the next few days together."

"That would be wonderful. I'll have to ask Mr Clayton-Jones, but I'm sure it'll be alright."

"How about driving down to the Zimbabwe ruins?" he suggested. "We met in the Zimbabwe Club, so maybe we should see the real thing. There's a hotel, and we can be on our own."

"I'd like that very much."

After a while she said, "I think I ought to introduce you to the Clayton-Joneses. After all they brought me here."

She took him over to Clayton-Jones' table, and Peter couldn't help noticing the looks of displeasure that were cast in his direction.

"Mr Clayton-Jones, I'd like you to meet Peter Johnson," she said rather formally.

Clayton-Jones nodded at Peter and said, "Jennifer, where on earth have you been? Archie was worried about you."

For the first time Peter looked at Archie. He was a good-looking lad with a healthy sun-tanned face and short light brown hair.

"Something came up," she said.

Clayton-Jones sighed. "Jennifer, I can't understand you. You're in the middle of a nice evening with my son, and then you disappear with a man you met less than five minutes before."

"I am sorry. I didn't mean to desert you, but something unexpected happened."

"It certainly did," said Clayton-Jones.

"I just got engaged."

"You what?"

"Got engaged. You know, we're going to get married."

Clayton-Jones choked and spilled whisky down his shirt.

"My God," he said, looking at Peter with sudden interest. "She's the catch of Johannesburg and you snap her up in five minutes. What on earth did you do?"

"We have met before," he said.

Jenny explained what had happened, and how she and Peter had known each other so well back in England, and eventually Clayton-Jones went on to congratulate them.

Time off to visit the ruins was quickly arranged, and then hand in hand they walked over to tell the Bishops their news. Peter was concerned about the way he'd left Melanie, but when she heard their story she understood. Soon she was toasting the newly engaged couple along with Gordon and Norma.

"So you're off to the Zimbabwe ruins, are you?" said Norma. "You don't have to go that far you know, all the important items are here in this room."

Jenny stared at her with sudden interest. "You mean these things are from the Zimbabwe ruins?"

"Yes. These are copies of course, but the real ones look just the same."

Jenny pointed to the big black birds standing on the altar. "Those birds, did they come from Zimbabwe too?"

"They were the most important items there."

"My mother had secret pictures of them." She paused, collecting her thoughts. "Something very strange happened a long time ago when I was a little girl. My sister and I were playing hide and seek, and I hid in my mother's bedroom cupboard. She came in and I watched her take some pictures out of a drawer and spread them on the bed. She stared at them for a long time, looking terribly sad. I even thought she was going to cry. Then she knelt down and started to pray. It was really weird."

"How do you know they were pictures of the birds?"

"Well, eventually she put them back in the drawer, and after she'd gone I had a look. There were pictures of those birds, and other things as well."

"How odd," said Peter. "What other things?"

"Pictures of statues and things like that. Looking back I think they were Egyptian. And there were photos of a man, a frightening looking man with straight black hair and dark staring eyes. And there was an old map, yellow and torn. But the things I remember most clearly were the birds and a picture of a woman with horns on her head."

"Perhaps they were postcards she'd picked up on holidays," Peter suggested.

"No, they were special. You see my mother came back and caught me. She got very angry and gave me a spanking. She said they were wicked pictures and I must never tell anyone I'd seen them or ever look at them again. It was strange because I'd really done nothing wrong and my mother hardly ever spanked me. That's why I remember it so well. Next time I looked in the drawer it was empty and I never saw them again."

"And you're sure they were pictures of these birds?"

"Certain. The instant I walked in the door this evening I was struck by two astounding things. You Peter, and those birds standing on that ghastly altar. I was right about you, wasn't I? And I'm right about the birds."

There was a moment's silence, then Norma said, "Perhaps you shouldn't go to Zimbabwe after all."

"No, I've got to go," said Jenny slowly. "I've got to see the place where the things came from. There's so much about my mother that I don't understand."

Chapter 29

Mark Wooding's pulse quickened as he opened the envelope. Inside was a formal invitation:

Dr and Mrs Charles Cudmore
request the pleasure of the company of
Dr Mark Wooding
at a dinner party
to be held at Overton House, Cedar Road, Woking
on Friday, March 24, 1961, at 7:30pm.
R.S.V.P.

Mark was standing by the mail slots at the entrance to Guy's. There were similar envelopes for two of the senior surgical registrars, but Paul Ellison's slot was empty.

When he'd finished his year in Brighton Dr Radcliff had asked him to stay a second year, but careers were made in London and he'd managed to get a post at Guy's. It was one of the less important jobs but it allowed him to keep his foot in the door. He'd worked very hard since he'd been back and his efforts were finally paying off. The next year would be critical. In July he would have a chance to become a registrar on Dr Cudmore's firm, but Ellison was also in the running. Paul was still as smooth and well-spoken as ever, however it was rumoured that he was not such a skilful surgeon as Mark.

On the evening of the dinner party he dressed carefully in a grey suit with a crisp white shirt and a Guy's hospital tie. He combed his hair and pulled faces at himself in the mirror. At the age of twenty-seven his features had filled out and he thought he looked pretty good.

He'd sold his old MG and now he drove a white Triumph TR3. Woking lay twenty miles southwest of London and the drive took about an hour. Overton House looked far too big to be a private home. It was set in a couple of acres of parkland, with a large semicircular driveway where a Rolls and two Jaguars were already parked. He didn't want to be the first to arrive, and certainly not the last.

A maid in a black and white uniform showed him into an elegant drawing room where Dr Cudmore and his wife were entertaining the first of their guests. Cudmore looked as impressive as ever with his reddish hair and beard. Mark glanced nervously at the other guests, a couple of consultants and a senior registrar, all with their wives and all impeccably dressed.

"Ah, Mark," said Cudmore. "I'd like you to meet my wife."

He shook Mrs Cudmore's hand.

Cudmore introduced the other guests and finally he said, "And what about my daughter? You must have met her already."

"Not officially, sir."

He smiled and formally shook Pat Cudmore's hand.

Pat was a redhead, big and tall, with a handsome face and a firm chin like her father. Mark regarded her as good-looking rather than pretty. She was a medical student in her final year so he'd seen her about the hospital. It was rumoured she'd been having an affair with Paul Ellison but she'd recently broken it off.

"Come with me and I'll get you a drink," she said, and she led him over to a table set up as a bar.

"I'm so glad you could come, Mark," she went on. "My father's guests are usually much too old for me. I hope you don't mind if I monopolize you a bit."

A dinner party like this was a golden opportunity to meet influential members of the staff, and to have the Director of Surgery's only daughter at his side would be an enormous advantage. Perhaps Ellison was in decline and his own opportunity had finally arrived. Even as they talked another group of important guests arrived.

He reached down and briefly touched her hand. "I'd like to be monopolized," he said. "Perhaps you could introduce me to some of your father's friends."

He made sure he sat next to her at dinner too, and before he left he invited her to the theatre the following week.

Mark's affair with Shirley Fuller had ended when he left Brighton. He'd been fond of her but his career came first. When he got back to Guy's he'd been too busy for female company, but as he settled in he found he was missing not Shirley but Beverley Morton. His affair with her had been running on and off for over five years, and he'd come to regard her as part of the Guy's Hospital scene. But Beverley had gone. Six months after he'd moved to Brighton she'd emigrated to Canada.

She had sent him a letter from Toronto explaining her decision. He had disappeared to Brighton and Jeremy Blakelock had married the only daughter of a wealthy country family. There was nothing left for her in England, she'd written. It hadn't bothered him at the time because of Shirley, but now he missed her.

His association with Pat Cudmore was quite different from his previous affairs. For one thing it was not spontaneous. He didn't find her attractive, either physically or emotionally, and he would never have cultivated her friendship if she hadn't been the Director of Surgery's daughter. He started to take her out about once a week, always to expensive restaurants or theatres. He quite enjoyed her company, particularly when they had got to know each other, but he was never as relaxed as he'd been with Beverley or Shirley.

It might have worked out better if he hadn't been living at the hospital. The house staff lived in an old Victorian building where everyone could see who came and went. And his room was dreary and cramped, not a place for entertaining. They sometimes kissed and cuddled in the car but that was as far as it went.

At Easter he had a few days off and he took her down to Salcombe to stay at Maplehurst. The weather was perfect. Jack Ross was home on leave and he had a girl with him too. The four of them went sailing on the estuary during the days and spent the evenings in the pubs. Pat got on well with Mark's mother and that weekend the reserve that separated them melted away. His association with Pat did not pass unnoticed at the hospital and his chances of becoming Dr Cudmore's next registrar were rated higher every week. This was not merely because of his relationship with Cudmore's daughter; everyone could see he was a highly competent young surgeon, an ideal candidate for the job.

In May Pat asked him to a party given by some friends in Woking.

"It's on a Saturday and my mother has invited you to spend the night with us," she said.

"I don't know," said Mark doubtfully. He was nervous about staying at Overton House with her father there.

"Don't be silly," said Pat. "I spent the whole of Easter at your place."

The registrar appointments were to be announced in June, and he didn't want to offend the Cudmores so he agreed.

Woking lay in the stockbroker belt southwest of London, the domain of the wealthy upper middle class, and the party was held at another mansion similar to Overton House. It was a young people's party, but there was an expensive buffet and live music, and everyone was fashionably dressed.

Mark felt uncomfortable from the start and he was sure it showed. Most of the guests knew each other already, but he was a stranger, and there were no other medical people to whom he could talk. If Pat had taken the trouble to introduce him to her friends he might have been able to fit in. But she didn't bother. She seemed to ignore him and flit from group to group, chatting and dancing, oblivious to his plight.

In fact she wasn't quite oblivious. Once, when he was standing alone with no one to talk to, she came up to him with a chinless but well-dressed young army officer and said, "Mark, why don't you join in with everyone else?"

"Yes, I'll introduce you to the chaps," said the youth. He made chaps sound like chaaaps, but he meant well, and he took Mark over to a group of young Guards officers.

They eyed him briefly and he asked if they knew Jack Ross.

"What Regiment?"

"The Royal Army Service Corps, I think."

"Oh dear," laughed one of them. "No, we don't associate with the Service Corps. It's a bit N.O.C. you know."

"N.O.C.?"

"Not Our Class."

He asked if they knew any army doctors, but he got the impression that the Royal Army Medical Corps was a little beneath them too. The conversation quickly returned to the Ascot race weekend.

Then he spotted an opening in another group, so he moved in that direction, drink in hand, ready to join in. But as he approached the gap closed and he was left self-consciously on the outside. Next he tried to join a third group of young men who worked in the city, stockbrokers and bankers he thought. They were discussing the stock market, and he hunted for something to say.

"Oil is bound to go up," he blurted, repeating something he'd heard at the hospital. They stared at him in silence for a few seconds. Embarrassed, he walked over to the bar where he could drink on his own, unnoticed.

Pat did dance with him once or twice, but just when he seemed to be getting her attention she'd be off with one of her friends. He recalled Shirley Fuller's behaviour at the party in Brighton over a year before. He'd felt humiliated at the time, but later he realized her actions had been intended to produce a reaction in himself. Could Pat Cudmore want a spanking too?

He stood by the bar aware that he was drinking too much, but he had nothing else to do. At 1:00am the guests started to leave. He found Pat and told her he thought it was time to go. It was the first time he'd spoken to her for an hour, but she meekly agreed.

"I think we'd better have a little talk when we get home," he said, recalling his approach to Shirley.

"What about?"

"You and me."

"Alright," she said submissively, then added with a smile, "Come to my room when you're ready for bed."

When they got back to Overton House Mark was relieved to find the place in darkness. The older Cudmores were already asleep. All the bedrooms were in the same wing of the house, but Pat's was some distance from her parents', so he thought they'd be safe.

He went to his room and undressed, washed and brushed his teeth. Then he sat on the bed for a while thinking about Pat. Her behaviour had been just like Shirley's. He could guess what was going to happen and he found he was looking forward to it.

After a few minutes he crept silently along the corridor. Her door was open a fraction so he went in. The room was illuminated by a night light and she was lying on the bed in a silk nightie. It looked loose and easy to pull up, and he imagined her naked bottom underneath. He was still a little drunk and the thought of smacking it was exciting. He climbed onto the bed beside her and she started kissing him as if nothing had been wrong.

At Easter they'd done this but they hadn't gone any further. Now he slipped his hand up inside her nightie and slowly moved his fingers up her thigh. She caressed him back but he found it rather dull and the feeling of excitement drained away. He should be ready to make love, but somehow he was not. She'd been awful at the party and now he realized he didn't even like her. She felt flabby, not neat and firm like Shirley.

For five long minutes he tried to get aroused, all the time pretending there was nothing wrong. Eventually she reached down and felt him with her fingers, and he was filled with shame.

"What's the matter?" she asked. "Is it me?"

He was about to say No, the fault was all his own, when something inside him rebelled. She'd behaved atrociously at the party, and now he was about to lose his self-esteem because of her. He remembered what had happened with Shirley and he felt sure she wanted the same thing. He wanted it too. He was certain he'd be alright then.

"Yes, it is you," he said, sitting up in bed.

"Why?"

"The way you behaved at the party. Flirting with everybody but ignoring me."

"Don't be silly. I can dance with whom I please."

That was exactly what Shirley had said; the very same words. He slipped his legs over the side of the bed and sat on the edge.

"You deserve a good spanking," he said.

"A spanking?"

There was a funny little smile on her face, and he thought he noticed something sexy about the way she said the word. Now she was sitting up too. He was sure he knew what was going on in her mind, and suddenly he grabbed her and put her across his knees. She was a big girl, but he was quick and strong and he caught her by surprise. She was across his lap before she could resist.

"You wouldn't dare," she said.

It sounded like a challenge, a test of wills. He slowly pulled up the silk nightie until her bottom was exposed. The sight of her naked buttocks was exciting and he felt himself respond.

"You wouldn't dare," she repeated.

He smacked one buttock hard with his open hand. She seemed to catch her breath and choke, but she didn't cry out, so he raised his hand again. The second smack turned out to be much harder than he intended. His hand landed absolutely flat. It even stung his fingers.

Then she screamed.

She didn't merely scream, she shrieked at the top of her voice, over and over again.

He was horrified. Instantly he knew it was a disaster. He wanted to put his hand over her mouth to shut her up, but he knew that would only make things worse.

He pushed her aside and did up his pyjamas, but before he could escape there were footsteps in the corridor and Dr Cudmore burst in.

"What the devil's going on?" he yelled.

Pat hurriedly pulled down her nightie. There were no more screams, she just sat there sniffing.

"He started to beat me," she stammered.

Cudmore stared at Mark in amazement.

Then he looked at Pat. "Are you injured?"

"I don't think so," she sobbed.

At that moment Mrs Cudmore arrived. She ran straight to the bed and threw her arms around her daughter. "Oh, my darling," she cried. "Are you alright?"

Cudmore had a reputation for a cool head in an emergency. He didn't shout or throw a tantrum. He glared at Mark and his wife and daughter for a minute, then he ordered, "Wooding, go to your room and wait for me there. I'll deal with you later."

Mark dressed and packed his bag, and then sat miserably on the bed. Eventually there was a perfunctory knock on the door and Cudmore marched in. He looked calm and cold.

"Alright Wooding," he demanded bluntly. "Tell me your version of what happened."

Mark didn't know what Pat had said, so he gave a fairly accurate account. He finished by saying, "I thought she wanted me to spank her, sir, sort of in fun. So I gave her a couple of little slaps on the bottom. That was all. Then she started to scream."

He thought it sounded quite plausible, and it was more or less true. Perhaps what he'd done wasn't so bad after all.

Cudmore stared at him for a moment.

"Wooding," he began. "You went to my daughter's bedroom in the middle of the night, right here in my own home, right under my nose. She may have invited you, but for an up-and-coming member of the hospital staff that was an incredibly stupid thing to do."

Mark was relieved. Being caught in the boss' daughter's bedroom was pretty careless, but it wasn't a mortal sin. In fact it was a bit of a joke. Perhaps Cudmore was going to ignore the spanking bit. It was rather embarrassing and maybe Pat had glossed over it. Perhaps he was going to get off lightly after all.

Cudmore continued, "I know the two of you are not children, and I'm perfectly aware that young people nowadays are more liberal than they were a few years ago."

Good old Cudmore, thought Mark. What a sport.

"Patricia has told me that in actual fact nothing improper has happened between you, but she's very upset and you're not to see her again. I order you to keep strictly away from her in the future."

After tonight that would be a relief. And he hadn't said anything about the registrar appointment.

"Now, what about this spanking business?"

"Well, it was all a bit of a misunderstanding," said Mark lightly. "Just a couple of little slaps on the bottom as a kind of a joke."

Finally Cudmore's voice grew harsh. "Wooding, I've examined my daughter's backside and those were not little love-slaps given in fun. For some reason that only you can understand you hit her as hard as you could.

I'm satisfied that you didn't try to rape her, so I'm not going to call the police, not at the moment anyway."

Well, thank God for that, thought Mark.

"But when your present job finishes at the end of June, you will leave Guy's Hospital and you will never work there again."

Chapter 30

Jennifer White was walking on air, hardly able to believe what had happened. But already there was a cloud on the horizon. She made her way down to the foyer of Meikles Hotel at 9:00am to meet Peter. They were going to buy her engagement ring. Last night it had seemed a lovely idea, but now she wanted more time to choose the ring herself.

It was hard to believe that six years had passed since she'd last seen him. She recalled the first few months with such terrible sadness that tears came to her eyes. Even now she didn't understand what had happened. Could her mother really have stopped all his letters?

The early months had passed in a sort of numbness. But eventually she'd recovered. Then she'd made friends, gone to college and become happy again. Her mother had returned to England, but she liked South Africa and she'd never heard from Peter, so she didn't go back herself. She'd become a secretary, moved to Durban, then Johannesburg, and now she had a wonderful job.

Just then she spotted him coming up the hotel steps and her heart leapt. His face was tanned and his hair had bleached to the colour of gold in the African sun. He was wearing grey slacks, a white open necked shirt, and a sports jacket that flew in the breeze as he strode along. His eyes lit up when he saw her.

"You're even better than I remembered," he said. "Are we really going away together?"

"We'd better be. It almost cost me my job."

"I've got something for you," he said, pulling a little gift-wrapped box out of his pocket.

Her heart fell. It was obviously a ring.

"Can I take it back if I don't like it?"

"No, I'm afraid you can't."

Perhaps it was a family heirloom, some clumsy Victorian thing.

"Why not?"

"Well, it's not quite new."

"You mean it was someone else's ring?"

"You mustn't think of it that way."

"Did you give it to somebody, Peter?"

He hesitated. "Well, to tell you the truth, yes I did."

She felt angry and disappointed. She didn't know him at all. Perhaps it was all a mistake. She began to unwrap the package and inside was a tiny jewellery box.

"I thought we were going to choose a ring together," she said bitterly. "I don't want some second hand thing you gave to someone else."

"Why don't you open it?" he said.

She pulled open the lid and caught her breath. Inside was the blue and silver eternity ring he'd given her at the church in Rye. That ring had been her one connection with him after they were parted and she'd been heartbroken when it disappeared.

"Is it . . . ? Is it real?"

"Yes."

"Oh Peter," she stammered with tears on her cheeks. "It's so silly of me. It's the most wonderful present I've ever had. However did you get it?"

"Someone sent it to me after you went away. It was on its own in a box with no letter. At the time I thought you'd sent it back."

"I would never have done that. I wore it all the time. Then one day I took it off to shower and it disappeared. My mother thought the houseboy had stolen it, but my aunt wouldn't believe that. We searched and searched but we never found it."

"Jenny, don't you think it would be better to wait and choose a proper engagement ring later, when we've got more time?"

"That's exactly what I think."

Driving through the Rhodesian bush in a Land-Rover was a new experience for Jenny. She had lived in Africa for six years, but she'd never been this far north. They were crossing a plain with small hills every two or three miles which Peter called kopjes. They had rocky outcrops at their summits like the rocky tors on Dartmoor.

The bush was dry and hot, more brown than green, with miles of stunted trees, cacti and sun-dried grass. There were hardly any people and she saw only three vehicles all morning. The bumpy road wound between the kopjes and dipped across dried-up river beds. They took turns driving but Peter wanted to stop whenever anything caught his interest so progress was slow. They got out to examine a dead lizard three feet long, a huge deserted ant hill by a dried up stream, and later, in a wide valley, an enormous baobab tree. Jenny had never seen anything like the baobab. Its trunk was twelve feet thick, but short and stunted and covered with bark which looked like an elephant's hide.

They stopped in a dusty one-street town called Enkeldoorn for lunch. In the afternoon they crested a hill at the head of a broad green valley more fertile than the rest, and in the distance lay the ruins. Jenny could make out a big circular outer wall with the tops of other walls and towers poking up inside.

"How about going to the hotel first?" she suggested. "We can look at the ruins in the morning."

"Do you realize it's the first time we've stayed in a hotel together since the Mermaid?" he said. "Let's take the best room they've got."

It was a small place with a cosy bar decorated with pictures of African wildlife. They showered before dinner and had a pleasant meal by candlelight with a bottle of wine. There were half a dozen other guests who gathered in the bar after dinner, but they went straight up to bed.

They had a large room with a big double bed, elegant furniture and a veranda which overlooked a lawn. Jenny was a little nervous and she was grateful when Peter suggested they sit on the veranda to enjoy the scents and sounds of the African night before going to bed. There was a bright tropical moon which bathed everything in silvery light and cast shadows across the grass. The warm air was filled with the fragrance of tropical flowers, and from all around came the sounds of crickets and frogs. It was beautiful, magical, the most magical night she'd ever known. They sat there together, touching, kissing, and caressing for a long time. Finally she nestled up against him and murmured, "Peter, let's go inside."

He led her back into the room and slowly, gently, with more kissing and touching they undressed each other in the moonlight that filtered through the window.

Next morning the hotel supplied them with a packed lunch and a guide book, and they set off in the Land-Rover to explore the ruins. As they approached Jenny realized the circular ruin that they'd seen from the hilltop was massive, twice the size of Stonehenge. The outer wall towered above them. It was nearly forty feet high and fifteen thick, and the area it enclosed measured about three hundred feet across. It was built of roughly cut rectangular granite slabs each about a foot in length.

They followed a dirt track past some lesser ruins and parked close to the entrance. Inside there were more walls and passages, and three round towers. With the guide book in hand Jenny led the way along a narrow passage between thick thirty-foot walls. It was cool and eerily quiet after the hot African bush. Eventually they reached the end of the passage and emerged into the sunlight close to a stone platform at the foot of the tallest tower.

"This is where the priests brought their victims," she whispered, looking at the book.

"What victims?"

"The ones that were going to be sacrificed."

She looked around for anything that might relate to her mother's pictures, but there was nothing. Everything of importance had been taken long ago.

After they had explored they ate their lunch sitting on some rocks in the shade of a fig tree. Jenny read the guide book as she ate.

"The first outsider to see the ruins was an American hunter called Adam Renders in 1868," she announced.

"I wonder what it was like then?" asked Peter.

"A lot better than this. He found all kinds of things; carvings, ornaments made of gold and silver, things like that. The place was in much better shape back then."

"What happened?"

"Treasure hunters," she said, in a tone of disgust. "When Renders reported what he'd found, all sorts of ruffians came up here to steal the loot. They even blew up some of the buildings with dynamite trying to find more gold."

A quarter of a mile away stood a rocky hill with walls and terraces climbing its sides, and after lunch they explored that too. The hillside ruins were not as massive but they were more complex. Passages led from one terrace to another, and finally they reached a lookout at the top with a view of the whole valley. From the lookout Jenny realized that smaller ruins spread right down the valley, partly hidden by trees and scrub. There'd been a whole city there once. She fancied she could see patterns on the surrounding hills as well, roads perhaps, or irrigation canals, all that was left of some long-lost civilization.

After a while they climbed down to the Eastern Enclosure.

"This is where the birds were found," she said, looking around with disappointment. "But there's nothing here now."

That evening after dinner they went to the hotel bar with the other guests. The owner was an Englishman called Sam Milton who had lived in Africa for years. He claimed to be an authority on the ruins.

"Archaeologists have been coming to Zimbabwe for nearly a hundred years," he told them, "and each one has come up with a different theory about who built the ruins. Some had even suggested that Zimbabwe was Ophir, where King Solomon obtained his gold.

"Have you read *King Solomon's Mines*?" asked Jenny.

"Of course I have. This is the place Rider Haggard had in mind when he wrote it."

"But is it true?"

"The book was fiction but the gold was real."

"But there aren't any gold mines here."

"Oh, there are," grinned Sam. "The country around here is riddled with shallow mines, but the gold ran out centuries ago."

"Israel is a very long way off," said Jenny. "Solomon couldn't have had mines that far away."

"He may have had an alliance with the Egyptians," said Sam. "The ebony birds look as if they came from ancient Egypt."

Jenny pricked up her ears. "The birds came from ancient Egypt?"

"Probably. There are similar carvings in Isis' temple."

"Who was Isis?" asked Jenny.

"The Egyptian Goddess of Love."

"Really?" said Jenny. Some of her mother's pictures had looked Egyptian. "Do you have a picture of her?"

"Well, as a matter of fact I do," he replied with a smile.

He disappeared into a room behind the bar and emerged after a minute or two with a book about antiquities.

"There." He held it open at a stylized picture of an Egyptian goddess.

Jenny was shocked. It was a grotesque picture which she recognized immediately. Isis had horns growing out of her head, and impaled on the horns was a round object that looked like the moon. It was the same picture that she'd seen in her mother's bedroom all those years ago.

Underneath was a description. Isis had usually been worshipped in conjunction with her husband, the God Osiris. He was her own brother, and together they'd produced a son, the young God Horus, an ancestor of the Pharaohs. Horus was the last true god to appear in human form and actually rule the world.

Jenny was surprised to read that Isis-worship had rivalled Christianity in the Roman era, and it had been important even in recent times. Could her mother have been mixed up with a modern Isis cult?

She looked up. Sam was still talking about the ruins.

"Tell me more about Isis," she asked.

"Well, Isis-worship has cropped up from time to time since long before the Christian era. It's similar to Christianity in a way, because the followers believe there will be a second coming. One day Isis and Osiris will return to earth to rescue mankind, and their son Horus will once again rule the world for a thousand years."

"Did people worship Isis here?"

"Apparently. A lot of the artefacts found here resemble things from ancient Egypt."

Jenny had an odd feeling she was on to something, but her parents had lived in Canada, not Africa.

"Do you know about the Aquarians?" she asked.

"Who were they?"

"Some sort of religious group, I think."

"Sorry, I've never heard of them," said Sam. "But Isis has inspired a lot of odd little cults."

The group began to break up and Jenny moved towards the door.

"But there's something strange about Zimbabwe," Sam added as they left. "Just when you think you've got the answer, another question always pops up."

Another question, she mused, as they walked up to their room. She had come here to find out about the birds, but she'd discovered the Goddess Isis. How did she fit in?

Peter wanted to go somewhere special to celebrate their reunion and the Leopard Rock Hotel in the Vumba mountains sounded just the place. The road wound through lush foothills and forests, and after the dusty plateau of central Rhodesia the scenery was spectacular. The mountains were not high enough for snow, but there were miles of blue-green tree-covered slopes and majestic peaks of bare grey rock.

The hotel had a steeply pitched roof with pointed turrets like a French chateau, and it was surrounded by lawns and gardens and a copse of flowering trees. It was a romantic place and they spent the next day walking hand in hand through the gardens making plans.

Peter knew they couldn't marry immediately. He was on his way to Nyasaland, and Jenny couldn't walk out on Clayton-Jones in the middle of the mining venture. She said she wanted a big wedding at home in England, but he was locked into the Rhodesian health service for another five months. They were sitting in the shade of a flowering tamarind tree when he took her hand and said, "Look, I love you and you love me. Let's wait until I get back from Nyasaland and you finish your job, and then get married here in Africa. You'll like it on the Copperbelt. We'll get a nice new house, and there's a sailing club, and you'll make lots of friends."

"A sailing club?"

He kept forgetting she'd never seen the prosperous Copperbelt.

"On a lake. It's nothing like Salcombe, but it'll do for a while."

"Done," she said, giving him a kiss. "Where shall we go for our honeymoon?"

"I heard about a little place on the Indian Ocean called Malindi."

"On the Indian Ocean?"

"In Kenya, a few miles north of Mombasa. There's a hotel with a sandy beach and a coral reef, and there's a quaint little African town nearby."

"It sounds wonderful, but Mombasa is an awfully long way away."

He paused, not knowing how to tell her what he really had in mind. Finally he said, "I don't fancy one of those honeymoons where you do nothing but lie on a beach."

"Well, there is something else I want to do."

But then she looked at him suspiciously and said, "You've got something else in mind, haven't you?"

"Have you enjoyed touring in the Land-Rover the last few days?"

"You know I have. They've been some of the best days I've had in Africa."

"But we haven't seen anything yet. Malindi is in East Africa, near Mount Kilimanjaro and the big game reserves."

"Well?"

"Let's drive up there in the Land Rover, climb the mountain, see the animals, and visit Nairobi, Mombasa, Dar-es-Salaam and Zanzibar. We can have a week or two on the beach at Malindi, but let's have our own East African safari as well."

"Could we really go all that way in the Land Rover?"

"It would be hard, but it would be a real adventure."

She threw her arms around his neck. "Oh Peter, it sounds a wonderful thing to do."

Chapter 31

Peter stared at Gerry Rossiter in disbelief. "What did you say?"

"There's an outbreak of smallpox in the northern district. I want you to drive up there tomorrow and have a look."

"But I'm getting married tomorrow."

It was March 1961 and Jenny was arriving that afternoon. He was about to pick her up at Ndola airport, and the day after the wedding they planned to leave for their honeymoon in East Africa.

Gerry looked tired and worried. "The trouble is I'm not sure it really is smallpox. The doctor up there has never seen a case, but you have, in Nyasaland."

Peter recalled the big ugly barn near a place called Lilongwe. It was an old building with a great high roof of rusty corrugated iron. There'd been armed guards at the doors so no one could escape.

He shuddered. "Yes, I've seen smallpox."

There'd been two hundred people in the barn, all Africans, all desperately sick, lying in rows on blankets on the floor. There were hardly any beds and only rudimentary sanitary arrangements. The heat and smell were impossible to forget.

"The outbreak is in a village near a place called Luwingu. I must have it confirmed as quickly as possible."

"But Gerry, tomorrow's my wedding day. Surely someone else can go?"

"You're the only one who's seen a case, apart from me. The others don't know what smallpox really looks like."

Peter could recall the patients now, lying in rows, their half-naked bodies dotted with pustules. He'd seen simple pustules before but these were deep festering ulcers half an inch across. They seemed to be more numerous on the head, and sometimes they were so close together that there was no skin left, the face a shapeless mass of scabs and pus. Sometimes the pustules spread over the whole body so there was no position in which the patient could lie without rubbing off the scabs.

They had to leave the windows of the old barn open because of the heat and smell, so flies buzzed from patient to patient, settling in swarms on anyone too weak to brush them off. He remembered one little girl whose face was seething with their fat black bodies, her eyes swollen shut and her nostrils caked with crusts.

"We're leaving for East Africa the day after tomorrow," he said.

"I know, and I want you to drop into Luwingu on the way. If it really is smallpox we'll have to set up an isolation hospital. Forced isolation and vaccination are the only things that will stop it spreading."

An isolation hospital. That was what they'd called the Lilongwe barn. Rossiter was right, of course, nothing else would stop the spread of smallpox, but confining a lot of very sick people in one place always led to trouble. It was impossible to feed them properly or keep them clean. Uncontrollable dysentery was the usual result.

The Lilongwe barn had been a hellhole. Five or six people had died every day, and others had arrived to take their places. No one had managed to escape, but a few had eventually recovered and returned to their villages, carrying their pock marks for the rest of their lives.

"Well?" asked Gerry.

Peter knew Rossiter had to be sure of the diagnosis before he ordered anything like that, and wedding or not, how could he refuse?

"We're sailing up Lake Tanganyika on the old lake steamer, and she leaves on Sunday."

"If you start first thing tomorrow morning you can reach Luwingu in one day. You'll be able to see the smallpox cases and still have time to drive on up to Lake Tanganyika by Sunday. You needn't get involved with any treatment, just let me know whether it's smallpox or not."

"Gerry, the wedding's tomorrow. You're one of the guests, remember?"

Rossiter looked exhausted. "Of course I remember, but there are lives at stake. Why don't you and Jenny have your honeymoon in East Africa, and then get married afterwards?"

"Oh boy. How am I going to tell her that?"

"I'll tell her if you like."

"You don't know anything about women. You've never been married, and now I can see why. No, I'll have to tell her myself."

"Good, that's settled then," said Gerry with relief. "Now, Luwingu's a long way west of the main road to Lake Tanganyika. You'll have to take the old road that cuts across the corner of the Congo."

"I thought the Congo road was closed because of bandits."

"It's not actually closed, people just haven't been using it, that's all. And they're not really bandits, just small gangs of robbers, mostly unarmed. You can borrow my revolver if you like."

Peter watched the DC-3 circle Ndola's small airport before it made its approach. Jenny climbed down the steps to the runway in a light summer dress, looking as fresh as a daisy.

He kissed her and took her bag. He was uneasy about the change of wedding plan, so he thought he'd tell her later. He'd booked the bridal suite at the Savoy, the best hotel in Ndola. The porter took her luggage and showed them to the rooms.

"Peter," she said as soon as they were on their own, "I've got something terrible to tell you."

She stood close in front of him with her arms around his neck. "Will you promise you won't be angry?"

He loved her so much he didn't care what she had to say.

"I promise."

"I can't marry you tomorrow after all."

"Why on earth not?"

"My mother wants us to wait. She wants a big wedding back at home."

He didn't trust her mother. Why should they put off their wedding just to please her? But he'd been prepared to put it off for a lousy epidemic.

"Oh."

"You're not angry?"

"Well, I've got a confession of my own."

He told her about the smallpox and his own change of plans.

"Can I come?"

"Of course. It's on the way to Lake Tanganyika."

"Good," she said as she pulled him down onto the bed.

When they left Ndola next morning in the heavily laden Land-Rover Peter figured they had enough equipment to drive right home to England. There were spare parts for the engine, tools, medical supplies, extra fuel, food, clothes, even blankets in case they had to sleep in the bush.

They filled up with fuel in the small Rhodesian mining town of Mufulira and soon they reached the Congolese border. The difference in appearance between the British colony and the Belgian one was striking. The buildings on the Congo side of the border looked as if they'd come straight from continental Europe. A sign proclaimed, "Vive Katanga," and another, "Katanga ma patrie."

"What's that about Vive Katanga?" asked Jenny.

"Well, Katanga's the richest province of the Congo, and when the Belgians left, it declared itself independent so it wouldn't have to share its wealth with the rest of the country."

"I see."

"But the rest of the country needs the money, so the United Nations is trying to force Katanga to rejoin."

"Force it?"

"U.N. troops are fighting against the Katangese in the western part of the province right now. But it won't bother us, the fighting's miles away from here."

An African customs official with a Belgian pillbox hat looked at their passports and jabbered at them in animated French, too fast to understand.

"What did he say?" asked Jenny.

"I think he's trying to warn us to drive on the right-hand side of the road."

"He's certainly trying to warn us about something."

The customs man stamped their passports, and Peter took the narrow bumpy road that led into the interior of the Congo. It was rough and full of potholes which hadn't been repaired for a year. He'd driven that way a year ago and it had been in much better condition then.

The first thing that surprised him was the lack of other vehicles. The road had never been crowded, but last time he'd seen an occasional truck and a few Africans on bicycles. Now there was no one at all. After a few slow bumpy miles they came to a village he remembered from before. There had been several thatched huts, with children, dogs and chickens playing by the side of the road. Now it was deserted. The huts lay in ruins and the only brick building, the police station, had been gutted by fire. They stopped to examine it and found bullet holes in the walls.

Jenny was aghast. "What on earth could have happened?"

"I don't know," he said. "There's not supposed to have been any fighting in this area, but Gerry Rossiter lent me his revolver just in case."

"Really?"

"It's in the glove compartment of the Land-Rover. But we'll be through the Congo in a couple of hours."

They got back into the car and he drove on in silence. A couple of miles beyond the deserted village he got his first hint that something was wrong. They were climbing a hill when he felt the engine falter. At first he tried to ignore it but the problem got steadily worse.

"What is it?" asked Jenny.

"I don't know."

"Oh God, I don't want to break down here."

He nursed the Land-Rover to the top of the hill, but on the next hill he had to stop.

He got out and looked at the engine. It was pinging with heat but otherwise it seemed alright. They chatted nervously while it cooled, but nobody came along. When the engine had cooled he checked everything that he could. There was some dirt in the carburetor but he could find nothing else wrong. They climbed back in and when he turned the key the engine sprang to life.

"Well done," said Jenny with admiration.

They made good progress for a couple of miles and Peter's spirits rose. They might reach Luwingu before nightfall after all. But then it happened again. They were running along a straight flat stretch of road with forest on either side when the motor faltered and died. He pulled to the side of the road and they waited in silence for the engine to cool. This time he did find something wrong. The carburettor bowl was nearly empty. There was fuel in the tank but it wasn't reaching the engine.

"It's the fuel pump," he announced. "I'll have to take it apart."

Before long he had the fuel pump disassembled with the pieces spread out on the front quarter-panel of the Land-Rover.

Then Jenny called, "Peter, I think I can see something moving down the road."

He looked up. There was no wind and the road shimmered in the heat of the midday sun. He had to shield his eyes with his hand. Eventually he saw it too, a black dot, several dots, in the far distance, moving from side to side.

"Probably a troop of baboons," he said. "I don't suppose they'll bother us."

He went back to the pump. One of the valves was sticky, but he had a nasty feeling he still hadn't found the problem. Before reassembling it he tried sucking on the pipe that came from the fuel tank, and there he found the problem. No fuel would flow. There was a small filter on the bottom of the tank which must be plugged. Perhaps they'd picked up dirty fuel in Mufulira.

Jenny was still staring down the road.

"I'll have to get underneath the car," he called.

"I think those baboons are getting nearer."

He glanced up, but they were still a long way off. There were only five or six of them which was odd, baboons usually travelled in larger groups.

Once he was under the Land-Rover he had no difficulty disconnecting the fuel pipe. There was a wire mesh filter in the opening at the bottom of the tank which was clogged with dirt. He removed it and put his thumb over the hole to stop the fuel running out.

"Jenny," he called, holding out the filter from underneath the car. "Clean this, please. There's a brush in the tool box."

She cleaned the filter and handed it back but he found it impossible to install without fuel leaking out. In the end she had to get under the car to help. When they'd finished she climbed out and stood up to brush the dust off her clothes while he tightened the bolts.

Suddenly she called, "Peter, quick."

He had one more bolt to tighten.

"I won't be a minute."

"Now. You must come now."

He tightened the last bolt, climbed out from under the car and scrambled to his feet. It took a moment for his eyes to adjust to the bright sunlight, but two hundred yards away stood five men, one of them carrying a gun. His first thought was to get away, and if the Land-Rover had been ready they would have had time to escape, but the fuel pump was still in pieces.

The men were spread out across the road walking slowly towards them; five big unsmiling Africans, young and grim and strong. The one with the gun was in the middle and slightly ahead. They paused for a moment when they saw him, but the leader made a sign and they moved silently forward. He heard Jenny gasp with fear.

He thought about the revolver. It was a big Smith and Wesson that looked as if it had come from the American West, but it would be no match for a rifle, and getting it out might make the situation worse.

"Quick, get in the car," he said. "I'll try to get it running before they reach us."

He started to assemble the pump, but his hands shook so much he kept dropping the pieces. The Africans were getting nearer every minute. The leader wore an old army uniform and the others were dressed in scruffy jeans. One of them had an ugly scar across his face.

Peter finally got the pump together and began to bolt it into place. The men stopped thirty yards from the Land-Rover and stood silently watching him, the leader with his weapon ready but pointing at the ground. Peter even recognized the make, a modern semi-automatic FN, probably left behind by the Belgians. The man with the scar looked especially repulsive. He was a squat bull-necked individual with long arms like a gorilla. He carried a coil of rope which he swung slowly back and forth.

"Bwana," called the leader with a sneer.

Bwana. Master. The old colonial title by which an African addressed a white man, spoken with contempt.

"Bwana. You have trouble with your car?"

It was surprising that the man spoke English. He'd probably worked in Rhodesia or South Africa, and he must have seen the licence plates on the Land-Rover.

Peter replied as calmly as he could, "I'm a doctor on the way to treat Africans in a village up north."

"A doctor? You have drugs?"

"No. No drugs."

"Maybe we help you. Then you give us morphine, eh?"

"I don't need any help."

"Bwana," grinned the gunman. "I think you do need help. I think you never needed it more in your life." He barked something in African and two of the men started towards the Land-Rover.

Peter guessed they could see he wasn't armed and when they reached him one of them spat on the ground. He had finished his repair but he hadn't checked the fuel connections or primed the pump. He'd have to chance that.

"I've finished," he called. "They needn't bother to help me."

The men went to the back of the Land-Rover. The tailgate was open and they pulled out a box and dropped it on the ground. It split open and cans of food spilled onto the road.

"Sorry Bwana. They just clumsy kaffirs," sneered the leader, and they all began to laugh. One of them picked up a can and threw it to his friends.

Peter was sweating with fear, but he thought they still might get away if only he could get into the car. He took a couple of steps towards the door, forcing himself to smile. "You can have the food as a present," he called as casually as he could.

"Thank you, Bwana," said the leader mockingly. "Now, morphine and all your money."

Peter pulled his wallet out of his back pocket and threw it to the man. "That's all our money and we truly have no drugs." Then, trying to show as much confidence as he could, he turned his back and started to open the door.

Suddenly there was a tremendous explosion and something hit him in the back. For a moment he thought he'd been shot but he didn't feel any pain. The explosion echoed in his ears and startled a flock of crows in the trees nearby. Slowly he took his hand off the door and turned round. A cloud of dust was rising from the road a few yards away. The man had fired into the ground and he'd been hit by flying gravel.

"Move away from the car," ordered the gunman, gesturing with his rifle. Then he bent and picked up the wallet and carefully looked inside.

"Only twenty Rhodesian pounds. Now you give me the rest."

"That's all there is."

The man deliberately raised the rifle until it was pointing directly at Peter's face. "Twenty pounds and an ugly white cow," he sneered. "Bwanas have more than that. You give me or you die."

"For God's sake, there's nothing more."

For a long minute everyone stood rigid. Even the crows were silent. Peter was looking straight at the muzzle of the gun and he could see the man's finger tightening on the trigger. But then the scar-faced man said something in African and slowly the leader lowered his aim. Peter realized his knees were shaking and he felt so weak he almost fell.

Scarface beamed a crooked grin and began to tie a loop in one end of his rope. At first Peter was relieved to be alive, but when he saw what was happening he began to feel sick. The man was making a hangman's noose.

When scarface had finished he proudly held up his work for the others to see, a grotesque circle of rope with a thick slipknot at the top. Then he walked over to a tree, swung the rope, and expertly threw the end over a branch. He slid it back and forth to make sure it would slip, and tied the free end to the foot of the tree. The noose hung loosely five feet from the ground. He had obviously done it before.

The leader looked at Peter. "Maybe now you tell us where your money is hidden?"

"There is no money. You must believe me."

"A white bwana has more than twenty pounds, and doctors carry morphine. Show me then I let you go."

"There's nothing."

"We'll see," said the leader with a smile. Then he shouted at Jennifer, "Donna. Get out of the car."

Jenny sat frozen, as rigid as a statue.

He pointed his rifle directly at Peter's eyes. "Get out, or I blow his head off."

Still she hesitated.

Fire exploded in Peter's face. He felt the wind and smelled the cordite, but the bullet passed just above his head.

"No," screamed Jenny, throwing open the door. One of the men jumped forward, pulled her roughly out of the car and twisted her arm up behind her back.

"Over there," ordered the gunman, nodding towards the noose.

Peter was about to rush forward, when someone began to speak, and soon they all joined in. After a moment the leader held up his hand. When they had quietened down he looked at Peter.

"Well, Bwana, it is you they want to hang." Then he snickered. "They want the donna for something else."

Then Scarface began to speak. Soon he was shouting and waving his hands as he pointed at Peter and then at the noose. Before long the others joined in.

"They want to hang you, Whitey," said the leader with a smile.

Then Scarface pretended to jerk and twitch in a grotesque manner with his head to one side and his tongue lolling out.

"They want to see the white man dance at the end of the rope," the leader went on. "But you tell me where the money is and maybe I let you go."

"There isn't any money," Peter pleaded. "You can have the car and everything that's in it, but please just let us go."

They were all jeering at him now, jumping up and down like a bunch of kids. Jenny seemed forgotten. She was standing on her own by the car.

"They want to see the white man dance," repeated the leader. He gestured with his gun. "Go on Whitey, dance."

Peter was dazed. He had no idea what to do.

"Whitey," ordered the gunman, and everyone was quiet. "Whitey, I want to see you jump. I count to three. You jump. Understand?"

Peter only vaguely realized what he meant.

"One," the man called. "Two." He paused. "Three." Pause. "Jump."

Peter did a little hop and there was a mighty report as a bullet struck the road inches beneath his feet. The men laughed. Then scarface said something and pointed to the noose again.

"You jump higher," demanded the gunman. "Or they hang you. Eh?"

He raised his rifle and aimed at Peter's shins. The men fell silent.

"One."

No one moved.

"Two."

Peter bent his knees.

"Three."

He jumped as high as he could, but this time the shot was higher too and he felt its draft very close to his ankle. He landed on his feet and the men cheered and clapped their hands. For a moment they seemed satisfied. He felt a sense of relief, but it didn't last long. After a few moments one of them began to chant a single word over and over again. Hrup. Hrup. Hrup. He wondered what it meant.

Soon they were all chanting it in rhythm as they jumped up and down. Hrup. Hrup. Hrup.

Peter was terrified. "For God's sake take the Land-Rover and everything that's in it," he cried.

"Too late, Whitey, they want to see you jump. This time you jump higher, eh? Or the bullet break your leg."

Hrup. Hrup. Hrup.

"Are you ready, Whitey? One. And two. And three . . . "

Peter leaped with all his might and drew his legs up tight, but the gunman had aimed even higher, and he felt a sharp pain as the bullet struck him below the knee. He landed heavily and fell. The men jeered. He lay in the dirt sick with pain and humiliation. Now he was as good as dead.

He tried to move his leg. It didn't seem to be broken so he struggled slowly to his feet. It hurt but it would still take his weight. The bullet must have missed the bone. Once again he felt a sort of relief.

The gunman laughed. "Maybe next time, Whitey."

Blood was running from his knee. The men leered at him silently, fascinated to have him in their power. Then scarface began to dance up and down again, and the chanting started once more.

"OK, Whitey," grinned the gunman. "Higher this time. I shoot higher too."

He lifted the rifle.

"Ready?"

Peter's leg hurt and he didn't know how he could jump. All their eyes were on him. Slowly the gunman took aim directly at his knees.

"One."

A pause.

"Two."

Another pause.

"Three."

Suddenly there was a shattering explosion and even as he jumped he thought he'd already been hit. But it was the gunman who spun round as if he'd been struck by an invisible fist. The man flew backwards a couple of yards and fell in a twisted heap with the rifle by his side.

Peter landed on his feet. The other blacks stood motionless for a second, then one darted forward to pick up the rifle. There was another explosion. The man's head jerked sideways and he was thrown to the ground with blood gushing from the side of his face.

Peter turned. Jenny was leaning across the front of the Land-Rover. She held the big revolver in both hands, her elbows supported on the vehicle, her face a grim mask as she sighted along the barrel.

The remaining three men stood rigid and even as he watched she fired again. The shot went wide, but one of them started to run, and soon all three were racing back down the road as fast as they could go.

"Are you alright?" she stammered.

"I think so."

"There's blood all down your leg."

"It's just a flesh wound."

"I'd better drive," she said.

He nodded and took a couple of steps to try the leg. It seemed alright in spite of the blood, so he limped over to retrieve his wallet. The men were dead.

Peter picked up the rifle. The other three were still running, so he threw it into the bushes at the side of the road.

"For God's sake let's get out of here," said Jenny.

"Get the engine started while I put the tools away."

She climbed in and turned the key as he picked up their things. The engine cranked and cranked but it wouldn't start.

"Oh God, please let it start," cried Jenny.

"The fuel line's empty. Pump the accelerator."

She tried again and at last it fired, and by the time he climbed in it was running smoothly. They drove for a couple of miles in silence. When they came to a long straight stretch where they could see half a mile in both directions Jenny stopped the car and burst into tears.

He put his arm around her. "But you were wonderful. You saved my life, both our lives. I don't know how you did it."

She sobbed and sobbed.

"I'm terrified of losing you," she said at last. "Like I did the first time, when I was a girl. We must get married, I'll feel safer then. As soon as we get back to Ndola we must get married no matter what my mother says."

They travelled another five miles to get well clear of the robbers before stopping to bandage Peter's leg.

"We're never going to reach Luwingu tonight," he said as he looked at the map. "There's a place called Fort Roseberry which is almost on the way. It's inside Northern Rhodesia and there's a hotel where we can spend the night."

They were in the middle of Africa now, far from the civilization to the south. Fort Roseberry was little more than an outpost, rich with the atmosphere of the frontier. It reminded Peter of the one-street towns he'd seen in movies of the American West, with men in check shirts and wide-brimmed Stetson hats. There was a boma, a solid looking government building for the police and the administration. Further down the street stood a run down petrol station, a general store with hitching rails for horses, and the Mansa Inn.

The Inn had a long narrow bar decorated like an English pub which was crowded in the evening. There were young Englishmen from the Northern Rhodesia Police, Boer farmers from South Africa, army officers from the King's African Rifles, prospectors, administrators, big-game hunters and an assortment of other hangers-on. A few of the guests were women, but most of the company was male. They all drank freely and Peter had to tell his story over and over again.

He could see that Jenny was enjoying herself. She was the first new woman the town had seen for a month and she'd been surrounded by admirers all evening, especially after he'd told how she'd driven off the robbers.

"This was supposed to be the first night of our honeymoon," he said when he got her to himself. "I'm afraid it's not very romantic."

"I'm enjoying it," she said.

"I can see that. It's a good job we're leaving tomorrow."

"Jealous?" she asked, smiling at him. "Peter, this is good for me. I was in shock after what happened this morning and talking about it has made me feel better."

It was a hundred and twenty miles from Fort Roseberry to Luwingu. They arrived in the middle of the morning and went straight to the boma to pick up a native policeman. He guided them along unmarked tracks deep into the bush until they eventually reached the remote village where smallpox had been reported.

There were a couple of dozen thatched huts around a central area of trampled earth, with a few trees and bushes to provide some shade. At one end stood two small government houses built of brick, one for the Chief and one for the next most important person in the community, the Medical

Assistant. The arrival of a vehicle was obviously an unusual event because soon twenty or thirty people were milling around outside.

"I find Chief," said the policeman, who didn't speak much English.

"What shall I say I'm doing here?" asked Jenny as they waited.

"You can tell them you're my nurse if you like." And when the policeman pushed his way back through the crowd, accompanied by the Chief and the Medical Assistant, Peter announced, "I'm Dr Johnson and this is Sister White."

They shook hands, and Peter began to question the Medical Assistant about the number of villagers who had been vaccinated and his handling of the smallpox cases. There had been no isolation.

"It's impossible here, Doctor," said the Assistant. "Many of the cases are children. I can't separate them from their mothers."

He led Peter and Jenny to a circular hut with a conical roof at the far end of the village. The walls were made of sticks and dried mud with a thick roof of thatched grass. Outside the doorway stood a couple of rough wooden stools and a stone mortar for grinding maize. He pushed aside a curtain of woven reeds and ushered them in. After the bright sunlight, Peter found it gloomy inside. There was very little furniture, just some wooden boxes, a couple more stools, and a few other items of everyday use. Three half-naked children lay on the floor on mats with their mother squatting nearby.

Peter put his medical bag down on the packed earth floor and turned to the Medical Assistant. "Have they been vaccinated?"

"Not before they got sick, Doctor, but I've vaccinated them now."

"And the mother?"

"Many years ago."

Peter thought all three children looked very ill. They lay limp and silent as he examined them, and their skin was flaccid and dry. Their bodies were covered with small round blisters and pustules, some fresh, some already scabbed over. He examined them thoroughly and when he'd finished he turned to Jenny.

"Well, Nurse, what do you think of the rash?"

She stared at him in surprise. "Er, well, I don't know Doctor. I'm really not sure."

"Come now, Nurse," he said with a hint of a smile. "What about the distribution of the pustules? Are they thicker on the body, or on the face?"

She looked at the children again. "On the body."

"What about the arms and legs? And the axillae? You did notice the axillae, I suppose."

She shot him a look that could kill, but she replied calmly enough, "I'm afraid I haven't seen any cases of smallpox, Doctor, so I can't be of much help. But these children are dehydrated. What they need is fluids."

"Quite right, Nurse." He turned to the Medical Assistant, "I'd like to see all the patients before I decide what to do."

They visited half a dozen huts and saw ten patients altogether. They all looked ill but none of them had the terrible sickness he'd seen in Nyasaland. By the time he'd finished he was confident it was a virulent strain of chickenpox and not smallpox at all.

He had a conference with the Chief and the Medical Assistant, checked the supply of medicines in the village dispensary, and left instructions for the treatment of the patients. In an hour they were back on the road. They returned the policeman to the boma in Luwingu and Peter called Gerry Rossiter on the radio.

As soon as he got back to the Land-Rover Jenny turned on him. "Don't you ever do that to me again, Dr Johnson, or I'll stick your stethoscope up your bum."

"Sorry, Nurse." He bent to kiss her, but she turned her face away. Then she seemed to think better of it because she laughed and said, "Alright, you idiot, what's the axillae?"

"The armpits, dummy. Don't you nurses know anything?"

"Well, I can see I don't have to worry about you running off with another woman. No one else would have you."

The old steamship *Liemba* was far bigger than Jenny had expected. She looked exactly like an ocean-going tramp steamer from the days of Joseph Conrad. Her hull was painted white and she had an old-fashioned upright bow, a broad rounded stern, and a tall narrow funnel. She was moored across the end of a jetty and she dominated the tiny port of Mpulungu at the southern end of Lake Tanganyika. Jenny liked her immediately.

She parked the Land-Rover on the jetty between sacks of maize and stalks of bananas, and waited for Peter to find out what they had to do. While he was away she watched the African crew load cargo using the ship's davits as cranes. An ancient steam winch belched and puffed as it strained to lift the heavy loads.

After a while Peter returned with a bearded man smartly dressed in a white ship's officer's uniform.

"This is Captain MacKenzie," he said.

"Och, just call me Jock," said the Captain, with a broad Scottish accent. "There are only seven first-class passengers and we'll all be messin' together. There's no need to be too formal."

Their cabin was one of the best on the ship. It lay at the forward end of the upper deck with windows on the front and the side. There were two varnished mahogany bunks, one above the other. From the cabin window Jenny could see down onto the foredeck ten feet below. A dozen crewmen were loading sacks of maize into the hold and the steam winch chugged intermittently. Further forward was the fo'c'sle where the crew lived, and she couldn't help noticing that several young women were living there too. A goat was tethered near the fo'c'sle door, and chickens scurried about pecking at maize that had spilled from the sacks.

A white-uniformed African steward politely showed them round while a pair of cabin boys fetched their luggage from the car. There was a comfortable wood-panelled saloon on the same deck as their cabin, and further back the whole broad aft deck was reserved for the seven first class passengers.

"Please let me know if there's anything you need," said the steward. "Dinner is at 6pm."

Jenny stood on the aft deck watching the bustle below. A steady stream of people were climbing the gangway into the ship immediately beneath where she stood. Their accommodation was one large space open at the sides. Beds and food were not provided so they carried blankets, baskets of food, and even live chickens. She felt conspicuous with the whole upper deck to herself, but no one seemed to care.

After a few minutes Captain MacKenzie appeared with a crew to load the Land Rover. They swung a davit from the mizzen mast out over the dock and attached ropes to the wheels. Then the steam winch chugged and soon the precious cargo was suspended in mid-air. The crew swung the davit back in over the ship's rail and deposited the vehicle neatly on the aft deck.

The ship sailed at 5pm as the sun dropped behind the mountains on the western shore. The steward served dinner in the saloon and Jenny welcomed the opportunity to meet the other passengers. There was a middle-aged Australian couple on an extended tour of Africa, the First Engineer's wife who'd come along for the trip, and a couple from Kenya with their four-year-old son. Captain MacKenzie sat at the head of the big mahogany table opposite the Chief Engineer. The weather was calm, there was plenty of wine, and soon they were all good friends.

It was the Chief Engineer who interested Jenny most when he talked about the *Liemba*. The ship had been built in Hamburg in 1913 as an ocean-going tramp steamer. She had sailed to Dar es Salaam where the Germans had dismantled her, transported the parts seven hundred miles through the bush, and rebuilt her on the lake where she'd been sailing ever since.

"Well, not quite ever since," said the Engineer with a smile. "Tanganyika was German territory, so in 1916, during the First World War, they scuttled her to stop her falling into the hands of the British."

"You mean they sank her?" asked Jenny.

"Yes, and for six years she lay on the bottom. But in 1922 the Brits salvaged her, and the old girl really has been sailing the lake ever since, still running on the same old 1913 steam engine."

Jenny really took to the Kenyans, Rob and Jane Howlett and their little son Adam. Jane was only a couple of years older than herself, and after six years in South Africa Jenny wanted to hear about life in another part of the continent.

After dinner she and Peter sat out on the deck with their new friends, sipping drinks and enjoying the balmy evening air. The moon shimmered on the water as the *Liemba* plodded steadily forward, pushed by her ancient engine. This was the way to travel. No more dusty roads for four whole days.

She wondered whether the Captain or the steward had guessed they weren't married, and if marriage really mattered. But it did matter. Love and marriage went together. They'd do it as soon as they got back to Rhodesia. She wouldn't even let her mother know.

When Jenny woke the first rays of the sun were creeping across the calm water and lighting the mountains in the Congo thirty miles away on the western shore. They had breakfast early, then lounged on deck as the lush green eastern shore slipped by a mile away on the right. Lake Tanganyika was huge, four hundred miles long and nearly thirty wide.

They were in the very heart of Africa now and it seemed to Jenny that they'd stepped back in time. The *Liemba* steamed sedately on, past palm-fringed beaches and timeless African villages where smoke curled lazily from cooking fires. She saw natives fishing from motorless dugout canoes, but no vehicles, no roads, no sign of modern civilization at all.

At midmorning the *Liemba* made her first stop, at a village called Kapembe. They lined the rail as the ship dropped anchor a couple of hundred yards offshore. Soon a flotilla of dugout canoes came out from the beach to fetch passengers from the lower deck. Jenny called to a boy in an enormous canoe and after some bargaining in broken English he agreed to take them ashore along with Jane, Rob and little Adam.

The village was much larger than the one where they'd seen the chickenpox, but the huts looked just the same. They were round with conical thatched roofs and walls of mud and sticks. Some were nestled among the palms at the top of the beach while others had been built along a path of trampled earth that ran inland for a couple of hundred yards. There were many dugout canoes pulled up on the beach, some of them big heavy boats over twenty feet long. Nearby a group of men sat on the sand mending nets, and further along rows of fish lay on wooden racks drying in the sun.

Kapembe was no tourist trap. Jenny didn't imagine the people saw anyone from the outside world, apart from an occasional visit from the *Liemba*. They were scantily clad in ragged shorts or loincloths, and neither the men nor the women wore anything above the waist. She couldn't help noticing the beautiful firm breasts of the teenage girls, and how quickly they seemed to sag. Most of them carried babies on their backs which was probably the reason. They walked inland along the path escorted by a group of children and a couple of dogs. Chickens darted between the huts and there were goats and pigs. She saw a battered bicycle but no other machinery.

As they penetrated deeper she noticed women staring from the doors of their huts, and she realized that Adam was the reason. He looked cute, bouncing along with his button nose and his freckled face, and he stood out among the native children. They looked cute too, of course, but in a different way.

"Perhaps they haven't seen a white child before," Jenny suggested.

"Perhaps they want to eat him," Peter whispered in her ear.

"Shut up. How could you say such a thing?"

"What was that?" asked Jane.

"Perhaps they want to give him something to eat," Peter lied, and Jenny had a feeling that was just what they wanted to do.

Nearby stood a hut with a woman and two bare-breasted teenage girls at the door. The girls had copper bracelets on their arms and rings in their ears. The woman looked friendly and she beckoned them in. It was dark inside but Jenny's eyes soon got used to the gloom. There wasn't much to see, just some stools and wooden boxes, a low table, and sleeping mats on the floor.

The woman offered them stools and they all sat down. Then she held out her hands to Adam and to Jenny's surprise he immediately sat on her lap. She smiled and spoke to one of the girls who fetched a bowl of something that looked like porridge. First she tasted it herself from an old wooden spoon, then she offered it to Adam. He took a little from the spoon, but then he pulled a face and started to cry.

Jenny felt sorry for the woman so she smiled and pointed to the porridge and then to her own mouth. The girl passed her the bowl. It was made from a gourd and half full of thin brown mealie porridge which didn't look too clean. She could understand Adam's response, it was like boiled oatmeal without a hint of sugar or salt, and it tasted strongly of fish. She grinned and pretended to enjoy it as she finished up the bowl.

When it was time to leave the girls accompanied them back to the beach, walking one on either side of Adam, holding his hands and making detours to show him off to their friends.

Back at the waterfront a single toot came from the *Liemba*'s whistle announcing she was ready to sail.

Peter was worried. Adam Howlett had run a fever for two days. He had some mild nausea and Jane thought it might be due to the porridge he had tasted in Kapembe, but there was no diarrhoea or vomiting, and Jenny wasn't ill. Peter had examined him carefully but he could not see what was wrong. He had prescribed chloroquine, but so far it had not been effective.

They'd been on the *Liemba* four days now, four lovely peaceful days. They'd stopped at two more villages like Kapembe but they had seen no other ships. In fact they'd seen no other signs of modern civilization at all.

They docked at the Tanzanian port of Kigoma a little before midday. By the time Peter had unloaded the Land-Rover it was too late to drive on, so they booked into the Stanley Hotel. Adam had been awake all night, so he wasn't surprised when the Howletts booked into the Stanley too.

After they'd checked in he went for a walk with Jenny. The town looked shabby and run down. The harbour was in disrepair with rows of boats in need of paint, and there were no waterfront cafes or modern shops. When they got back to the hotel Peter found Rob Howlett searching for him.

"For God's sake come at once," said Rob. "Adam's had a convulsion."

He rushed to the Howletts' room and found Adam lying bleary-eyed on the bed with Jane holding a wet cloth to his forehead. She looked terrified.

"He started to twitch," she stammered. "I thought he was going to die."

Peter tried to appear calm. "Tell me exactly what happened."

"Well, this evening he felt very hot, and when I tried to make him take his medicine he seemed to hold his breath. Then he began to shake and next thing he was unconscious, and . . . Oh God, I thought he was dead."

"Has he ever had a fit before?"

"No. Was it something I did?"

"It was probably a febrile convulsion."

"We've got to get him to a hospital."

In a way Peter was relieved because the chloroquine wasn't working. He examined Adam quickly. The child was conscious but drowsy.

"Alright," he said to Rob. "I'll phone the doctor while you get the car."

The hospital looked run down like the rest of the town. The examination room was dingy and when the doctor finally arrived he looked very young and nervous. He didn't pay much attention to Adam, but he studied Peter closely.

"I say, weren't you at Guy's?" he said with a very proper British accent.

"Yes." Peter felt embarrassed.

"Splendid. So was I. Johnson, isn't it? Weren't you one of the chaps who lived on Comeragh Road?"

"Yes, I lived there." If only he'd get on with the job.

"I went to one of your parties. Splendid do. My name's Potter, Chris Potter. But I don't suppose you'd remember me because I was a year or two behind you. Have you been in Africa long?"

"A couple of years."

"A couple of years! I've only been here a couple of weeks."

Peter shuddered. "Well, this little boy's had a fever for three days. It hasn't responded to chloroquine, and now he's had a convulsion. Is there a pediatrician here?"

"No, but Dr Buckler is a specialist physician. He's the chief of staff."

"Let's give him a call."

Chris Potter hesitated. "He doesn't like to be called after 6pm."

"Well, who else have you got on the staff?"

"Actually there's only Dr Buckler and myself. I'm supposed to deal with the emergencies."

Jane looked doubtful, but Dr Potter seemed to do an adequate job of examining Adam. When he'd finished he looked at Peter and said, "I can't see anything wrong. What do you think we should do?"

"Get a white count, urinalysis, throat swab, a blood smear for malaria, and take it from there."

Chris called in a lab technician and within an hour they knew that Adam's blood smear was positive for malaria.

"But I thought you'd been giving him chloroquine," said Chris.

"I have, but his tummy was upset so he may not have absorbed it. Why don't you set up an intravenous and give it to him that way? Then we can be sure it's getting in."

Chris tried to get an i.v. running, but Adam's arms were so small he couldn't get the needle into a vein. In the end Peter had to do it himself. The nurse admitted the child and soon he was tucked up in bed with the chloroquine running into his arm. Peter was worried about another convulsion so they added phenobarbitone as well. Eventually they went back to the hotel.

Peter had planned to start the 350-mile drive north to Lake Victoria in the morning, but Jenny wouldn't hear of it.

"We can't leave the Howletts with Adam in that dreadful hospital," she said.

"It's just an old colonial hospital. It's really not too bad."

"The doctor's just a boy. I don't know what would have happened if you hadn't been there."

"Poor Chris Potter. He does seem a bit green. But Dr Buckler will be there in the morning."

"We're not leaving until we know Adam's alright."

But next morning Adam was worse. The fever was the same but now he was vomiting. Peter was there with Jane when Dr Buckler made his rounds accompanied by Chris Potter.

Buckler was a thickset man in his fifties, with bad teeth, a red face and a bulbous nose. His hands shook as he examined Adam, and Peter could guess why he didn't like to be called after 6pm. He was obviously annoyed that there were visitors in the room and he disregarded Jane completely. After a very brief examination he ordered more tests.

"Probably malaria," he said gruffly to Chris as he left the room. "Keep him on chloroquine and add penicillin."

"But, Doctor, he can't keep his medicines down," pleaded Jane.

Buckler ignored her and looked at Chris. "Give them by injection, then it doesn't matter if he vomits."

Peter paid for another night at the hotel. After lunch he drove Jenny down the lake to Ujiji, where Stanley met Livingstone in 1871.

"What happened to Livingstone in the end?" Asked Jenny.

"He died of malaria."

"Oh Peter, what are we going to do about Adam?"

"Nothing. He'll recover as soon as the chloroquine starts to work."

But the next day Adam was sicker than ever. Again Peter was there with Jane when Dr Buckler made his rounds.

"He's no better, Doctor," said Jane wretchedly.

"But he's not much worse," said Buckler, as if that were an achievement.

When Peter called at the hospital in the evening he got a shock. Poor little Adam's condition had deteriorated still further. His temperature was higher and his eyes were sunken like those of a corpse. Peter couldn't help thinking of the policeman who'd died of malaria a couple of years before. No matter what they'd tried he'd just gone downhill. He remembered the autopsy and the pathologist's report. The tissues had been loaded with malignant tertian malaria in spite of the chloroquine they'd given.

Jane was worn out. She'd been with her little son all day, and now when she kissed him he didn't even know who she was. She burst into tears.

"Peter, he's dying. Is there nothing you can do?"

He took her hand. "They're doing all they can."

"But it's not working. There must be something else."

He shook his head, but he did have an idea.

When Chris Potter came in the nurse gave him a report on Adam's condition, but he had nothing new to offer.

Peter made up his mind. "Do you have any intravenous quinine?"

"I don't think so. Dr Buckler always uses chloroquine."

The nurse looked up. "There's some in the pharmacy," she said. "It's right at the back of the cupboard."

"Perhaps you should try that?" suggested Peter.

Chris looked doubtful. "I'd have to ask Dr Buckler."

"Well, call him."

"He doesn't like to be disturbed after 6pm."

Peter felt his temper flare. "For God's sake man, the child's dying." He shouldn't talk like that in front of Jane but he was desperate. "Either act on your own, or call Buckler."

When Dr Buckler arrived Peter's suspicions were confirmed, the man's speech was slurred and he smelled of alcohol. He looked angrily at Chris Potter. "I told you not to bother me in the evenings."

"It's Adam Howlett. He's getting worse. Dr Johnson would like us to try him on quinine."

"What the devil for?"

"Well," Peter started. "I think he's got malignant tertian malaria. I saw a case once in Rhodesia which didn't respond to chloroquine ... "

"And you cured it with quinine, I suppose?" Buckler interrupted sarcastically.

"Well, no."

"Then why the hell do you want to use the stuff now?"

"Well, he's not responding to chloroquine. Perhaps it's some type of malaria that's resistant to the drug."

"Malaria's never resistant to chloroquine."

Peter stared at Adam in silence. The child was unconscious now, his skin had a yellowish tinge and his breathing was fast and shallow. The nurse was having difficulty getting his blood pressure.

"It's just that what we're doing doesn't seem to be working."

"Doctor, please try something," pleaded Jane, tears running down her face.

Buckler ignored her, but he glared at Peter. "You're not using intravenous quinine in my hospital, it's far too dangerous. I've been practising here for twenty years. Chloroquine always works."

"What is quinine?" sobbed Jane.

"An old treatment for malaria," said Peter. "It's not used anymore."

"Well, I want you to try it." Her voice was rising. "He's my son and he's dying. You've got to do everything you can."

"Don't get hysterical," said Buckler curtly. "I haven't got to do anything. We're not using quinine on your son or any other patient I'm responsible for."

There was a silence as Jane stared at her little boy. There were still tears on her cheeks but she was struggling to pull herself together. After a minute she turned to Peter. "What do you think? If Adam was your son would you give him the drug?"

Peter hesitated. He really didn't know much about the effects of quinine given intravenously, but in the end he nodded.

"Well, he's not getting it while I'm on the case," retorted Buckler angrily.

Finally Jane turned on him, her voice unexpectedly firm. "Dr Buckler, I have the right to choose my own doctor and I'm dismissing you from this case. If you object I shall report you to the Director of Medical Services for being drunk, because that's what you are. I don't want you to see my son again. Is that perfectly clear?"

Everyone was quiet. The nurse stopped trying to take the blood pressure and nobody moved. Peter watched Buckler carefully. The man was obviously an alcoholic and anything could happen. It would all depend on whether there'd been previous complaints. For a minute Buckler stared at Jane in disbelief, then he glowered at Peter, turned on his heel and marched out of the room.

Jane burst into tears. "Please don't waste any more time," she sobbed. "Just give him the quinine before it's too late."

But now Peter wasn't sure. He knew hardly anything about the drug. He seemed to remember that when given intravenously it could occasionally cause blindness, and perhaps there were other complications. He had no authority in this hospital. If anything went wrong he'd certainly be blamed. Buckler was a drunk, but he might be right.

"Hurry," begged Jane. "Adam's burning up."

Well, it couldn't do any harm to look at the package. It would have instructions with it and a list of the side effects as well.

"Nurse," he said. "Would you fetch that quinine, please?"

The nurse looked at Chris. For a moment Peter thought he was going to refuse, but in the end he nodded, and off she went.

When she got back he was dismayed to find that the instructions had been lost. The box contained six small glass vials of yellow liquid, and the only information was the dose stamped on the outside of each vial. He was trying to read it when he heard Jane say, "Look at his face."

Adam's mouth had started to move and for a moment Peter thought he was waking up. Perhaps they wouldn't need to use the quinine after all. But relief turned to horror as he watched one side of Adam's mouth twist into a horrible grin. Then his lips curled back unnaturally, baring his teeth like a snarling dog.

"Oh, my God," cried Jane.

Next his mouth began to twitch and slowly it spread across his face.

She put her arms around him. "Oh, my dear little Adam."

The jerking spread down his neck and soon one arm was twitching. She tried to hold him still, but in half a minute his whole body was racked with convulsions.

"Quick, Chris, an airway," called Peter.

He struggled to get the rubber airway between the child's teeth before his jaw clamped shut. It was either another febrile convulsion or cerebral malaria, malaria of the brain. The three of them hung on to the child to stop him falling off the bed. In a couple of minutes the spasm passed, but it made up Peter's mind.

"Chris," he said, as soon as Adam was still. "We've got to risk that intravenous quinine."

"Alright."

"Nurse, a syringe please, and open one of the vials."

He injected the yellow liquid slowly into the i.v. tubing. Everyone watched nervously, but there was no immediate reaction, and he followed it with phenobarbitone to prevent another convulsion. Adam remained unconscious.

A couple of hours went by and Peter could see no change. The child did not wake up but there were no more convulsions. By midnight Jane looked exhausted and he suggested she went to bed.

"I can't," she said. "He's been such a wonderful little son, I couldn't leave him now. But there's no need for you to stay. I'm sure the nurse will call you if anything happens."

So he put another dose of quinine into the i.v. bottle and then went back to the hotel.

"Are you sure you shouldn't have stayed?" asked Jenny as they went to bed.

He felt uneasy. The nurse was responsible to Dr Buckler and Chris Potter, not himself. She'd call them first. Anything could happen.

He slept poorly, troubled by a recurrent dream. He'd see Adam tucked up in bed with a gentle smile on his face, but slowly the smile would get too wide and he'd turn into a snarling dog. He waited for dawn so he could go back to the hospital to set his mind at rest. But just as it came he fell asleep and it was 9am before he or Jenny awoke.

They drove over to the hospital immediately. Peter led the way through the entrance hall wondering why the receptionist ignored him. They walked down the corridor past the nursing station, and nobody said a thing. He went straight to Adam's room. The door was shut and his heart pounded as he turned the handle. Adam was sitting up in bed and he smiled as they came in.

Chapter 32

Mark Wooding stood in front of a bank of X-ray view-boxes in the Radiology Department of Vancouver General Hospital looking at films of a patient's stomach. He was wearing the white jacket and pants which was the standard uniform of Canadian interns and resident doctors.

"There's an ulcer in the posterior wall of the duodenum," said the radiologist standing by his side. "Right there." He tapped one of the films with his finger.

"You're sure it's not stomach cancer?"

"Quite sure. Just a simple duodenal ulcer."

Mark had been in Canada for a month. His rapid departure from Guy's in June 1961 had taken a lot of people by surprise. The fiasco with Pat Cudmore had occurred in May, which had left him insufficient time to find a suitable registrar's post in England. There were several Canadians on the staff at Guy's and one of them steered him through the process of getting a job as a surgical resident at Vancouver General. He'd told no one the real reason he'd been forced to leave, simply saying he thought there were better opportunities overseas.

He had expected a resident's job in a big Canadian hospital to be much the same as a registrar's job in England, but he'd soon found there were differences. The interns and residents worked just as hard as their British counterparts, but they were more closely supervised. They were never allowed to do important operations on their own. He missed the emergency cases, usually at night, when in England he had the operating theatre and its staff at his command. The names of things were different too. Here the operating theatre was the operating room, a postmortem was an autopsy, and of course petrol was gasoline.

He looked at his watch. He was supposed to have the afternoon off but it was already 4pm and he still had a patient to examine on the ward. He thanked the radiologist, switched off the view-boxes, and set off across the hospital towards the surgical wards in the new Centennial Block.

The buildings of Vancouver General Hospital were arranged around a central open area that sometimes reminded him of the Guy's Hospital park. The resemblance was superficial because the area was much smaller than the Guy's park and it had long ago been paved as a car park. A huge oxygen tank stood in the middle, and there were none of the trees and flowers which made the Guy's Park such a pleasant place.

He walked across the car park and past the oxygen tank missing his old hospital a lot. Even the cars were different here, Cadillacs, Pontiacs and Fords. The Centennial Block was new. It had four big rectangular wings joined in the middle like an X. It was a big modern building but Mark thought it looked dull. He entered through a door at the back and walked down an impersonal corridor to the elevators. Other white-coated residents and interns crowded into the elevator, but VGH was such a big hospital that he didn't know any of them.

He got out at the surgical floor and went straight to the nursing station to find his patient's chart. He wondered if he'd ever get used to the system of nursing in Canada. The nurses all wore the same sort of uniform so you couldn't tell who was what. The head nurse in charge of the ward had no special uniform to indicate who she was, and she seemed to have none of the authority of a ward sister in England.

"The patient's name is Sharon Smith and she's in 512," said the head nurse curtly. She was middle-aged and busy, and she didn't have much time for residents.

Mrs Smith had gallstones. She was plump and cheerful, and he recalled Mrs McIntosh on Queen ward all that time ago. He hadn't thought of the episode for years and he wondered why it came back to him now. He even remembered Paul Ellison with a sort of strange nostalgia.

He took the patient's history, examined her abdomen and went to the residents' room to write up her notes. He was tired and the room was empty, and before he opened the folder he sat for ten minutes staring through the window at the mountains and the harbour. Vancouver was a beautiful city, but he couldn't help dreaming of home.

Finally he opened Sharon Smith's folder. She'd been in the hospital with a gallbladder attack a few months before, so he thumbed through her previous notes to see what had happened then. He was flipping the pages, still daydreaming, when an entry caught his eye. He looked again and his heart missed a beat. It was the handwriting that was familiar, but in his present state he seemed to imagine familiar things everywhere he looked. The entry ran over the page so he couldn't see the signature. For a minute he held his breath, hardly daring to move. Then he slowly turned the page, and at the bottom of the entry was the name, Beverley Morton.

Beverley in Vancouver. He felt like jumping for joy. She was supposed to be in Toronto, thousands of miles away, and he hadn't heard from her for a year. Anything could have happened in that time. Did she know he was in Canada? Had she been avoiding him? Was she married or engaged?

He wrote up Sharon Smith's medical history and her orders, and hurried back to the nursing station.

"Excuse me. Is Beverley Morton working here?"

"She was." The head nurse didn't bother to look up.

"Was?"

"That's right."

He wanted to shake her, but he asked politely, "Do you know where she is now?"

"Gone back to England, I think."

"How can I find out?"

"I'm afraid I don't know," she said, getting on with something else.

Mark felt gloom descend on him again. He wanted to be on his own so instead of taking the elevator he made his way down the stairs. Eventually he reached the car park, but he couldn't get Beverley out of his mind. Maybe she was back at Guy's. He pictured her on Victoria ward with Dennis Weeks. The obstetrical wing at Vancouver General was called the Willow Pavilion. He walked across to look at it and then he lingered outside wondering if she had worked there. Finally he pulled himself together and set off towards the Department of Surgery on the far side of the car park.

"Mark."

He recognized the voice immediately, a clear-cut British accent amid a sea of Canadian. He turned. The blond ponytail had gone and now she wore her hair cut in a bob, but her face was just the same. She smiled and his mood began to soar.

"Beverley."

"Mark. What on earth are you doing here?"

She was in nurses' clothes, plain white, different from the familiar blue and white uniform worn by British nurses, but it was the same Beverley and she looked lovely.

"I thought you were in Toronto."

Seeing her was like a glimpse of home. They chatted for a while and then he remembered his half day. The afternoon was gone but he still had the evening.

"Let's go somewhere this evening. How about dinner?"

"I'd like that very much."

"Can I pick you up in an hour?"

"Better make it an hour and a half to give me time to change. I live in a flat in Kitsilano. They call it an apartment here. It's a fifteen minute drive."

He collected her at 6:30 in the old Pontiac he'd bought when he arrived in Vancouver. It had none of the personality of the TR3, but it was cheap and reliable, and gas was only forty cents a gallon. She looked fabulous in a simple dress of emerald green. Her skin was darker than it had been in London, tanned by the seaside sun, and her blond hair shone like gold.

He took her to a new restaurant called Dine In The Sky at the top of the Sylvia Hotel on the waterfront, downtown. They had a table with a spectacular view across English Bay. It was a gentle summer evening; pleasure boats dotted the bay and a couple of freighters were anchored further out. To the right of the harbour stood the mountains of West Vancouver, with expensive homes climbing their lower slopes, and to the left was the residential district of Kitsilano. Beyond that Point Grey jutted out into the ocean with the smart new buildings of the University of British Columbia along the top. Across the water, on the far horizon, he could see some little humps of land.

"They're the Gulf Islands," she told him. "I visited them once on a yacht."

"I didn't know you were a sailor?"

"I'd like to be. They're beautiful islands, almost uninhabited, with lots of little creeks and harbours just waiting to be explored."

She chose shrimp bisque followed by Chateaubriand steak. Mark had discovered that North American steaks were far better than those he was used to in England so he had the same, and he ordered a bottle of wine.

They took an hour over dinner and then sat sipping coffee for another thirty minutes, watching the people stroll along the waterfront below. There seemed to be so much to talk about. Beverley was hungry for news of Guy's, and for the first time he found himself interested in Vancouver. Previously he'd thought of it merely as a place to pursue his career after he'd been thrown out of Guy's, but she saw it in an entirely different light.

"Just look at the setting," she said. "Look at the mountains and the ocean and the beautiful harbour. And behind the city there's a great fertile valley with the Fraser River running down the middle."

"Do you want to stay here?" he asked. "I mean live here for the rest of your life?"

"Perhaps. Vancouver's just getting started. A hundred years ago there was nothing here but forest, and now there's a city that's growing at a fantastic pace. Soon there'll be great glass-fronted buildings thirty storeys high, with convention centres, shopping malls, and marinas for yachts. It'll be the most beautiful city in North America."

"What about medical services?" Peter asked. "Do you think they will expand?"

"They'll have to as the population increases. They'll need surgeons and specialists of all kinds. It's a golden opportunity to get in at the ground floor."

After he'd paid the bill they strolled along Beach Avenue to look at the ocean. He took her hand and she squeezed his in return. They stopped to watch the sun disappear below the horizon, and again he saw those mysterious little humps that were islands waiting to be explored. In just one day everything had changed; now he felt a zest for life that had eluded him for months.

She seemed to sense it too. "Mark," she said. "It's so good to see you ."

"Do you really mean that?"

"Yes I do. Let's go back to my apartment for coffee and a nightcap."

As night approached the boats on English Bay began to head for home and he felt that somehow he was going home too.

Her apartment was the top floor of a three-storey house on Cornwall Street. He parked the car and followed her up the stairs, watching her legs as she climbed ahead of him. He recalled the scruffy staircase in her old place at the Elephant and Castle. How different this was. Everything looked new. She unlocked the door and he followed her into a small entrance hall off the living room. The furniture was modern and there was a big picture window in the wall. Before he had time to take in anything else she turned towards him and put her arms around his neck. How vividly he remembered the first time she'd done that when he was not much more than a boy.

"Oh, Mark," she whispered. "How marvellous you feel."

He bent to kiss her again, but she turned her head.

"We're going too fast. Let me put a record on and make some coffee."

He nodded and soon the romantic strains of *Hollywood in Rhythm* were filtering through the room. He sat on the sofa and while Beverley was in the kitchen he picked up a magazine. It fell open at an article headed Brother XII's Treasure and there was a picture of a man with dark staring eyes.

"Cream and sugar?" she asked as she came back into the room.

"Please."

"What about a liqueur?"

He remembered the night they'd bathed together, back in London years ago.

"Do you still have Drambuie?"

"It's my favourite."

She walked over to a cabinet and filled two small crystal glasses.

"What's this about treasure?" he asked.

"There's supposed to be treasure hidden in the Gulf Islands."

"Really?"

"A man called Brother XII started a religious commune there before the war. He swindled a lot of rich people and changed their money into gold. Apparently it's still buried on an island called De Courcy."

"Brother XII? What a strange name."

"It has some religious meaning, but he must have been quite a character. A lot of people gave him all their money, and according to that article he often took their wives as well."

"Perhaps we should go over there and have a look."

"We'd need a boat."

"I can handle a boat. My father owns a boatyard, remember?"

He read a little more.

"It says Brother XII left gold worth $2,000,000 at the present day value and it's never been recovered."

"That's right."

"Well, to hell with exploring the little creeks and harbours, let's go for the gold."

She sat down on the sofa close to him and they drank their coffee and sipped the liqueur. She stroked his cheek and soon they were in each other's arms, but the sofa was too small.

"Let's go and lie on your bed," he suggested.

"No," she said, looking embarrassed. "There's something I've got to show you, but first I need another drink."

"Something you've got to show me? What is it?"

"Don't be silly. If I could tell you as easily as that why would I need a drink?"

He wanted to see it at once, of course, but she wriggled up against him and after a few minutes nothing seemed to matter. From time to time they stopped to sip the liqueur until finally the drinks were gone.

"Would you like to see the rest of my apartment now?" she asked with a smile.

"I'd like to see whatever it is you're scared to show me."

She took his hand and led him through the hall and along a short passage, but she stopped outside the bedroom door and said, "Mark, I had no idea this was going to happen. It's wonderful and I don't want to spoil it."

"How could you possibly spoil it?"

"I don't want you to be shocked."

He took her in his arms and said, "Beverley, I love you and I don't care what your bedroom's like."

I love you. He hadn't meant to say those words, they'd just slipped out.

"Do you really mean that?"

"Yes, I do."

"Oh Mark, so do I. You're the one I always wanted."

She kissed him and then without a word she threw open the bedroom door and switched on the light.

He stepped inside and gasped. He'd been too excited to think about her warning. If anything he'd supposed the room might be impossibly untidy or something like that. But it wasn't untidy at all. It was a neat room with a double bed right in the middle, but all the walls were lined with mirrors and so was the ceiling.

He was so surprised he couldn't speak.

"Well, what do you think?" she asked.

"Did you do this?"

"No. It was like it when I moved in and it would cost the earth to change."

He guessed what the mirrors were for, of course, but he couldn't see much from where he was standing. He walked over and sat on the end of the bed, wondering what to say.

"Would you like to see how it works?" she asked.

He nodded.

"Climb onto the bed and lie right in the middle on your back."

He did as she instructed but he still couldn't see much in the mirrors because it was too dark.

"Now turn the pink knob in the middle of the headboard."

He found the knob and when he turned it the room was transformed. Soft pink spotlights illuminated the whole centre section of the bed, and the further he turned the knob the brighter they became. He quickly realized that the mirrors were angled so that whichever way he looked he could see his body in one or more of them.

"Wow," he exclaimed. "Have you tried this?"

"Only with my clothes on."

"Well, perhaps we should . . ."

"Let's wait and see what happens," she said. "Tonight is special. I want to make love with you in the old-fashioned way tonight."

Chapter 33

As soon as she saw Malindi Jenny knew it was the perfect place for a honeymoon. The white sand beach was shaded by palms and protected by a coral reef. The water inside the reef was calm and translucent blue. Outside were the darker hues of the Indian Ocean, dotted with the sails of fishing boats.

It had taken three weeks to drive there from Kigoma, via Lake Victoria, Nairobi, the Amboseli game reserve, and the colourful city of Mombasa. The Eden Roc Hotel was about a mile up the coast from the little town. The food was delicious and there was plenty of time to swim and soak up the sun. One day they hired a native to take them fishing on the reef in a primitive sailing catamaran. Another day they visited the ruined Arab town of Gedi, abandoned three hundred years before. The town of Malindi was a pretty little place with a mixture of Arab and African architecture, a colourful Swahili market, and a small whitewashed mosque by the sea. They stayed ten days. Jenny would have liked to stay longer but Peter had arranged to join a safari climbing Mount Kilimanjaro, so they had to move on.

After leaving Malindi they drove inland for a whole day across the great plains of Kenya and Tanzania. The grassland was dotted with deciduous trees and it seemed to go on for ever. Herds of zebra and wildebeest roamed by the side of the road, and giraffes cropped leaves from high in the trees. For most of the day they could see the snow-capped peak of Kilimanjaro in the distance, hovering mysteriously above the clouds. In the evening they passed through the town of Moshi and twenty-five miles beyond, on the green lower slopes of the mountain, they reached the Marangu Hotel which was organizing the climb.

Peter found the first part of the climb easy because they were not high enough to be affected by the altitude. Their safari resembled a snake as it wound its way up the narrow jungle trail. There were fourteen porters, three African guides, and six climbers, all spread out in single file or walking in pairs. It was easy to distinguish the porters because they were barefoot and carried wooden boxes on their heads. The guides wore better clothes and leather boots, and Jomo, the head guide, spoke passable English.

The mountain was an enormous extinct volcano 19,000 feet high and 50 miles across at the base. The peak was still 15 miles ahead, hidden in the clouds, and already the brown veld of East Africa lay far below.

They had reached the level of increased rainfall so everything looked green. The trail led past streams and waterfalls, through lush banana groves, and under trees hanging with vines. Tropical birds darted from tree to tree and there were brightly coloured flowers.

Before long they came across a group of fearsome looking tribesmen carrying spears with wicked blades. They all wore the same reddish-brown robes, with rings in their ears and metal bands on their arms. The path was not wide enough for both parties and the tribesmen stood glowering to one side as the safari passed. Jomo called a greeting in Swahili but they did not reply.

"Masai," he murmured disapprovingly. "Make trouble."

Peter had met the other climbers in the hotel the previous evening. They were Roy Metten, a middle-aged American biologist travelling with Bruce, his twenty-year-old son. And Glen Littleton, a Canadian school teacher, with his wife Nancy who worked in a museum.

Peter walked with Glen and Nancy for half an hour, while Jenny chatted to the Americans. She was wearing trim khaki shorts and a white bush-shirt tucked in at the waist. She looked lovely even on safari, he thought. He caught her eye and they dropped back to talk.

"The Canadians come from British Columbia," he told her. "Isn't that where our parents misspent their youth?"

"Yes, it is. Did you ask them about Brother XII?"

"I don't suppose they've ever heard of him," said Peter.

They walked on in silence for a while. Then he asked her what the biologist was doing in Africa?

"He's with the World Health Organization."

"Really?"

"Studying malaria."

"Did you tell him what I think?"

"I told him about Adam Howlett, but I didn't mention your theory about malaria becoming resistant to chloroquine. No one else seems to believe it."

At midday they stopped in a grassy clearing for a meal. The porters opened a box and produced sandwiches and lemonade, and the six climbers sat in a circle to enjoy their lunch. The guides and porters relaxed in a group to one side, but no food was provided for them.

"Jomo, aren't you going to eat?" Peter asked.

"Africans eat only two meals a day," he replied, and Peter wondered if he thought it decadent to eat more often, especially if one had nothing to carry.

He sat down on a box next to Roy Metten, the biologist. "Jenny says you're interested in malaria."

"That's right," replied the American with a southern drawl.

"I've treated a lot of malaria in the last couple of years."

"I guess you would. What drugs do you use?"

"The usual stuff. Chloroquine."

"Any problems?"

"Not really." He decided not to mention his theory. Specialist biologists often knew more about their particular disease than a doctor and he didn't want to look ignorant.

"That's good," said Roy. "Chloroquine works pretty well in Africa so far as I can find out."

He was tempted to tell Roy it didn't always work, but he let it slip. "How long have you been out here?" he asked instead.

"A little over a month."

"Enjoying it?"

"I've been working most of the time," said Roy, "but I'm enjoying this. Your wife told me about your trip. That's what I'd like to do."

"Did she tell you about the old steamship on Lake Tanganyika?"

"Yes, and the little boy who got sick."

"I think that child had cerebral malaria," said Peter. "That's why he took so long to respond."

"I see."

"Malaria doesn't always behave in the way it's supposed to, you know."

"That's what the World Health Organization is worried about," said Roy. "That's why I'm here."

Peter wondered if he should take a chance. He would like to hear what the biologist had to say.

"Have you ever come across any chloroquine resistant strains?" he asked, trying to sound casual.

"Chloroquine resistant malaria? That's just what I'm looking for, but it doesn't seem to occur in Africa."

Peter felt a glow of excitement: "Well, I think I might have seen a case."

"It would have to be properly documented," said Roy doubtfully.

By this time the others were listening and he wished he'd kept his mouth shut, the biologist would probably ask a lot of technical questions that he couldn't answer. But it was too late to back out, so first he told them about Adam Howlett, and when Roy didn't laugh he went on to describe the death of the policeman in Ndola. Roy took in every detail and by the time he'd finished Peter had everyone's attention.

"And you did an autopsy on the policeman?" asked Roy.

"Naturally."

"Were samples of the liver and spleen examined by a proper pathologist?"

"Of course they were. This was Rhodesia, not the backwoods of Texas!"

Roy laughed. "There'll be records, I suppose."

"Certainly. They'll still have the microscope slides I expect."

"Well, it looks as if I'll have to make a trip to Rhodesia. What about the little boy?"

"He had positive blood slides which will still be available at Kigoma Hospital, and he eventually responded to quinine. I spoke to his mother on the phone last week. He's seeing a doctor in Nairobi now."

"Would they let a WHO doctor examine him, do you think?"

"I'm sure they would if I ask them."

"Oh boy," the biologist drawled. "In all the big centres everyone says no way, malaria's never resistant to chloroquine. Then I meet a guy in the bush who's actually treated two cases. If it's confirmed, your little boy may be the only documented case in the world to survive."

By this time the porters were packed up and waiting, and soon they were all back on the trail. They covered another five miles during the afternoon. As they climbed it got cooler and the vegetation gradually changed. By late afternoon the tropical jungle had given way to deciduous woods that reminded Peter of England, and at 6pm, as dusk was falling, they reached the hut where they were to spend the night. There were bunks and an old iron stove but nothing else.

Jomo gave orders in Swahili and soon the camp was a hive of activity. First the porters unpacked the wooden boxes they'd been carrying on their heads. Peter was astonished by the amount of gear they had brought: there was food for twenty-three people for four days with everything needed to cook it; there were pillows, sheets and blankets, and lastly the equipment for the final ascent.

Some of the porters swept out the hut, made up the bunks for the climbers, and lit the stove. Others gathered firewood, and soon two separate campfires were burning and two quite different meals were cooking, one for the Africans and one for the whites. The hut was too small for everyone, so the porters slept in a lean-to outside.

After the meal the two groups gathered round their different fires to talk about their day. The younger guides remained with the porters, but Jomo joined the climbers' fire to tell them about his experiences on the mountain, and what to expect in the days ahead.

"Cold up there," he said, pointing up the slope. "Lots of ice."

Peter sat on a log next to Jenny with his feet stretched out towards the fire. It was dark apart from the glow of the flames flickering on people's faces. After a while Jomo returned to the Africans' fire, and Roy brought up the subject of malaria again. Soon everyone joined in.

"Tell us what you're up to?" asked Glen Littleton, the Canadian.

"Well, rumours of chloroquine resistance started to come from South America about six months ago," Roy explained, "but no one believed them, so they weren't published in the medical journals."

"I expect that's why no one here has heard of it," said Peter.

"How is the WHO involved?" asked Nancy.

"Malaria kills about a million people a year," said Roy. "So when the WHO heard these rumours of chloroquine resistance they decided to investigate. There'd been no reports from Africa, but they sent a couple of us out here to check, just in case."

"And you hadn't discovered any cases until today?"

"None. There's no record of it in any of the bigger centres."

"How on earth did you recognize it?" asked Roy's son Bruce, looking at Peter with admiration.

"Well, I knew there was something wrong when I found malaria parasites in patients who'd been getting adequate doses of chloroquine."

"But that's a difficult thing to prove," said Roy. "Sometimes chloroquine is poorly absorbed from the stomach."

"But in both my cases the drug was given intravenously, and still the parasites persisted."

"Then I suppose there can't be any doubt."

"The little boy was on chloroquine for several days, getting steadily worse, but as soon as I gave him old-fashioned quinine he started to improve."

"What made you think of using quinine?"

"Well, I couldn't help remembering the policeman who'd died in spite of all the chloroquine we'd given. That was when I first wondered if malaria could become resistant. The little boy seemed to be dying too, so I had to try something different."

"I think you saved his life," said Roy, kicking another log into the fire.

Everyone was silent for a minute and Peter enjoyed the warmth from the flames. There was no wind, but it was cool at this altitude, like an English autumn.

"How could malaria become resistant to a drug that worked before?" asked Glen.

"Chloroquine's been misused," said Roy. "In tropical countries it's been given to almost anyone who had a fever. Isn't that right, Peter?"

"I'm afraid so."

"And on top of that they've handed it out to whole populations as a prophylactic."

"But isn't that the best way to eradicate malaria?" asked Nancy.

"No. The best way is to get rid of the mosquitoes. Drain the swamps, use repellent, that sort of thing. Widespread use of drugs just encourages resistance. With chloroquine prescribed the way it is, resistant strains are bound to take over."

"Well, they're hardly taking over, Dad," said Bruce. "You've been looking for a month and this is the first time you've found any."

"It'll happen," said the American. "It happened with penicillin when that was misused and now it's happening with chloroquine. Peter's uncovered the tip of an iceberg. When his findings are published other doctors will come forward and soon we'll find there are cases all over the world."

Jenny lay awake on the hard wooden bunk. She wasn't used to sleeping in a room with five other people, and after weeks of sleeping with Peter she missed the feel of his body.

She felt so proud of him. His hair had become even fairer while they were in Malindi, and she loved the set of his face and chin. But it wasn't just his looks. This evening round the campfire it had been Peter they wanted to hear. His stories of medicine in Africa and his experiences in the bush. And he made no secret of the way he loved her, everyone could see.

Her mother's objection to their marriage troubled her terribly. She felt sure it had something to do with the Aquarians. She would talk to the couple from British Columbia tomorrow to see if they could help. Her thoughts wandered back to Peter and she drifted off to sleep.

Next day they started out through deciduous woods of birch and alder. As they climbed higher it got steadily cooler and they passed through different climatic zones.

"It's like walking from the equator to the north pole," Roy Metten explained, "and getting a brief look at all the trees and plants along the way."

Towards the end of the morning they plunged into a forest of strange moss-covered trees. The path was hemmed in on both sides and branches draped with moss passed right overhead. The trail was steep and narrow and they had to walk in single file so Jenny had no opportunity to talk to the Littletons.

In the afternoon they reached a belt of conifers and the trail was wider, but for a whole hour the Littletons talked to Roy about the conifer forests of British Columbia. By 3:30 she'd almost given up when Roy dropped back to be with his son.

Finally she pulled in beside Nancy. "Peter tells me you come from British Columbia," she said as casually as she could.

"That's right."

"My parents used to live there before the war."

"Really?" Nancy smiled. She was an attractive woman in her late thirties. "We live on Vancouver Island."

Jenny felt sure that was the place where the Aquarian colony had been located and she felt a tingle of excitement. "Have you heard of the Aquarians?"

"Oh yes. I work at the museum in Nanaimo."

"Nanaimo?"

"It's a town a few miles north of where the Aquarians lived."

"Then you're just the person I've been looking for. My parents were Aquarians and I want to find out more about it."

Nancy looked at her suspiciously. "Did your parents actually live in the Aquarian colony?"

"I believe so."

"When were they there?"

"1936, I think. They must have left before July 1937 because that's when I was born."

"Well, the Aquarians were a semi-religious group who had a colony on Vancouver Island in the 1930s. It was a little isolated community with its own houses, a meeting hall, and a farm where they grew their own food. Everyone was supposed to live together in harmony and share everything they had."

"That sounds rather nice."

"I think it was alright at the beginning," said Nancy. "But eventually people quarrelled and lost their faith, and then it all fell apart."

"What sort of faith did they have?"

"Basically Christian. But they believed mankind had become so evil that the Gods would direct a meteorite called Aquarius to strike the earth and destroy everything except their colony. After that it was their duty to start a new civilization based on the Aquarian ideals of honesty, equality and love."

That didn't sound so terrible. "Did you ever hear of a man called Brother XII?"

A wary look crossed Nancy's face. "He was their leader."

"What was he like?"

"He had a very strong personality. He could persuade people to believe anything he wanted. The Aquarians gave him everything, including themselves sometimes."

Including themselves sometimes, Jenny mused. She remembered her mother's photographs of a man with dark penetrating eyes and thick black hair.

"What did he look like?"

"He had a powerful face with dark eyes and black hair. It was a face you'd never forget."

"Did he believe what he preached?"

"I think he did at the beginning, but later he developed some weird pagan ideas."

"What sort of ideas?"

"He believed in the reincarnation of the gods and goddesses of ancient Egypt."

Jenny felt a throb of excitement. "Really? Was one of them a goddess called Isis?"

There was a pause while Nancy stared at her in surprise. They were walking side by side with Glen a pace behind, and she sensed he'd been listening to every word. Now he interrupted: "That's enough. Nancy doesn't know any more than she's told you. She just works in the museum. That's her only connection with the Aquarians."

"I just wanted to hear about Isis."

"Well, that's all we know. I'm sorry we can't be of any more help." He took his wife's arm and hurried on ahead.

That night it was much colder and Jenny began to notice the altitude. She had a headache and when she fetched firewood she found herself panting for breath. They slept in a hut like the night before but it was too cold to spend the evening around a campfire and after a meal they all went to bed. Next morning was sunny but cool. As she watched the porters pack up the camp, Jenny noticed they were gathering bundles of wood.

"Very cold tonight," said Jomo. "No more trees. No firewood."

Soon after they set off the forest got thinner and then it came to an end. The tree line was abrupt. On one side there were small coniferous trees and on the other a vast open plain of grass and heather like an English moor. The treeless landscape stretched away for miles, sloping gently upward until it disappeared into the cloud that hid the summit of the mountain. Although the summit was hidden Jenny could see a rim of snow just below the cloud and she felt an icy draft of wind from higher up. They pulled on sweaters and even the hardy porters donned extra clothing. Then Jomo led them out onto the moor and they followed him steadily uphill in single file across the empty landscape.

About noon he stopped and pointed to a black speck far ahead at the edge of the snow. "Kibo hut," he announced with pride, but Jenny was too exhausted to care.

By this time the grass and heather had given way to a jumble of small lichen-covered rocks with tiny cactus-like plants between them. It was a bleak cold desert with no birds or animals to be seen, although there were occasional animal droppings between the rocks.

"Wooly antelope," said Jomo. "Sometimes we see them here."

Jenny wondered how the porters managed, still barefoot, still carrying their loads, four with large bundles of firewood on their heads.

By this time they were at over 16,000 feet. Peter had given her pills to stop altitude sickness but they didn't work. She had a headache and she felt nauseous, but she struggled on with thoughts of her mother, Brother XII, the Aquarians and Isis going round and round in her head. Presently she noticed the Littletons walking on their own so she slipped into line beside them.

"Nancy," she began. "I wish you'd tell me more about Brother XII. He had some sort of influence over my mother and I've just got to find out what it was."

Nancy looked ill herself. "I don't know any more than I told you yesterday," she said.

"What happened to the colony in the end?"

"Well, the end came shortly before the war. Everything went wrong. People distrusted each other. Aquarius did not strike the earth. And then the colony broke up."

"What actually happened?"

There was a terrible trial in the Nanaimo courthouse. People accused Brother XII of stealing their money. And other things."

"What other things?"

"He had an affair with one of his followers."

An affair. Jenny remembered her mother's secret photos. One of them had shown her mother gazing rapturously at the Brother's face as he gestured out to sea. But she was born in 1937 so her parents must have left the colony well before the end. Thinking of the pictures reminded her of Isis.

"What about the Goddess Isis?" she asked.

Nancy's mouth fell open. "So you know about Isis?"

"Not very much, but my mother has pictures of the colony and one of them shows Isis."

That seemed to make things worse. "Your mother actually has a picture of her? Can you see who she is?"

Jenny didn't know what Nancy meant, but she answered, "Well, I didn't recognize the picture at the time because I didn't know what Isis looked like then. But now I know who she is. I wish you'd tell me about it."

Nancy went white. "I . . . , I can't."

"Please tell me. I really want to know," Jenny pleaded.

But before Nancy could reply she put her hand to her mouth and vomited on the ground. Jenny felt quite nauseous herself and she thought it was probably the altitude.

Glen went to help her and eventually he said, "Does your mother's picture show who it is?"

"Who what is?"

"Isis, of course."

"What do you mean? It's only a picture postcard of an Egyptian goddess."

He stared at her for a moment.

"Look," he said. "Nancy just works at the museum, please leave her alone."

When they reached the Kibo hut Jenny could see why they'd brought firewood. The place was like the south pole, cold and bleak with wisps of snow blowing between the boulders. It was still the middle of the afternoon but a ceiling of dense grey cloud hung a couple of hundred feet overhead shutting out the sun. Beyond the hut the side of the mountain rose into the cloud like a sloping wall of rock and snow. One of the porters lit the wood stove and another cooked a meal. No one felt hungry and after a few mouthfuls they all went to bed.

Jomo woke the climbers before dawn with a pot of coffee, and they put on thick clothes and nailed boots. The porters couldn't climb the snowy peak without shoes, of course, so they remained at the camp for the day. Nancy Littleton had altitude sickness and felt too ill to climb, so she stayed in bed.

As the first light of dawn filtered through the sky the little party of five climbers and three guides made their way to the foot of the final peak. It was bitterly cold. Jenny wore a heavy parka, a thick woollen cap, goggles and gloves, and an ice axe swung from her wrist.

Before they started Jomo gave them instructions. "If you slip, drive the blade of your axe into the ice and hang on. We will come to get you." He showed them how to do it and even made them practise.

Then they started up the steep snow-covered slope. The rocks were covered with ice, and Jenny felt clumsy in her nailed climbing boots. She could feel them slipping as soon as they set off, and after only three hundred feet both her feet slipped at the same time. She frantically drove her axe into the crust of the snow. The slope was no more than forty-five degrees and the axe stopped her sliding down. She wasn't the only one to slip, but nobody slid very far.

For an hour they climbed through cloud, and just as the sun was rising they broke through. The scene was spectacular. They seemed to be standing on an island of rock and ice above a flat white ocean of cloud that stretched to the horizon. Jenny had never seen the sky so blue. To the right there was nothing but rock and snow, but to the left the edge of a glacier shimmered with pale blue light.

By this time they were at 18,000 feet, and she felt exhausted and breathless. None of them could climb more than a few yards before stopping for a rest. Eventually the lip of the crater came in sight and one by one they struggled onto the top. The guides produced flasks of coffee and they stood around congratulating one another, eight heavily dressed hooded figures wearing goggles, like explorers at the pole.

The crater was a mile across and for the first time Jenny could see what an enormous volcano Kilimanjaro must have been, but she was disappointed to find that the highest part of the rim was on the other side.

"How high are we here, Jomo?" she asked.

"19,000 feet."

"What about over there?"

"The highest place is 19,340 feet."

"Well," said Peter. "Who wants to reach the very top?"

Bruce still seemed to have some energy and his father agreed to go as well. Glen looked exhausted. He made the excuse that he should get back to his wife, and finally Jenny saw an opportunity to get him on his own.

"You go ahead," she told Peter. "I'll stay here and rest."

She watched the three of them stumble off around the crater rim, panting in the thin air. Jomo and another guide went with them. Finally she was left alone with Glen Littleton and the third guide who could speak no English. She took a seat beside him on a rock.

"Glen," she started tentatively. "I'm sorry about yesterday."

"That's alright. But please don't bother Nancy again."

"Would you tell me about Brother XII, then? I really need to know."

"Nancy told you yesterday."

"But there are still lots of things I don't understand. My mother had secret photos of a man who must have been the Brother."

"Well?"

"Nancy said he had an affair with one of his followers."

"Oh, I see what's bothering you," said Glen. "When was your mother there?"

"1936 I think."

"The affair Nancy was talking about took place later than that."

She forced a little laugh. "Well, that's a relief," she said. "But there's something else."

"What else?"

"Isis. My mother kept a picture of the Goddess Isis."

"I thought you said it was just a postcard."

"But it must have had some special significance because she got so angry when I found it. She had pictures of carvings from Isis' temple as well."

"Was there anything else?"

"There were photos of a man with straight black hair and staring eyes. He must have been Brother XII. In one of them he was with my mother, and another showed him in front of a little house with a peaked roof."

"I see." He sat staring at the horizon deep in thought. Then he asked, "Was your mother living in the commune in 1937?"

"Yes."

"You're sure about the date?"

"Pretty sure. Why is it important?"

"Because . . . " He stopped.

"Please tell me."

"Jennifer, why don't you ask your mother what happened in 1937?"

"She won't talk about it, and my father's almost as bad."

"Where were you born?" He asked after a short silence.

"In England."

"And you've never been to Canada?"

"No."

"Then it's really none of your business, is it?"

"You mean you're not going to tell me?"

"Look. Lots of people were Aquarians and the Brother swindled most of them out of their money. They're embarrassed about it. They don't want to talk about it. I expect that's all it is."

Perhaps he was right. She sat gazing at the view. The sun was higher now and there was no wind. She'd never seen snow so white or the sky such a vivid blue. Even the rocks seemed to glow with different shades of grey. A thousand feet below, a flat carpet of cloud stretched away to the horizon shutting off the rest of Africa. It was impossible to imagine that there were trees and grass and animals down there.

But she must have the answer.

"There's something I don't know, isn't there? Please tell me. I must know because it involves my family, and Peter's parents were Aquarians too."

He stared at her in surprise. "Your husband's parents were Aquarians?"

Husband. If only he were.

"Yes."

"What an extraordinary coincidence. When were they there?"

"Early on. Before 1936."

"Good. Well, you seem to have plenty of people you can ask."

"Please," she implored. "It's about Isis, isn't it? My mother won't tell me and Peter's parents don't seem to know. Please tell me what it is."

"Does your mother love you?"

"Yes, of course she does."

"Jennifer, the Isis affair is none of your business. If your mother loves you and she still won't tell you what happened, then perhaps it's better not to know."

Going down the mountain was a great deal easier than going up. They spent the night at Kibo hut and the next morning the cloud had cleared so Jenny could finally see the huge snow-covered peak which they had climbed. On the fifth night they arrived back at the Marangu Hotel but she had learned no more about Brother XII. They said goodbye to Jomo and the guides, paid off the porters, and in the evening the six climbers had a farewell dinner. Nancy stuck to her husband like glue and finally Jenny gave up. That night was the first she'd slept with Peter since they'd set out five days before, but she didn't want to make love.

"I'm too tired."

"It's this Brother XII stuff, isn't it?"

"Oh, Peter, what am I to do?"

"Try to forget it. Your mother will tell you what happened when she's ready."

But she couldn't forget, so she went down to breakfast early, determined to confront the Littletons one more time. For half an hour she sat on her own and eventually Peter joined her, but Littletons never came.

After breakfast Peter went to pay the bill while she did the packing. She was putting their clothes in the case when she heard a knock on the door.

"Can I have a word with you," said Glen Littleton.

"Of course."

"Come to my hotel room, please. We mustn't be disturbed."

She followed him with her heart in her mouth. The room was empty and he explained that Nancy had gone for a walk. He motioned her to a chair and took another himself.

"We haven't treated you very well," he started off. "And Nancy wants me to apologize and explain. You see she was an Aquarian herself, but she doesn't like to talk about it."

"Nancy an Aquarian?" said Jenny in surprise.

"Yes. She had a terrible experience. She was only sixteen at the time."

"What happened?"

"Are you sure you don't already know?"

Jenny couldn't think what he meant. "How could I know?" she said.

"When you said your mother had a picture of Isis, Nancy thought you meant a photograph, and she thought you might have recognized who it was."

"Who what was?"

"The person in the picture of Isis. I told her it was just a postcard, not a photograph, but she still wasn't sure. That's why she was so embarrassed."

"I have no idea what you're talking about."

Glen looked at her carefully. "No, I can see that. You really don't understand what went on in that commune, do you?"

"That's what I want to find out."

"Do you know who Isis was?"

"The ancient Egyptian Goddess of love."

"What about her husband, the God Osiris, and their son Horus?"

"I've read about them, that's all."

"And you still can't guess Nancy's secret?"

"No."

"Well, Brother XII persuaded her that she was the reincarnation of the Goddess Isis. He hypnotized her, I guess. For a while she really thought she was a goddess."

Suddenly Jenny understood. Nancy must have thought the picture was a photo of herself posing as Isis. She was frightened that her secret was about to be revealed.

"And the Brother told her he was the reincarnation of the God Osiris," Glen went on.

"Why did he do that?"

"Because he wanted a son, the God Horus, who would be the next leader of the Aquarians. He persuaded Nancy it was her sacred duty to take part in special fertility rites with him, so she could bear him a son."

"Fertility rites? You mean they actually . . . ?"

"Yes."

"Oh, my God. Poor Nancy. Now I can see why she doesn't like to talk about it. Did she have a baby?"

"No, she didn't get pregnant. And the Aquarians split up soon after it started, so she was saved. But she thought you knew about it, and that was why you were asking all those questions."

"Oh, poor Nancy. I'm so sorry."

Jenny wondered how any woman could be persuaded she was a goddess, but then she remembered Brother XII's extraordinary personality. Even Peter's father had said the man could convince anyone of anything. She recalled her mother's pictures of him, and she had a dreadful thought.

"Were there any other Isises? I mean before Nancy came along?"

"Yes, there was one. She was already married to another Aquarian, but that didn't stop the Brother. She suffered even more than Nancy, poor woman."

There was a hollow feeling in Jenny's stomach.

"What happened?"

"She left her husband and lived with Brother XII in his house in the woods. He got her pregnant alright. The Aquarians thought she really was a goddess and they worshipped her. When the time came she had the baby right there in the commune, with no proper facilities and everybody watching. She had a terrible labour from all accounts."

Jenny felt faint.

"What happened?"

"The baby was a girl."

"A girl?"

"Yes. Horus was supposed to be a boy. Obviously the baby couldn't be Horus, so they decided the woman must be a fraud."

Jenny hardly dared mention what was in her mind.

"What happened to them?"

"The Aquarians threw them out of the colony with the poor mother still bleeding from childbirth."

"Oh, my God." Jenny thought she was going to pass out.

Glen must have seen it too because he asked, "Are you alright?"

"You don't think . . . My mother . . . "

"No, she couldn't have been your mother. When we were talking on the mountain I thought she might have been, but Nancy says she couldn't."

"Are you sure? Mother kept a picture of the Goddess Isis, and photos of herself with Brother XII. And some of them were taken by a little house in some woods."

"No. Nancy says that woman died. The baby too."

"Oh no."

"She had a terrible labour and there were no facilities. She died in Nanaimo a few days later."

It was a long drive back to Ndola down the rough gravel roads of Africa. The dust swirled in through the open windows and covered everything. One by one the hot little towns of central Tanzania rolled by, Dodoma, Iringa, Mbeya. They took turns with the driving and spent the nights in scruffy hotels or government hostels. Peter had chosen a route that bypassed the Congo, but even getting near the place had a strange effect on Jenny.

"Do you still want to marry me?" she asked nervously.

"Of course I do."

"We must do it at once, as soon as we get home, before anything else goes wrong."

They arrived one afternoon, tired and dirty, and went straight to the Savoy Hotel. Peter phoned the District Commissioner's office and arranged for them to marry at 2pm next day. Gerry Rossiter and the Melforts agreed to meet them there.

"We've got another young fellow here now, just out from England," said Gerry. "I'll put him in charge of the hospital so we can all go out for a drink after the wedding. I want to hear about your trip."

"Jenny may have other ideas about what to do after the wedding."

"Nonsense. You've had the honeymoon already, remember?"

He dressed in grey flannel trousers and a lightweight jacket and tie. Jenny looked cool in a white linen suit with a wide-brimmed straw hat. Her hair had grown while they were away and he'd never seen her look more beautiful.

"Peter, sweetheart," she whispered as they sat in the waiting room. "Do you remember the first day we met, when you took me to that party on the beach in Salcombe? I knew one day we'd be married, even then."

She kissed him and he saw there were tears on her cheeks. The Melforts looked on approvingly, but Gerry wriggled with embarrassment.

The door opened and a clerk beckoned them in. The District Commissioner was sitting behind a big oak desk. He motioned them to chairs and the clerk fetched more chairs for Gerry and the Melforts.

"Now, let's get the paperwork sorted out first," said the D.C. "Were you both born in England?"

Peter nodded and handed him their birth certificates, passports and immigration papers. He looked at them all quite quickly until he came to Jenny's birth certificate. Peter had already noticed that it was different from his own, but he hadn't given it much thought.

"This is not a standard British birth certificate," said the D.C.

"Well, it's the only one I've got," said Jenny casually.

The D.C. turned to his clerk. "Better fetch Mr Craddock, he's the expert on this sort of thing."

An elderly bureaucrat came in. He took one look at Jenny's piece of paper and announced, "This is a TB 101. It's a temporary birth certificate, issued during the war to allow the bearer to obtain a wartime identity card and ration book."

"Why would she have something like that?"

"I expect her mother lost the original. That was the usual reason."

"Will it do for getting married?" asked Peter.

"I'm afraid not." Craddock's voice was expressionless.

"You must be joking."

"No. You can't get married with a TB 101. But if you were born in England you should be able to get a proper certificate in two or three weeks."

Peter couldn't believe it, but they were not beaten yet. It should be the D.C.'s decision, not Craddock's.

"We have already postponed our wedding for six weeks at Dr Rossiter's request so I could attend to a suspected smallpox outbreak up north," he said, looking at the D.C. "We don't want to delay it any longer, so in the circumstances I wonder if you would marry us with just the temporary certificate."

The D.C. glanced at the bureaucrat, but Craddock shook his head. "Very inadvisable, sir. If there is a problem with this young lady's origins you would regret it, and if there is no problem she should be able to obtain a proper certificate quite quickly."

The D.C. looked at Peter, "I'm afraid he's right."

"How did you get into South Africa?" Craddock asked Jenny suspiciously.

"It was years ago when I was a girl. I was on my mother's British passport then."

The D.C. picked up her present passport. "She seems to have a valid South African passport now, how could she have got that?"

"Easy" said Craddock. "If you're white and you don't cause trouble, they don't ask any questions."

Jenny looked utterly defeated. She wasn't making any noise, but tears were streaming down her face.

Even Mr Craddock looked sympathetic. "You were born in England?" he asked gently.

"In a village called Ashtead, south of London."

"Wait a moment." He left the room, and returned a minute later with a book.

"Is that Ashtead in Surrey?"

"Yes."

"Write to the Registrar of Births and Deaths for the County of Surrey, the clerk will give you the address. Tell them your family details. They'll send you a proper certificate. It'll only take a couple of weeks."

It was three weeks before Jenny heard from the Registrar of Births and Deaths and they were the most frustrating weeks of her life. Every day she called at the Post Office, and as the third week dragged by she became increasingly depressed. Eventually an official-looking envelope arrived from England. She opened it at once but inside there was just an impersonal letter stating that there was no record of her birth in the County of Surrey. She was overwhelmed by frustration and she had to fight back tears. She tried to call Peter at the hospital, but no one could find him so she went back to the hotel. They still couldn't find Peter, so she phoned her mother instead.

"I can't understand it, dear," said her mother. "That birth certificate has always been alright before."

"They said it was just a temporary one."

"Well, I lost the original during the war."

"Mum, they said there was no record of my birth. I was born in Surrey, wasn't I?"

There was a pause, then, "Yes. Yes, of course you were."

"It's so difficult doing things from out here. Would you sort it out for me?"

"But I don't understand why you need a birth certificate?"

She hadn't told her mother they intended to get married as soon as they got back from East Africa. Now she did her best to explain.

"But you promised," her mother replied. "You promised me you'd wait."

"Oh Mummy, Peter nearly got killed. That changed everything. We can't wait any longer."

There was a silence on the other end of the line, and then her mother asked, "And they won't marry you without a proper birth certificate?"

"No."

"Jenny, I don't think they'll let me sort this out. You're over twenty-one. You'll have to come home and do it yourself."

"But that'll take weeks. It's two weeks on the ship alone."

"Then fly. There's a flight on Thursday, the day after tomorrow."

Jenny was amazed. "How on earth do you know that?"

"Well, dear, it so happens I was thinking of coming out to see you, so I had the travel agent look up the flights. The plane lands at Gatwick and I'll meet you there if you like."

"Oh, Mum, flying is terribly expensive. I couldn't afford it."

"Your father and I will pay. We want to see you, and anyway I was the one who lost your birth certificate, wasn't I?"

"Oh, I don't know. What will Peter say?"

"Don't be ridiculous. If you want to get married you've got to have a birth certificate, and you've got to come home to get it. Tell him that."

"Alright," she replied.

"Now, dear, the flight is B.O.A.C. 121, and it leaves Thursday morning at 10:30. The Ndola travel agent is called Central African Travel. I'll have my travel agent wire the ticket to you there. Have you got all that?"

"Yes. And Mummy, thank you very much."

"It's perfectly alright, dear. I just want to do whatever is best for you in the long run."

"I know that."

"Oh, and Jenny, bring that temporary birth certificate with you. We may need it."

"I can't believe you're walking out on me." Peter was almost shouting. It was 9:00pm, he'd just got back from the hospital, and everything had gone wrong all day.

Jenny glared at him across the hotel room. "I'm not walking out on you, but I'm fed up with sitting here doing nothing."

"So you're running back to your precious mother."

"Don't be so stupid. I'm going to England to get a birth certificate."

"You can't go. I won't let you."

"Won't let me," she mocked. "I'll do as I like."

"Your mother's behind this, isn't she?"

"You never liked my mother."

"She wants to separate us again."

"Separate us? Who's paying for me to fly to England to fetch a certificate so we can get married?"

"I would have paid."

"You should have said that three weeks ago."

"Don't be silly. Three weeks ago we thought the whole thing could be fixed by mail."

"And I suppose you still think it can be fixed by mail. If it were left to you we'd never get married. Maybe that's what you want."

The phone rang and he picked it up, grateful for the interruption.

"Dr Johnson? This is the hospital," came the voice. "Please hold the line for Sister Morrison."

Elaine Morrison ran the African maternity ward. They had just admitted a woman in obstructed labour who might need a Caesarean section.

"I'll be right over," said Peter with a sigh.

It was midnight before he finished at the hospital so he slept in his room at the hostel and drove over to the Savoy to have breakfast with her. He tried to explain and she said she understood, but when he kissed her goodbye at the airport next day he sensed their relationship had changed. The plane took off, circled once and headed north. When it had disappeared he drove slowly back to the hostel feeling lonely and miserable.

For three weeks he heard nothing although he wrote every day. He phoned three times but he always got her mother, and she always said Jennifer was out. She took messages but Jenny never called back.

Finally a letter arrived:

Darling Peter,
Please, please write. I know we had a row but it was nothing. I miss you terribly. You are my lover and my best friend, and I think of you as my husband. Please let me know you still care.

They can't find any record of my birth in the local office, so today Mother has taken my temporary birth certificate up to Somerset House in London, so they can search through the national files. Hopefully she'll return with a proper certificate and I should be back with you in a few days.

Please do write, I miss you so.
With all my love,
Jenny.

It had to be her mother. The woman must be intercepting his letters just as she'd done before. He phoned immediately, but after a long delay the operator announced that the Whites' line was out of order. He wrote another letter right away and sent it by express mail. A week dragged by and the phone remained out of service, but on the eighth day another letter arrived and his heart fell when he read the first line:

Darling Peter,
You must help me. Everything has gone wrong and I need you more than ever. They could not find any record of my birth at Somerset House. They even took my temporary birth certificate away from Mother.

Then a letter arrived from the South African Consulate. Someone has reported that I obtained my South African passport using a false birth certificate, so the passport has been withdrawn. Now I have nothing.

Peter, I can't return to Rhodesia without a passport. I have applied for a British one, but with no birth certificate it may take months. And still I haven't heard from you. I have tried to call but the African phones don't work.

For God's sake don't desert me now.

I love you.

Jenny.

He had to go to England, he knew that immediately. He went straight to Gerry Rossiter and explained what had been going on.

"Women," said Gerry. "Much better not to get mixed up with them."

"There's a plane on Thursday. You've got to let me go."

"What about the army? Won't they grab you for national service as soon as you set foot on English soil?"

"I'll have to chance that."

"A week, that's all. I can't spare you for a day longer."

The plane was a four-engined Bristol Britannia. It stopped at Entebbe and then flew directly to Gatwick. From there it was only fifteen miles to Ashtead, so he took a taxi.

As the taxi wound its way through the Surrey countryside he wondered what approach to take. He was frightened Mary White would try to turn him away at the door. Perhaps she would deny that Jenny was there at all. What would he do then?

"Drop me off at the gate," he told the driver.

Six years had passed since he'd last seen Strathbrook and the laurel hedge had grown. He set off down the drive with his feet crunching on the gravel. When he reached the door he rang the bell and waited. There was no reply.

After a couple of minutes he rang again and eventually he heard someone moving about inside. The footsteps were light. A woman? Mary White? His heart fell.

The door opened a crack. "Who's there?"

"Jenny?"

Suddenly the door was thrown wide open and she was in his arms. "Oh, thank God," she cried. "Oh, Peter, thank God you've come."

For three whole minutes Peter held her tight. He thought there'd be so much to say, but neither of them spoke. Eventually she explained that her parents were away and they had the house to themselves. As she pressed against him he began to experience an unexpected desire. He felt guilty because he hadn't come all the way to England just for that, but she seemed to be feeling it too.

"You as well?" he whispered

"Yes."

Her bedroom was just as he remembered it. The satin curtains, her furniture, the bed, soft and warm and filled with memories of their childhood love. Even the pink night-light. They were all the same. After a while he realized there were tears on her cheeks.

"What is it?"

"I'm sorry," she sniffed. "It's so stupid. It's because I've got you back."

They made tea and sat at the kitchen table.

"You've got a week?" she asked.

"I'm afraid that's all."

"Oh, Peter. I've got you back, that's all that matters."

"How long before you can get a passport?"

"I don't know. I've given them my mother's old one, with me included on it, as proof of identity. But they really want a birth certificate. It'll take several weeks I think. How about you? How much longer have you got to stay in Africa?"

"Only a couple of months. But if I return before that I'll be conscripted into the Army."

She groaned. "Two whole months. But we can write."

That raised a tricky subject. "Jenny," he said. "When you first went to Africa do you think your mother stopped my letters?"

She looked at him warily. "Yes, now I do. But she thought it was for my own good."

"Well, just to be on the safe side I'll address your letters to Poste Restante, Ashtead. Then you can pick them up at the Post Office. And when you write to me post the letters yourself."

"Alright. It feels awful not to trust one's own mother, but there are things about her that I don't understand."

"What things?"

"The secrecy about Brother XII, Isis and the Aquarians. The Littletons told me the Aquarians used to worship Isis, you know."

"But how could that relate to us?"

"I don't know, but I think something happened to my mother when she was there, something so evil that she just can't talk about it," said Jenny. "I'd really like to go to British Columbia to see what I could find out for myself."

"So would I. That's exactly what I'd like to do. Do you remember Mark Wooding?"

"Your friend from Salcombe?"

"He's in British Columbia now, working at a hospital in Vancouver. I had a letter from him last week."

"Oh, Peter, let's go there together."

"I'd like to sail there."

"On a ship? That would make a wonderful holiday."

"I mean sail there on a yacht. You see, my father doesn't need me to join him in Salcombe yet, and when I leave Africa I won't have anything to do. I thought we might buy a yacht and sail it out to British Columbia to see Mark. And if you liked it there I could get a job."

There was a silence while she sipped her tea.

"What's the matter? Don't you think we'd be able to sail that far?"

"I know you can sail, Peter, you've been around boats ever since you could walk. No, it's us I'm worried about. What about you and I getting married?"

"That's just it. I can't get an ordinary job in a medical practice in England if we're not married. We couldn't live together, people just wouldn't accept it. But on a boat it would be no different from when we were on holiday in East Africa, nobody would know or care."

"You're right." She took his hand. "Peter, it's a wonderful idea. I'd love to do it. Which way shall we go?"

He felt a thrill. "Sailing boats have to follow the old trade routes because that's the way the wind blows. We'll go south to Gibraltar, out to the Canary Islands, and on across the Atlantic to the West Indies. Then through the Panama Canal, across the Pacific to Hawaii, and finally northeast to British Columbia."

She threw her arms around him. "Oh, Peter, life is such a fairy tale. An hour ago I was in despair. Now I've got you back and we're off on another wonderful adventure."

Chapter 34

Mark Wooding and Beverley Morton were married in Vancouver in October 1961. It was a small wedding with only a few local friends as guests. His parents did not attend, saying they would rather visit British Columbia in the summer when the weather would be better; however his father sent money for a wedding present.

"Buy a boat," he'd written. "Whatever you think is suitable for B.C."

The B.C. coast consisted of miles of bays and islands, and often there was not much wind. They decided on a powerboat and settled on a twenty-five-foot Chris-Craft called *Sundance*. She was nearly new and she had a sleek white hull, a teak deck, a varnished cabin, and a large open cockpit aft. There were a couple of bunks in the cabin, and a neat little galley. *Sundance* was no laggard, she could do thirty knots on a calm day.

They kept her moored at a dock in Vancouver's inner harbour, tucked in behind the peninsula of Stanley Park. During the winter months they explored the harbours within a few miles of the city, but Mark was still intrigued by the treasure on De Courcey Island, and when spring arrived that was where they decided to go.

They both had a week off in May so Mark checked the compass and the charts while Beverley stocked up with food. Then one spring morning they slipped the lines and nosed out under Lions' Gate Bridge. English Bay was dotted with boats, but once they reached the open Strait of Georgia they were on their own.

Mark felt as excited as if they were heading off across the Pacific Ocean. He set a course southwest for the tiny harbour of Silva Bay on Gabriola Island, thirty miles away. It was flat calm so halfway across they stopped, and for twenty minutes they sat in the cockpit sipping coffee and enjoying the sun.

Behind them lay the city of Vancouver. To the north the water stretched away to the horizon where the snow-capped mountains on the Canadian mainland shimmered in the haze. In the distance to the south lay the mountains on the Olympic Peninsula of the U.S.A. and directly ahead sat the mysterious Gulf Islands.

"We'll be in Silva Bay by midday," Mark said as they set off again. "There's supposed to be a pub so maybe we'll get lunch."

A couple of miles before they reached Gabriola Island he spotted the beacon on Thrasher Rock sticking straight up out of the sea, and soon he saw the narrow passage that led into the harbour. Silva Bay was sheltered by low wooded hills on every side. There were a few fishing boats and yachts at anchor, and on the far side of the harbour Mark saw a dock with dinghies tied alongside and a narrow road running up the hill behind. They moored *Sundance* to the dock and climbed some steps to the road where they found a little general store, a boatyard with a fishing boat on the slip, and a small hotel with a cosy pub inside.

"What a neat little place," said Mark. "I feel as if we've crossed an ocean and reached a foreign land."

After lunch at the pub they walked up the country road behind the dock, past fields with cows and hedgerows full of flowers.

Mark felt Beverley take his hand. "Isn't this wonderful?" she said. "I feel like I'm sixteen again, in the country back at home."

"What did you do in the country when you were sixteen?" he asked with a smirk.

"None of your business."

Gabriola Island was six miles long. It was one of several long narrow islands that lay end to end, forming a barrier which sheltered the water between themselves and Vancouver Island. This protected area measured about ten miles wide and fifty long, and within it lay dozens of smaller islands, one of which was De Courcy, the stronghold of Brother XII.

Late in the afternoon they took *Sundance* through the narrow channel between Gabriola and Valdes, and Mark got his first glimpse of the inner Gulf Islands. The beauty of the place took his breath away. Tree-covered islets stretched away to the south as far as the eye could see. The water was calm and the air was warm with hardly any breeze. There was a slight haze that made the more distant islands look mysterious and indistinct. Ahead lay the island of De Courcy, a couple of miles long, and near its southern tip the chart showed a small natural harbour called Pirates Cove.

The entrance was only a few yards wide, but once inside the cove broadened out into a tranquil lagoon a quarter of a mile across. A heron flew slowly overhead hardly moving its wings, and in the distance came the wavering call of a loon. There were no other boats, but on the far shore Mark spotted an old wooden dock and he headed for that, very slowly so as not to disturb the peace. Beside the dock was a small beach, and nearby he saw a ramshackle shed and an overgrown track leading into the woods.

As darkness fell Mark maneuvered *Sundance* alongside the dock and Beverley helped him tie up. When they were moored he began to rig the canvas cockpit cover, while she prepared the cabin for the evening.

"Hi there," came a man's voice.

Mark jumped. He hadn't heard anyone approach.

"Hello," he said.

"This is a private dock, you know. It belongs to the farm."

Beverley stuck her head out of the cabin door. "Is there a farm?" she said. " We'd like to buy eggs and milk."

"I see," said the man, changing his tone. "Do you have cash?"

"Of course. If we can stay here for the night we'll get them in the morning."

"OK."

He seemed to hang around as if he were lonely and Mark wondered if he knew about Brother XII.

"Would you like a beer?" he asked.

"Thanks."

"Come aboard. I'm Mark Wooding and this is Beverley."

"Bert Hogarth," said the man, holding out his hand. He was tall and lanky, about forty, wearing a red check shirt and jeans.

Mark opened three bottles of Molson Canadian, and they sat in the dim light of the cabin and drank them straight from the bottle. Bert talked about the weather and the crops, and the salmon fishing around the islands.

"Do you live here on your own?" asked Beverley.

"Me and the wife"

"Anyone else on the island?"

He shook his head. "There used to be. Back in the thirties lots of people lived here."

Mark nodded. "Did you ever hear of a man called Brother XII?"

"Brother XII and the Aquarians? Of course I did. This used to be their dock and the shed up there was their storehouse."

"Really?" said Mark. Then he added, as casually as he could, "Isn't there supposed to be treasure buried here?"

Bert smiled. "So you're after the gold, eh? Well, I'm afraid you're not going to find it."

"What do you mean?"

"The Brother took it with him when he fled. There's nothing left here now."

"How can you be so sure?"

"Lots of people have searched for it, not just on this island but in the other two settlements as well."

"What other two settlements?"

"They had one at Cedar and another on Valdes Island, but this was the main one."

Mark felt disappointed, although of course he'd never really expected to find any treasure. He was about to change the subject when Bert said, "I know where they kept it, though."

"You do?"

"Yep. I found their secret hiding place a couple of years back." He took a swig of beer. "There's a vault hidden in the floor of one of the houses."

"I see," said Mark. "But how do you know it's where they kept the gold?"

"It's the place alright. I got proof." He grinned, exposing a row of irregular teeth. "I'll show you in the morning if you like. That'll make sure you come to buy those eggs."

He finished his beer and Mark handed him another.

"Do you know how much gold there was supposed to be?"

"Thirty or forty jars of it."

"Jars?"

"Anyone who joined the colony had to sell everything they owned and give the money to Brother XII. But he didn't believe in banks, see? So he used to change the money into gold coins which he stored in big glass jars. In the end there were about forty of them."

"Forty jars of gold coins. How much do you think they were worth?"

"They figured it was half a million dollars at the time, but it would be far more now, of course."

"And you're sure it's not still on the island?"

Bert grinned again. He was already halfway through his second Molson. "Of course I'm sure. The wife an' I moved here five years ago to try to find it and we've searched every inch. No, it's gone. The Brother and Zee took it with them."

"Who was Zee?" asked Bev.

"Madame Zee. His mistress. His last mistress to be exact, because from all accounts he had several of 'em. But she was the only one who had any influence over him. She was a real bitch."

"What do you mean?"

He paused to drain his bottle. "Well, she was their overseer. She made 'em work."

"Made who work?"

"The settlers, the ordinary members of the colony. At the beginning it was a friendly little community and they all helped with the work. But as time went by any Aquarians who could think for themselves got fed up and left. Eventually the only ones remaining were completely in the Brother's power. They were brainwashed, I guess, and he used them like slaves to work the farm and do anything else he wanted."

"I see," said Beverley. "So where did Madame Zee fit in?"

"Well, he got tired of having to boss them up himself, so one day he arrived back with a big black-haired woman. He announced that her name was Zura de Valdes and she was to be their overseer. She would organize them and make them work, a job which she seemed to thoroughly enjoy."

"Why was she called Madame Zee?"

"The Zee was for Zura and Madame was her title. She insisted that everybody called her Madame. If they forgot she'd give them a whipping."

"Jesus," said Mark.

"Oh yes, wherever she went Zee carried a horsewhip. If anyone displeased her she'd whip them, with everybody watching. Man or woman, boy or girl, it made no difference."

"My God. Why didn't they run away?"

"I don't know. It's a strange thing. The Brother had too much influence over them, I guess."

"How did you discover all this?" asked Beverley.

"From people who were there. And a lot of it came out in court when the colony came to an end."

"Tell us what happened then."

"There'd been rumours about what was going on in the Aquarian commune for years, but no one dared give evidence against the Brother, so nothing could be done. But when Zee got going with her horsewhip eventually some of them did run away. They reached Nanaimo cold, wet and broke, and they had nowhere to stay."

Bert paused and stared at his empty bottle. Mark handed him another.

"Thank you," he said, putting it to his mouth. "Now where was I?"

"You were telling us about the end of the Aquarian commune."

"Oh, yes. Well, the Aquarians who'd run away were destitute. They'd given the Brother all their money, see, so they had to sue him to get some of it back. That's when the stories came out in court."

"What stories?"

"What I've been telling you about the gold and Madame Zee. And there were even stranger things like black magic and fertility rites."

"Fertility rites?"

"In the summer they'd have weird ceremonies round a big fire deep in the woods. Brother XII would pretend to turn into a god. Then he'd pick one of the young women and turn her into a goddess, and they'd . . . Well, you know . . . ," He snickered. "The girls thought it was a great honour, I believe."

"How disgusting," said Beverley. "But you still haven't told us what happened in the end."

"Well, when all this came out in court there was a public outcry and the police decided to raid the place. But they were too slow. By the time they arrived the Brother and Zee had gone, and so had all the gold."

"But how could they have carried it?" asked Mark. "Gold's heavy stuff."

"You don't have to tell me about gold. I've spent the last five years searching for it. They had a tugboat which they used for hauling barges between the settlements, and that was quite big enough to carry the gold. Some of the last remaining settlers saw them leave the island in the tug and head out across the Strait."

"Do you know where they went?"

"The tug was found abandoned in a harbour on the mainland. The Brother and Zee were supposed to have escaped to Switzerland by rail and ship."

"Didn't the police track them down?"

"By the time they'd found the trail the war had started, so they couldn't follow them then. After the war they found that the Brother had been living in Switzerland and eventually he died there in some sort of a clinic. They even got a copy of the death certificate."

Mark found the story fascinating, far more interesting than the bare facts he'd read in Bev's magazine. But he wondered how reliable Bert Hogarth was likely to be.

"Is all this written down anywhere?"

"There isn't any book, if that's what you mean, but there's quite a lot of stuff in the museum in Nanaimo."

By the time he was ready to leave the moon was up, bathing the island in silver light. Mark watched him walk unsteadily along the old wooden dock and up the trail until he disappeared among the trees.

"Well, what do you make of that?" asked Bev when he'd gone.

"It's obvious we're not going to find any treasure by scratching around on the beach," said Mark.

"I mean all that stuff about fertility rites and Madame Zee."

"I don't know. Things like that can get awfully exaggerated if they're not written down."

"Let's go to Nanaimo tomorrow," she said. "Then we can have a look in the museum."

He climbed out onto the dock to check the mooring lines while she made up the bunks for the night. Brother XII's actual dock. The moon glinted on the water and in the background he heard the gentle sound of frogs. When he got back on board he found Beverley in her nightie.

"I've been thinking about those fertility rites," he began.

"So have I," she said. "Hurry up and get undressed."

The morning was sunny and warm. Mark and Beverley were walking up the narrow road to the farm. Mark could see that a thriving little community must have lived there once. The road was overgrown and among the trees were the ruins of houses abandoned long ago. The island seemed much larger now they were ashore. It was far too big for them to search on their own so he was looking forward to seeing what Bert Hogarth had already found.

A few hundred yards from the dock they came to a clearing with a derelict tractor, a couple of cows and some chickens. At the far side stood a pretty little farmhouse with a peaked roof and gables, and nearby there was a vegetable garden fenced off to keep out deer. A dog barked as they approached, and Bert came to the door. He gave a shout and soon he was joined by a tired-looking woman with straggly blond hair. He gave her some instructions and she went to fetch the milk.

"We're not supposed to sell it like this," said the woman when she returned. "It's all supposed to go to Nanaimo."

"Is it fresh?" asked Beverley.

"Of course it is. I milked the cow this morning."

The eggs were still in the chicken house and Bert sent her off to collect them while Bev gave him the money.

"You were going to show us Brother XII's secret vault," said Mark.

"It's a long way and I haven't got much time."

In the cold light of morning he didn't seem so friendly, and Mark realized they should have seen the hiding place before they paid for the food. "We'd really like to see it," he said. "Then we'll leave you alone."

"Alright. But this is a private island. I don't want you poking around on your own."

After Mrs Hogarth had given them the eggs, Bert led the way to the remains of a house that stood on its own overlooking the water.

"This was one of Brother XII's personal houses," he said as he led them through the broken-down porch. "It was the best house on the island."

They walked across a hall and past a ruined living room into what had once been the kitchen. Everything was a shambles. The windows were broken and plaster hung from the ceiling. Bert pointed to a large cupboard with a full-length door.

"Take a look in there," he said.

Mark eased open the door but the cupboard was empty.

"Have a look at the floor," said Bert.

The cupboard had a linoleum covered floor that matched the floor in the kitchen. Mark could see nothing remarkable.

"Take a closer look," said Bert.

When Mark knelt down for a closer look he found the cupboard floor was loose. It was made of plywood and he was able to lift it out, exposing the concrete pad on which the house was built, but there was nowhere to hide any gold.

"You still can't see it, eh?" said Bert with a smile. "Feel the concrete with your fingers."

Mark finally realized that sand had been sprinkled onto the concrete to conceal its surface. He felt about and found an iron ring hidden in a recess. The ring was attached to a concrete lid that looked like part of the pad.

"Look underneath," said Bert.

Mark had to stand with one foot on either side to raise the heavy lid. Eventually he lifted it out. Underneath was a dark cavity.

"Here, try this," said Bert, passing him a flashlight.

He crouched on his hands and knees and peered into the hole. It was a dusty vault, about three feet square and two feet deep, with rough concrete walls. He probed the whole area with the light, but it was empty apart from a rolled up strip of black paper.

"Now are you convinced?" asked Bert.

"Well, it looks like a hiding place for something, but how do you know it was the gold?"

"Look at the paper."

Mark reached inside and pulled out the roll of paper. It was a strip of thick black building paper of the type used in the walls of wooden houses, impregnated with tar and impervious to rot. Slowly he uncurled the springy strip. On the inside was a handwritten message in large white letters, scratched on with hard chalk which would never fade.

"FOR FOOLS AND TRAITORS, NOTHING."

"It's the Brother's writing," said Bert. "I've had it checked."

"We're never going to find any treasure," said Mark with a smile as they ate a late breakfast on *Sundance*, still tied to the dock.

"Of course we're not," said Beverley. "But it's Zee and Twelve I'm interested in. I hope there's something about them in the museum."

At mid-morning they left Pirates Cove and headed north along the wooded shore of De Courcy Island towards Nanaimo. Bert Hogarth had told them of a narrow channel between De Courcy and Link Island that they could squeeze through if the tide was high enough.

When they reached the end of De Courcy Mark turned into the little bay that led to the channel, and he slowed the Chris-Craft to a crawl. The banks were lush with fir, cedar and twisted arbutus trees which overhung the water. A kingfisher darted across the bow calling loudly as they invaded its territory. Eventually Mark spotted the channel that Hogarth had described.

"How deep is it here?" he called.

"Three and a half feet," said Beverley, looking at the depth sounder.

He nosed in with Bev holding a boathook to push off if they got too close to rocks. The narrow bit was only a few yards long and soon they were through.

"Whew," said Bev. "Do you think that's a natural channel?"

"Looks like it was blasted out by dynamite to me."

"Who would have done that?"

"The Aquarians, maybe? They built those houses and the farm. They must have had a much bigger organization than I imagined."

He turned north along the rocky shore of Link Island. Link was only three-quarters of a mile long, and most of the western shore consisted of a cliff that dropped sheer into the water. Cormorants nested on the ledges and eagles circled overhead. About halfway along there was a prominent outcrop of rock at the top of the cliff, and below the outcrop he spotted a small cave with the sea running into its mouth. Nearby, standing on a ledge, he saw a sleek furry animal with a pointed snout.

"Look at that. It must be an otter."

"Oh, isn't he sweet," said Bev. "Let's go in close and have a look."

The otter slipped headfirst into the water with barely a ripple, but immediately another appeared and then a third. It seemed a whole family of otters were living in the cave. Mark edged in close to the cliff and stopped the motor so they could watch. Soon the otters surfaced in a group and stared at them with curious little eyes, their heads held high above the water to get a better view.

From Link Island it was only a couple of miles to Dodd Narrows and another seven to Nanaimo. They rounded Gallows Point at the entrance to Nanaimo Harbour a little before noon. The town was spread out on the side of a hill behind the harbour. He motored slowly in, past fishing boats and yachts; there were even a couple of floatplanes waiting to take off. Ahead lay the wharves and boatyards of a busy waterfront, and near the middle he spotted the public dock.

Bert had told them the museum was in an old Hudson's Bay Company fort called the Bastion. Mark saw it right away, an angular black and white tower directly above the waterfront, within walking distance of the public dock. They moored among the commercial salmon-fishing boats, walked up the hill, and in fifteen minutes they were at the Bastion's massive wooden door.

The fort had been built in the middle of the nineteenth century, but it looked like a relic of the seventeen hundreds. It was a broad eight-sided tower, three storeys high, with a pointed roof and black-edged gun ports round the upper two levels. The base was built of stone, but the rest of the structure was made of heavy rough-hewn lumber several inches thick.

Mark could see that the Bastion was a very small museum. On the main floor there were glass-fronted cabinets of artefacts and some filing cabinets. A dark-haired woman of about forty sat at a desk studying papers.

"Excuse me," said Mark. "Do you have any information about Brother XII?"

The woman looked up. "Brother XII? What sort of information do you want?"

"Do you have a book about him?"

"No, there isn't any book."

"What about old magazine articles or newspaper cuttings?" asked Mark.

"Yes, we do have some stuff like that."

She walked over to the filing cabinets and pulled out a folder.

"A couple of men were looking at this just last week," she said.

She handed him the folder and nodded towards the table. "You can sit over there if you like."

The folder contained newspaper clippings and faded photographs but little else. The photos were mostly of groups of people dressed in 1930's clothes, under a huge maple tree. Only three showed the Brother. He was a dynamic-looking man in his forties, with dark eyes and black hair brushed straight back. Even in the photos he seemed to dominate the surroundings.

But another picture caught Mark's attention, a photo of a wrecked two-masted sailing vessel lying half on her side. He recognized the lines immediately. She was an old Brixham trawler. A similar boat, the *Provident*, was still afloat in Salcombe.

"What's this boat?" he asked the curator.

"The *Lady Royal*. She was Brother XII's yacht."

"He had a yacht?"

"Oh yes, he sailed her out from England. She was his pride and joy, but in the end he scuttled her in Pirates Cove just before he left."

"Why did he do that?"

"To stop anyone else from having her, I guess."

"How big was she?"

"Seventy or eighty feet long."

Mark felt a wave of excitement. A boat that size could go anywhere in the world. No one would scuttle an ocean-going yacht if they had gold to transport, particularly if they'd already sailed the boat halfway around the world. The Brother would never have chosen a tugboat over a Brixham trawler if he was taking the treasure with him, so it must be still on the island.

The curator went back to her desk, and they started to read the press cuttings.

"My God," said Beverley after a while. "I can see why the settlers didn't run away, the Brother had them completely in his power. Listen to this, it's testimony one of the runaways gave in court:

"Brother XII has the most tremendous mental power I have ever known. He controls the very soul of everyone who comes near him. If you raise one finger in opposition you get implacable hatred from that time on; and if need be he can even use black magic to work on people's minds until they die."

"Black magic? Was anyone actually killed?"

"That's just what the judge wanted to know," said Bev. "Here's the reply:

"Yes, sir. He forced us to work together on several people."

The judge: "Can you give me an example?"

"Yes, Mr Hargreaves the accountant was one. I should say ex accountant, because soon after we went to work on him he disappeared and he was never seen again. There were several others."

"Will you describe how it was done."

"The Brother uses black magic of the most devilish kind, Your Lordship. First he would make us sit in a circle, usually at night. Then he would call out to invisible powers from the darkness beyond. Next, in imagination, he would stand his victim in the centre of the circle and begin a tirade of implacable black hatred, cursing and damning the victim's spirit. Then he would cut him with an invisible knife, to sever his etheric spirit from his body, so the body would wither and die."

"Did you believe in this? Did you think it would work?"

"Yes, sir. I was utterly convinced."

"Then why did you take part?"

"I had to, sir. He controlled my soul. If I had disobeyed him in the slightest way he would have condemned my soul to torment for a thousand years."

"Do you still believe that?"

"I don't know, sir. That's a difficult question to answer."

"That's actual testimony that came out in court?" asked Mark.

"That's what it says."

"Jesus."

"Here's something else. This is a different witness:

"He has made us all distrust each other, so the entire colony is seething with fear and suspicion. It is impossible to describe such hell on earth. The whole scheme is to drive you into such intense fear and confusion that you are desperate to get away, even if you have to leave all your money and goods behind. We had to surrender everything. We believed it. We did it."

Then Mark came across a map. He spread it out on the table and saw that it was a copy of part of the navigational chart of the Gulf Islands, enlarged and drawn by hand on heavy paper. He recognized Silva Bay, De Courcy and Link Islands. The Aquarian settlements at Cedar-by-the-Sea and on De Courcy and Valdes Islands were shown as well. Some of the names were marked, and even some individual houses and the farm.

It looked like a simple map of Brother XII's empire except for one thing: a red line had been drawn along a crooked path from one side of the map to the other. The line started at the settlement in Cedar and ran east to Link Island, then it turned south across De Courcy Island where it ran through the farm. From there it turned east near Pirates Cove, and out across Pylades Channel to Valdes Island.

"What do you think of this?" he asked.

"It looks like a map of the Aquarian settlements," said Bev.

"I can see that, dummy, but what about the red line?"

"I don't know. It could be anything."

"Perhaps this is a treasure map?" Mark suggested.

"Oh, dummy to you. You wouldn't find a treasure map in a public museum, would you?"

"Look. The line goes right through the house where Bert Hogarth found the secret vault," said Mark. "How do you explain that?"

"It also goes through Cedar, Link and the farm. It even goes through the cliff where we saw the otters' cave."

There were no other visitors and the curator was still at her desk, so Mark got up and showed her the map.

"Excuse me," he asked. "Do you know anything about this?"

She looked at it in surprise. "I had no idea that was in there," she said. "It must have been found on the *Lady Royal* after she was scuttled."

"But what is it?"

"Just a map of the Aquarian settlements."

"But what's this red line supposed to show?"

"It marks the track where they thought the meteorite Aquarius was going to pass overhead."

"The meteorite Aquarius?"

"The Brother said that a meteorite was going to collide with the earth and destroy everything except the Aquarian settlements. This map was supposed to show the course it would follow before it struck."

"A meteorite wouldn't follow a course like that," said Mark.

"I'm just telling you what the Brother said."

"But a meteorite would travel in a straight line. He couldn't have said that."

"He did," she replied stubbornly. "As a matter of fact I heard him."

"You heard him?" Mark was amazed. "Were you an Aquarian?"

"A lot of people were Aquarians. I was just there for a few weeks at the end."

"I think that's wonderful," said Beverley. "It must have been an incredible experience. I wish you'd tell us what it was like."

The woman smiled. "Well, actually it was awful and I don't like to talk about it. Brother XII himself was alright, a charming man really. When he talked to you he'd look straight into your eyes and it felt like magic. Madame Zee was the one who caused the trouble."

"What did she do?"

"I think she was a sadist. She had absolute power and she could be really beastly to people, particularly other women if she thought the Brother was interested in them. It was horrible. I'd be embarrassed to tell you the things she'd make people do."

But Mark was more interested in the map. "I wonder if this map could have shown where the treasure was hidden," he suggested.

"There isn't any treasure. Brother XII and Zee took it with them when they left," said the curator.

"How do you know?"

"Because when they ran away to the mainland they took the colony's tugboat. Why else would they have used a slow old tug to escape when they could have gone in one of the faster powerboats?"

"What do you mean?"

"The Aquarians had several powerboats which were much faster than the tug but they couldn't carry much weight. As soon as we saw them leave in the tug we knew they must be taking the gold."

Mark didn't say anything, but he was sure that if they'd wanted to take the gold they'd have used the *Lady Royal*. Perhaps they had travelled on the tug to make people think the gold was no longer on the island.

"Bert Hogarth certainly thinks they took it in the tug," said Beverley.

The curator raised her eyebrows. "You know Bert?"

"We met him on De Courcy yesterday," said Bev. "He sent us here."

"Well, Bert may be a bit of an oddball, but he's spent five years searching the island. If the treasure was there I'm sure he would have found it."

"Perhaps this map shows where it used to be stored before they removed it?" Mark suggested.

"I don't think so."

But he saw her look at it again, more carefully this time. He watched her check the houses which the red line crossed and pick out the one where Bert Hogarth had discovered the secret vault.

But in the end she said, "I'm sure it's got nothing to do with the treasure. I distinctly heard Brother XII say it showed the path that Aquarius would take."

"Can we made a copy of it?" asked Mark.

"I'm sorry, we don't have a copying machine."

"What about a tracing?"

"You're not allowed to make copies of documents without written permission from the directors of the museum."

Chapter 35

Peter Johnson left the Rhodesian health service and returned to England in June 1961. He'd been out of the country for over two years and he was no longer required to do military service. Jenny still had no birth certificate but she'd been able to get a British passport because she was included on her mother's passport when she was a child.

Peter immediately started looking for a yacht. He contacted several brokers and eventually found himself in the upstairs office of Laurent Giles and Partners, in Lymington. The office was old and quaint with a latticed window, an ancient brass sextant on the mantelpiece, and prints of boats and ships on every wall. Captain Cawthrope, the broker, sat behind an antique desk. He was a big friendly man, retired from the Royal Navy, who'd been sailing all his life.

"So you want to sail to western Canada, eh?" asked the Captain with a very proper British accent. If he'd added "My boy," it wouldn't have sounded out of place.

"That's right." Peter almost called him "Sir."

"Will you be on your own?"

"With a friend, a girlfriend."

"By God, you're a lucky young fellow."

Captain Cawthrope got up and walked over to a map of the world. "You'll have to follow the old trade wind route south to the West Indies. I've sailed yachts down there a couple of times myself."

"Really? Do you have any tips?"

Peter spent two and a half hours with Captain Cawthrope, most of the time discussing the voyage. Before he left Cawthrope gave him some advice.

"It'll be harder than you think," he said. "The Bay of Biscay will be rough and you'll get tired and seasick. But as you sail south the weather will get warmer and the sea will turn a brighter shade of blue. England to Gibraltar is the toughest bit. Don't give up before you reach Gibraltar."

Jenny took a week off from the secretarial job she was doing in London to help inspect the yachts that Cawthrope had listed. Eventually they settled on a thirty-five-foot sloop called *Bluebell* at Elkins' boatyard in Christchurch. She looked smart and strong and seaworthy, with a light blue hull, a single mast and a stern cockpit. The cabin was bright and cheerful, with curtains and cushions in blue and white stripes to match the hull. They both fell in love with her at once.

Peter had her surveyed the following week and bought her the week after that, and in May they sailed her down the coast to Salcombe. Soon after that Jenny gave up her job and they lived on *Bluebell* in Salcombe harbour. At first they made short trips up and down the coast, then a shakedown cruise to the Isles of Scilly. When they were not sailing or partying, they were preparing for the voyage. July slipped by, then August, and when September arrived it was time to go.

One day in early September the weather forecast was good so they announced they would sail next morning. They had a last evening in the Ferry Inn with their friends and spent a restless night, too excited to sleep. Next morning when they hoisted the sails to leave half a dozen boats were waiting to see them off. Finally they let go their mooring and turned *Bluebell*'s bow to the sea.

The next week was the worst in Jenny's life.

She enjoyed the morning they set off. The sea was calm and it was fun to have an escort of friends in other boats. The wind came from the west, so they were able to head straight for the northwest tip of France a hundred miles away. One by one their friends turned back and eventually they were alone. Slowly the cliffs of Devon fell astern and in the early afternoon they shared their last look at England.

"Excited?" asked Peter, who seemed to be enjoying himself.

Yes, she was excited, and homesick, and a little apprehensive too. She yawned. All she wanted to do was go to sleep. As soon as the coast of England had disappeared she made an excuse and went below, feeling guilty for leaving Peter on his own.

For a couple of hours she lay on her bunk listening to the creaks and groans of the boat, and during the afternoon she heard Peter trim the sails as *Bluebell* heeled further to the wind.

They'd arranged no strict division of duties, but it was mainly her job to prepare the food, and his to sail the boat. She was happy with that arrangement. She didn't want to struggle on the foredeck changing sails, or crouch over the engine getting grease in her hair; but now she realized they hadn't eaten since they'd put to sea and the thought of cooking turned her stomach.

At 4:30 she forced herself off her bunk and up the steps to the cockpit, and she was shocked by what she saw. The sun had gone and now the sea was grey. They were alone in a circle of empty ocean, with white-capped waves stretching to the horizon in every direction. The deck was wet, and even as she watched spray flew from the bow and whipped back into her face. She ducked behind the canvas dodger that sheltered the cockpit and smiled at Peter sitting at the helm, his yellow oilskins dripping with water.

He smiled back. "You alright?"

She nodded. "Shall I fix you something to eat?"

"Are you hungry yourself?"

"No," she said, realizing she actually felt like throwing up. "But I'll get you something if you like," she added as bravely as she could.

"Don't bother. The bloody weather forecast was wrong. The wind has backed to the southwest and the barometer is falling. I think we're in for a blow."

When she took another look she could see that the wind was much more on their bow. They were close hauled, sailing into the wind, and *Bluebell* shuddered as she pitched into each wave.

"I'm going to change to a smaller jib and roll a couple of reefs into the mainsail," Peter said. "Will you stay up here in the cockpit and handle the ropes while I'm on the foredeck?"

All she wanted was to go back to her bunk, but instead she struggled into foul weather oilskins, stiff and cold, to look after the cockpit while he crawled forward along the tilted deck. It took three quarters of an hour to change the sails and when they'd finished she could see he was exhausted. There were no ships in sight, so he left the tiller connected to the self-steering vane and they both went below for a rest.

That was when she started vomiting. She managed to do it into the galley sink so there wasn't any mess, but she felt thoroughly ashamed.

"Don't worry about it," he said, putting his arm around her. "I'm just sorry you feel ill."

"Don't look at me, I must look awful."

"A bit green, that's all. Lie down and wait it out."

The boat was heaving about so much that it was difficult to do anything, but he helped her out of her oilskins and rigged the canvas flap along the edge of her bunk to stop her falling out. She climbed in but it was impossible to relax. She watched him pull a chunk of bread off the end of a loaf and wash it down with a cup of water, but she couldn't face anything herself.

As evening faded into night she was vaguely aware that the howl of the wind was even louder and the motion more violent. She'd never felt so ill in her life. She struggled to the sink to vomit a couple more times, and after that there was nothing left in her stomach. Peter was in the cockpit most of the time but occasionally she saw him lying on his bunk still wearing his yellow oilies. The wind-vane was steering the boat, of course, but it was pitch dark outside, and with no one on watch they might collide with a ship.

"Let me take a turn on deck," she suggested weakly, not knowing how she'd manage if he agreed.

He looked at her carefully. "No. There's no shipping around and the coast of France is still forty miles away. We're perfectly safe, so stay where you are and get well. And try to take a few sips of water, I don't want you to get dehydrated."

A little before dawn he announced he could see the flashes of the lighthouses along the French coast, but she hardly heard. The gale was even stronger now. The wind howled through the rigging with a continuous whine, and the boat shuddered as each wave struck.

When it finally got light Peter wanted to change to an even smaller jib and further reef the main. She had to struggle up to the cockpit to help. The waves looked enormous, with big white crests and streaks of foam on their backs. Spray flew from the bow and blew back along the deck, but she was too ill to feel any fear. The sails were as taut as drums and the new jib cracked like a whip as Peter fought to winch it up. When it was set he pointed to a low grey line along the horizon: "That's the coast of France."

Land, solid land. She gazed at it with desperate longing. Harbours where the sea was calm, shelter from the wind.

"Couldn't we go into a port?"

"We can't risk it in a gale with no detailed chart. I know it's horrible out here, but there are no rocks. At least it's fairly safe."

The wind had pushed them too far east, and they spent the morning beating down the French coast fifteen miles offshore. The weather remained about the same, with rain squalls intermittently blotting out the horizon. Jenny spent most of the time in her bunk, retching periodically, but she did manage to crawl up to the cockpit to help when she was needed.

As the day wore on conditions in the cabin deteriorated. Everything was wet. Peter was too tired to take off his wet clothes when he came below, and water dripped from the hatch and the ventilators overhead. At first she tried to keep the drips off her bunk with her waterproofs, but soon she felt too ill to care. Books fell from the shelves, and cutlery, dishes, clothes, and food slid back and forth on the wet floor as *Bluebell* rolled and pitched.

Jenny could eat nothing at all. Just the thought of food revolted her. Peter insisted she took sips of water which he gave her from a dirty cup, but even that came back up. She could no longer make it to the sink, but there was nothing in her stomach except greenish slime which she vomited into a sodden towel that she kept beside her head.

During the afternoon it seemed a little less rough so she climbed up to the cockpit to have a look. The coast was only five miles away and it was giving them some shelter. Ahead lay a wide gap in the cliffs and beyond that a high rugged island.

"What's that?" she asked.

"The Isle of Ushant."

"But the gap before the island? Doesn't that lead to a harbour or something?"

He looked doubtful. "It's the northern approach to the port of Brest."

"Well, couldn't we go in there?"

"The channel's full of rocks, and we don't have a detailed chart. I'd hate to try it in this gale."

"Oh."

"Jenny, I know you feel awful. We probably could get in, although it would be risky." He looked towards the shore for a minute. "You decide. Whatever you say, I'll understand."

She hesitated. The idea of relief was overwhelming, and she felt so ill she hardly cared if she drowned. But she couldn't make him risk their lives just because she was seasick.

"I think we'd better press on," she said.

He squeezed her hand. "You look so soft, but you're the toughest person I've ever met."

Eventually the wind backed further to the south and they began to get shelter from Ushant, so she stayed on deck to keep him company. *Bluebell* crept laboriously along the rocky coast, but as they approached the end of the island she spotted bigger waves ahead. Beyond Ushant the coastline fell away to the southeast into the dreaded Bay of Biscay, and as they rounded the headland they felt the full force of wind and sea. With the last of her strength she helped him harden in the sails on the port tack. Biscay lay to the left, whitecaps stretching to the horizon, and ahead was the open Atlantic, dark and savage and cold.

Dusk came early. Lights winked on the land and faded gradually as they struggled out to sea. Soon they were alone, hunched together in the cold wet cockpit, surrounded by darkness and lashed with spray.

"There's nothing to do up here," said Peter. "You go inside."

"OK."

Even the dirty cabin seemed comforting as she climbed down the steps like a wounded animal retreating to its cave.

By the next afternoon Jenny felt seriously depressed. They were well out into the Bay of Biscay, a hundred miles from land, with no hope of shelter for several days. The seasickness went on and on, and in addition to the nausea and retching she had a splitting headache. She thought it would go on forever, getting worse and worse until she died. How she longed for the land. She dreamt of it, pictured it, just a few minutes of peace in a field, sitting under a tree.

Peter was getting irritable. She could hardly blame him. He'd done nearly all the work and had hardly any sleep. Her friends had warned her that men became bossy and demanding at sea. Well, he hadn't been like that at all, but last night there'd been ships around, so he'd asked her to keep watch in the cockpit for a couple of hours while he slept. But she'd gone to sleep herself, and when he'd come back on deck a freighter was passing only a hundred yards astern. She'd read the reproach in his eyes when he woke her.

"We could have been run down and drowned," he'd said.

"Big deal," she'd replied. "Anything would be better than this."

Another night dragged by, and then another day. She had lost count so she didn't know which one it was. Peter had stopped bringing her cups of water and she was thirsty, but she couldn't be bothered to drink. Still the wind howled in from the southwest, right in their teeth, and still *Bluebell* pitched and rolled without a moment's rest. Conditions below were worse than ever and the cabin was beginning to smell. She hadn't undressed for days. Her hair was matted and dirty, but she simply didn't care.

She woke and it was dark again, yet another night. In the dim cabin light she could see Peter fast asleep on his bunk, still wearing his oilskins. No one was on watch. She imagined a big ship's bow ploughing through *Bluebell*'s side, but nothing seemed important and she just went back to sleep.

However she gradually became aware that things were changing, and the next time she opened her eyes sunlight was streaming into the cabin. She looked across at Peter's bunk. He was still in his oilies, sound asleep.

Then she realized the noise had gone, the whining sound of the wind had disappeared. The boat's motion was different too. She could relax without being thrown out of her bunk. Her seasickness had gone, but she daren't move for fear it might come back, so for a few blissful minutes she just lay still.

After a while she very gingerly climbed out of her bunk and made her way up the steps to the cockpit. Everything had changed. The wind was down to a gentle breeze that was just enough to fill the sails. The waves were smaller too. Those horrible white crests had gone and their tops were round and smooth.

She made her way slowly back into the cabin just as Peter woke up.

"My God," he exclaimed. "What's happened? I must have been asleep for hours." Then he smiled. "Are you feeling better?"

She nodded, hardly daring to speak for fear the nausea might come back.

He got up and went on deck to look around. When he came back he said, "The south-westerly has blown itself out and the wind's veered round to the north." He tapped the barometer. "The glass is rising too."

Jenny felt weak and dirty but she was well enough to help him reset the sails. The wind was behind them now, so they furled the mainsail and set a pair of jibs held out by booms, one on each side of the mast. *Bluebell* rolled a bit, but it was gentle, and she realized it was the violent pitching into head seas that had made her so terribly sick. When the wind and waves came from behind she felt perfectly alright. She drank some orange juice and ate a bowl of cereal, and then she washed, brushed her teeth and changed her clothes.

Next they opened the hatches to air out the boat, and then they put their wet clothes and sleeping bags on deck to dry. She was surprised how quickly they were able to clear up the mess, but of course their cabin was quite small.

By midday she was hungry. She felt like something spicy, so she lit the stove and heated a can of spaghetti Bolognese. She spent the afternoon in the cockpit, and for the first time she began to notice what was going on around them. The surface of the ocean was deep blue now, and smooth, but it wasn't flat. Huge low swells rolled in from the west, so wide and far apart they hardly rocked the boat.

The sea was alive with birds, white-winged gulls and skuas flecked with brown, little flocks of petrels, and shearwaters riding the updrafts ahead of the swells. There was no land in sight, but a mile or two away she saw a group of fishing boats not much bigger than *Bluebell*. They had brightly painted hulls, blue, yellow and red, with flat decks and flared bows, and each had a flock of gulls jostling overhead.

"Sardine boats from northern Spain," Peter told her.

"So we're getting down there at last." She'd been too ill to pay much attention to their progress. "How far are we from the land?"

"A hundred and fifty miles if my navigation is correct. Another couple of days and we'll reach the Spanish coast."

On the horizon to the right she spotted a freighter travelling north, and further off lay two deep-sea fishing trawlers which Peter thought were French. *Bluebell* might be a long way from the land but they certainly weren't alone. She thought of the nights they'd sailed for hours with nobody keeping watch.

"I'll stay on deck tonight," she said.

"We'll take it in turns. Why don't you get some sleep now? Then we'll have supper just before the sun goes down, and you can take the first shift."

For supper she opened a can of stew which tasted delicious after the near starvation of the last few days. It was still light after they'd washed the dishes and trimmed the sails for the night. Presently she heard a sharp blowing noise nearby and the black body of a dolphin surfaced alongside. Before long a whole school of them were playing around the bow.

"Let's go forward and watch them," she suggested.

The breeze was still blowing gently from astern. The sea remained calm, and they sat on the foredeck for twenty minutes as the sun went down. There were half a dozen adult dolphins and a couple of calves. They could easily outpace *Bluebell*, and they circled right round the boat, or swooped back and forth beneath the bow. Sometimes they would look up towards the deck, and Jenny felt sure they could see her and recognize her presence. Their game seemed like a show of friendship and she hoped they'd stay for the rest of her watch.

Peter put his arm around her waist and gave her a kiss. "I'm so glad you're better. I was terribly worried about you."

"I'll be OK if it stays like this," she said. "But I don't know what'll happen when we have to sail against the wind."

She dreaded it.

He seemed to read her thoughts. "Captain Cawthrope warned me it would be tough at first. He said we must stick it out as far as Gibraltar. After that it'll get warmer and calmer, and everything will be better. Do you think you can hang on till then?"

They had almost reached Gibraltar when Jenny decided to give up.

Sailing down the coast of Spain and Portugal had been easy although she'd felt seasick once or twice. They'd called at several little ports and spent a week in the historic city of Cadiz, only sixty miles from Gibraltar.

They left Cadiz on a hot sunny afternoon with a gentle westerly breeze and Peter said they'd reach Gibraltar next morning. At first everything went smoothly, but as they approached Cape Trafalgar the wind died, leaving them utterly becalmed on a glassy sea. The sun beat down from a cloudless sky and it became oppressively hot. To the north lay the rugged cliffs of Spain, and far off to the south Jenny saw a strip of sand shimmering above the horizon, a heat mirage from the Sahara many miles away. In another direction a broad tower seemed to be rising out of the sea. It slowly got bigger until she could see the distorted image of a freighter still below the horizon. A few miles to the east a mysterious cloud of mist appeared to hover above the sea.

"What do you think of that?" she asked Peter.

"Perhaps it's another type of heat mirage," he suggested, but it didn't look like a mirage to her.

Peter stripped naked and swam around the boat. She would have joined him, but she felt strangely apprehensive.

After a couple of circuits he climbed back on board.

"What was it like?" she asked.

"I felt sort of vulnerable so far from the land, particularly with no swimming trunks. Do you think there are sharks?"

"The sharks won't notice whether you've got trunks," she laughed.

"Well, it didn't feel right."

"I don't feel right either. I tried to get a forecast but everything's in Spanish."

The heat became more oppressive by the hour and the patch of mist seemed to be getting closer. The sails hung limp with not a breath of wind and not a ripple on the surface of the water. She gazed down into the depths and many feet below there were flashes of silver as big fish chased smaller ones, hungry for a meal.

Every time she looked the misty cloud was closer.

"What on earth's going on?" she said at last.

"I've no idea," said Peter.

The first breaths of wind came late in the afternoon. It was unlike anything she'd experienced before, a cruel hot dry wind that felt as if it had come straight from the heart of the desert. It got stronger by the minute and it filled her heart with dread.

Peter knew what it was. "A levanter," he said. "A strong easterly that blows out of the Mediterranean."

"Very strong?"

"It can reach gale force. Too strong for us to sail against."

"So what can we do?"

"We'll have to ride it out."

"How long do they last?"

"Two or three days."

"Oh, no." She felt a stab of despair.

Within an hour they'd changed down to their smallest jib and set the storm trysail. The sea was a mass of small white-crested waves, and already bigger ones were building.

"Well," she said, "I'll make you some sandwiches and anything else you need, but once it gets rough I'm not going to be much use"

He kissed her. "Oh Jenny, I'm so sorry. But maybe you'll be alright this time."

"I'm feeling sick already."

"Don't bother about the sandwiches, all I need is bread."

The wind howled out of the east the whole night long and she was as sick as a dog. There was shipping around so Peter had to stay on deck while she lay in her bunk quite unable to help. He came down to see her once or twice, and towards morning he announced that they had been blown almost as far as the coast of Africa. The chart showed an unnamed bay behind Cape Spartel a few miles away, and he promised that when it was light he would try to get in there.

It was a precarious anchorage, sheltered from the east but completely exposed to the west, however as soon as they reached it she felt better. Peter set the anchor, and there they sat for three whole days waiting for the levanter to blow itself out.

It was not a good time for Jenny. She was no longer seasick, but they had almost reached Gibraltar and she had to decide if they should carry on with the voyage. In fact she had already decided that they would quit when they reached Gibraltar. There were other ways of getting to B.C. What she had not done was tell Peter. She spent hours searching for the best way to do it, but she kept putting it off.

"Captain Cawthrope said things would be better after Gibraltar," he told her.

"To hell with Captain Cawthrope," she snapped. "We haven't reached Gibraltar yet. I don't have to make up my mind till then."

On the third day the wind moderated and they had a leisurely sail to Gibraltar. The harbour was easy to find, nestled at the foot of its huge bare rock. They tied up in an old naval destroyer pen among a dozen other boats, British, French, and American.

After struggling with Spanish and Portuguese for the last few weeks, it was a delight to deal with officials who spoke English and mix with English-speaking crews. But everybody wanted to know where they had come from and where they were going, and she still hadn't told Peter her decision.

In the evening he insisted they go to the yacht club for a drink. She was trying to avoid other crews so they sat at a table on their own. Peter went off to sign the visitors' book and she resolved to tell him as soon as he got back.

He was gone a long time, and when he returned he said, "What a fascinating place. There's a visitors' book from before the war with the names of all sorts of famous yachts."

"Really?"

She must tell him now. She drew a breath.

"Yes. Your mother was here," he said.

"My mother?" she repeated in surprise.

"Well, a Mary White anyway. I guess it's a fairly common name."

"Oh, I see."

She was just about to tell him when a voice said, "Hello," and she recognized a couple from another yacht. She knew they were heading south and she didn't want to talk to them.

"I think I'll go and look at that visitors' book," she whispered to Peter, slipping away from the table.

She found the old leather bound visitors' book but there were many pages. Searching them took a long time but eventually she found it: Mary White, her mother's writing, even her signature. There could be no doubt. She read the details.

Yacht's name: *Lady Royal.* She'd never heard of it.

Owner or Captain: Amiel de Valdes. Who on earth was he?

Passengers: Mary White. The name was clearly written.

Crew: Three names she'd never heard before.

Port of origin: Chichester. That was in the south of England, so Mother must have crossed the Bay of Biscay too.

Destination: British Virgin Islands, West Indies. The other side of the Atlantic Ocean. It was astounding.

Date: 20 September 1936. She counted on her fingers. Only ten months before she was born.

There was no mention of her father. Her pulse raced. What could Mother have been doing here on a yacht? During all the talk about their sailing plans she had never uttered a word. She didn't know whether she loved her mother or not. The woman had led a secret life and shut her daughter out. Jenny didn't know what to think but there was admiration in her heart, and a sense of competition too. This changed everything.

She closed the book and walked back to Peter. The couple from the other yacht were still there.

"Peter says the two of you haven't decided where you're going next," said the woman.

"Oh, it's just the details we haven't decided," Jenny replied. "We're heading for the British Virgin Islands."

"Where are they?"

"In the West Indies. The other side of the Atlantic."

Captain Cawthrope had been right, everything was better after Gibraltar. They sailed down the African coast to Casablanca then called at Las Palmas before heading out across the Atlantic. They reached the northeast trade wind on the fifth day and it blew steadily for the next three weeks. *Bluebell* hurried forward, her sails full, flying fish leaping from her bow wave, and with the wind coming from astern Jenny was no longer sick.

Once they were in the trade wind they began to see more wildlife. There were birds, speckled brown shearwaters, a kittiwake, and as they got further south white tropic birds with long streamer tails. But it was the flying fish which interested Peter. He'd seen them from the ship on his way to Africa, of course, but from *Bluebell*'s deck they were only a few feet away. They'd launch themselves from the crest of a wave and skim across the water two or three feet up, gliding on big translucent fins. Sometimes they'd land on the boat during the night, and Jenny would fry them for breakfast, crisp and delicious, straight from the sea.

Jenny sat in the stern of *Bluebell*'s dinghy daydreaming while Peter rowed.

After the Atlantic crossing they'd spent Christmas in Antigua, partying in Nelson's old dockyard which was being renovated as a haven for yachtsmen. Now they were exploring the British Virgin Islands on their way to the Panama Canal.

She liked to watch Peter as he rowed. She often gazed at him for minutes at a time but he didn't seem to mind. She'd never seen a man look so tanned and healthy. He was wearing a white T-shirt and his muscles bulged as he pulled back on the oars. She smiled and he grinned back, his face alive with happiness.

"Is this really the island Robert Louis Stevenson wrote about?" she asked.

"That's what it says in the sailing guide."

She looked around. They were on uninhabited Norman Island, one of the smallest of the Virgins, rowing across a sheltered bay called the Bight. Behind them *Bluebell* lay at anchor on her own, a hundred yards off a sandy beach, and ahead she could see the rocky point that would lead them to the treasure cave. Peter had his back to it because he was rowing.

"Keep me headed for Treasure Point," he said.

"Go a bit more to your left."

It was a hilly little island. There was a palm grove behind the beach, but the hills were covered with bushes and small deciduous trees. Ahead she saw some cliffs and Treasure Point.

Eventually they reached the point and Peter took a rest. There was not a soul in sight. As they sat and drifted she read aloud from the sailing guidebook:

Stevenson used Norman Island as the model for his book Treasure Island, because in the nineteenth century a native fisherman discovered real treasure in the southernmost of three caves which lie 250 yards south of Treasure Point. The treasure consisted of a hoard of gold doubloons of Spanish origin in an iron-bound chest. It was probably hidden by pirates during the golden age of piracy in the first quarter of the eighteenth century.

"Do you think there'll be any left?" asked Peter with a grin.

"Of course not. But I want to see the cave just the same."

They found the caves easily enough at the foot of the cliff beyond Treasure Point, and they headed for the southern one. It had a low narrow entrance at sea level, with the water surging in and out.

"I don't like it," said Peter. "Suppose we get washed against the rocks."

She looked at the small black hole and gave a shiver, but she felt a strange compulsion to go in. "It says in the sailing guide you can go in if it's calm."

"But it's not calm."

"The cliff is sheltering it from the wind," she persisted.

"But there's a swell."

"Oh, don't be such a chicken. I'll swim in if you like."

That seemed to do it. He manoeuvred the dinghy into position and eventually they slid through the entrance on a wave, just grazing the rock.

Inside it was dark, particularly after the bright sun, and she couldn't see a thing. She felt for her flashlight, cursing that she hadn't got it out before. Then she heard a fluttering sound and something brushed against her face.

"Oh my God," she said.

"Bats," said Peter. "Keep your head down or you'll hit it on the roof."

Next moment the boat crashed into the side of the cave and they rocked wildly back and forth. It was impossible to keep balance in the dark, but just when she thought they were going to capsize her fingers found the light. She flicked the switch and at last they could see.

Peter soon had the boat under control and steadied it with the oars while she looked about. The cave was bigger than she expected, about eight feet high and twelve wide, although the entrance was much smaller. The walls were smooth black rock which glistened wetly in the light, and they dropped sheer into the water which looked as black as ink. She searched the walls with the light but the cave disappeared into the darkness and she couldn't see the end. Dozens of bats hung from the roof, their furry little heads turning in unison as she shone the light on them. Several were fluttering around on their pale skin-like wings, and she wondered what she'd do if one got tangled in her hair.

"I wonder where they found the treasure," said Peter. "See if you can spot a ledge."

He slowly paddled the boat farther in while she examined every inch of rock. The cave extended for about sixty feet. It curved round to the left, so when they reached the end the entrance was out of sight and it was pitch dark. The sound of dripping water echoed off the roof. Everywhere the walls were smooth and flat without a ledge of any kind.

"Where on earth could the treasure have been?" Peter repeated after a few minutes. "There's nowhere here to stand a matchbox, let alone an iron-bound chest."

They were looking around, about ten feet from the end, when the flashlight slipped from Jenny's hand and they were plunged into darkness. There was no splash, so she thought it must have fallen in the boat, but she couldn't find it anywhere. Eventually Peter shipped the oars and began to search as well. Sitting in the wobbly boat, in the dark, with the fluttering bats was not a pleasant feeling, and soon she became disoriented.

"How are we going to find the way out?" she asked, trying to sound calm.

"I think I can see the way to the entrance," said Peter. "Look, there's light filtering through the water. It must be over there."

She could see it too, a pale glimmer a few feet below the surface. But it seemed to be coming from the wrong direction. "I thought the entrance was the other way."

She was still searching for the light and finally her fingers found its familiar round handle. She tried the switch and the light came on. For a moment they sat blinking with relief.

"You're right," said Peter, after a minute or two. "The entrance is the other way. I wonder why there was light coming from under the water over there?"

She tried shining the flashlight where she'd seen the glimmer, but the water looked black. She was still trying to see, moving the light one way and another, when she spotted some marks on the wall.

"Look at that," she said excitedly.

"What?"

"There's writing on the wall at the end of the cave. Perhaps it's a message from the pirates."

Peter paddled over to the wall, but it was just where people had scratched the names of their yachts on the rock. There were a dozen or more, some fairly recent, others very old.

"Look at this," he said. "*Otter*, 1948. That's nearly fifteen years ago."

"Well, here's one from before the war: 1939, The schooner *Annette*."

"This one's dated 1936," he said. "Give me the light a minute, it's hard to see the name."

She passed him the flashlight and he read out slowly, "*Lady* something. I can't make out the last word, but it's dated December 1936."

Jenny felt her blood run cold. That was seven months before she was born.

"*Royal*," she said.

"What's that?"

"*Royal*. The yacht's name is *Lady Royal*."

"Yes, that's it. How did you know?"

"Peter, that's the boat my mother was on. Give me that flashlight."

She examined the writing with a racing pulse. It must have been scratched into the rock with something sharp, because although it was old, it was clear enough to see.

"My mother was here," she said at last. "In this very spot. I can feel it. She was already carrying me."

"Don't be silly. The *Lady Royal* may have been here, but I expect your mother was back in England, especially if she was pregnant."

"Look at that writing. Just look at the R. No one else does Rs like that. No, she was here alright, and so was I. But God knows what she was doing."

Peter found the passage from the Virgin Islands to the Panama Canal straightforward. The northeast trade wind was steady and strong, and at noon on the eighth day he could see the twin concrete breakwaters that formed the harbour. Soon they were safely inside.

They anchored in the wide outer harbour designed for big ships, hoisted the yellow quarantine flag to show they were new arrivals, and waited for the harbour master's launch.

The American officials were friendly and efficient. The canal dues were levied according to tonnage, and the measurer quickly ran his tape over *Bluebell*'s decks, did some calculations, and announced she was eight tons.

"But you haven't weighed her at all?" Peter queried.

"It's all done by measurement. That's how much cargo we reckon she'd be able to hold."

"But we couldn't possibly carry eight tons of goods."

"That's what they all say," replied the measurer with a deadpan face. "The fee is $1.20 a ton, so that'll be $9.60 altogether. Of course you can sail her south round Cape Horn if you think we're overcharging!"

When the officials had left Peter pulled up the anchor and they motored over to the yacht club and tied up to the visitors' float.

The Panama Canal Yacht Club was one of the great yachting crossroads of the world. A couple of dozen boats were waiting to pass from the Atlantic to the Pacific, or resting after going the other way. They had met some of the crews before, in Antigua, or the Virgin Islands, or even faraway Gibraltar. There was a friendly bar and stories to be swapped, and a week slipped by before they were ready for the canal.

Peter had been warned about the Panama Canal. Most of it was not really a canal but a big tropical lake in the jungle of central Panama. The lake was ninety feet above sea level, so ships had to be raised or lowered at either end in huge locks. That was the danger. Water swirled into these locks so fast that yachts on their own were often dashed against the walls, and those tied to bigger ships for stability were sometimes crushed.

A yacht needed four stout mooring lines with extra crew to handle them to hold her in the centre of the locks. He and Jenny volunteered as line handlers on an American yacht to gain experience, and when it came to their own turn they took along a couple from another British boat.

It was a hot sunny morning. They rode the up locks without incident, and when they reached the top they found a good sailing breeze to push them across the lake. The big ships had to stick to a specified route, of course, but that didn't apply to small yachts. They wanted to see some Central American wildlife, so they made a detour through a group of islands and anchored for lunch in a quiet channel with lush green jungle on either side. Brightly coloured parrots fluttered through the trees, and basking on the banks Peter spotted a couple of fat crocodiles.

It was a memorable day and Peter felt sad as they rode the down locks back to the ocean. *Bluebell* was the only boat going north, all the others were heading for the south seas.

Panama to the Hawaiian Islands was the longest leg of the voyage, over five thousand miles along the curved route a sailing vessel must take to make the best use of the wind. For the first few hundred miles they sailed through the doldrums. Sometimes there were thunderstorms and they'd rush out on deck naked to shower in the rain. Sometimes the sea was glassy smooth and the sun burned from the dome of a cloudless sky. Then they'd rig the awning, or use a bucket on a rope to toss seawater onto each other.

Peter found it trying. The wind might blow for an hour but as soon as he hoisted the sails it would die. Jenny fared better. She read and cooked and studied the ocean. The Pacific was teeming with wildlife. Turtles with barnacle-covered shells three feet wide poked their heads above the water to stare at *Bluebell* with big round eyes. There were whales and sharks, and sea snakes swimming in groups of fifty or more. The snakes were short and thick, with yellow and black stripes, and they looked wickedly dangerous.

"I think they can swim both ways," Jenny announced, looking over the side.

"What do you mean?"

"Backwards or forwards, both ends are the same."

"Don't be silly," he replied from the shade of the awning. "Snakes have a head and a tail."

Before he could stop her she'd caught one in a bucket which she stood on the deck. It looked wickedly poisonous and the sailing guide said it could kill. But she was right, or almost right, its tail was camouflaged to look like a head, and it could dart backwards as fast as swim to the front.

They reached the trade wind on the fifteenth day. It was gentle at first but steady and cool, and the sky looked different too. Gone were the great islands of cumulo-nimbus cloud, with their white tops and black lower layers. Gone were the showers of rain. Their hearts lifted and *Bluebell* seemed to feel it too. With her mainsail and genoa pulling she bounded forward as if the Hawaiian Islands were calling her. The wind-vane steered the boat, of course, but there was always something to do.

They were well south of the shipping lanes, a thousand miles from land, crossing a bit of ocean rarely seen by man. A favourite topic of conversation was what they'd do if they found an uncharted island. Peter didn't think it entirely impossible. The Pacific was huge. They'd been sailing for nearly a month without any sign of a ship or a plane, and it seemed feasible that there might be an island which had never been seen before.

"It's got to have trees on it," said Jenny. "I want one that's big enough to build a house among the palms."

"And there'll have to be a lagoon," Peter said. "We've got to have a sheltered anchorage for *Bluebell*."

"And a stream with pools to bathe in, and breadfruit trees and ferns. Oh Peter, wouldn't it be wonderful. Our own secret island where it didn't matter whether we were married or not."

"It doesn't matter now."

"Yes it does. It matters to me."

On the morning of their fifty-fourth day at sea Peter saw a pile of cloud on the horizon that did not move along with the wind. It was still there at noon when he worked out their position.

"It's the big island of Hawaii alright," he announced. "It's 14,000 feet high. No wonder it's easy to see."

In the afternoon the cloud cleared and they could make out the island's shape. The twin peaks of its mountain seemed to glow in the light of the sun. After fifty-four days at sea it was the most beautiful landfall in the world.

They wanted an anchorage sheltered from all directions, with a quiet beach and palm trees. So far as Peter could see from the chart there was no such place on the island of Hawaii, so they decided to sail on to Maui.

When dusk came Hawaii was still twenty miles ahead so they took turns on watch and by morning they were sailing along the island's northeast shore.

Peter had never seen such a sight. The brown upper slopes of the mountains reached into the clouds. Then came a belt of blue-green forest, and below that bright green fields of sugar cane were shining in the sun. Here and there stood a sugar mill, a village or a road. Along the shore there were palm trees waving in the breeze, and small black cliffs of lava rock, and narrow strips of sand. The water along the beaches was a pale turquoise blue, then came a strip of white where the sea broke on the reef, and finally the deep blue of the ocean, flecked with waves.

It took all day to sail the length of the island. He warned Jenny that they would have a boisterous night ahead crossing the channel to the island of Maui, but she was too excited to go below.

The night was rough as he expected but Jenny was no longer sick. Morning found them off the southern tip of Maui. The wind was light in the shelter of Maui's mountain so they dropped the sails and motored the last fifteen miles, past little Molokini Island, deep into Maalaea Bay.

Peter knew they'd made the right decision as soon as he saw the bay. At its head there was a long sandy beach, completely sheltered from the Pacific swells and backed by palms and wild shrubs. At one end stood a village with an old stone pier, and at the other the little sheltered harbour of Maalaea.

They spent three weeks on Maui, most of the time in Maalaea harbour with *Bluebell*'s stern tied to the dock. It was a lazy place with a fish market under a great spreading banyan tree, and an old-fashioned general store which smelled of herbs and had a rusty iron roof. One week they sailed round to the old whaling port of Lahaina to buy provisions. There they wandered through the streets looking at huge sun-bleached bones and enormous iron pots for boiling blubber.

Peter didn't want to reach Canada before the summer weather arrived, but in the first week of May he thought it would be safe to leave. Jenny secretly feared the journey north because the first five hundred miles would be against the wind, but the wind was only moderate and she wasn't sick at all.

On June 8 they saw two freighters, a sure sign they were nearing a port, and during the night the flashes of the Cape Flattery lighthouse appeared ahead. At dawn the cape itself was in view and they entered the broad mouth of the Juan de Fuca Strait.

This was their first view of North America and they both looked about in awe. The strait was several miles wide with snow-capped mountains on either side. To the south lay the Olympic Peninsula of the U.S.A. and to the north Vancouver Island. Nearby was a group of fishing seiners, similar to those in France or Spain, and further off there were freighters bound for the ports of Vancouver and Seattle. There were tugs pulling barges, a coastguard vessel, and even another yacht.

As they penetrated further up the strait the weather got warmer and it turned into a lovely afternoon. The wind fell light and eventually Peter started the engine, but it was 9pm before they finally tied up in the harbour at Victoria. Nine o'clock and still daylight, so they went ashore for a walk.

They had called at Victoria to clear customs and immigration. Their real destination was the much larger city of Vancouver, eighty miles farther on. Peter phoned Mark Wooding from the dock to discuss their plans and find temporary moorage for *Bluebell*.

"On your way to Vancouver you must visit the Gulf Islands," Mark told him. "That's where the Aquarian settlements were."

They left early but the wind was light and *Bluebell* made slow progress. As they travelled north between the islands Jenny began to understand why Mark Wooding had insisted they went that way. The most southerly Gulf Islands were pretty, but as they penetrated into the sheltered northern area the tranquil beauty took her breath away.

For nine months she and Peter had lived closer than most married couples ever did and she'd never known such harmony. But it was nearly over now and still they could not marry. Soon they'd be mixed up in the red tape of society once more. He would get a job in a medical clinic and they'd have to live apart. She couldn't bear to think of it.

And then there was the business of her mother. She'd come to Canada to find out about her mother, but after what she'd learnt in Gibraltar and the Virgin Islands she wasn't sure. Her mother must have been in both those places soon before her birth, but there was no mention of her father. Perhaps there was something secret about him too. Glen Littleton's words, spoken on Kilimanjaro, echoed in her ears: *"If your mother loves you and she still won't tell you what happened, then perhaps it's better not to know."*

North of Sansum Narrows the real magic began. They entered what seemed to be a huge landlocked lake, twenty miles long and ten from side to side. Islands dotted the surface as far as she could see, some wooded, some covered with grass, some mere rocks and sand. There was not a breath of wind, and a slight mist hung in the air making the islands in the distance look mysterious and indistinct. The water was like glass. She watched a group of loons swimming lazily on the surface or diving below for fish.

"Let's stop and drift awhile," she said. "I'll make a pot of coffee."

"I thought you wanted to get to Vancouver."

"Peter, this is an enchanted place. I want to spend the night here. One more day won't make any difference."

He stopped the engine and there was utter silence. A heron winged slowly by, floating in the warm air, and high above eagles circled effortlessly in the sky.

"I do hope there's somewhere we can spend the night," she said.

"There are plenty of places," he replied with his finger on the chart. "Look, we've got to go up here, and then through this narrow pass. There are sheltered harbours everywhere."

"What about that little cove?" She pointed to a bay near the south end of one of the islands. "It seems to be on the way."

"Yes, I think that would do nicely." He read the name off the chart. "Pirates Cove, and it's on De Courcy Island."

Chapter 36

"So all four of your parents were Aquarians," said Mark. "That's amazing. Bev and I have been searching for information about them."

He'd met Peter and Jenny when they arrived in Vancouver and found them a place to moor near *Sundance*. Now they were back at the Woodings' apartment having dinner. They were finishing dessert when Jenny brought up the subject of the Aquarians.

"That's the main reason I wanted to come here," she said. "To find out more about them."

"But if your mother and father were in the colony you probably know as much as anyone," suggested Beverley.

"That's the problem, they won't talk about it. I think some very strange things went on in that commune, but they're as tight as a couple of clams."

"What sort of things?" asked Bev.

"How about idolatry, black magic, and fertility rites for a start." said Jenny.

"Yes, we read about that in the museum."

"Did any of your parents talk about the gold?" asked Mark.

"What gold?" queried Peter.

"Brother XII is supposed to have left a fortune in gold coins buried on De Courcy Island."

"You've got to be kidding."

"I'm perfectly serious," said Mark. "The Brother amassed a huge amount of money and I think it's still there."

"Well, I don't believe my parents knew anything about that."

Jenny shook her head as well. "It was the spiritual side of the operation that affected my mother."

"Do you know about Madame Zee, the sadistic overseer?" asked Beverley.

"No I haven't heard of her. My mother was more concerned with an Egyptian goddess called Isis."

"You know," said Beverley, "Finding out about the Aquarians is like trying to do a jigsaw puzzle when everyone has different pieces."

"Bev's right," said Mark, finishing his dessert. "We all have different parts of the puzzle. Let's take it one at a time and each give an account of what they know. Peter, your parents were there first. Why don't you begin?"

"Well," said Peter, collecting his thoughts, "I think pooling our knowledge is a very good idea, but this is not the right time to do it. Jenny and I are tired after a very long voyage and we need time to get our facts together. I suggest we meet in a few days when we've had time to think."

Beverley accepted the telegram by phone.

"Jennifer White's not here," she told the operator. "She lives on a boat, but if it's urgent I can deliver a message."

It was a couple of days since Peter and Jenny had arrived and *Bluebell* was still moored close to *Sundance* in Vancouver's inner harbour.

"Oh, how awful," said Beverley when she'd written down the message. "I'll take it to her immediately."

She drove north across Burrard Bridge and turned left onto Georgia. It was 4:30 and the rush hour traffic had begun. The road was packed with cars heading for the Lions' Gate Bridge and it took fifteen minutes to reach Stanley Park.

Poor Jenny, she thought. This whole Brother XII thing was just a diversion for Mark and herself, a chance to dream about treasure and puzzle over Madame Zee, but for Jenny it was deeply important.

The traffic crawled into the park and eventually she reached the moorage floats. Peter was busy on *Bluebell*'s foredeck. Putting her finger to her lips to silence him, she whispered, "There's a telegram for Jenny. I'm afraid it's bad news." She had written the message down and now she handed him the paper.

PARENTS IN CAR CRASH. MOTHER GRAVELY INJURED. COME AT ONCE. JO.

"Oh, my God," he said. "It sounds as if her mother's dying. You'd better let me tell her."

Jenny phoned her sister immediately. Both her parents had been badly injured, but her mother was the worst. The first flight she could get was in the morning. Peter wanted to go with her but she knew she'd be better on her own.

The plane refuelled at Edmonton and again in Greenland, and it took fourteen hours to reach London. There was an eight-hour time difference between Vancouver and London, so it was morning again when she arrived, and she hadn't slept at all.

She called Jo from the airport. "Is she still alive?"

"Yes."

"Is she going to live?"

"I think so. Now. Yesterday no one seemed to know."

"What about Dad."

"He's better than she is. He'll be alright."

Suddenly she felt tired and dirty, and there were tears on her face.

"Are you still there?" asked Jo.

"Yes." She sniffed. "Can you pick me up?"

"Of course. I'll be there in an hour."

Her parents were in the Epsom District Hospital, and on the way Jo told her the details.

"Some idiot crashed into Mum's side of the car. She's got fractures of the ribs and pelvis, a ruptured spleen, a perforated bowel, and a torn mesentery."

"What's a mesentery?"

"It's the tissue that attaches the bowel to the inside of the abdomen. It's very serious and she lost a lot of blood. They operated on her the night before last."

"And Dad's not so serious?"

"He has a fractured femur. It's been pinned, but he'll be in hospital for a couple of weeks."

Her mother was in a room on her own, and Jenny was shocked by her appearance. Her eyes were sunken and her face looked pale and thin. An intravenous was running into her arm, and tubes led from her nose and abdomen to containers under the bed. For the first time Jenny noticed that her hair had gone grey. She looked like a sick old lady who'd soon be dead.

For several years she'd addressed her mother as "Mum", but now she reverted. "Oh Mummy," she cried, putting her lips to the old lady's cheek. "Oh Mummy, thank God you're alive."

"Jenny," her mother murmured, her lips moving very slowly. "My own . . . darling . . . little . . . girl . . . You've come . . . at last."

She tried to raise her arm, but it was tied to a board to protect the i.v. A nurse stepped forward and caught her wrist.

"Keep your arm still please, Mrs White," she ordered. "It's alright, your daughter won't go away."

"She's been asking for you ever since she came out of the anesthetic," said Jo with a smile.

Soon she started to speak again. She was half delirious and most of what she said didn't make sense. Try as she might, Jenny could only make out fragments: ". . . come back . . . something to tell . . . never see you again . . . important. . ."

"She's just had some morphine," explained the nurse.

She seemed to be making a tremendous effort but the harder she tried the more difficult it was to understand: ". . . terrible secret . . . the Brother . . . take you away . . . ," she tailed off.

"A secret?" Jenny prompted.

She tried again with desperate urgency. This time she had a frightened look on her face and Jenny wondered if she sensed she was going to die before she could tell her secret. Eventually the nurse stepped forward and said, "That's enough, Mrs White. Dr Robinson says you must rest. You can talk to your daughter later, when you've got stronger."

Jenny saw her father in a separate room. He seemed to be recovering from the operation on his leg. He was more concerned about her mother than himself.

"If only we'd left five minutes earlier," he kept saying.

"You're both alive," she replied firmly. "That's the main thing. And in the end you're both going to get better."

Jenny spent most of the day at the hospital and as the afternoon wore on her mother became more lucid. She still seemed to have something on her mind, and when Jo was out of the room she tilted her head forward shakily and whispered, "Jenny, I must have a talk with you."

Jenny nodded.

Her mother looked at the nurse. "A private talk."

"Nurse, would you mind leaving us alone for a few minutes," Jenny asked.

The nurse hesitated. "I'm sorry, Dr Robinson says she must have someone with her at all times."

"Well, I'm someone."

"He meant a nurse."

"You could wait just outside the door."

"Why don't you ask Dr Robinson if it'll be alright tomorrow," the nurse suggested.

Jenny saw the doctor late in the afternoon. "Of course she can talk to you on your own," he said. "I think she's over the worst now anyway. I'll leave instructions that you can have your talk in the morning. But don't come before 11am."

That evening Jo had to go back to London, leaving Jenny alone at Strathbrook. She was too tired to cook a meal, and she wandered around the big empty house feeling nostalgic. Now that her mother seemed to be getting better she became obsessed by thoughts of the Aquarians. Then she remembered the secret pictures and she had an overpowering desire to find them.

She made her way up to her parents' bedroom. It had hardly changed since she was a little girl. There was the mahogany dresser with the very drawer that once held the pictures. With a pounding heart she eased it open. Inside were some odds and ends but nothing else. She tried the next drawer and the next. Eventually she searched the entire bedroom and the rest of the house as well. There was nothing, not any sign that her mother had ever been anything but a respectable stockbroker's wife.

She went to bed at midnight, but it was still only 4pm Vancouver time and she couldn't sleep. Thoughts of Brother XII and Isis went round and round in her head. Eventually she dozed off, but even when she was asleep she had a feeling that the answer to the puzzle was about to slip away.

During the past year Mary White's life had become a living hell. Several times she'd considered suicide and she'd even been to the doctor for sleeping pills which she'd been saving up.

Of course the root of the problem was the secret of Jenny's birth, but it was only after Peter Johnson's return from Africa that the real trouble had begun. When Jenny had told her their plan to buy a yacht and sail it out to British Columbia she'd been flabbergasted. Even the route they'd chosen was the same as the one that she and Amiel had followed.

Jenny had been so excited. She'd brought home books about sailing, and she and Peter had discussed their plans right in front of her. How she'd longed to tell them about her own yachting experiences, but of course she had to keep quiet. After a while they'd mistaken her silence for disinterest, and then they began to ignore her altogether which almost broke her heart. Finally Jenny had moved down to Salcombe and she'd hardly seen her daughter since.

 Philip had seen what was happening. He'd advised her to tell the truth, but how could she after all these years? She'd hoped that in the narrow confines of a boat they'd get tired of one another, but judging from Jenny's infrequent letters they'd grown closer. The letters had come from the very same places she'd visited with Amiel: Gibraltar, the Virgin Islands, the Panama Canal. Oh, what sweet memories those names evoked. How she longed to discuss them with her daughter. How she yearned to be reconciled. She was worn out by deceit.

One evening she and Philip had been going out to dinner with friends. She didn't want to go, and they'd been late. Philip had jumped a traffic light, crossing before it was green. There'd been a squeal of brakes, a crash, the door had caved in and glass flew everywhere. She hadn't cared. She didn't even care if she died.

After that the images were blurred. She remembered being surrounded by people, then she'd been in an ambulance, and then on a stretcher in a hospital. There'd been doctors, an operating theatre, an injection to put her to sleep.

Later she'd had dreams: lights, pain, half-heard voices, roll over, lie down, keep still. There were nurses, her daughter Jo, even Amiel, black-haired Amiel, and darling little Jenny. Then she was standing on a road holding Jenny's hand, a long straight road with pillars down either side. And far away in the depths of space was Brother XII, calling to his daughter, spiriting her away. She must tell Jenny the truth, now, before it's too late. The dreams went on and on, the same scenes over and over again.

And then a miracle. The mist cleared, and there was Jenny, modern grown-up Jenny, right beside her bed. Jenny kissed her on the cheek, a real kiss, there was no mistake.

She had to tell her daughter now.

"Secrets?" Jenny asked. She actually asked. Now it would be easy. But there were other people in the room, she must wait till they were gone.

The people stayed all day, but she heard Jenny arrange for them to talk alone tomorrow. That was a tremendous relief. It was her happiest day for a year.

Until the evening.

As afternoon wore into evening she sensed something was terribly wrong. She'd never felt so cold. The nurse gave her extra blankets, but her whole body shook and she had a dreadful feeling of doom. If only Jenny were there. If only they'd had their talk and she'd already told the truth.

The next few days were a nightmare, a kaleidoscope of hallucinations and cruel glimpses of reality. And over it all hung the conviction that her chance of reconciliation with her daughter had slipped away. The periods of reality got shorter and shorter. Then she was in the operating theatre again.

Jenny was feeling much more positive when she woke on the morning after she'd arrived in England. The previous evening her mother had seemed better and she was looking forward to the private talk they were about to have.

As soon as she arrived at the hospital she knew something was wrong. The sister caught her before she reached her mother's room. "Dr Robinson would like to talk to you before you go in," she said, and there was something about her unsmiling face that sent shivers down Jenny's spine.

She saw the doctor in his office. "Her temperature's gone up again," he said. "I hope it's a temporary setback. We had to remove her spleen, you know. It was a big operation."

Jenny stayed at the hospital all day. Her mother was delirious and there was no question of a private chat to discuss family secrets. As the day wore on she went further downhill and the following day she was even worse.

"It's infection," said Dr Robinson. "She had a ruptured bowel, you know. The bacteria from the bowel have spread into her peritoneal cavity."

During the next few days they gave her penicillin, streptomycin, oxygen and intravenous fluids, and a nurse was with her day and night. Jenny stayed by her bedside most of the time, but she had her father to comfort as well.

Slowly her mother slipped downhill, and by the sixth day after the accident she was unconscious. They did X-rays, blood cultures, an ECG, and eventually Dr Robinson called Jenny aside.

"The infection has collected under her diaphragm," he said. "She's developed a subphrenic abscess, and I'm afraid it will have to be drained. That means another operation."

Jenny was stunned. "Are you sure, Doctor? I don't think she could stand another operation."

"It's her only chance."

"Will she get better? Do you think she's going to live?"

"You want me to be frank?"

"Of course I do."

"Well, it's touch and go. There's only a fifty-fifty chance."

That was when it really sank in. Jenny felt shocked, guilty too, because of all the horrible thoughts she'd had about her poor mother during the past year. If only they could have just one last talk before she died.

They did the operation that afternoon, and afterwards Dr Robinson told her that technically it had been a success.

"We drained pints of pus," he said. "She would never have survived."

"But will she survive now?"

"We'll just have to wait and see."

She regained consciousness during the evening, but she couldn't move or talk and they thought she must have had a stroke. Jenny was dreadfully upset. She waited by the bed for hours, but there was never any change, and at 2am she went home exhausted to get some sleep.

"Don't worry about the eleven o'clock rule," said the nurse as she left. "Come back at any time."

In spite of everything she slept soundly and when she woke it was already 9am. She'd been sleeping like a baby while her mother lay dying. With a pang of guilt she pulled on her clothes and hurried to the hospital.

The ward was busy. Junior nurses scurried about and a group of white-coated doctors crowded around a bed. She couldn't see Dr Robinson. Perhaps he was in her mother's room. Perhaps she was already dead. With trembling fingers she turned the handle, telling herself that she must keep calm whatever she found inside.

Mother was propped up in bed, not cured, but certainly not dead. She smiled weakly when Jenny came in.

"The doctor's been already," the nurse explained. "The toxemia seems to have passed now that the pus has been drained."

"Oh Mummy, I'm so glad." She kissed her on the cheek. "I've been so worried."

"Jenny dear," said her mother right away. "Do you remember we were going to have a little talk?"

"Yes."

"Well, I think we should have it now, before anything else goes wrong."

Jenny's pulse quickened. "Alright, but are you sure you're strong enough?"

"I want to get it off my chest." She turned to the nurse. "Would you mind waiting outside the door? I want to have a private conversation with my daughter."

The nurse looked doubtful, but before she could say anything Jenny interrupted. "Dr Robinson said it would be alright."

"Very well," she replied primly and left the room.

But her mother didn't seem to know how to begin. "Have you any idea what this is about?" she asked at last.

Jenny thought she'd better take a chance. "Brother XII, perhaps?"

"Yes dear. I must say that does make it easier, but you're going to be terribly shocked. Sometimes I think I'm the most wicked woman in the world. But I've got to tell you what happened for both our sakes."

"I may not be so shocked. I think I know some of it already."

"What do you know?"

"Well, I know you were with Brother XII in Gibraltar on the *Lady Royal*."

Her mother looked astounded. "How do you know that?"

"I saw your name in the yacht club visitors' book."

"Why didn't you tell me before?"

"Mum, having secrets is a two way street. You haven't been able to talk to me, so I haven't been able to talk to you. I've been dying to find out what you were doing on a yacht in Gibraltar. I know you were in the Virgin Islands too. We've got a lot of things to talk about."

For the first time her mother smiled. "Where shall I begin?"

"Do you remember telling me you heard Brother XII give a talk in Southampton?"

"That's right."

"Was that the beginning?"

"Yes."

"Well, how about starting there?"

As her mother's story unfolded Jenny was surprised how much she already knew, but when Mother explained how she'd come to believe she was a reincarnation of Isis, Jenny was amazed. Finally the answers began to fall into place. She realized her mother was holding back some details, but she heard quite enough to understand what had happened. She felt sympathy rather than shock. Who could stand up to Brother XII? The story finished in 1937 and Mother knew nothing of Madame Zee, the treasure, or what happened at the end.

As she got the secrets off her chest her mother appeared more relaxed, and soon she was chatting about her yachting experiences as if nothing had happened. For half an hour they discussed their ocean crossings, the tropical islands and the Panama canal. It was wonderful. But then her mood changed.

"Jenny," she began. "There's something else I've got to tell you, something so dreadful I can hardly bear to think of it. I just don't know how to say it, but I must."

Somehow Jenny knew what was coming. It was something she'd refused to acknowledge for half a year.

"When I was Isis I became pregnant," her mother whispered.

"When was that?"

"On the *Lady Royal*. In the Virgin Islands."

"And Father?"

"He wasn't there."

Jenny's heart was thumping. "It was . . . ?"

"Amiel."

"Brother XII?"

"Yes."

"Oh Mum, how terrible."

"It didn't seem terrible at the time. I . . . , I thought I was in love."

"What happened?"

"I had a baby. A little girl."

Jenny was trembling. "When?"

"In the summer of 1937."

"Me?"

"Yes." Tears were streaming down her mother's face. "A darling little baby girl, whom I loved with all my heart."

Jenny was stifling tears herself, but she still wasn't quite ready to accept it.

"But I thought Isis died."

"We both nearly died. As far as the Aquarians were concerned we were dead. They threw us out."

"Oh Mum, how dreadful. What happened then?"

"Your father, you know, Philip, took us back. He came all the way out to B.C. to fetch us. Jenny, he's a wonderful man. I hope you'll always think of him as your real father."

She had suspected it for some time and now it finally sank in.

"But Brother XII was my biological father? I'm his daughter?"

"Yes."

"And I was born in Canada?"

Her mother nodded.

"And that's why I couldn't get a birth certificate in England?" said Jenny accusingly.

"Yes dear," her mother whispered.

"You knew it all along, and you did nothing?"

There was a silence.

"How could you? How could you do such a horrible thing?"

"I couldn't let you marry Peter Johnson."

Jenny was trying not to shout. She had to remember her mother was sick. The nurse might come in.

"Why? Why do you hate Peter? What's the matter with him?"

"I don't hate him, but you can't marry him."

"For God's sake why not?"

"Because he's your brother."

Jenny froze. Her mouth fell open and she stared at her mother in silence for a whole minute. Finally the nurse came in to see what had happened.

"It's alright nurse," she stammered. "We haven't quite finished."

"I'm so terribly sorry, dear," said her mother when the nurse had left the room. "I knew you'd be shocked."

"I don't believe it. How could Peter possibly be my brother?"

"I wasn't the first woman to fall for Amiel."

"Angela Johnson?" she whispered.

Her mother nodded.

"How do you know?"

"I learned a lot of secrets when I was living in the House of Mystery."

The Johnsons had left soon after Angela got pregnant, Jenny remembered. It had to be true.

"Oh, God," she breathed, her face deathly pale. "Oh God, I just don't know what to do."

It was evening and Jenny sat alone in the living room at Strathbrook, staring at the floor. The house was in darkness. She hadn't taken off her coat, eaten, or even drawn the curtains. Her whole world had collapsed and she couldn't even think.

She sat there for an hour before a plan slowly began to form. Her first idea was to phone Peter, but she wondered if his feelings for her might change. No, she wouldn't tell Peter yet. His mother was the key. She must talk to Mrs Johnson. It was too delicate a subject to deal with on the phone, so she'd have to go to Salcombe. As soon as she'd made up her mind she couldn't bear to wait.

She got up, dialled the Johnsons' number and got Peter's mother right away. First she explained why she was in England.

"An accident? Oh Jenny, how terrible. Is your mother going to be alright?"

"She is now, but for a day or two she didn't look too good." She hesitated. "Mrs Johnson, could I meet you in Salcombe in the morning?"

"Well of course you can, Jenny. But why?"

"It's a personal matter," she said stiffly. "I can't tell you on the phone."

"How are you going to get down here?"

"I'll drive my mother's car."

"You mean drive down during the night? I don't want you to have an accident too. Why don't you leave in the morning and see me after lunch?"

"Oh, Mrs Johnson, I can't wait."

There was a pause. "Jenny, are you alright?"

"Yes, I think so. I'll see you in the morning." She hung up.

It was already getting light when she left Strathbrook at a little after 4am. The road was empty so she made good time. She was still frightened of Stonehenge, so she took the southern route along the A30, through rolling farmland most of the way. The dawn was beautiful, with mist hanging in the valleys and the hedgerows glistening with dew.

When she reached Salcombe there were already sails on the estuary and fishing boats on their way out to sea. She drove down the hill feeling increasingly nervous. Soon she'd have to confront Peter's mother with being unfaithful to her husband, and suggest that another man was the true father of her son. She parked in the driveway at Wiscasset. Mrs Johnson was at the door even before she got out of the car, smiling and friendly, with no sign she knew what was wrong.

"I'm glad you've got here safely," she said. "I worried about you all night. Come in and I'll make you some breakfast."

Peter's father was out doing house calls, so they had the kitchen to themselves. Jenny still wasn't sure what to say, but when she finished breakfast she knew she had to begin.

She cleared her throat. "Yesterday I discovered something absolutely terrible."

Mrs Johnson looked at her sympathetically, as if nothing could be that terrible.

"Do you remember Brother XII?" she went on.

"The leader of the Aquarians?"

"Well, he's my father."

Mrs Johnson stared at her for a minute. "I'm not sure I understand," she said. "If you mean your spiritual father, he was a sort of father to us all at one time."

"I mean he was my real father."

There was another pause. "I see," she replied at last. "You're quite sure about that?"

"Yes, I am."

"May I ask how you found out?"

"My mother told me."

"Because she thought she was going to die?"

"I think so, yes."

Mrs Johnson didn't reply at once and Jenny thought her fears were about to be confirmed.

"Does Philip know about this? Does he know you're not really his daughter?"

"Yes, apparently he's always known."

"And he's never treated you differently?"

"No. At least, I've never noticed."

"Well, in that case it doesn't matter," said Mrs Johnson, reaching across the table to take Jenny's hand. "He's your real father, dear. He brought you up and cared for you. I don't think it matters who your biological father was."

"So you're not shocked?"

"Well, I'm a bit surprised, if that's what you mean. Poor Mary. She must have had this on her conscience all these years. I always wondered why she was so sensitive about the Aquarians. Now I understand."

Jenny looked at her for a moment. "I'm so relieved you feel that way. I didn't know what you'd think."

"But the important question is what do you think yourself, Jenny? Are you shocked by what your mother did?"

"I don't know. I think I am a bit."

"Well, you mustn't be. I'm sure it wasn't her fault. Brother XII had unbelievable power. No one could resist him. Remember, she's your only mother and she loves you. She must have suffered terribly all these years."

"I hadn't thought of that."

"You've got to let her know you understand and you still love her just the same."

"I will."

Jenny felt tears at the back of her eyes, but she kept them under control. She hadn't reached the most difficult part of her mission yet.

"Your father must be a very fine man," Mrs Johnson went on. "Does he know your mother has told you?"

"I don't think so, but I'll have to tell him. Everything's different now."

"That's just the point, Jenny, everything is not different now. They're still your mother and father just as they were before."

Jenny squeezed her hand. "Oh, Mrs Johnson, it was worth the drive to Salcombe just to hear you say that. I don't want my parents to change."

But then she remembered what she'd really come about.

"I'm afraid there's something else," she whispered.

"Well?"

"It's very personal."

"Just say it, Jenny. It's probably not as bad as you think."

"It's . . . It's about you."

Mrs Johnson looked surprised. "Well then, that's all the more reason for you to tell me what it is."

This was it, there was no going back. "Mother said that when she was at the colony she heard the Brother had been interested in you."

"In me?"

"It was just a rumour."

But Mrs Johnson's face blushed red and Jenny knew it must be true. The bottom seemed to drop out of her world.

"I can't believe it, after all these years. Yes, I have to admit the Brother did show an interest in me at one time."

Jenny waited. She must be sure, but she didn't know how to carry on.

"Did he . . . ?" Her voice tailed off.

"Did he what?"

"It's about Peter," Jenny stammered. "Mother thinks Peter is Brother XII's child too. Don't you see? That means he's my brother. I've been wanting to marry my own brother."

Mrs Johnson looked shocked. "Oh, my God," she said. "Now I see it. Now I understand why Mary has tried so hard to keep you two apart."

"Well, is he?"

"No. It's true that Brother XII showed a bit of interest in me for a while. I was flattered at the time, but I was already pregnant with Peter, although of course the Brother didn't know." She smiled. "Don't worry, both my sons are James' doing."

Jenny phoned the Epsom District Hospital from Salcombe at lunchtime. Both her parents were doing well, so she left a message that she'd visit them next day, and spent the night with the Johnsons at Wiscasset.

Before she left next morning, Peter's mother had another talk with her.

"You must remember that Brother XII was not an ordinary man," she said. "Don't judge your mother too harshly. She loves you and she thought that everything she did was for your own good. Even taking you to Africa."

"But if only she'd told me the truth."

"She has, now. And even at your age you've found it hard to accept. What would you have thought of her if she'd told you when you were only seventeen?"

"I don't know."

"Being a mother isn't easy, Jenny. I hope you'll be a mother to my grandchildren one day."

"Oh, I do hope so."

"Give your father a kiss, and tell him that he's always been your real father and he always will be."

Jenny gave her a hug. "I'm so glad I came down here and talked to you. I'll never be able to thank you enough."

"Just make it up with your parents, and then go and marry Peter. That's all the thanks I need."

Jenny could hardly believe how much better Mother looked. Her temperature had returned to normal and she was sitting up in bed.

"And you're quite sure Peter's not Brother XII's son?" her mother asked.

"Absolutely."

"Angela Johnson couldn't have been hiding it?"

"I'm certain she wasn't," said Jenny.

"But I overheard Ken Martin give her name: *Angela Johnson, the doctor's wife*. I couldn't mistake a description like that."

"Apparently the Brother was interested in her at one time. That's how the rumour started. But there was nothing to it. He wasn't Peter's father."

"You mean I tried to keep you and Peter apart for nothing?"

"Yes."

"How can you ever forgive me?"

She put her arms round her mother. "You did it because you love me and you thought it was for the best. Of course I forgive you."

"Was Angela disgusted by what I did with the Brother?"

"She said it wasn't your fault. No one could resist Brother XII for long."

Now that she'd cleared up the problem about Peter, Jenny began to think of her mother's pictures. She was curious to see what her real father looked like.

"Mum," she began. "Do you remember years ago you caught me looking at some old pictures?"

"What old pictures?"

"They were photos of people in old-fashioned clothes. You kept them in the drawer in your dressing table and you got very angry when I looked at them. You even spanked me. You must remember that."

"Well, I do recall something about it," said her mother warily.

"I'd like to look at them again?"

"Alright."

"Do you know where they are?"

"In the drawer I expect."

Jenny could hardly tell her she'd already searched the whole house.

"Mum, I want us to begin our relationship over again and I think the pictures would make a good start." She looked directly at her mother. "I do hope we can find them."

Her mother observed her equally directly for several seconds. "You know, dear," she said at last, "I think I hid them on top of my wardrobe."

Jenny found the pictures immediately. They were tucked in behind a wooden rim at the top of the wardrobe where she never would have looked. She was disappointed with most of them, and surprised they'd made such an impression when she was a girl. If her mother hadn't spanked her she would have forgotten all about them.

There were about a dozen photos of groups of men and women dressed in 1930s clothes, sitting in the woods or on the beach. Three of the photos stood out from the rest, and one glance was enough to know they were pictures of Brother XII. His charisma shone like a beacon. Two of them showed him on his own, beside a huge maple tree and outside a small house in the forest, and in the third he was with a woman.

With a pounding heart she held them under the light to see him better, and he stared back at her with such vitality she caught her breath. Everything about him radiated power, the dark eyes, the thick black hair, the nose, the chin. His mouth was sensitive but strong with no hint of a smile. He could be an Egyptian god, she thought, the reincarnation of Osiris.

The woman in the third photo was her mother. Brother XII was standing on a beach, gesturing out to sea with his eyes on some faraway shore. There were people at the edge of the picture, so she guessed he was preaching. Her mother stood beside him, but she was not gazing at the horizon. Her eyes were fixed upon his face with such a look of rapture that Jenny was transfixed. Suddenly she understood. So that was her father, his blood ran in her veins. She could sense his strength and she felt a wave of pride.

The pictures of the Egyptian carvings were little more than postcards, and even the great Zimbabwe birds were disappointing. The one of the Goddess Isis was bigger and more elaborate, and she recognized the horns which had impressed her so much when she was a child.

And then there was the map. It was much bigger than the pictures, about eighteen inches square, but dirty and tattered round the edges. She recognized it immediately as a hand-drawn duplicate of a navigational chart, and when she looked more closely she realized it was a copy of the Gulf Islands chart that she and Peter had used only a few days before. And there was the crooked red line running from the top to the bottom just as she remembered.

Jenny's father was discharged from the hospital first. She made a special effort to look after him at home so he would see that their relationship was unchanged. She visited her mother every day and soon they became close. They spent hours discussing yachting and the places they'd visited. Jenny described her seasickness and how seeing her mother's name in the visitors' book in Gibraltar had inspired her to carry on.

"And when I recognized your writing on the wall of the treasure cave it nearly blew my mind."

"Did you find the secret chamber at the end of the cave where the treasure had been hidden?" her mother asked.

"What secret chamber?"

"Oh, I'll never forget that. Amiel nearly drowned."

Her mother went on to tell her how their native guide had shown them an underwater passage to a hidden chamber. When she heard what had happened to Amiel she felt thankful it wasn't mentioned in the sailing guide because Peter would have tried it too.

"But in spite of nearly getting trapped Amiel still explored the pirates' secret hiding place," said her mother. "There was nothing that man wouldn't do."

Jenny wanted to know more about him. "Did you really love him, Mum?" she asked.

Her mother stared out of the window for a whole minute with a faraway look in her eyes.

"Yes, dear," she replied eventually. "I love your father in a wonderful equal way. No one could ever be as important as he is to me. But I was intoxicated with love for Amiel. His face, his voice, his touch, I could think of nothing else. But we were not equals. I wanted to share in his world but he had no interest in mine."

"Do you love him still?"

Again that faraway look.

"No, but sometimes I picture him. We are on the boat. It's evening and the warm air drifts across the deck. There are palm trees and a beach, and moonlight on the water. Then I feel his arms and see his face, and for a moment the ecstasy comes back. I've learnt to separate the memory from the hurt that came later."

"Oh, Mum, he's my father. Was he good or bad?"

"Both. He was just a man; a rather special one with an extraordinary ability to make people believe in him. At the beginning he was good. He really thought he'd make the world a better place."

"Why did he turn bad? Towards the end he got positively evil, or so everybody says."

"Jenny, he believed he was the new Messiah, like Jesus Christ, who'd save the world and make it a better place. He was higher than a king, and we treated him that way. Imagine how he must have felt when he discovered it wasn't true. When he realized he was just the broken leader of a group of misfits on an unimportant island. But his power over his followers was still intact. I think he just got angry and began to play with them like puppets on a string."

There was something else she was curious about.

"Among the pictures there was a map."

"That's right. It showed the path Aquarius was supposed take before it hit the earth. I don't know why Amiel thought it was so important."

"He did?"

"Yes. There were a pair of maps. He kept one on the *Lady Royal*, and the other in the House of Mystery in his private desk."

"How did you get it?"

"I don't know how I got any of the pictures. They belonged to Brother XII. When I was taken to the hospital in Nanaimo someone threw my things into a bag and I think they got in by mistake."

"Could I have the map? I know Peter would like it. I'd love to have a photo of Brother XII as well."

"I don't know dear, they're all I have left, but there's a photographic shop in Epsom that would copy them."

Chapter 37

Peter parked the second-hand Thunderbird he'd bought the previous week and walked across to the airport lounge. After the airports in Africa Vancouver International seemed palatial. He settled into a seat in the glass-fronted waiting area and watched the new Boeing 707s come in from across Canada and the U.S.A. Eventually the loudspeaker announced the arrival of the flight from London. He went over to the customs area and waited for the passengers to emerge through the big swing doors. Finally he spotted Jenny and in a few moments she was in his arms.

"Sweetheart," she said as they set off across the arrivals hall on the way to the car. "You'll never believe what I discovered while I was away."

"Well?"

" For a start I'm not even English."

"I always thought you looked a bit odd," he smirked. "What are you? A Hottentot?"

"It's not funny."

"Well I ought to know what I'm marrying."

She looked at him seriously. "You might not want to marry me at all when you hear the truth."

"Don't be silly, it makes no difference to me what you are."

"It's too complicated to tell you here. Wait till we get to the car."

She hadn't seen the Thunderbird before. He was rather proud of it but she didn't show much interest. As soon as they were inside he gave her a kiss.

"You'd better let me tell you what I've found out," she said.

"Is it more important than this?"

"It's the reason we couldn't get married."

So he sat quietly while she described everything her mother had said. Some of it he already suspected but when he heard the Isis part he was truely amazed.

"You mean your father was Brother XII?" he said at last.

"Yes," she whispered.

"And your mother actually thought she was a goddess and he was a god?"

"I told you it was hard to believe."

"And you were born out here? And that's why you couldn't get a birth certificate in England?"

"Yes."

"But I still don't understand why she tried to keep us apart. Even if you are Brother XII's daughter, why should that make any difference to us?"

"Because she thought you were Brother XII's son. She thought you and I were brother and sister."

"That's ridiculous." But even as he said it he started to wonder. He really didn't look like either of his parents.

"I know that," said Jenny. "And now she does too."

"How can you be sure?"

"I asked your mother."

"You what?"

"Peter, it's terribly important, so I drove down to Salcombe and asked her. She was sweet. She understood completely, and she assured me that James is your father."

"Well, thank God for that. But if you could ask her so easily, why couldn't your mother have done it years ago?"

"Because she was so ashamed of what she'd done. She couldn't bear to talk about it. Oh, Peter, how are we ever going to forgive her?"

He didn't know what to say. He thought of all the trouble Mary had caused over the years; the dreadful time when she'd banished Jenny to Africa; the way she'd stopped his letters and even lied about Jessica Clark. And all because she was embarrassed about some stupid secret of her own. No, he could never forgive her for that.

"You mean that if she'd told you this before, we could have married years ago without any fuss?"

Her voice was very small. "I think so."

He didn't just feel angry with Mary, he began to despise her too. The Brother had actually persuaded her that she was a goddess and he was a god. It was unbelievable. How could anyone be stupid enough to believe something like that?

"Will you try to forgive her?" asked Jenny.

"I don't know." He couldn't say what he really thought.

"She's terribly sorry for everything she's done."

"Oh Jenny, she's caused us so much trouble. What on earth can I say?"

There was a silence as they sat and stared through the windshield at the car parked in front. After a while he decided to change the subject. "So you finally got to see your mother's secret pictures?"

"Yes," she said. "I had copies made of the map and the three photos of Brother XII. I've got them here if you want to see them."

Anything to take his mind off Mary White. "Yes please."

She opened her bag and handed him an envelope. He looked at the first photo and gasped with surprise. All thought of Mary White flew from his mind. Staring up at him was a face he remembered well. Remembered, feared, admired, respected, despised. Every detail of that face was etched into his mind. The straight black hair, the dark unwavering eyes, the firm chin. He examined the next one, and then the next, but they were all pictures of the same man. They all looked just like Gordon McNair.

It couldn't be McNair, of course, because of the dates, but he felt like a frightened boy again, sitting on a hard chair in a small dark room beneath a naked light. He could see McNair's face, his eyes, his mouth only a few inches away from his own. He could even smell the cigarette smoke on the man's breath.

With a shudder he recalled the disgusting things they'd done in that room. A form of medical treatment Mr McNair had said. How could anyone have believed that? He looked at the pictures once more and suddenly he understood what had happened to Mary White. Brother XII had not been the only man to convince people that black was white, and Mary had not been the only dupe.

"Well, what do you think of him?" asked Jenny.

"I don't know." He could still hardly bring himself to talk about what had happened with McNair.

It took forty minutes to drive from the airport to Stanley Park and they spoke hardly at all. Peter spent the whole time brooding about Gordon McNair. He'd never told anyone except Jenny. He knew he ought to have told his parents, but somehow he found the subject impossible to discuss.

"Peter," said Jenny as they approached the dock. "Please don't be too hard on my mother."

"What makes you think I'm being hard on her."

"The way you're sitting there with nothing to say. I don't want anything to come between us."

"I was thinking about your pictures."

"I thought you didn't like them."

"Brother XII looks exactly like the homosexual teacher at my boarding school."

"I see."

"He made me believe things which seem ridiculous now, and I can't bear to think of the ghastly things he persuaded me to do. It was medical treatment he said. I'm terribly ashamed of myself because I was stupid enough to believe him. That's partly why I never talk about it."

"And my mother?"

"I'm sure she feels the same way. I don't know what to think about her yet, but I'm beginning to understand."

He parked the T-bird by the dock and they sat in silence for a minute.

"What shall we do next?" she asked.

He grinned. "Get you a birth certificate and find a church. That's if you'll still have me?"

"I've been having you regularly for the last year and a half," she giggled. But then she looked serious. "Sweetheart, I really think it's finally going to happen."

She started to kiss him and presently she asked, "How do you think one gets a birth certificate?"

"Why not try the hospital where you were born?"

Jenny got the number of Nanaimo General Hospital from directory assistance.

"Sorry," said the hospital clerk. "We don't issue duplicate birth certificates."

"Oh. But couldn't you just confirm that I was born there?"

"Sorry. We only keep detailed records for seven years."

"But I don't need a detailed record, just confirmation of where I was born."

"I'll put you through to Medical Records."

After a delay a records clerk came on the line. "Patients' records are destroyed after seven years," she said, sounding just like the clerks Jenny had come up against in England.

"But don't you have a ledger of births? I just want to confirm that my name is there?"

"You mean a birth register? Yes, of course we keep one of them."

"Well, do you think you could see if my name is in it, please?"

"What year?"

"1937"

"It will take a few minutes."

Eventually the clerk came back on the line; "I'm sorry. The 1937 volume is missing."

"Missing?"

"It was sent to the Division of Vital Statistics in Victoria a few weeks ago. Sorry I can't be of assistance." The line went dead.

Vital Statistics wasn't much better.

"We can't give out information over the phone."

"But do you issue birth certificates?"

"You'll have to come in person."

"Alright. Are you open tomorrow?"

"You'll have to provide proof of identity. We can't do anything without that."

Peter said it would take too long to go to Victoria in *Bluebell*, so they took the car ferry to Nanaimo on Vancouver Island and drove south from there. It was a lovely sunny morning in July, and Jenny was awed by the size and beauty of Vancouver Island. There were towns and villages, mountains, forests and miles of rolling green farmland. It seemed far too big to be called an island.

The contrast between modern bustling Vancouver and colonial Victoria was startling. She found quiet streets and elegant old houses that reminded her of England, and downtown there were double-decker buses like the ones in London.

The Division of Vital Statistics was on the second floor of an old office building on Government Street. There was no elevator and the stairs looked shabby and run down. They went through a scruffy glass-fronted door and waited at the inquiries counter while the clerk finished some work at his desk. He was a small downtrodden man in his thirties and there was no sign of a smile when he eventually walked over to see what they wanted.

"I would like a copy of my birth certificate," said Jenny politely.

He asked to see proof of her identity and she produced her British passport, half expecting he'd reject it.

"You were born in B.C.?"

"Yes."

He walked wearily over to his desk to fetch a form.

"Your full name, please?"

"Jennifer White."

His writing was meticulous and slow.

"The place where you were born?"

"Nanaimo."

"Date?"

"July 19, 1937."

"Your mother's name?"

"Mary White."

"And your father's name?"

She hesitated, but Amiel was her father. The clerk waited, his pen poised above the paper.

"Amiel de Valdes," she replied.

He looked up. "Would you repeat that, please?"

"Amiel de Valdes," she said nervously. "It's a Spanish name, I think."

He stared at her in surprise.

"Would you wait here a minute, please," he said. Then he picked up her passport and walked out of the room.

"What was all that about?" asked Peter.

"I don't know. Government offices make me nervous. I just want to get my certificate and run."

After a few minutes the clerk returned, accompanied by a plump man with a sallow complexion and greasy brown hair. He looked at her suspiciously.

"Jennifer White?"

"Yes."

"Your father is Amiel de Valdes?"

"That's right."

"Is he also known as Brother XII?"

"Yes. That's correct."

He turned the pages of her passport. "It says here that you were born in London, England."

"I'm afraid that's a mistake."

"Really? What makes you think so?"

His tone was unpleasant, but she needed the certificate so she answered politely, "My mother told me. And there's no record of my birth in England."

"Your mother? Is that Zura de Valdes?"

Jenny recoiled in horror. "No. Her name is Mary White."

He turned the page. "Your country of residence is England?"

"That's right. But I was born over here and I need a birth certificate. Couldn't you just look up the details in your records?"

"Miss White," he said slowly, fixing her with his eyes. "If you want me to help, you'd better answer my questions. Do you understand?"

She swallowed. "Yes."

"So you claim your father is Brother XII and your mother is Mary White?"

"Yes."

"Do you live with your parents?"

"I live with my mother. Brother XII is dead, I believe."

"How do you know he was your father?"

"My mother told me."

He raised his eyebrows. "You'll have to provide more reliable evidence than that."

She was tempted to spit at him and walk out, but she stifled her anger and tried to think of something to show that she was related to Brother XII.

"My mother has some personal things of his," she said at last.

"Really? What things?"

"Personal photographs, pictures and a map," she replied, doing her best to make them sound significant.

"A map?"

"It's a map of the Aquarian settlements. Brother XII drew it himself and he said it was important."

At last he looked interested. "I'll have to see it. And the other things too."

"I'm afraid my mother keeps most of them at home in England, but I do have a copy of the map and three photos of Brother XII."

He held out his hand so she opened her bag and passed him the copies. He only glanced at the photos but he spent some time studying the map, turning it over and over and holding it up to the light as if he were trying to find some mark hidden in the paper.

Eventually he asked, "Are you sure your mother has the original of this?"

"I've seen it myself."

He snapped his fingers at the clerk. "Make a copy of this and put it on my desk." Then he picked up Jenny's application form. "We don't seem to have your English address."

She gave him the Ashtead address which he wrote down carefully in a notebook. When he'd finished he looked up.

"Well," he said. "I'm afraid I can't give you a birth certificate."

It took a minute to sink in.

"Why not?"

"There are no records of any children born to Brother XII."

"But you haven't looked."

"We searched the files a few weeks ago. No children were registered to Brother XII and you have no proof that you're his daughter. We can't issue birth certificates on a whim, you know."

He turned towards the door.

"But there must be a record of my birth somewhere," Jenny pleaded.

"Try Nanaimo Hospital."

"They said they'd sent the 1937 record book to you."

He glanced at the clerk. "Nonsense. I expect they've lost it."

Then her temper flared. He'd known it all along and she'd put up with his rudeness for nothing. She wanted to scream at him, but he'd already left the room. Tears of frustration filled her eyes.

"I'm sorry, Miss," said the clerk. "Mr Serano can be awfully hard."

"What can I do?" she sobbed. "I was born in Nanaimo, and I need a birth certificate so much. We can't get married without one."

"Get married?"

"That's why I need the certificate."

"I see. So it's got nothing to do with Brother XII?"

"Nothing at all."

He seemed to consider that for a moment, then he asked, "Do you think your mother might have given someone else's name as the father?"

Jenny was beyond embarrassment. "She might have said it was Philip White. He's her husband."

"Look, Mr Serano will be away this afternoon. Why don't you come back then? We'll look in the records under Mary and Philip White."

"Will you be here?"

He nodded. "Don't worry, Miss. If you were born in Nanaimo I'll give you a certificate. But I can't do it now."

"Oh, thank you so much."

She turned to go, but before they left Peter asked, "Is it true that you've already searched the records for children born to Brother XII?"

"Yes."

"Why was that?"

"We had a request."

"From whom?"

"I don't know. Mr Serano has the details."

When Mark picked up the phone he heard a woman's voice which he didn't recognize. She sounded very upset.

"This is Mary White, Jennifer's mother. Can I leave a message for my daughter?"

"You can talk to her directly," he said. "They're having dinner here tonight. Just hang on a minute." He handed the phone to Jenny.

"Hello, Mum," said Jenny, and then a moment later, "What on earth's the matter?"

There was a pause while she listened, then she said, "Oh Mum, how dreadful. And the police are there already?"

If there was anything Mark hated, it was listening to one side of a telephone conversation.

"Nothing of value?" said Jenny after a minute. "How very strange."

She listened a little longer, then she said, "They've gone? I don't believe it"

They continued for a few more minutes, then finally Jenny said, "Well I'm terribly sorry Mum, but at least you and Dad are alright. I think you should take one of your sleeping pills and go to bed. I'll call you in the morning."

"What was that all about?" Mark asked as soon as she'd hung up.

"Someone broke into their house while they were out this evening."

"Oh no. Was much stolen?"

"That's the funny thing. Nothing was stolen. Almost nothing anyway."

"Vandals?"

"No, there was hardly any damage. The burglars cut a neat hole in one of the windows, reached in, and opened the door from the inside. The police think it was a professional job."

Mark felt a tingle in his spine. "What was taken, Jenny?"

"Just the old photos of the Aquarian colony that I told you about. That's why Mother's so upset, she can't replace them."

"Just the photos?"

"The whole package. The photos and the Egyptian pictures."

"Professional burglars don't steal worthless things," he said. "Something in that package must have been important."

"What about the map?" suggested Peter.

"That was in the package too," said Jenny.

"That's what they were after. That sleazy Serano man in Victoria was interested in your mother's map."

"But he couldn't have carried out a burglary in England."

Mark's pulse began to rise. "He must be working with some organization, a gang or something. They must know about the gold. There's a lot of money involved."

"Well, he certainly knew about Brother XII," said Jenny.

"It's bound to be the map." Mark felt more convinced than ever. "Your mother's had it all this time and now we've lost it. I just can't believe our bad luck."

"I've got a copy," said Jenny.

"You have?"

She took the envelope out of her handbag. "There are copies of the photos as well."

Mark went straight to the map. It looked much like the one they'd seen in the museum and it even had a crooked line running through the middle. He studied it carefully but there were no other clues.

"The Brother said it was important," said Jenny.

"It looks similar to the one in the museum," he replied. "Perhaps if we could get the pair of them together we'd be able to see what they mean."

"You really believe in that treasure, don't you," said Peter.

"This burglary just confirms it. Look, Bev and I both have time off. Let's go to Nanaimo in *Sundance* and have a poke around."

The thirty-mile trip in a fast powerboat was a new experience for Jenny. It was exhilarating to feel the boat fly over the water and reach the horizon in only fifty minutes instead of four or five hours. They got to Nanaimo a little before midday and nosed slowly into the harbour, past fishing boats and yachts.

"That's the Bastion," called Beverley, pointing to the black and white tower behind the public dock. "The museum's inside."

Jenny wondered if Nancy Littleton still worked there. Nancy hadn't been very helpful when they'd met on Kilimanjaro two years ago, but she knew a lot about the Aquarians. Perhaps when she learned the truth about the first Isis she'd be more willing to talk.

They moored *Sundance* at the dock and walked up the hill. It only took ten minutes to reach the old fort with its massive wooden door. Once they were inside she spotted Nancy sitting behind the curator's desk. She was a little plumper than before but Jenny recognized her immediately. She looked up as they walked in and then dropped her eyes. They were the only visitors and Jenny waited for the others to go upstairs so she could get Nancy on her own.

"Do you remember me?" she said when they were alone. "Jenny White. We met on Kilimanjaro eighteen months ago."

Nancy looked up. "Yes, I thought I recognized you."

"It's good to see you again," said Jenny. "Did you enjoy your stay in Africa?"

"Yes."

"I was wondering if we could have a chat about the Aquarians?"

"My husband told you what happened. There's nothing more to say."

"I recently discovered that I was born in the colony."

Nancy looked at her in surprise. "Really?"

"Yes. My mother told me a couple of weeks ago. It explains a lot of things, but I still want to find out more."

"I see." She paused, then started to get up. "Well, there's some stuff here in the museum. I'll fetch the folder."

"Nancy, Brother XII was my father. I want to know more than what's in the folder. I need to find out what he was like."

"Your father?" She sat down. "How do you know?"

Jenny reached into her handbag. "My mother finally told me the truth. Look, I've even got a Canadian birth certificate."

Nancy looked stunned. "I don't believe it."

"My mother was the first Isis."

"The first Isis died."

"No. They took her to the hospital and everyone thought she'd died. They thought the baby had died too but eventually we both recovered."

Nancy didn't reply.

"Could we have a private talk? Just you and me?"

There was a long silence, but eventually she nodded. Then she got up and led the way to a small room at the back of the museum where they sat at a table littered with magazines and coffee cups.

Slowly Jenny told her mother's story and as it unfolded Nancy seemed to relax. By the time it was finished she was even asking questions and talking freely about her own life in the colony. It was just what Jenny wanted. At the end Nancy took her hand and said, "The Brother wasn't all bad, you know. You'll hear about the wicked things he did, but there was a good side to him as well. He was your father so you should remember that."

"Thank you."

"Do you know," she went on. "This is the first time I've been able to talk about him like this. I can't tell you how much better you've made me feel."

"Well, thank you," said Jenny. "I think we should look at the Aquarian folder now."

Mark noticed a change in the curator's attitude as soon as she came back into the room with Jenny. On their earlier visit to the museum she'd been reluctant to talk, but now she smiled as she walked over to the filing cabinet to fetch the Aquarian folder.

"It's strange," she said. "A couple of men were in here looking at this just yesterday. I didn't like the look of them."

"Why not?" asked Mark.

"They looked like a couple of gangsters."

"Gangsters?"

"Yes, you know, like the mafia."

"The mafia don't hunt for treasure, they're in the drug trade."

"That's just it," said Nancy. "They came in a big narrow powerboat with American registration. It was at least forty feet long and painted dark grey. It looked like a drug runner to me."

They spread the contents of the folder out on the table but Mark couldn't find the map.

"I saw it yesterday," said Nancy. "Those men were looking at it."

"I can't believe it," said Mark. "There are two maps and now they've both been stolen. They're bound to show where the treasure's hidden."

"I've still got my copy," said Jenny. "Do you want to have a look at that?"

He nodded, and she took it out of her handbag and spread it on the table where they could all see it.

"It's not quite the same as the one we had in the museum," said Nancy.

"What's the difference?" asked Mark.

"Our one had a red line running from side to side. On this map the line goes from top to bottom."

"I thought Brother XII said that line was the path the meteorite Aquarius was supposed to take," said Beverley.

"That's right," said Nancy.

"Well, the Brother couldn't have believed a single meteorite would take two different paths," said Mark.

"I guess not," said Nancy. "But I thought that's what he said."

"But he couldn't have believed it, so he must have drawn the lines for some other reason."

There was a silence while they all stared at the map.

After a minute Peter said, "I wonder if the treasure could be hidden at the point where the lines cross."

"What do you mean?" asked Mark.

"If you laid one map on top of the other and held them up to the light, you'd see a place where the two lines crossed."

"I bet that's it," said Nancy. "That's why the Brother drew two maps and kept them in different places."

"We've only got one of them."

"But I expect the treasure's hidden somewhere along that line," said Peter.

Mark stared at the map with dismay. "Look," he said. "The line runs through Gabriola Island, then Mudge, then along the shore of Link Island, then De Courcy, and finally right through Ruxton. Unless we have the other map the treasure could be almost anywhere."

There was another pause, then Beverley said, "But it completely misses the house where Bert Hogarth found the vault. How do you explain that?"

"Maybe the vault was just a blind to throw people off the scent," Mark suggested. "If I had treasure to hide I'd put it where I could retrieve it by boat." He pointed to where the line ran along the shore of De Courcy Island. "If Peter's theory is correct it's probably hidden along there."

"But the line on the other map didn't cross the shore of De Courcy at all," said Beverley.

"It didn't? How do you know that?" asked Mark.

"Because it crossed the shore of Link Island by the otters' cave."

"What otters' cave?"

"Don't you remember? The first time we came here we saw a family of otters living in a cave on Link Island. The line on the other map crossed the shore close to the cave. That's why I remember it."

"Are you sure?"

"Certain. There was a rocky outcrop at the top of the cliff directly above the cave. Perhaps I can find it on the map."

Beverley ran her finger up and down the shore of Link Island. "There," she said at last. "There's the outcrop, and that's where the line crossed the shore. The otters' cave is directly underneath."

"And the line on Jenny's map runs right along the shore at that point," said Peter. "So that's where the two lines cross. Congratulations, Bev."

"Thank you," she smiled.

Mark slipped his arm around her waist. "Fantastic. I'd never have remembered that otters' cave in a hundred years."

Peter grinned at them. "Come on, let's go."

"Watch out for the Mafia," warned Nancy.

By the time Mark eased *Sundance* out from the dock a cold breeze was raising little wavelets in the harbour and there was a hint of rain in the air. He left Nanaimo and turned south, down Northumberland Channel, towards Brother XII's domain. The wide channel looked sombre and deserted, with the cliffs of Gabriola Island on one side and the dark forest of Vancouver Island on the other. He set a course for Dodd Narrows near the far end of the channel. Soon it began to drizzle and for a while nobody spoke.

Eventually Jenny said, "What a horrible place. Where are my beautiful Gulf Islands?"

"It's often like this just here," said Mark. "Wait till we get to Dodd Narrows; that's the gateway to the islands."

Dodd was a narrow gap in the cliffs between Mudge and Vancouver Island. It was only a hundred and fifty feet wide and the flood tide was rushing through at ten knots, creating whirlpools large enough to swamp a boat. Mark headed in gingerly. The current gripped the boat and twisted it back and forth. He eased the throttle open. The big engine roared and *Sundance* surged forward. As soon as they were through the scene changed. The rain cleared, and ahead lay a tranquil vista of quiet water and tree-clad islets that stretched away for fifty miles. In the distance there was a break in the clouds and shafts of sunlight were bursting through.

"That's better," said Jenny. "The Brother knew what he was doing when he chose this place. How did he keep other people away?"

"He didn't have to," said Mark. "There weren't many fast powerboats like *Sundance* in those days. They were isolated by the Strait of Georgia to the east, the forests of Vancouver Island to the west, and cold dark Northumberland Channel to the north. And to the south there are fifty miles of mostly uninhabited islands before you reach Victoria."

"The otters' cave is a couple of miles ahead on the left," said Beverley. "It's at the foot of the cliff on Link Island." She pointed through the windshield. "Link is the next island beyond that sandy bay."

Mark screwed up his eyes. The cliff was still a long way off and he couldn't see much detail, but even at that distance he had a feeling that something was wrong. Instead of heading directly for Link he set a course a little to the west. As they drew nearer he became certain he could see something in the water at the bottom of the cliff. A whale perhaps? Killer whales sometimes passed through the area but they usually swam in groups. A dead whale, or a sick one? Sick whales could be dangerous. A killer whale could sink a boat like *Sundance* with one butt of its head.

He stopped the engine.

"What's the matter?" asked Beverley.

"There's something in the water by the otters' cave."

"I'll get the binoculars," she said, ducking into the cabin.

Even when they were not going along there was still some motion, so he waited impatiently as she braced herself against the cabin to steady the binoculars.

"It's a boat," she announced at last. "A long grey boat anchored close in beside the cliff."

"It's bound to be those gangsters," said Mark. "How many long grey boats are there? They've got both maps and now they're picking up the loot."

"Perhaps they don't know about the cave," suggested Peter. "Let's take a closer look."

"There's a tiny channel called the gap between Link and De Courcy islands that Bev and I went through once," said Mark. "If I head for that we'll pass a quarter of a mile to the west of them, close enough to see what's going on without looking suspicious."

He started the motor and they moved forward again, a little slower so they'd have more time to look. Beverley continued to study the distant boat through the binoculars, and as they got closer she went into the cabin and used one of the portholes so she wouldn't attract attention.

When they were only a few hundred yards off Mark gave her the wheel and took the binoculars himself. The grey boat was anchored about twenty yards from the cliff. She was a sinister-looking craft, long and narrow, with a low cabin and a small flying bridge. Painted on the stern were the words *Seawolf, Seattle*. He spotted a man on the aft deck watching them and he was surprised to see the man was wearing a grey city suit.

Then a white dinghy appeared through a cleft in the cliff. He focused the binoculars and saw that it was a modern Boston Whaler with a powerful outboard on the back. So they'd found the cave already. The dinghy headed for the landing platform at *Seawolf*'s stern and three men climbed out. Two of them were young and strong and dressed for boating in sweaters and jeans. The third was older and overweight, and he also wore a city suit.

"I'll have to head in towards the gap now," called Beverley, gently turning the wheel. "Do you want to take over?"

Mark put the binoculars down and climbed out of the cabin to take the wheel. They had passed *Seawolf* by this time, and *Sundance* was heading in towards the narrow channel between Link and De Courcy islands.

"There are at least four men," he said. "Two of them look young and strong."

"And the other two?" asked Peter.

"It's strange but they do look like a couple of Mafioso gangsters."

"Well, they've found the cave, so we can't do much to stop them taking the gold."

"I'm not giving up yet," said Mark. "We'll go to Pirates Cove and think it over."

They had not been through the gap from the west before. It started to get shallow long before they reached the narrow part and Mark could see underwater rocks on both sides. He slowed the boat to a crawl and Beverley picked up the boathook in case they needed to fend off.

"Can we really get through there?" asked Peter.

"So long as the tide is high enough."

The sides of the channel were a mere three feet high, but they were solid rock and close enough to touch. The really narrow part was only a few yards long and soon they were in the little bay beyond. Everyone breathed a sigh of relief. It was only a mile and a half to Pirates Cove. Three other yachts lay at anchor in the cove, rafted together in a group. The crews waved as *Sundance* came in, but Mark continued on to the far shore and anchored near the beach where they would be on their own.

"There are trails on the island," he said as they lowered the dinghy off the transom. "If we walk up to the north end we'll be able to watch *Seawolf* from the top of the cliff. Bev and I hiked up there once. There's a small farm and we'll have to watch out for the farmer's dog."

They left the dinghy on the beach and set off walking carefully in single file and talking in whispers. They'd almost passed the farm before the dog started to bark. Mark held up his hand for silence and motioned them to hide behind trees. Eventually the barking stopped, and without a sound he motioned them forward again.

Beyond the farm the path got narrower until it petered out and he had to lead the way through the woods. It took an hour to reach the low cliff at the northwest corner of the island, but eventually he found a spot from which they could watch *Seawolf* and the otters' cave while they lay hidden by bushes and grass. The sun had come through and it was hot. Crickets chirped nearby and swallows swooped overhead.

Seawolf was still anchored in the same place less than half a mile away. The man in the incongruous grey suit was still standing on the afterdeck. He was talking to one of the younger men, while the other two sat in the Boston Whaler near the base of the cliff. The tide had risen making the entrance to the cave too low for the Whaler to get in. It looked as if high tide would cover the entrance completely and Mark wondered what it would be like to be trapped inside.

"Do you think they've got the gold?" whispered Peter.

"I don't know," said Mark. "There's no sign of it on deck but they'd probably take it below."

After a while the Whaler returned to *Seawolf* and he watched the two younger men hoist it aboard. A puff of exhaust came from *Seawolf*'s stern and he heard the growl of a powerful engine. Then there was another puff as a second engine fired. Twin V-eights, enormous power, she could probably top thirty knots.

Mark watched in silence as the anchor came up and she headed out from the cliff. Wild schemes flew through his mind. Perhaps they could follow and board her at night, or sink her and dive for the gold. But soon exhaust and spray were billowing from her stern as she gained speed and turned to the south.

"What a boat!" exclaimed Beverley.

"She's a drug runner alright" said Peter. "We saw boats like that in Panama."

"I wonder where she's headed."

"The States I expect. They can slip across the border at night and no one will see. She's not painted dark grey for nothing, you know."

"What shall we do now?" asked Mark bitterly. "Go home and get drunk?"

"I want to have a look in the cave," said Bev.

"The tide's too high. We'll have to wait till the morning."

He picked up the binoculars and watched *Seawolf* disappear to the south.

"That's odd," he said after a while. "They seem to be passing inside Thetis Island. That's not the way to the States."

Jenny stood in *Sundance*'s cockpit looking at the otters' cave thirty yards away. The entrance was a low arch about six feet across and three or four feet high, with deep water running right inside. They would have to explore it by dinghy, but she thought it looked dark and dangerous.

They had spent the night in Pirates Cove and returned through the gap early in the morning. Once they had anchored Jenny helped lower the dinghy and then she climbed in with Mark and Peter.

"Take care," said Beverley who was staying on *Sundance* to keep watch.

"We won't be long," Mark said as they pushed off. "Give a blast on the foghorn if you want us to come back."

Jenny was sitting in the bow and she ducked her head as the dinghy slid through the entrance of the cave. It was cold inside, with seaweed hanging from the walls and water dripping off the roof. They had a flashlight, of course, and when she switched it on she realized the cave was much bigger than she'd expected, about twelve feet wide, seven high, and at least forty feet long. It curved round to the left so she couldn't see the end. There was a dank fishy smell, but the otters had gone. She probed about with the light but the walls dropped straight into the water with no sign of a ledge where anything could be stored.

"I'll go in a bit further," said Mark, dipping the oars.

After a few yards they turned the corner and the light from the entrance was cut off. Jenny tried to see what lay ahead but the wet rock seemed to absorb the flashlight beam. Mark eased the boat slowly forward but thirty feet beyond the corner the cave came to an abrupt end. They sat in silence for a few minutes while Jenny examined the walls with the flashlight but there was nothing to see. Eventually Mark said, "Well, there's nothing here so I suppose we'd better get back to Beverley."

"We explored a cave like this in the Virgin Islands," said Peter as they paddled back towards the entrance. "It was supposed to be the place which Stevenson wrote about in *Treasure Island*."

"Was there any treasure?"

"Not when we were there, but apparently somebody found some once."

Jenny recalled the bats in the Norman Island cave. Well, at least there weren't any bats in here. She also remembered the name *Lady Royal* scratched on the wall. That was when she'd first suspected Philip might not be her real father.

"It's a funny thing," Peter said. "But we couldn't see where the treasure had been hidden in that cave either."

They rounded the corner and Jenny was relieved to see the narrow crack of daylight at the entrance. Mark pulled in the oars so they could squeeze through.

She pictured her mother and Brother XII in their dinghy in the Norman Island cave twenty-six years ago. He was her real father and she wondered what he'd been like. What was it her mother had said? Something had happened when they'd been in that cave. He had tried to swim through a tunnel to a hidden chamber and almost got stuck. Suddenly she felt a flush of excitement.

"Wait," she said. "I think I know the answer."

"What answer?" asked Peter.

"Do you remember the Norman Island Cave?"

"Of course I do."

"There's an underwater tunnel to a hidden chamber deeper in the cliff."

"We didn't see anything like that."

"When my mother was there with Brother XII they had a native guide who showed them where it was."

"Are you sure?" asked Mark.

"My mother told me about it. Brother XII actually swam through the tunnel."

"I think we'd better take another look," he said, slipping the oars back into the water.

"Shouldn't we check on Bev first?" asked Peter.

"We won't be long, and she hasn't blown the horn."

He rowed gently back to the head of the cave but the walls looked sheer and solid with no sign of any tunnel.

"Try probing with an oar," Jenny suggested.

Peter steadied the boat with one oar while Mark poked about under the water with the other. He insisted on going right round the end of the cave but he couldn't find a thing.

"Maybe when the tide is lower?"

"It's pretty low now."

"Well, I'm certain there was a hidden passage in the other cave."

"But there doesn't seem to be one here," said Mark irritably. "Those maps were probably just another trick to mislead people, like the vault Bert Hogarth found."

"But my mother remembered the Brother saying they were important," she persisted. "Here, let me have a go."

This time Mark steadied the boat and Peter held the light, while she probed under the water with the oar. She was determined to prove she was right and she made them go right round the end of the cave. When she held the oar at the very end she could reach down five or six feet, but the walls felt smooth and unbroken.

"Well," she said at last, "I suppose you must be right."

"We'll have another look at your map," said Mark. "I'm certain the treasure's on the island somewhere, but it's obviously not here."

She felt disappointed but really she was more interested in her biological father than the gold.

"Perhaps we should go back to *Sundance*," she suggested, handing Mark the second oar. "Bev must be wondering what's happened to us after all this time."

"Wait a minute," said Peter. "Do you remember, when we were in the Treasure Island cave you dropped the light and it went out?"

She recalled it only too clearly; the bats fluttering around her head in the dark.

"Yes."

"It fell into the boat, but you couldn't find it for three or four minutes," said Peter.

"Well, it was dark so I couldn't see."

"But while it was dark I saw a light coming from under the water," Peter persisted.

"That was just light filtering through from the entrance of the cave."

"No it wasn't. When you finally located the flashlight we found the entrance was in the opposite direction."

"So?" said Mark.

"Perhaps the light was coming through the hidden tunnel."

"Let's try it," said Mark, steadying the boat with the oars.

"OK." She switched off the light and for a few moments it was totally black. No one said a word. The sound of dripping water echoed eerily off the walls.

Then Peter said, "Look. Over there."

She had no idea which way he was pointing, but then she saw it too, a pale patch of light shimmering mysteriously several feet below.

"By Christ, you're right," said Mark. "There is a hidden passage. But it looks pretty dangerous. Do you think Brother XII swam through there?"

"I don't know about this cave," said Jenny. "But he certainly swam through the one on Norman Island."

"Jeez, he must have had some guts."

"He was my father," she replied with a hint of pride.

There was a silence, then Peter said, "Well, if your father could do it so can I."

She hadn't expected that. She remembered her mother saying Brother XII had almost drowned.

"No," she said. "I mean, we'll have to get diving equipment and stuff like that."

"Think of all the diving I did on our trip," said Peter. "I'll just swim down there and have a look."

Peter regretted what he'd said immediately. Diving in warm tropical water with sunlight filtering down was very different from a narrow tunnel in a cold dark cave.

"It might be difficult to find the way back," he wavered. "It's dark in here. The passage might not show up from the other end."

"Why don't you pull a rope behind you?" Mark suggested. "Then you can follow the rope back to the boat."

He could see that at least he'd have to try and he reluctantly took off his clothes. Eventually he was sitting in the stern of the dinghy in only his underpants.

"Here's the rope," said Mark. "Tie the end round your waist. I'll pay it out as you go so it doesn't get tangled. If you need help give four short jerks on the rope."

The water looked black and cold.

"Are you ready?" asked Mark.

"I guess so."

Peter secured the rope round his waist and slid gingerly over the back of the boat. He'd hoped to be able to stand, but it was much too deep.

Finally there was no excuse to delay. "Alright," he said. "Here goes."

"Do be careful," Jenny pleaded.

He took several deep breaths, ducked his head, and swam straight down to the glimmer of light. It was only about eight feet below the surface and he could see that Jenny had been right, the light was coming along a short tunnel about six feet long and quite wide enough to swim through. After a moment he started. It was easier than he expected because he could pull himself along with his hands while his body floated weightlessly behind.

He was about halfway through when the rope got caught, and as he reached down to free it his back scraped on the rock. He jerked instinctively, hitting his head, and he felt a twinge of fear. He tugged on the rope, but it wouldn't budge, so he tried to untie the knot. For half a minute his fingers made the same frantic movements over and over again, but the knot remained tight.

Desperately he tried to wriggle backwards out of the hole, but his body was trapped by the rocks and the harder he tried the more firmly it stuck. By this time his head was throbbing and lights were flashing before his eyes.

Then his hands found the rope again and he gave it one last tug. A miracle. Somehow it came free. For a moment his mind cleared and he reached forward with both hands, pulling himself towards the light. He felt

his back scrape against the rock but there was no pain. Then he was
through, looking up at the silvery glint of sunlight on the surface above his
head. There was a swish of water rushing past his ears, and then his head
broke the surface and his lungs exploded as he drew a breath.

For several minutes he clung gasping to a ledge of rock, but when he
finally looked up he was stunned by what he saw. He was in a small
chamber about ten feet across. This part of the cliff was composed of
sandstone that was easy to chip away. The chamber was neat and square,
with vertical walls, and steps and ledges that could only have been carved
by human hands. The roof rose in a natural vault to a small aperture in the
cliff far above. That was why he could see. The aperture let in a beam of
sunlight which reflected off the pale sandstone walls and filled the room
with a ghostly shimmering glow. The chamber looked as clean and tidy as if
it had just been built, and it was as silent as a Pharaoh's tomb.

And there was something else. At first he hardly dared to look.

Carved into the wall that faced the tunnel was a broad ledge, well
above the waterline. It was set back into the sandstone, so it was protected
from above. On the ledge stood what he first thought was a heavy wooden
altar like the one at the Zimbabwe Club. However, when he looked again it
was not an altar but three rows of dark wooden boxes, stacked neatly one
on top of another. He counted eight boxes in each row, twenty-four in all.
There was nothing remarkable about the boxes themselves, but some of
them were rotting and at one end the wood had completely fallen away
revealing what they held.

Each box contained two big glass jars, and each jar seemed to glow
with a rich yellow light of its own.

He was still in the water clinging to the ledge, and now he noticed that
steps had been cut in the rock nearby. They were slippery with seaweed
and he nearly fell, but he was too excited to care. Nor did he feel the cold,
or even notice the blood still oozing from his arms and back. He climbed
the steps and crept along a man-made ledge that led to the boxes and jars.

At first he just stood there staring at them, lightheaded with
excitement and too awed to touch. Every one of them was filled with gold
coins. Their tops had been sealed with wax, and the coins were as bright as
the day they'd been minted. He'd seen gold before but nothing like this,
hundreds of pounds of it shimmering with soft yellow light. Here was more
money than he'd have in the whole of his life.

Eventually he reached out and touched one of the jars, gingerly at first,
and then he tried to pick it up. It was cold, slippery and very heavy, and he
had to use both hands. It must weigh twenty pounds, he guessed, so it

would be impossible to swim back through the tunnel with even a single jar. They could open them and carry a few coins at a time, of course, but that would take too long.

He sat down on the ledge and tried to think. The gold was still there, undisturbed, it was just a matter of getting it out. There were two jars in every box, so the Aquarians must have brought them in two at a time. They must have used a system of ropes, he imagined, and right beside him was an iron ring set firmly into the rock. Then he noticed the remains of a large canvas bag on the ledge nearby. It was still attached to a brass hook which was obviously designed to slide on a rope. The bag was rotten but the hook looked perfectly sound.

So that was how they'd done it.

Before swimming back to the dinghy, he broke the wax on one of the jars and took out an American double-eagle. Then he had a final look around, popped the coin into his mouth, gripped the brass hook in one hand, and lowered himself into the water. The passage back was easy. He knew how long the tunnel was and what to expect at the end. He'd forgotten how dark it was in the other section of the cave. He had to come up carefully to avoid bumping his head on the boat.

"Thank God you're alright," cried Jenny as soon as he surfaced. "I've been worried sick."

"Mmmmmm," he replied, with the coin still in his mouth.

First he handed them the brass hook, which Mark examined with the flashlight. Then he took the double-eagle out of his mouth and held it up for them to see.

"Jesus, you did it," shouted Mark, bouncing up and down. "By Christ, you did it."

"There are forty-eight jars of them," he said, "Every one is full of gold."

He climbed into the dinghy and as he dried himself on his shirt he described everything he'd found. "The jars are heavy," he concluded. "But I know how we can get them out. We'll need more rope and a large bag made of something tough."

When he'd finished drying there was blood on his shirt and Jenny said, "You've got cuts all over your back."

"It's nothing," he replied. "We've got the gold. Those thugs on *Seawolf* didn't find it after all."

"Come on," said Mark, "We'd best get back to Nanaimo to buy the equipment that we need, so we can start the salvage tomorrow morning."

Chapter 38

Mark unhooked the heavy Dacron bag from the guide rope and Beverley helped him lift it into the dinghy. They put it on the floor and he lifted out two big jars of gold. They'd been working for over two hours and he was tired. Most of the initial excitement had gone.

"That makes another twelve jars," he said. "That's all this boat can carry so we'd better take them back to *Sundance*."

Bev untied the dinghy from the mooring buoy which they had anchored in the cave, and he began to row the dinghy back to the Chris-Craft, leaving Peter in the treasure chamber.

Their system was like a mountain cableway. A strong rope ran from the iron ring in the treasure chamber, through the tunnel, and up to the stern of the dinghy, which was tied to a mooring buoy in the middle of the cave. The gold was carried in a thick Dacron bag which hung from the rope by the same brass hook the Aquarians had used. They pulled the bag back and forth with cords attached to the hook.

Mark untied the dinghy, eased it out of the cave, and blinked in the bright sunshine. Jenny waved from *Sundance*'s cockpit and called that everything was quiet. Then he rowed over to her so they could unload the gold.

"That's twenty-four jars altogether," she said when they'd transferred them to *Sundance*. "We're half way through and we haven't broken a single one." She looked at her watch. "It's 1:30. Do you think we'll get it all done today?"

"I certainly hope so," said Mark.

"How's Peter?" asked Jenny. " I hate the way you've left him in the cave on his own."

"He's perfectly alright."

"Why don't we swap places?" suggested Beverley. "You go back with Mark, and I'll stay here and keep watch."

"Good idea," said Jenny.

Mark rowed back to the cave and took a last look around before going inside. It was a sunny afternoon with a blue sky and a few small clouds. They were completely sheltered by the cliff so there were no waves. A mile and a half away a sailboat ran slowly north towards Dodd Narrows, and in the distance he spotted a big powerboat, but it was too far off to see any details.

He guided the dinghy into the cave, and Jenny tied the bow to the mooring buoy while he fastened the guide rope to the stern. He gave the rope two sharp tugs to signal that they were ready and then he waited for Peter's signal in return. Next he began to haul the loaded bag through the tunnel. Jenny helped him lift it aboard, and he peered inside with the flashlight. The two jars were still in their wooden box. It was easier for Peter to leave them in their boxes if the wood was not too rotten, but it made a heavy weight to handle in the dinghy.

He lifted out the jars of gold, hooked the bag back onto the guide rope, and gave a single tug. The pull cord tightened and the bag disappeared beneath the water on its journey back to the treasure chamber. Nothing could be smoother. Fifteen minutes for each load of gold. Fifteen minutes for fifty thousand dollars, and already it was becoming routine.

The foghorn could not have come at a worse moment. Mark had just begun to haul the second load of gold towards the dinghy when he heard its low-pitched "mooo." The cave was insulated from the outside, so the sound was faint and easy to ignore.

But then it came again. Mooo. He knew it was *Sundance*'s horn. They'd agreed that whoever was on watch would blow the horn if anything went wrong. Obviously he should check with Bev but he didn't want to abandon the present load of gold.

Mooo.

"I think Bev's trying to call us," said Jenny.

Mark's pulse ran faster.

"Let's get this load aboard, then we'll see what she wants," he said, pulling the bag up to the dinghy's transom.

The horn sounded again, more urgently this time, mooo, mooo, mooo.

"We've got to go," said Jenny. "You'd better signal Peter."

"As soon as we've got this gold aboard. We can't just drop fifty thousand dollars into the sea."

She helped him lift the heavy bag into the boat. Then he said, "OK. Untie us from the mooring buoy."

"But what about Peter?"

"We'll come back for him later."

"We can't leave him, the tide's coming up."

Mooo, mooo, mooo.

He felt a twinge of panic. "It'll only be for a minute."

Mooo. The sound stopped abruptly.

"I'm not leaving here without him," said Jenny.

He turned and gave three sharp tugs on the guide rope, the signal that Peter should come out. There was an agonizing pause, and after a minute he gave three more tugs to make sure the signal was understood. Several minutes passed with not a sound from outside, while Mark sat sweating, wondering what was going on.

Finally the rope began to jerk. He guessed Peter was using it to pull himself through the tunnel, and a few seconds later his head broke the surface.

"What's up?"

"Quick, get aboard," said Mark. "Something's wrong outside."

He started to paddle towards the mouth of the cave before Peter had climbed over the transom, and in a couple of minutes he was easing the boat out of the cave. *Sundance* lay at anchor just as she was before, but there was no sign of Beverley and a hundred yards away lay *Seawolf*'s sinister grey hull.

The gangsters were in the process of anchoring. They didn't seem to have spotted the dinghy, so he warned the others to keep quiet and began to row gently towards *Sundance*, trying not to attract attention. At any moment he expected a shout, but they reached the Christ-Craft undetected, and he brought the dinghy alongside the cabin where it would be out of sight.

"Keep your heads down, and for Christ's sake don't let them see that gold," came Beverley's whisper from the cabin top.

Mark looked up and to his amazement she was lying on her back on a towel, stark naked.

"What the hell are you doing up there?"

"Pretending to sunbathe," she chuckled. "And what the hell took you so long?"

"But naked?"

"I had to do something to distract them. They circled around a couple of times, but they spent more time looking at me than the cave."

"I'm not surprised."

"Now listen," she went on. "They didn't see you come out of the cave, and I don't think they've guessed what we're doing. They probably think we're just a bunch of boaters enjoying the sun."

"So what do you suggest?"

"Let them go on thinking that. Act like we're ordinary people on holiday. Peter, you're in swimming trunks, go for a swim. Then you can climb up here and join me."

"Make sure you keep your pants on," said Jenny with a grin.

Peter slid into the water and dived under the boat.

"How much gold have you got in the dinghy?" asked Beverley.

"Four jars," said Mark.

"Well, let's get that aboard and then slip away as quickly as we can."

"What about the gold that's still in the cave?"

"We'll have to leave it. Either they find it or they don't, but we can't go back for it now."

"I guess you're right," he replied. "It'll be hard enough to unload this lot without them seeing."

By that time Peter had reached the stern and started to climb out onto the swim grid. "Why don't you come for a swim?" he called loudly to Bev.

Mark looked across at *Seawolf* and he could see that it was working. The *Seawolf* crew were not paying any attention to the Chris-Craft. Two of them were launching their Boston Whaler while the other two chatted on the bridge.

"Now's the time to unload the gold," he said. "Jenny, you climb into the cockpit. I'll pass you the jars one at a time while Peter and Bev entertain the guests."

He waited while she clambered onto *Sundance* and braced herself to take the first jar.

"It's heavy," he warned as he passed it across.

They got the first three jars aboard without much difficulty, but the fourth one slipped and hit the gunwale with a loud bang. Fortunately it didn't break, but it almost fell overboard, and for a minute they struggled as it teetered on the side of the boat.

"Look out," whispered Peter from the swim grid. "They're all watching us now."

Beverley stood up and stretched, still naked, with her legs apart and her hands behind her head. Her figure looked superb. Then she walked slowly round the cabin top springing on her toes. She finished standing at the edge of the cabin, facing *Seawolf*, as if she were about to dive in.

"Oh boy, that's got their attention," said Peter with admiration.

"Alright," said Mark as soon as the gold was safely in the cockpit. "Now we'll get ready to go. But I don't want them to see that we're leaving until the Boston Whaler is inside the cave, then if they want to follow us they'll have to retrieve the Whaler first which will take several minutes."

"Well, what do you want us to do, Skipper?" asked Peter.

"You and Bev had better get dressed. And Jenny, you make some coffee. Then we can all sit casually in the cockpit while they launch their Whaler and go into the cave."

Soon they were sipping coffee in the cockpit pretending to carry on a normal conversation. Mark kept an eye on *Seawolf*. The men were passing equipment down to the Whaler as they prepared to explore the cave, apparently unaware of what was happening on *Sundance*.

"Peter," he said. "When I give the signal you and Jenny get the dinghy onto the transom. Make sure it's firmly tied to the swim grid with a rope around the back."

"OK."

"And Bev, can you get the anchor up on your own?"

"So long as it doesn't get stuck."

"Good. I'll take care of the engine. Don't move till I give the word."

He knew the deception was working when he saw the Whaler set off towards the cliff. Three of the men were aboard, leaving one behind on *Seawolf* just as they'd done before.

"They'll know something's wrong as soon as they get inside the cave and see our mooring buoy," said Peter.

"We'll sit tight till they're nearly there," he replied. "Drink your coffee as if nothing's wrong."

He waved as the men went past and the fat one gave a casual nod. Now they were only thirty feet from the cave. The timing was critical.

"Don't leave it too late," said Beverley. "Suppose our engine won't start."

"Not yet."

The outboard slowed as the Whaler approached the mouth of the cave. He wanted them to go right inside so it would take them longer to get the big Boston Whaler out again and back to *Seawolf* before they could give chase. But Bev was right, *Sundance*'s engine might not start at once.

"Alright," he said at last. "Let's go. Peter and Jenny hoist the dinghy, Bev pull up the anchor, and I'll start the engine. Smoothly now, we don't want to look as if we're in a hurry."

Sundance's engine was sometimes difficult to start, but this time it sprang to life immediately with a resounding roar. He throttled back at once, but the Whaler was still outside the cave and the men looked up suspiciously. Mark thought they might go straight back to *Seawolf*, but after a minute they began to maneuver their boat through the entrance, and soon they disappeared inside.

"Hurry," said Mark. "It'll take them a while to realize what we've been up to, but as soon as they do they'll come after us."

He revved the engine a little to warm it up, while Peter moved the dinghy round to the stern, and Beverley started to pull up the anchor. It all took longer than he expected. He watched the cave nervously, wondering what they were doing inside. Suddenly there was a patch of white as the Whaler reappeared. The fat man in the suit stared at *Sundance* for a minute, and then they headed back towards *Seawolf*. Mark knew the long grey boat would be faster than the Chris-Craft, but it would take them ten minutes to get the Whaler aboard and haul up their anchor.

"Come on," he said. "We've got to get going before they do."

The Boston Whaler was fast. It had a powerful outboard engine and soon it was halfway back to *Seawolf*. Mark revved his own engine impatiently and immediately regretted it when he heard the noise echo off the cliff. The *Seawolf* crew must have heard it too because they changed course and headed directly towards *Sundance*.

Beverley had pulled up about half the anchor line and the loose rope lay in a coil beside her on the foredeck.

"For Christ's sake hurry up," he called.

"I can't go any faster."

He looked back towards the Whaler. It was only fifty yards away now, with the two younger men crouched in the bow ready to leap aboard *Sundance*. One of them held a heavy fishing gaff with a wicked-looking hook on the end.

He could see that Bev would never get the anchor up in time, so they'd have to leave it behind. The end of the rope went through a hole in the foredeck to a ring inside the boat. There was no time to untie it, so he grabbed a knife from the cockpit drawer.

"Cut the line," he shouted, passing her the knife. "Cut the rope and let the anchor go."

Then, above the noise of the engine he heard Peter shout. He looked round and saw the Whaler only thirty yards away and closing fast. It was approaching on the port side and the men were preparing to jump. Peter seemed to have spotted the fishing gaff because he was searching for a weapon of his own. Jenny already had the boathook, which she held in both hands like a spear.

He glanced forward again. Beverley was crouched on the foredeck trying to cut the anchor rope. The coils of rope she'd already pulled up lay beside her. He knew what to do. Shouting for her to keep clear, he jammed the shifter into forward gear and threw the throttle wide open.

Sundance was no sluggard. She sprang forward like a stallion, her bow high and spray flying from her transom. He cranked the wheel to starboard which swung her stern towards the Boston Whaler throwing back a wall of foaming water. The Whaler's helmsman turned as sharply as he could and the other two men lost their balance and tumbled heavily into the bilge.

As the Chris-Craft gained speed the slack anchor line began to snake out over the bow. "Get back," he called to Bev. "It's too late to cut the rope now."

He didn't know what would happen when the rope came taut. Perhaps the fitting would tear out cleanly and they'd leave the anchor and its line behind. Perhaps the whole bow would burst apart. Or perhaps they'd come to a sudden stop and the *Seawolf* gang would catch them. Beverley was still struggling with the knife while the loops of slack rope whipped past a few inches from her face.

"For God's sake keep clear," he shouted.

They were travelling faster now and the rope snapped and hissed as it flew out over the bow. He could see she'd sliced it partway through and he hoped that would be enough."

"Beverley, get back."

But she didn't hear. She went on cutting the rope.

The last loop of slack flew over the bow.

Bang. In an instant the rope snapped tight, the whole boat shuddered and Beverley was thrown across the deck. Her legs went over the side but at the last moment she grabbed the rail with both hands. Then the rope parted and they were free.

He glanced back towards the stern. Peter and Jenny had abandoned their attempt to get the dinghy aboard, and it was trailing behind, bouncing from wave to wave. He knew it would soon capsize and then it would drag them back.

The men in the Whaler had seen it too. They'd recovered from their setback and now they were continuing the chase. The Whaler could never overtake the Chris-Craft on its own, but with a swamped dinghy tied to the stern it would soon catch up.

Even as he watched, the dinghy half filled with water, and he felt *Sundance* slow down. Peter had seen it too, and he was trying to untie the rope.

"For Christ's sake hurry," Mark shouted.

"I can't. The knot's pulled tight."

"Then cut the rope."

The Whaler was catching up fast, it was only fifteen yards behind. Again the two younger men were preparing to jump. This time one of them had a big steel wrench as a weapon while the other had the fisherman's gaff.

"Quick, Jenny, get him a knife," Mark called, and then he glanced forward again to make sure Bev was still hanging on.

Suddenly the rope to the dinghy broke and *Sundance* bounded forward. The helmsman of the Whaler did his best, but they were going fast and the waterlogged dinghy was directly in their path. There was a loud crash, the Whaler shuddered and splinters of wood flew into the air. Boston Whalers were tough and Mark imagined that most of the damage would be to the dinghy, but it was enough to stop the chase. The Whaler veered off to starboard and sped back towards *Seawolf*'s long grey hull.

He throttled down a bit to let Beverley crawl back off the foredeck, and when she was safely in the cockpit a cheer rang out from the *Sundance* crew.

"Round one to us," called Peter. "We've lost an anchor and a dinghy, and gained half a million in gold."

"We're not home yet," said Beverley as she rubbed her bruises. "They'll be after us, just you see."

"Where shall we go?"

"Well, it's no use heading for Vancouver," said Mark. "They'd catch us in the middle of the Strait."

"What about Silva Bay?" suggested Beverley. "They couldn't attack us in there, and there are lots of little nooks and crannies along the way where we could hide."

"Nanaimo's bigger," said Mark. "It's further to go, but we'd be much safer there."

He set a course for Dodd Narrows and Nanaimo, and then glanced astern to see what the *Seawolf* crew were doing. The Boston Whaler was still on its way back to *Seawolf*, but even as he watched, a puff of smoke appeared at the stern of the grey hull and he heard the roar of an engine.

"My God," he called. "The Whaler hasn't even reached her yet, and they're already getting underway."

He forced the throttle further forward, as wide as it would go, and pointed the bow directly at Dodd Narrows.

Looking back he saw another puff of exhaust as *Seawolf*'s second engine fired, and then the Whaler came alongside and he watched the men scramble aboard. The anchor came up immediately and she began to move forward. They made no attempt to retrieve the Boston Whaler, they just left it drifting free.

Seawolf was over a quarter of a mile behind, but her power and speed were phenomenal. He could clearly hear the roar of the big V-eights above the noise that *Sundance* was making, and spray flew from each side of her bow.

"Oh boy, she's fast," called Peter. "But we're going to beat her to Dodd Narrows."

But beyond Dodd lies Northumberland Channel, thought Mark, deep dark Northumberland Channel. *Sundance* and all her crew could disappear forever there.

"We'll never reach Nanaimo," he shouted against the wind. "Beverley was right. Silva Bay's our only chance."

He eased the wheel to port. They had to turn gently at the speed they were going, but even so there was a scream of cavitation from the propeller. Their wake streamed out astern in a smooth curve as they swung to the south. *Seawolf* was faster than the Chris-Craft, but less manoeuvrable. What she gained on the straights she lost on the turns, and for a while *Sundance* remained a quarter of a mile ahead. But the route to Silva Bay was round the south end of De Courcy Island, across two and a half miles of open water, and as soon as they got into a straight-line chase the distance between the boats began to close.

"Try a turn," shouted Peter.

Mark swung the wheel to starboard and *Seawolf* followed, throwing a great sheet of spray from her bow. Then he turned the other way, and soon the wakes of the two vessels were crossing back and forth like a pair of snakes racing across the sea. Mark stood braced in the cockpit with his head above the windshield, the wind whistling past his ears. One eye he kept on De Courcy Island two miles ahead, and the other on *Seawolf* a hundred and fifty yards astern. For a while they almost held their own, but *Seawolf* stuck to their tail like a dog chasing a rabbit, and gradually the distance closed.

"It's no good," he said at last. "We'll never reach Silva Bay."

It was then that he heard the first crack. Initially he thought something must have broken under the strain, but the engine gauges showed nothing wrong and the wheel felt firm and steady. He glanced behind. The gap had closed to a hundred yards. He put his hand on the throttle and jammed it as far forward as it would go.

Then there was another crack, and a sudden jolt at the stern.

"My God, they're shooting at us," cried Peter. "For Christ's sake keep down."

He looked back. *Seawolf* was even closer now. One of the younger men was on the flying bridge driving the boat, and crouched beside him was the fat gangster in the suit. He was leaning forward over the windshield with a pistol in his hand, sighting down the barrel directly at Mark's head.

Crack.

Mark flinched, and the windshield shattered. Glass flew everywhere.

"Jesus," screamed Peter. "Are you alright?"

"I think so."

"They want that gold and nothing's going to stop them."

For a moment they were silent. Mark felt stunned by what was happening. He swung the boat from side to side as two more shots rang out.

It was Jenny who came to her senses first. "If we keep on like this they'll kill us," she shouted.

"Well, what the hell do you suggest?" asked Mark.

"Go through the gap."

"There's not enough water."

"We went through yesterday."

"The tide was higher then."

Crack. The bullet was so close it hissed as it passed overhead.

"For Christ's sake try it," shouted Beverley. "We've got nothing to lose."

The gap lay a mile away to the left. Mark cranked the wheel and veered off in that direction. At first *Seawolf* kept straight on and for a while the shooting stopped.

"Perhaps they don't know about the shortcut," he said with a feeling of relief. "They probably think they can head us off at the south end of De Courcy."

But soon *Seawolf* curved back towards them with spray flying from her hull. After a few minutes she was close on their tail again. They were within easy pistol range and the fat man crouched on her bridge, his gun ready in his hand. Mark swerved from side to side and the long grey boat twisted back and forth, crossing and re-crossing *Sundance*'s wake. The man fired whenever he could, but he was being thrown about as the boats changed course, so most of the shots went wide.

Now they were nearing the gap. Mark strained to see if the water was sufficiently deep. He steadied the boat on a straight line course to get a better view.

"Watch out," screamed Peter, and a bullet clipped the cabin top inches from his head. As it whined away into the distance he stole a quick glance back. *Seawolf* towered above them only thirty yards behind. The fat man was grinning down at him from the flying bridge as he steadied his gun for the kill. Mark cranked the wheel to starboard and the bullet went wide.

He looked ahead. Only three hundred yards to go and the rocks were coming up fast. The sides of the channel looked awfully high, the water awfully low.

"Jesus," he cried. "There isn't much water. There can't be more than a foot and a half."

"How much do we draw?" asked Peter.

"Two feet."

"Oh, no."

"Eighteen inches if we're going fast enough."

He slowed down a bit and swerved from side to side while he decided what to do.

"I think we'll be alright if we take it flat out," he said. "But if we drop off the plane we'll hit the bottom."

"Go for it," shouted Bev. "They'll kill us if you don't."

But it seemed suicidal. He still couldn't make up his mind. There were a hundred and fifty yards to go. He was still weaving from side to side, but now there were rocks to avoid so he couldn't look back.

"Where's *Seawolf*?" he shouted.

"She's dropping back."

Dropping back? They were probably waiting for the wreck so they could help themselves to the gold. He eased the throttle a bit himself.

Suddenly there came a double crack of pistol fire.

"Holy Christ," shouted Peter. "Two of them are shooting at us now."

Mark made up his mind. He shoved the throttle fully open and *Sundance* jumped ahead. The shore was racing towards them less than a hundred yards away.

"I've got to line up with the channel now," he shouted. "Bev, call out the depth."

"Ten feet," she replied, looking at the sounder. "But there are rocks on either side."

"Watch out," shouted Peter, as two more shots rang out. This time one ripped into the deck, throwing splinters into the air.

"For Christ's sake zigzag."

"I can't, there isn't room."

Fifty yards to go. They were flying towards the shore at thirty knots or more.

"Depth, five feet," called Bev.

He held the boat as steady as he could, pointing straight towards the channel. There was a great wave on either side of the bow, and he wondered what would happen when all that water got trapped between the walls of the narrow passage.

Crack. A bullet smashed into the dashboard right beside his arm. They must make an easy target now they were travelling in a straight line. He was standing braced in the cockpit with his head above the shattered windshield and he imagined the next bullet smacking into the back of his skull.

Twenty yards to go and they were charging at the channel. Were they in the middle, or a touch too far to the left?

Brrrrrrrrrrrr . . . came a sudden high-pitched screech.

"Christ, what's that?" screamed Peter.

"The depth alarm," shouted Bev. "Less than two feet of water."

They were too much to the left. Mark turned the wheel to starboard a fraction and they were perfectly lined up.

Wham.

There was a tremendous jolt and *Sundance* was flung into the air. He clung to the wheel, but the others were thrown forward and fell in a heap. Somebody screamed and Peter swore.

Mark was sure they had hit the rocks. He steadied himself against the wheel and held it straight. Then he realized they were flying through the air in a cloud of spray, level with the land on either side. He knew what had happened. They'd entered the channel so fast that the water couldn't get out of the way. They'd been launched into the air by their own bow wave. For a few seconds they were airborne and he heard the motor race. Then they shot out of the far end of the channel like a cork from a bottle of champagne.

Crash.

He thought the hull must surely split, but they were back in the water, floating level, and the engine was still running. *Seawolf* had stopped a couple of hundred yards away on the other side of the gap. Already they were out of pistol range.

Jenny was the first to pick herself up.

"Jeez, we're through," she cried. "They'll never catch us now." And they all began to cheer.

The boat still seemed to be intact and when Mark gingerly opened the throttle the engine sounded fine. They were in the quiet little bay on the east side of the gap and apart from *Seawolf* there was not another boat in sight. He glanced back at her now, and caught his breath. Exhaust smoke was coming from her stern, and even as he watched he heard the roar of her engines as she began to surge forward. Soon they were all looking in her direction.

"They never give up," Mark exclaimed.

"What are they going to do?" asked Jenny.

"Turn south I expect. Go round the end of De Courcy and try to catch us that way."

"Can they do it?"

Seawolf's acceleration was amazing. Foam appeared on either side of her bow as she started to gain speed.

"Not a chance," said Mark. "We'll have a five-mile lead."

The wake began to stretch out behind her, straight as a die.

"She doesn't seem to be turning south to me," said Peter.

"Just taking a last look at us before she goes, I guess."

He looked at her again. She was flying now. The bottom of her bow came clear of the water as she raced ahead.

There was a sick feeling in the base of Mark's stomach. "My God, they're not going round De Courcy after all," he said. "They're coming through the gap."

"Can they make it?" asked Jenny. "How much water do they need?"

"Not much more than us so long as they're travelling fast enough."

They still had a hundred yards to go, but already the sleek grey hull was screaming along in a welter of foam and spray, the roar of the big engines echoing off the cliff.

"How wide is that boat?" asked Jenny.

"Ten feet, eleven maybe."

"And the gap?"

"Twelve," Mark replied. "They'll have to be dead in the middle."

Fifty yards to the narrow channel. She must be doing forty knots. A slight turn to starboard, another to port. He couldn't help admiring the helmsman's skill. Now she was perfectly lined up.

Her bow came level with the mouth of the channel and he saw it rise just as *Sundance*'s had. Suddenly the whole boat was lost in a cloud of spray. Then came a loud whamming sound, and he imagined *Seawolf* being forced into the air just as they had been.

His heart fell, they were going to get through.

But the sound went on and on, a horrible grinding rasping screech. Eventually the spray cleared and there was *Seawolf* wedged in the gap, still in one piece but twisted like a toy.

"Jesus," exclaimed Peter.

Then came a great thunderous roar as a sheet of flame flashed upward from the stricken boat. Sixty feet it rose, a vivid writhing ball of yellow and orange fire. Ahead of it flew chunks of wood and metal, and Mark saw a body in a suit, its arms outstretched like a doll as it tumbled through the air. He even thought he saw the gun.

He threw *Sundance* into gear to get out of the way, and when he looked back the fireball had gone. The burning hull of the *Seawolf* lay wedged in the gap with a plume of smoke rising into the sky.

"Holy shit," said Peter. "What the hell did that?"

"Two hundred gallons of gasoline exploding all at once."

Everyone was silent as they looked back at the shattered flaming wreck.

"Do you think we ought to search for survivors?" suggested Jenny.

"No way," said Mark. "No one could have lived through that. Anyway the explosion would have been heard in Nanaimo; the police will be here soon."

There was another silence. He guessed they were all thinking about the same thing. "What shall we do about the gold?" he asked of no one in particular.

"I wonder if the police will trace it to us?" said Beverley. "If they do, I guess we'll have to give it back."

"They'll trace us easily enough," Mark replied. "Our dinghy's floating outside the cave and our mooring buoy is inside. We even left the guide rope to lead them to the treasure."

"If only *Seawolf* hadn't come along."

Peter grinned. "Why do you think I took so long to come out of the treasure chamber?" he asked.

Everyone looked at him in silence.

"Before I left I stacked the remaining ten boxes neatly, so no one would suspect there were ever any more."

Then Mark understood. "You mean we're the only people . . . ?"

"We're the only people who know how many boxes there really were," said Peter.

"So we can say that *Seawolf* came along before we had time to take any of them?"

"Of course," said Peter. "No one will ever know about the ones we've got with us now."

Slowly it sank in.

"Equal shares?" somebody suggested.

"Of course."

Suddenly they were all shouting and cheering. "Whoopee."

"What are you going to get?" asked Peter of no one in particular.

"A forty-foot powerboat with twin V-eight engines," said Mark.

"A house in West Vancouver with a nice normal bedroom," said Bev.

Peter looked at Jenny. She threw her arms around him and gave him a kiss.

"We're going to have the biggest wedding Ashtead's ever seen," she said. "And then we're going to . . . "

"Live happily ever after," Beverley finished off.

Then they cheered wildly as *Sundance* pursued an erratic course towards Vancouver.

Chapter Index

Chapter Index

Keith Hammond was born in England and educated in British boarding schools. He did his medical training at Guy's Hospital in London before emigrating to Africa where he was a government doctor in the Federation of Rhodesia and Nyasaland (now Zambia, Zimbabwe and Malawi). On returning to England he married Gina and together they sailed a thirty-five-foot yacht out to the Caribbean. They spent a year cruising the Caribbean islands before heading north to the west coast of Canada. They now live in Cedar-by-the-Sea, the heart of Brother XII's domain. Dr Hammond has had articles published in yachting magazines and medical journals but this is his first novel.

www.ingramcontent.com/pod-product-compliance
Lightning Source LLC
Chambersburg PA
CBHW051440260626
47162CB00001B/175